Originally from London, Tony Cleaver has been a journalist, hippy, teacher, road sweeper, mountain guide, university lecturer and writer. He has lived and worked in Colombia, Chile, Singapore and the Netherlands and is the author of two economics textbooks published by Routledge. After many years teaching economics at the University of Durham, he has recently moved back to Colombia, where he lectures part-time, writes and plays cricket.

to Suzanne
with much love

Tony
xx

EL MONO

Tony Cleaver

Book Guild Publishing
Sussex, England

First published in Great Britain in 2014 by
The Book Guild Ltd
The Werks
45 Church Road
Hove, BN3 2BE

Typesetting in Sabon by
Norman Tilley Graphics Ltd, Northampton

Printed and bound in Great Britain by
CPI Group (UK) Ltd, Croydon, CR0 4YY

A catalogue record for this book is available from
The British Library

ISBN 978 1 909716 17 9

*For the women who have loved
and inspired me*

Contents

An Explanatory Note

Nicknames are common in Latin American Spanish. To call a friend *Gordo* (fatty) or *Negro* (blackie) is no insult. Similarly, a slim, sun-tanned, elegant woman might be called *Negrita* or *Flaca* (skinny). To foreign ears this may seem strange but such sobriquets are actually terms of friendship and affection and cause no offence. There are countless numbers of *Monos* and *Monas* in Colombia who may have hair or complexions only fractionally lighter than others (if at all). There is even a shop in Popayan called *El Mono*, though I found it only after this novel was written.

Prologue

This year James Mayor planned to celebrate Christmas out of the city, just with his wife and child. A number of reasons came together to prompt this decision: firstly he needed a release from working in Bogotá. It is a frenetic and teeming metropolis of over seven million people with chaotic traffic and he wanted a rest. Secondly, thanks to his firm, Transnational Mining Group or TMG, which operated extensively in the south-west of Colombia, he had found his family's favourite vacation hideaway in the Andes and they were delighted to be returning there once more. And, thirdly, his wife wanted to do some field research on indigenous languages for her university and there would be time over the Christmas vacation for her to interview a number of employees of TMG that were being recruited for the new mine in the region. All things taken together, a month on holiday away from the city and relaxing in the Andes seemed the ideal antidote to what had been a demanding year of work for all of them.

As soon as his son's school had finished in December, therefore, the three of them flew out on a company jet to Popayán, the capital of the department of Cauca – a beautiful old town a couple of hours' flight away. There they were picked up by jeep and ferried to their chalet in the mountains. Rest and peace at last!

1

James was deeply concerned by his twelve-year-old son, Daniel. He, most of all, needed a break from the city. Daniel had experienced all sorts of difficulties in school and his parents had been at their wits' end as to what form of education was most appropriate for him. Then, after a recent session with psychologists, Daniel had been diagnosed with dyslexia and at last his parents knew what was the cause of all his troubles. The reason why he had been a slow learner, why he had hated being in class, why he had been bullied for being different – it all made sense now. His mother had always been convinced that Daniel was an intelligent boy; it just didn't show in formal classwork. Of course it didn't. In what way other than reading and writing do traditional schools measure progress? His oral abilities, his quickness to follow instructions or second-guess his superiors, his excellent hand–eye coordination, these were attributes that were never really measured nor valued – except in his language classes in English and Spanish, the only subjects he seemed to do well in. The fact that Daniel came alive when on holiday in the mountains; his natural empathy with all creatures great and small; seeing that he thrived in the company of indigenous village people – none of this was observed by his teachers and educators in his expensive school in Bogotá. In retrospect, James considered that this was perhaps the most important reason why they were holidaying in the Andes once more.

Of course, it was not a complete holiday for James. The fact that his son would not be a continuing cause of concern now they were away – together with the absence of the niggling but time-consuming demands of the office – provided James with an opportunity to reflect and take a longer view of his firm's operations.

The rivalry between TMG and Triple F Corporation – two multinationals that were petitioning the Colombian government for licences to mine in the departments of Cauca and Nariño – had become increasingly intense of late. But TMG had been informally cultivating the government's minister for mines for some time now, with the result that their bid to purchase unique access to the region's mineral resources had been accepted. Such a success was real feather in the cap for James and his team, but he was sure that Triple F's anger and frustration at being out-manoeuvred on this occasion did not mean they had given up and retreated. All sorts of funny goings-on had been happening since, up to the point where a local staff member had been kidnapped and TMG had had to pay out on a big ransom demand. Word was that Triple F might have been somehow involved in this. Even if this wasn't true, James was sure they would be up to something – anything to make his life difficult. He would have to keep his eyes and ears open to see what developed in the New Year.

For now, it was time to enjoy a refreshing change. Well, almost a change. He had borrowed a company car and was going to drive his wife up to the new mine so she could meet some of the indigenous employees who had recently been taken on. Before operations started up big time and all labour became fully engaged, this provided a chance for his wife to quiz a number of them about their language and culture. Although James was regarded as one of the corporation's superiors from Bogotá, his was not an official visit. He would do nothing but meet a few of the mine's chief officers and say hello. He was not going to interfere.

That morning Daniel was left in the chalet with the maid, a local woman who doted on him, and his parents drove on up into the mountains on the new access road – a dirt track that wound round some precipitous curves in the Andes on the north-eastern slopes of Volcán Puracé. The drive required some concentration if you were to stay safe and away from the edge and its murderous drop below, but nonetheless James and his wife could afford to relax and enjoy the scenery and indulge in the precious time that they now had together on holiday. Until they hit a landmine. BOOM! The road exploded below them and the car was thrown up into the air and over the edge of the precipice. The two died instantly.

The death of two people in an unfortunate explosion caused no great fuss in the local media that day. The local police, when called to investigate, blamed the FARC for organising a war against foreign multinationals but the only people living in the area, indigenous Andean Indians, had seen no sign of the guerrilla organisation and they themselves had no cause to complain about the foreign enterprise that was offering them work. The view that guerrillas were responsible for this latest atrocity was, however, widely accepted. Who else would perpetrate such deeds? It was just another attack by fanatics who regularly spilt blood around the country as a means of promoting their nihilistic cause. Naturally, TMG was saddened by the loss of one of their executives, as was the Universidad Nacional in having its research set back once more in a volatile region of the country. But TMG had taken out insurance against the loss of senior personnel in overseas operations and no great inconvenience was felt by most people or most institutions in Colombia.

Except for poor, orphaned Daniel. What was going to happen to him? He could not now go back to his bilingual school in Bogotá so he stayed put in the place that he loved and with the people that loved him. His future was to be played out in the Andes Mountains of Cauca.

Part One

1

Juan Sebastián's Story

Juan Sebastián Torres had always been an excellent student at school – top of his class every year throughout primary – in maths, in Spanish, and best in the whole school in English – so much so that his devoted parents decided to make every sacrifice possible for him to continue into secondary. He was never required to join his older brother and work in the fields or mines to supplement the family's income. Even though Diego would sometimes complain about the easy life and the soft hands his brother was getting, none of them seriously disputed the decision that had slowly evolved between them with regard to Juan Sebastián's future. It was never directly referred to in this way, but Juan Sebastián was their joint investment for a better life for all of them.

From the moment he transferred into secondary – a thirty-minute, bumpy bus ride over unmade roads to the next pueblo – Juan Sebastián shone in his new school. He was keen, industrious, never late in attendance nor in handing in his work, and he was one of the brightest in his class, if not the entire school of 230 students. His teachers loved him and were stretched at times to keep him sufficiently challenged when others of his age were plodding behind in his wake.

Giving Juan Sebastián extra responsibility, from handing out and collecting classwork to helping organise class and school events, was one way to reward his efforts, keep him engaged and simultaneously develop his sense of solidarity with his community. Naturally, Juan Sebastián thrived on such a policy. His grades were excellent, his attitude impeccable. His initiative led him to discover when the radio was broadcasting a programme in English and he would eagerly try and outdo his teachers in pronouncing new words that he heard over the airwaves. It was not very long before his proud parents were informed that this young man had a very bright future indeed and that the head teacher himself, Dr Jimenez – who Juan Sebastián hero-worshipped – would recommend the family for state financial support to enable his education to continue in due course in the altogether more stimulating academic environment of the top school in the departmental capital of Popayán

Then, one evening at sunset when the family were altogether at dinner, the men with guns arrived at Juan Sebastián's house. They had already surrounded the tiny settlement where he lived, blocking the one path in and out, and were now systematically searching for able-bodied young men who could be press-ganged into joining them and promoting their cause.

Juan Sebastián's father protested loudly but to no avail. Diego, the oldest boy, was taken. However, his father put up such an impressive and energetic defence for his son that the two men who were at the door looked at one another, nodded in agreement and then promptly frog-marched the father out of the house as well.

Juan Sebastián and his mother were distraught. They watched, crying, fearful and powerless, as their livelihood was pushed at gunpoint away from them and out into the night. Worse, just as the armed group was disappearing into the bush, their leader paused, called out to Juan Sebastián and warned him to stop crying because, when they returned, 'he would be next!'

At school the next day, Juan Sebastián sat silent and in

shock. Where were all his dreams of the future now that his mother was alone at home and there was no income coming in? He would have to give up studying and find work.

Over the next week, he discussed his options with his mother, his aunt and young cousins, who lived across the way, and with his teachers in school. No matter all the protestations that they put forward, saying he was such a distinguished student and that he could not possibly give up on a potentially rewarding career, Juan Sebastián knew that his only real choice was to work in the fields or in the local mines. He went to school sad but resigned to tell his head teacher of this decision. But the men with guns had got there first.

His old bus arrived on the dusty open space in front of the main school entrance just as lines of students were being led to assemble in front of the Colombian flag. Dr Jimenez and most of his staff were already there, their faces gloomy and drawn, and behind them were several men in army fatigues carrying weapons.

Juan Sebastián and the others in his bus were all called to join the rest of the school and there was a buzz of subdued chatter and worried questioning as they disembarked and moved across the field to join their peers.

Bang! A shot was fired in the air and suddenly all attention was riveted on a dark, bearded individual who stood at the front of the lines of students, holding his AK-47 as if in salute.

'Youngsters, patriots, Colombians, welcome to the revolution!' The bearded leader shouldered his weapon and elaborately came to attention, parading in front of his audience. Then he dropped his arm and beckoned to the watching students, inviting them to follow him. 'Celebrate with me – you are today liberated from the clutches of international capitalism. From this moment on you can now join me in our struggle to free our beloved country from those who would despoil our lands, steal our wealth and impoverish our peoples.

'Sons and daughters of Bolivar, listen to me. Our glorious

Liberator fought against foreign forces who sought to enslave us. To what end? So that we may toil as wage slaves for imperialist mining companies and other foreign multinationals who continue to exploit our riches and ship them overseas to fill their own pockets? No! Colombia has suffered enough. We must take back our land; eject all those who wish to control our lives; shape our own destinies. Join us!'

At this point, Dr Jimenez the head teacher could remain quiet no longer: 'No, children! Don't believe him!' he cried out. 'Living by the gun is no life at all!'

Jimenez was quickly silenced by two men, who caught him around the head and dragged him away, out of sight of the assembly.

The bearded man continued, ignoring this interruption. 'Sadly, there are many so-called teachers who would want you to remain poor and subservient to foreign interests – either because they are ignorant of the evils of capitalism or, worse, they are in their pay. Such people must be re-educated. Ask yourselves: what do you want for your future? To be condemned to slave for a pittance, working for foreigners who live far away and yet who control all of Colombia's land and capital? Or will you rise up, join me and take back what rightfully belongs to you and your parents?

'Do you think that the capitalists will give us back our lands, our rights, our dignity just because we ask them? Or if we behave nicely to them? Of course not. They rob us of everything they can; they corrupt our own police and government; they enslave us; they poison the earth and waters we live by and they fling anyone who protests into jail. Will you remain weak, docile and helpless for ever? No! You must join with us and follow the example of Simón Bolívar, Che Guevara, and all of Colombia's heroes who seek to throw off our chains and regain our freedom.

'From now on this school is closed. No more classes in capitalism. Your re-education is to begin. You will join us in training for a free future for all our peoples. *Viva las Fuerzas Armadas Revolucionarias de Colombia! Viva Bolívar! Viva Colombia!*'

A roar of applause erupted among the men in battledress around them and everyone else was encouraged to join in. Shots were fired into the air. The youngest students were grinning and shouting – cheered as much by the suspension of classes as by the strong words of the lead guerrilla. Some of the older students had clearly been stirred into a patriotic fervour and were saluting the flag.

The assembly broke up. Teachers, school administrative staff and the one or two bus drivers were kept well away as the armed men went among the students, separating the older from the younger, the immediate converts from those who needed further persuasion.

Juan Sebastián was subdued and confused. He wanted to see Dr Jimenez. As soon as he could, he slipped away into the main building, taking the stairs and then the corridor that led to the head teacher's office.

It was empty. Dr Jimenez and the two men who had taken him away were nowhere to be seen. Juan Sebastián ran back out. He retraced his steps to the field, making for the group of teachers, looking for the school secretary or indeed any of the adults he trusted.

'Where's Dr Jimenez?' he whispered to one. No answer; no one knew.

Juan Sebastián looked for the two guerrillas who had led his head teacher away. He was not sure if he recognised them but he thought they might be those ones walking towards the bearded leader from the direction of the river bed behind the main building that marked the edge of the school field. So where was their captive? No sign of him. Juan Sebastián melted away.

By running across the front and then around the side of the school, Juan Sebastián could keep the buildings between him

11

and all the people busying about on the field. No one could see him searching. He crossed over the short distance to the trees that bordered the course of the small, muddy river at the back of the school. It was lower than usual – trickling down in between wide, heavily vegetated banks. The river bed was clogged in places by junk that thoughtless people had thrown in there and then suddenly he saw a body sprawled below him like a discarded doll. It was lifeless - like all the rest of the junk. Juan Sebastián had never seen a dead body before but he did not need a second look. He recognised the corpse immediately, of course. It was Dr Jimenez. Shot through the head.

Juan Sebastián took to his heels and ran. Away from his school, across the road, ducking into a field of potatoes nearby and off in the direction of his home. He did not slow down until he had put a fair distance between him and the armed men who had taken over his school. His face was flushed; his head was spinning, inside he was boiling with anger and frustration. Still he crashed through plants, bushes, stumbled over stones and loose earth, half running, half walking, desperate to get away from the sight he had just witnessed and all the implications it now held for his future.

He could forget ideas of continuing his education, gaining help and financial support thanks to his head teacher. All those dreams had vanished. What options did he really have now? Only to get away before the FARC came to take him – just as they had taken his brother and father and now most of the boys in his school. He would never join them. He was not so stupid as to be taken in by their lies. Poor, dear, heroic, dead Dr Jimenez. His eyes burned with tears and fury at what he had seen, what they had done to him, what he could not erase from his memory. His last words were so right: they echoed around his head. There was no future in a life with guns. Always on the run, living a life filled with hate, killing or being killed; so many good people being hurt in the process.

A short cut across another field of potatoes and Juan

Sebastián was nearly home. He broke into a run again, his mind racing faster than the rest of him. Where could he go from here, earn some form of income and yet remain safe? And his mother – what would happen to her?

The second question was quickly answered. His mother, worried but wonderfully calm, met him at the front door and told him what would happen. She would remain, close to her sister and her girls. There was no way that she could leave their home so long as there was the remotest chance that her husband and sons would return some day. She insisted, however, that Juan Sebastián should leave as soon as possible and look for his fortune elsewhere.

Where? They talked this over between them for as long as they dared. To start with, he might go to the Río Negro gold mine in the volcanic region of Parque Puracé. This was a long way north of his pueblo but it was open to all-comers and had been worked for decades by a host of refugees, displaced farmers and Andean Indians. More importantly, it had the reputation that you could still strike it rich there and hence it still attracted scores of hopefuls every year.

How long he stayed, if and where he would go afterwards, that depended on all sorts of incalculable factors that mother and son could not assess for the time being. Juan Sebastián assured his mother that he would be fine. Friends and relations who worked at the mine – either at the rock face or outside, panning for gold in the rivers and streams – would be con-tacted, and support requested, advice taken. He would make a success of it somehow. He had to.

So it was decided. Juan Sebastián embraced his mother and said his goodbyes. It was time to go.

For the next three years, Juan Sebastián learned the life of an artisanal gold miner: whom to trust; whom to avoid; the skills needed in panning and, as he grew older and stronger, how to use a pickaxe below ground. As before, he was quick to learn

13

and many of his elders recognised his willing, cooperative nature and his strong sense of what were his rights and obligations. He developed bargaining skills. Paramilitaries would demand a cut of his product as protection money and he would pay it, up-front and on time, but not a penny more than he thought fair. And he learned to fight hard to defend his position.

Small-scale gold mining involved the use of mercury, and sometimes cyanide, to separate traces of gold from the surrounding ore. Juan Sebastián at first kept his distance when such chemicals were being employed, but when he, in due course, learned that this was the cheapest and most effective means to make the most money, he too started using these dangerous additives to help in the almost impossibly difficult search for tiny glimpses of sunlight in the black and desperate darkness.

Hugo Rosas, a bright twenty-year-old who had mastered the technique, showed Juan Sebastián how to heat the ore on his shovel over a small fire, adding mercury in order to mix and separate the amalgam. Whenever he could afford it, Juan Sebastián did the same, though he knew the risks. As he followed the procedure below ground, stirring carefully, watching intently, breathing in the fumes, Juan Sebastián knew that this was a danger that he had not counted on in his appraisal of the costs and benefits involved in mining gold.

It could not continue. Juan Sebastián's eyesight began to suffer. When Hugo realised this he took his friend above ground and told him to stop. The two young men argued. Was gold so precious that it was worth losing your sight for? Was there no other way of earning your living that carried less risk? Juan Sebastián was no fool – despite his need to make money, he realised his friend was right. He had to give up mining.

Their argument did not last long. It was interrupted by a distant buzz of motorised transport that gradually became louder and louder until it became an insistent roar. A line of army trucks had come into sight and were labouring up the mountainside towards them.

The trucks zigzagged slowly uphill on a badly rutted path that rapidly deteriorated under the many passing wheels. Mud, stones, great chunks of the mountainside were thrown up as the trucks slewed and struggled their ways onward. Hugo counted eight trucks in all and watched as each in turn eventually slowed to a halt and disgorged its cargo of soldiers some distance below him. These men milled around their transport at first and then, as order was gradually established, two lines of soldiers emerged, climbing the muddy slopes up towards where Juan Sebastián, Hugo and a number of others were standing.

The mood at the entrance to the mine changed rapidly. There were shouts, whistles and a banging of sticks and shovels as word passed around among the watching miners and on down to their colleagues working below ground. Men, boys and a smaller number of women began streaming out of the tunnel that disappeared into the mountain and took up positions around the gaping entrance, staring at the two ribbons of soldiers as they slowly weaved their way upwards.

Trouble was coming; everyone sensed it. Well before the first soldiers drew level, the assembled gathering of miners started jeering and calling out:

'Go home!'

'Leave us alone.'

'Nothing here for you – leave us in peace!'

This was all to no avail. One by one, the soldiers arrived; each man stony-faced, each equipped with helmet, gasmask, full battledress and carrying an automatic rifle. They drew up and took guard at the entrance to the tunnel: two lines at either side, facing outward at the assembly of angry and abusive people awaiting them.

A whistle blew, a command was shouted and, with an

ominous mechanical clattering, every soldier armed his weapon and stood ready for action.

'This is General Alfonso González Duarte, commander of the third infantry troop, responsible for establishing security in this sector. In accordance to Presidential Decree 1382 and under the terms of the Mining Code approved by Congress, orders have been issued to the armed forces of the Republic of Colombia to eradicate all illegal mining activity in the area known as Río Negro. You are henceforth required to immediately depart from this site which is being occupied illegally.'

A barrage of catcalls, jeers and curses met this announcement.

'This area must be cleared of all those who have no licence or any other official permission to mine here,' the general continued. 'Anyone with such a permit should present this to the lead vehicle below. Everyone else should move away immediately … *immediately*, or we will begin to forcibly remove you.'

Juan Sebastián turned to his friend. 'Lead me away from here, Hugo,' he said. 'This sounds like trouble!'

Hugo agreed, 'You're right. There'll be bloody panic in a moment – I've seen it before. We've got to get away now!'

As a number of men drifted away, Hugo and Juan Sebastián stumbled and slid away down as quickly as they could. But still an angry and resentful crowd remained where they stood, daring the army to do its worst. Stones flew at the soldiers. Someone heaved a rock down from above.

An order was shouted by the general in charge and – bang! bang! bang! – a number of tear-gas canisters were fired into the air: some arching into the open mouth of the tunnel and vanishing below; others falling among the assembled throng outside. Things happened very quickly then. Waves of people rippled out and away from each canister discharging gas. Most stumbled, tripped and barged their way downhill, some of these overtaking Hugo and Juan Sebastián as they picked their

16

way more carefully in the front. Others surged back and forth and returned to challenge their opponents. More stones and rocks were thrown; jeering and shouts rent the air and then, from somewhere, shots were fired.

The response was terrifying. A fusillade of rifle fire crackled forth. Juan Sebastián could hear the bullets whizzing above him. Hugo slid quickly down on his back, pulling his friend to the earth with him.

'Keep as low as you can,' he shouted. 'Who knows how this will end?'

More shouts, curses and commotion sounded above them. A second deadly chattering of rifle fire followed and this time rocks splintered and the stones and earth spat all around them, accompanied by a chorus of screams and piercing cries.

Scrambling, sliding and tumbling down ever faster, the two friends descended as rapidly as they could to get out of harm's way. Blood was being spilt among the miners higher up the mountain, but there was nothing they could do to help anyone other than themselves. They were now some distance below the soldiers and passing level with, though not too close to, the vehicles that had brought the army on to the mountain.

Hugo was fuming with anger. 'There's a jeep or pickup over there with the Transnational Mining Group livery. I knew there was something more to this.'

Further down, as the slope eased, it became wetter and muddier, but now it was possible to walk quickly upright without too much fear of falling. The two young men kept going for another half-hour before at last stopping to rest in a corner of tangled woodland where they could not be seen.

Hugo was still spluttering with rage as the two drew breath. Juan Sebastián asked him: 'What did you mean back there … that you've seen all this before?'

'It was a couple of years ago – at the mine I worked at before here. Just the same: the army moved in and said "Only registered businesses allowed." People – whole families – who

17

have worked the mine for years and years are kicked out. Anyone who protests risks getting shot.'

'What about getting a permit?'

'That's a joke! Most of the people we work with can hardly read or write. How are they going to apply? I asked one about it once. The process means filling out all sorts of forms, visiting different offices here and in Bogotá, for all I know – it all takes ages and costs a fortune. None of the miners can afford that. No, it's all a stunt pulled by the Transnational Mining Group. They bribe the government to pass the laws they want and we are cleared out of the way so that they get all the gold. First one mine, then another ... In time they will buy up the mining rights for all the country.'

'So what do we do now? We can't fight the army!'

'No. We can maybe fight, or do a deal with, the FARC or the paramilitaries, but we cannot fight the law – they are cracking down on people like you and me in one place after another. I think we are both done with mining. It's time to look for other work. Anyway, with your poor eyesight you are going to have to change. What do you think you want to do?'

'Where do we go now? Dunno. Maybe Popayán?. I've got some relations who work the street market there and might be able to help out a poor, half-blind cousin.'

'Well, I've got some money saved up. I think I'll just take my chances and travel for a bit. Maybe I'll stop by Popayán some time to see how you are getting on.'

'That would be fine with me, you know that. I'll need a while to find my feet in Popayán but when you've finished your travelling, however long that takes, I'll always be glad to see you ...'

The two agreed to part. They embraced and slapped each other on the back. For the second time in his life Juan Sebastián set out alone in search of his destiny.

The Sunday market in the centre of Popayán was formed by

two lines of stalls that led around the main plaza. All sorts of foods, clothing, handicraft, paintings, posters and various entertainments were on sale to the throngs of local townsfolk, indigenous people down from the surrounding mountains, and tourists who came from further afield.

It was some time before Juan Sebastián could settle in and become productive at his cousins' stall. He had to find a way in which his partial sight could be used to some advantage and thus he could become an asset, and not a liability, to his generous relations. After months of trying, his first success came as a painter and designer of pottery and woodwork. Since he could only really see big, bold, bright colours, that became the medium he worked in. The surprise was he was helping to produce artefacts that sold well.

As he kept at his work and became more and more accustomed to his new environment, he took to moving around the town with a white stick, trading for the materials needed for his stall and buying and selling whatever other items could make a profit. He became known as El Ciego – the blind man. Many people treated the blind as if they were deaf or stupid, or even non-existent, and he was quick to exploit this. A private conversation between two people would not normally be carried on within earshot of a third party – but if El Ciego came tapping his stick nearby that did not seem to interrupt the exchange. He would just be ignored. Many useful bits of information could be picked up from idle chatter overheard in this way, especially useful when this involved passing by officers who congregated outside the police station, or dealing with people in the mayor's office and the town hall.

Which people were in trouble; who was trading without a licence; who was next in line for a visit from the authorities – such pieces of gossip would find their way to him and when he could he would pass them on to interested parties, for a profit. All and any such news had to be sensitively handled, of course, and Juan Sebastián developed a reputation for being discreet, trustworthy and, above all, accurate. There was no profit in trading rumours and idle speculation; nor would he pass on sensitive material to all and sundry. Thus El Ciego became the vital storehouse and exchange for all sorts of important communication.

When the Farming, Fishing and Forestry Corporation, better known as Triple F, started hiring people locally, this was no surprise to Juan Sebastián. He had known that the multi-national corporation would be coming to the region for some time. The fitting-out of a branch office in the town centre and, more interestingly, the purchase of a mining licence in the region, he had picked up months earlier. What was un-expected, however, was the arrival of a smartly uniformed security officer from Triple F at the Sunday market, who, as word was quickly passed on, was apparently searching for his stall.

Juan Sebastián discerned a tall, dark shape hovering nearby that he intuitively knew was familiar.

'Good morning, Officer, and how can I help you?'

'Hello, Juan Sebastián. I see your eyesight hasn't got any better.'

'Hugo! Is that your voice? I didn't recognise you. You don't even smell the same!'

'I should hope not! I haven't been down a mine for two years now and I have an official, above-ground job with clean clothes and regular showers. You, on the other hand, look even scruffier than usual! How are you my old friend?'

Much slapping of backs, laughter and the exchange of news followed.

'So what's this with Triple F?' asked Juan Sebastián. 'How long have you been with them?'

'About a year. They're building a road some way south of here and are having trouble with the FARC – who are placing landmines and capturing the odd truck or two. I hate the FARC and I heard that Triple F were recruiting security staff, so I applied. I got lucky. They needed people who have some knowledge of the area and I guess they liked me. How about you? How's business? I see that lots of people around here seem to know you.'

'Well, we don't do too badly. We do well when it's sunny and when there's a religious festival. At Easter, it's crazy. We make enough money then to last us almost six months. And as for people who know me, well, that's our security. The more we all look after each other the better. I have some very good friends here.'

'Certainly, asking for you around here was not difficult. They all seem to know El Ciego. But I've often wondered how you were getting on and whether, what with your poor eyesight, you might suffer from thieves and other dishonest folk.'

'Well, sometimes it's been a problem. Not so much now. ... Can you see a man sitting by a row of trees beneath the big white cathedral over there? He is not here very often but I gather he's there today.'

Hugo looked about him. The cathedral was at the head of the plaza and there was a line of five trees below the steps in front. There was what seemed to be a young man leaning against one of the trees. Standing as he was in the shade of the biggest tree, it was not too easy to pick out his features.

'Yes, there is one figure over there. Near a horse and a couple of dogs.'

'How many dogs?'

'Not easy to see. Two, maybe?'

'Are they doing anything?'

'No. Should they be? They are just lying there.'

'Are they looking at the man?'

'I guess so. They are too far away to really be sure. What's this all about?'

'I'll tell you in a minute. But look here – first of all take hold of one of my bigger pots; go to the end of this line of stalls and you'll see an indigenous woman selling food. Fried rice and a variety of meats. Tell her you've come from me, and you are going to see El Mono. Ask her to fill the bowl – she probably won't need asking – and then take it and give it to the man under the trees. That's El Mono – "The Fair One". You'll understand why we call him that when you see him close to. Then come back here and I'll tell you all about him.'

Intrigued, Hugo set off on his mission. His first stop, the little old Indian woman dressed in the bright colours of the *indígenas*, needed no persuasion – she filled up Juan Sebastián's pot with a variety of foods and a big smile. Then Hugo set off across the plaza towards the trees in front of the cathedral. The young man waiting there watched him all the way – a young man with sandy-coloured hair, unusual for these parts, and striking blue eyes. There were two dogs that Hugo passed en route. Both were rather lazily unconcerned with him until he reached the young man, but on his return he noticed that the dogs were now looking at him intently. Odd. Rather disconcerting.

'OK, Juan Sebastián. Now tell me what's this all about?'

'Well, you have now had the honour of meeting El Mono. The local people love him. As for me, he really helped me out a couple of weeks back.'

'How so?'

'Being blind, some people think they can rob me. Some even try it. One of my cousins is usually here to stop them and the stallholders also help out. There was one occasion, however, when some big brute knocked me over, took what he wanted from my stall and dared anyone to stop him. He also stole some clothes from the stall opposite. Bold as you like, as only a big bully can be. Then there was this fearsome growl, enough to make your blood run cold, a noise of a collision ... and suddenly the big man was bellowing in pain and rolling around on the floor, thrashing about, and bringing down a table-load of my pots on top of everything. Absolute chaos!

22

'Above all this, a calm voice, speaking impeccable Spanish, quietly says: "You have your calf in the jaws of a bulldog. He won't let go and the harder you try to get free the harder he will bite. You must try and calm down or he will cripple you."

'The big man screams louder: "Get him off me!"

'The calm voice – it was El Mono, of course – says: "No. I do not control him. He will only let go if you play dead."

'I was feeling quite sorry for the man by now. That dog was really stuck into him and nothing would shift him. Impressive if you were not the one he was biting, of course. Well, at last the man stops thrashing about and tries to keep still. He was in terrible pain, so he must have had some will-power to achieve it. El Mono says something to the bulldog and that animal lets go immediately and backs off, but even I could see it was still focused on the leg of its foe. Scary stuff! The poor man crawls away on all fours as fast as he could, under the stall opposite, whimpering and dripping blood. There is a big crowd around now and a huge cheer goes up. Everyone starts applauding. The bully got what he deserved. He certainly did not get any sympathy and people tell me he can hardly walk now. Meanwhile El Mono and the bulldog slip away. I tried to thank him but he just smiled and nodded and disappeared in the crowd. How about that?'

'Good for him and his dog!'

'Absolutely. I hadn't seen him before but asking around they tell me he turns up now and again. The local *indígenas* see him up in the mountains behind the town and maybe he follows them here on market day. He speaks their language, too, which is interesting because you can tell by his looks and by his perfect Spanish that he is not one of them. But wherever he comes from, I always ask now if he is sitting over there, keeping watch.'

'So he is your guardian angel; your security?'

'I'd like to think so. Like I say, I'd never seen or heard of him before – he seems very distant – but I'm certainly glad to have him around now.'

Hugo was glad, too. In a changeable, violent and uncertain world he wanted his friend to be free from trouble. Being a security guard for a large multinational corporation it was now part of his career to think in terms of how people and property could be kept safe. He explained to his friend that, despite his experience at the Río Negro mine, it was now a case of having to seek employment where he could: a case of 'if you can't beat them, join them'.

'I was as outraged as you by how we were treated, and how unfair it all was,' he told Juan Sebastián. 'But like you said – what could we do about it? Big business will always get its way. So I swallowed my pride and joined a big business. Farming, fishing and forestry – though ironically, they've recently got into mining as well. Not the same company as TMG but another multinational.'

Juan Sebastián sniffed. 'Yeah, I suppose so.' He still could not forget the bloodshed he had witnessed at the time. 'But what are you doing? You are not responsible for assaulting and injuring more poor miners and their families, surely?'

'Of course not, Juan Sebastián. They couldn't get me or any other of the security personnel they hire to do that. No – we are the ones who try to safeguard the work of the others in the company. The FARC have been detonating explosions and blowing up the road we are building south of here. It's our job to try and provide protection. I've got a couple of days off at present so I came to look for you, but tomorrow I'll be on my way again, patrolling Triple F property and checking everyone in and out.'

'Well, good luck to you. I guess any business must look after their own. It's just a pity that people like us remain so vulnerable. Nobody looks after us except ourselves.'

The next day Hugo set off into the mountains. His superior, Miguel Cortés – Triple F's head of security for Popayán and Cauca – had been crystal clear in his briefing: get in, gather as much evidence as you can about who is causing trouble up there, and then get out before dark.

The access road into the mountains was a rough track – uneven, unfenced and winding its way through a series of curves, higher and higher until the newly acquired site was reached. Triple F had already sent an armed and equipped advance party into the site to clear the area, but one of the road-making machines, a grader and leveller, had been sabotaged and they wanted to know who was responsible. Hugo was to join a team to investigate what had happened.

'It was probably the FARC that did it,' said Carlos, the driver of the jeep as they left the main trunk road and started up the company track, 'but I dunno how we are going to prove it even if it is them.'

'Well, it's not our job to prove anything,' responded Hugo. 'You heard Cortés – we just have to investigate and bring back whatever information we can. If we search the site, we might find something, some clue that helps ... but who knows until we start looking?'

'I'm not too bothered whether we find anything or not. I just don't want to see any trouble,' said the third man of their team, sitting in the back of the jeep. He was the newest recruit to Triple F security and nervous about entering what he believed to be bandit country.

'Don't worry, *amigo*,' replied Carlos. 'Our people have already been here before us; they've swept the road for mines and have searched the area all around where we are going. Nothing is going to happen.'

And so it seemed. The first three-quarters of an hour on the rough, unmade surface of the access road were uneventful and the four-wheel-drive Toyota motored along without incident. The terrain on all sides at this altitude was dense rain forest, thinning out as they climbed higher. As the gradient steepened and the curves came quicker so Carlos had to take more care on the unfenced single track, but still there was no great difficulty that slowed their progress. Finally, they rounded one bend and the road sloped down a little way in front through thickly vegetated borders to a clearing in the distance where they could see the bright yellow of the stranded road-making machine they had come to look at. Even from where they were, bouncing along in their jeep, they could see that at least three large tyres were flat and shredded, with chunks of rubber strewn all around the clearing.

Thirty yards short of their destination, just as they were all peering out of the windows and trying to figure out what exactly lay before them – BOOM! – the jeep leapt in the air, flipped in a somersault and, with an almighty crash, hit the side of the road and disappeared over the edge.

Crashing down through bushes and shrubs, the jeep tumbled first on to its roof, then its side, and finally came to rest sitting on its backdoor, half upside down, half vertical, its cabin crumpled, its front wheels spinning in the air.

The noise of the incident sent shock waves across the mountain and it seemed as if all of nature around echoed the crash. Then silence descended, broken only by a buckled wheel still spinning but slowing down with an eerie groaning that sounded as if the vehicle itself was crying in pain.

But there was not a sound within the bent and broken cabin of the jeep. Of the three passengers, none moved. One was not yet dead, however. Hugo lay twisted and trapped by the contorted metal.

He was losing blood and consciousness came and went in waves. He lay there unable to move and unable to feel any of his limbs for he did not know how long. The silence outside and all around him was complete: he tried shouting for help but he could only manage a feeble squeak and it only reinforced his helplessness and fear of the worst. It was a bright day, around midday, but his sight was going.

What is the point of struggling to stay alive, he thought. Just close your eyes and make peace with yourself.

He did precisely that. Just as every one of his senses was shutting down, however, he heard something. Was it someone talking? Somebody laughing above him as they surveyed the scene of destruction? They sounded strange ... but also, somehow, familiar. Why was that? It was a puzzle whose solution was lost somewhere deep in his past but it was something at least to latch on to, something to keep him alive. What was it? Oh yes ... now he remembered ... now he could die in peace. They were talking in a language that took him back to those gold-mining days that he had shared with Juan Sebastián, and that language that his friend had once tried to teach him. The people who had blown up the road and who had succeeded in killing him and his team were speaking ... were speaking ... English!

2

The Exchange Student

Santa Fe de Bogotá sits 2,600 metres high on an intermontane plateau of the easternmost arm of the Colombian Andes. The capital of Colombia, it is located almost at the geographical centre of the nation – which means it is a long way in any direction from the city to either the Pacific coast or the Caribbean coast or, indeed, its land frontiers with Venezuela, Brazil, Peru or Ecuador.

The Universidad de los Andes is at the very heart of Bogotá, close to its oldest foundations, but built right up against a dramatic curtain of forested mountain slopes that soar skyward an additional 500 metres and prevent any further eastern urban growth. A jumble of new university blocks and old colonial-style buildings rises in a series of steps on this eastern fringe of the city, as high as can be safely constructed, up to the cable-car station that serves the sanctuary of Monserrate, perched way above in the clouds. It is a spectacular setting and cannot help but impress any first time visitor.

Karin Roth walked, almost skipped, down the steps leading away from the university's Plazoleta Lleras and could not stop herself from grinning. It was a Friday in mid-August, the sun was high, the heavens bright blue and she had just finished her first week of classes. A recent arrival in Colombia as an exchange student from the UK, she was loving every minute of it.

'Wait up, Karin,' called out Claudia, her new-found class-mate. 'What is all the hurry?'

'Sorry, Claudia, I'm getting carried away! Let's go for lunch somewhere where we can sit and … and … and relax.' Karin's Spanish could not quite find the right words to express her sense of excitement, relief and exultation at having found her introduction to her new environment so enjoyable and trouble-free.

They picked out one of a number of cafés and bars popular with students on the next street corner. Karin found a table near the window and they both ordered a *corrientazo*, the cheap and cheerful set lunch of the establishment.

Claudia looked at the beaming expression of her new friend and smiled in return. Happiness was infectious. 'Well, how is it going, now you are established here in Los Andes? You look as if you like it.'

Karin burst into English: 'I love it! Before coming here I was really worried that I wouldn't be able to understand all they say, but that last lecture, for example, I followed nearly all of it. And even if I didn't catch the meaning of every word he said, I could follow the logic of where he was going and the argument he was developing. *Fantástico! Qué alivio!*'

Claudia laughed. She did not need her own bilingual education to understand the sentiment of her friend's out-burst. 'You have some really Spanish Spanish expressions! In Colombia we say things a little differently – but you'll soon pick that up. Your language is very good.'

'I have to say that here in Bogotá people speak so clearly. In Spain it wasn't always like that. So many different accents and forms of expression. Also, many of you in class use English.'

'That's because you are in Los Andes. We have to be good in English to be accepted and to read all the reference material. People outside the university and on the streets won't be the same.'

29

'But everyone is so welcoming,' Karin insisted. 'They ask me where I'm from and when I say I'm English they all try and say something to me in my own language. Even the porter in the building where I'm living. It's so friendly!'

'Well, you do stand out as a foreigner, what with your pale skin and blue eyes. So, of course, people are interested in where you've come from and what you are doing here.'

'I'm sorry to say that it is not always like that at home. I don't think foreigners there are treated quite so well as I have been here, so far.'

'Where is home exactly? Tell me about it,' Claudia said.

Their lunch was served by a young waitress and that meant arranging space for fruit juice, soup, plates of chicken with vegetables and fried plantain, and rice. It took a few moments before Karin could respond.

'Well, my university is Durham, as you know. That's up north in England, not so far from the border with Scotland. But I have been brought up in a number of different places – in and around London, mostly. Also, when I was very young, in Germany.'

'I've holidayed in Europe,' Claudia replied. She spoke in English: 'I went to a language school in Bourne-mouth – is that how you pronounce it? – and then travelled to Paris, Madrid, Rome, Berlin. All cities very different. Such a lot of contrast in places so near to one another. It is not like that in América Latina! Where were you in Germany?'

'Munich. My father is German but my parents separated when I was very young so I don't remember very much about him or his country. My mother took me back to England when I was four. But that was some holiday, you mentioned – a tour that …'

A sudden interruption stopped Karin in mid-flow.

'Hi, Claudia! How's my favourite *caleña*? And who's your beautiful friend?' A handsome young man looked down at their table. He was tall, wore a smart, pinstriped business suit, sported shiny, black patent leather shoes, and was towing a blonde-haired girl in his wake.

Claudia grimaced. 'Hello, Martín, how are you? Let me introduce Karin Roth. She has just arrived from England. Karin, this is Martín García. He's a recent graduate of Business Administration from Los Andes.'

'Now a Triple F executive,' boasted Martín in English with a strong American accent. 'Hi! Pleased to meet you.'

Karin smiled guardedly. 'How do you do?' Then in Spanish: 'Please introduce your partner.'

'This is María Fernanda.' García pushed his girlfriend forward. 'Say hello, María Fernanda.'

'Hello,' she dutifully obliged.

Karin's mother had once told her that you can judge a man's character by the company he keeps. In this case, Karin observed, the company in question tottered on very high heels, wore very tight, white jeans and a very tight, pink, low-cut top. She had naturally dark eyebrows, unnaturally light hair and more curves than a highway interchange.

'Are you a student at Los Andes, too?' Karin asked politely.

García answered for her, still in his American English: 'No. We met at the night club she works for. *No cierto, amor?*'

'*Qué?*' Clearly María Fernanda spoke little English.

'So you have just arrived in Colombia? What are you going to be studying here – languages?' Martín focused all his attention on Karin, ignoring his companion who smiled vacantly beside him. Claudia turned her head away to stare out of the window.

'Economics. I've just finished my first week of classes.' She kept it in English.

'Economics? Like Claudia here. Two bright academics, eh? I just love your accent, by the way. Which part of England are you from?'

'Durham. You've probably never heard of it.'

'You're right.' He changed the subject. 'So are we all going out together tonight? Friends of mine are having a party. It is going to be a really plush affair and I'd love you two girls to come along with me. I've room in my car to give you a ride. You *must* come!'

Claudia's head spun around immediately. She spoke quickly in Spanish so that Martín's girlfriend would not be left out of the conversation: 'No thank you, Martín; we can't come to your party tonight. You take María Fernanda and forget about us. We have already made plans for this evening and we cannot possibly change them without disappointing others. But it was very kind of you to invite us both. Another time maybe.'

Martín smiled broadly and winked at Karin. 'OK. I can take the hint. But there will be another time and I'll make a point of looking for you.' He turned back to his companion, switching on the charm in his native language: 'We'll leave these two to their *corrientazo*. Come, beautiful, let me take you to the bar next door. What would you like to drink …?' He turned and led her away through the crush of incoming students thronging the entrance of the café.

'Yuuuck!' Claudia exploded.

Karin laughed. Nothing could spoil her good mood at the moment and her friend's reaction made her laugh all the more.

'So you know Martín Garcia and don't think that much of him. Tell me about it!' She was all ears for some juicy gossip.

'No. I'll not say anything until I hear first what *you* think of him. I don't want to influence your opinion in any way at all.'

'Well, he is very full of himself, isn't he? And very direct. Invites us to go to a party with him when we've only just met, and this with his own girlfriend beside him.' Karin couldn't resist her own rapid judgement: 'And what a bimbo she is!' she concluded in English.

'Yuck!' Claudia snorted again. 'Bimbo? Is that an English expression? I can guess what it means and if it means a cheap tramp you would be exactly right!' Disgust was written all over her face.

32

'Well, of course I've heard all about macho Latino men,' Karin said, 'but I have to say I haven't met any so far ... until now. So come on, Claudia. I've told you what I think. Now give me your side.'

Claudia hesitated, looked pensive for a moment, and then decided to open up: 'Well, I met Martín in my first year here and I regret to say that, young innocent girl as I was, he swept me off my feet. He comes from a very wealthy, well-connected family and you can see how handsome he is. He can have the pick of any girl he wants and within a few months of me being here he picked me. I was so flattered, I fell for him completely. But after he had got what he wanted with me he treated me like a door-mat. I was so stupid and love-struck that I let him do it. Only, of course, to find out later that he was two- and three-timing me with other girls. It hit me hard. I was absolutely heartbroken. Can you believe it? That was a couple of years ago and now he is an even more attractive bastard. He knows it, and he still wants me and other old flames to keep on acknowledging it. I don't know whether I hate him or hate myself more!'

She poured out the emotion and Karin found herself drawn to this open, honest and, she admitted, very good-looking young woman.

'Claudia, I know exactly how you must have felt. But don't blame yourself for falling for such a brute. It happens to so many of us – me included. Put it down to experience. You have learned from it, haven't you?'

'Oh yes!' Claudia replied emphatically. 'Can't you tell? I cried rivers then ... but no way now. Can you believe it? He still has the cheek to ask me to some fabulous party he knows just so that I can be part of his adoring entourage. In his dreams! The bastard!'

Karin laughed yet again. What a week; what a university; what a country! After a moment Claudia began to see the funny side of it too: she laughed as well.. The girls' nascent friendship was cemented.

They had long finished their lunch, but there were no more academic demands on either of them on this Friday afternoon, so they ordered more fruit juice and drew their chairs closer together to prolong their intimate discussion.

After a while, Karin asked what Martín García had meant, calling Claudia a *caleña*.'

'That is what someone from Cali is called. Do you know Cali? It's Colombia's third city – some way south and much lower down and in a hotter climate than Bogotá. My family owns a large finca – that's a farm – and some other property down there. I'm living with an aunt here in Bogotá while I'm studying, but my home is in the department of Valle del Cauca, in Cali.'

'Well, I've heard of Cali, of course, but you know I can't say I really know anything of anywhere in Colombia – other than what I've seen here in Bogotá since I stepped out of the plane a little over a week ago. And that's precious little!' Then she added: 'But what's this about plans for tonight and disappointing others? Have you been arranging something I don't know about?'

'Hardly. That was just something to get Martin out of our hair. Now I realise I was very rude in doing that and not giving you any chance to decide for yourself. I'm really sorry if you wanted to go with him ...but I just couldn't stop myself. The bastard!'

They both laughed out loud together. They were two of a kind.

'That's OK, but as it happens I have nothing planned for tonight and you're the only real friend I have found so far. Can't we do something together? Is that possible, or do you have something on this evening?'

'No, nothing's arranged. But there are some of the other students in our class that would definitely like to see more of you. You've said how friendly we are here; well, there are some boys you've met this week who would definitely like to be get even friendlier with you ...' Claudia grinned knowingly. 'how would you like that?'

Karin smiled back. 'I'm definitely not looking for any commitments just yet, thank you very much. I've only just got here and I'm not tying myself down with anyone! Do warn any admirers off. Besides, all the boys in our class are a bit younger than I am. For me, they're all very nice, so far as I can see, but they are boys.'

'Surely you can't be that much older than us?'

'Well ye...e...s. I took two years out before going up to university – I went waitressing in Madrid to work on my Spanish. So I'm an old woman compared to everyone in our class'

'Hardly an old woman,' Claudia smiled, 'but I think I get the idea. I'll see if we can find some of the more mature Andes students to add to the numbers of your admirers. Martín García not included, of course! I'll phone around and contact you later. Go back to your apartment now and I'll let you know what's happening as soon as I can. I have your number; you have mine. This is going to work out fine!'

'Claudia, I can't thank you enough! You don't know how good I feel here now, knowing you. This has been a wonderful week and you have helped so much to make it that way. *Gracias, gracias, muchísimas gracias*!'

The two girls hugged each other. They left the table, arm in arm, and walked out into the street: the start of a beautiful friendship.

Friday evening at the Black Cat night club was salsa night. Well, it was salsa night almost every evening, but Friday night there was a seven-piece band rather than recorded music and that guaranteed to fill the place almost to bursting point. Claudia had phoned Karin to say they all had to get there relatively early in order to be sure they could reserve a table. There were eight of them in all: two other girls from Claudia and Karin's class – Simone and Diana – and Diana's boyfriend, Pablo, with his older brother, Ricardo, and two of his friends,

Felipe and Nicolas. Claudia had done her job well: Ricardo and his mates were all more mature postgraduate students and Karin liked the look of them.

Introductions were quickly made. Nicolas was interested in this newcomer from England, so he asked: 'Do you know how to dance salsa?'

'Actually, yes. It is very popular in the UK now and salsa classes and clubs are popping up everywhere. I have to say that this is the salsa as practised in Britain – it might well be different here. I have yet to try it in Colombia.'

Nicolas smiled. 'You should go to Claudia's home town. Cali is the capital of salsa and we say that everyone born there is born with it in their blood ... Not that we are far behind in Bogotá. Wait until the band starts playing – this place comes alive!'

Karin looked round. All the tables on the ground floor were now taken and people were standing by the bar. Around three sides of the club on the first floor there was a long, narrow gallery set with tables, reached by two wooden staircases that came down to the entrance below. At the back of the club was a stage set with the usual amplifiers, speakers, microphones, drum set and also bongos and an electric piano. There were musicians sorting out trombones and trumpets, tuning guitars, joking with friends, or chatting with helpers - all generating an atmosphere of expectation and excitement.

Pablo and Diana had ordered a bottle of the local white rum – *Tres Esquinas* – for the table, plus a lot of ice and a jug of fruit juice. Claudia warned Karin that when the dancing started she should drink frequently to keep hydrated – but to keep an eye on her glass and what went into it. Karin grinned – she had heard the same advice in Durham, Newcastle, London and Madrid. Night clubs were night clubs all over the world! But now the musicians were ready; the spotlights were trained on the stage; the drummer counted them in and, with a one, two, three, four, the band started up.

The rhythm was infectious. Two percussionists, the bass and piano set the beat and the singer started with a popular number that half the audience seemed to echo. There was no delay: couples immediately took the floor and it seemed to Karin that the whole place started to swing.

'Come on, Karin,' prompted Nicolas, 'Let's see what you think of our salsa!' He rose from the table, holding out his hand and there was no choice. When in Bogotá, do as the *bogatanos* do. Dance.

Karin loved it. Soon Claudia, Simone, Diana and all their friends joined her and time passed quickly as their feet flew, their bodies swayed, their partners changed, and changed again. The whole club pulsed with music, song and laughter.

At last, the Karin and Claudia had to take a break. They headed for their table and sank into the chairs. The music was still throbbing loudly so Claudia leaned across to her friend to speak: 'Karin – you dance so well; like a native, I'm sure.'

'Thank you, Claudia. That's a real compliment coming from a *caleña*, but you are too kind. I dance like a robot compared to you. You are so relaxed and rhythmical. I've been trying to copy how you do it.'

Claudia laughed, poured ice cubes into Karin's glass, and passed it over. 'Well, if that is your secret, you copy very well.'

'I should say so,' said a familiar American voice, 'quite the salsa queen, I must admit.'

'Martín!' Claudia cried, 'What are you doing here?'

'What happened to your party?' Karin echoed.

'It's still going on. I was so bored I came looking for you. I know this is one of Claudia's favourite night spots ...'

'Where's your bimbo?' asked Claudia, relishing her command of colloquial English.

'Bimbo? Well, I guess that must mean María Fernanda? She's enjoying the party – I left her fending off a horde of admirers. Meanwhile, I was thinking of you ...'

'Oh save us,' groaned Claudia. She looked round, saw

Ricardo and stood up. 'Excuse me, Karin, but I will have to leave you with this man while I go and salsa.' With that, she grabbed Ricardo and disappeared into the swaying crowd of dancers.

Karin was now left alone with this handsome vampire. Sure enough, Martín sat down close to her, his eyes twinkling. 'Enjoying it here? You look as if you've danced salsa all your life.'

'Only in my last year in Durham. Also a bit in Madrid, though I didn't have much time I was so busy working.'

'Well, you're a natural.' Martín smiled, turning on the charm. 'You were working in Madrid recently?'

'No – I was waitressing there before going to university, improving my Spanish. Where did you learn your English?' Karin was as polite as ever.

'My father runs a business here and in the States. We own land and export flowers from here and run a chain of retail outlets there. Over the years I've always spent my holiday time helping the business and travelling to and fro.'

'But you're now with Triple F?'

Martín visibly swelled. He was proud of his new appointment and even more pleased that this attractive English girl had noted this from their first conversation.

'You remembered! Yes – I didn't want to stay in the family business; it would have been too easy. I wanted to learn more, which meant either doing an MBA or getting a job with an international organisation. Triple F have always been big in Latin America and I've regularly done business with them. So I applied via their graduate recruitment programme and, knowing so much about them, I sailed through their selection process. I started work in June here in Bogotá. But that's enough about me. How long are you here for?'

'I'm on a year's exchange from my university. It could be just two terms or right up until next September – depending on whether I like it and if I can afford it.' Karin smiled. 'So far I love it. How far the money will stretch I have to wait and see ...'

There was an opening here for Martín; he recognised it straight away and lost no time. 'Well, I can help you there. We have property where you can live for next to no rent and offices that pay a decent salary for someone as talented and attractive as you.'

Alarm bells rang for Karin. She backed off immediately. 'Oh no! Please, I wasn't looking for any help. You are too kind, but I've only just arrived here and I need to settle in first. I couldn't think of accepting anything like you suggest. Really ... no!'

'Well, come and dance with me first!' Martín stood beside her and offered his hand. 'We can talk it over later. Come on, salsa queen!'

Karin rose blushing from her seat, wondering how she could retreat gracefully from this very forward young man. He led the way to the dance floor, found a space, then turned and confidently beckoned her forward – the prince among his courtiers. Karin approached, allowed him to hold her at arm's length, but no closer. They danced, but the more he tried to subtly move his body into closer contact, the more she swayed out of his reach. She was determined: this mouse was not going to play with this cat.

After two dances Karin noticed that Claudia and the others had returned to their table so she stopped, feigning tiredness, thanked her partner and quickly made for the safety of her friend. Martín followed.

What with the loud music and the buzz of the conversation around the table, Karin could lose her suitor for a while. The four girls chatted and closed ranks together and meanwhile Martín knew Felipe and Pablo so they exchanged news between them. A few minutes later, the band took a rest and, in the break, the music changed to records.

Martín looked at Claudia. 'For old times' sake, *caleña* – come and dance with me.'

Claudia grimaced but she rose from the table. Karin could see the conflict in her face as she went with him: he was a handsome devil after all and she could not help her feelings for him despite how he had hurt her in the past. Watching them dance together, Karin could see how Martín was smiling, joking, sparkling with conversation and doing all he could to reconquer his old flame. Claudia was doing her best to resist but inevitably could not help but respond to his charm. She returned to join Karin and the others with laughing eyes and a sheepish grin on her face.

Martín saw his chance. He sat between the two friends and put his arms round both of them, drawing their heads towards his. 'So are you two beauties going to come with me to dance the night away? The best of the music has stopped here.'

Karin answered for them both. 'Please, Martín, we've told you already not tonight. And you have María Fernanda still waiting for you. How can you suggest such a thing?'

'She would not mind at all. We are all friends, aren't we?'

Claudia seemed to wake up from her bewitchment. She spoke to him in English: 'The answer is no. The word is the same in English and Spanish!'

'OK, OK! But you girls are breaking my heart. I've got to work away from Bogotá over the next month so I don't know when I'm going to see you again. Wait! I've got it! Los Andes will have a study week at the end of September when there are no classes timetabled. That'll be the perfect opportunity for us to meet up again …'

Claudia was quick to interrupt. 'Sorry again, Martín, but that week we are both going to be away at my family's finca. But never mind – there'll be other times, if you haven't forgotten us by then!'

The handsome prince was not used to repeated rejections but he was not going to let his annoyance show. His face broke into mock grief. 'How you two mistreat me! When shall I ever get to be with these two angels? I shall leave you now but I'll never forget you, be sure of that!' He made his goodbyes and, with one last tragic glance back at Karin and Claudia, he moved away and out of sight through the crowded dance floor.

Karin turned to her friend. 'What's this about a week away, Claudia? Is this another way to stall his advances?'

'Well, actually, every year, I always spend that week with my family and, again, I just guessed you'd need that excuse as well. But it's not just an excuse. If you'd like to come, I'd love to show you around my family farm. Of course, you are not obliged to, if you'd prefer to be elsewhere with other people. Even with Martín.'

Karin laughed and hugged her friend.

'You know I've nothing planned for tomorrow, let alone for next month and beyond. Even if it wasn't necessary to avoid Martín, I'd love to go with you and meet your family and see where you live. I simply don't know how to thank you enough.'

'No need for thanks. It's settled!'

The next few weeks saw the friendship between Karin and Claudia deepen and strengthen. They went shopping after classes, visited street markets, the occasional club or pub at night and lunched together most days. They exchanged notes on economics, boyfriends and the best places to go clubbing. By the last week of September they were eagerly discussing what they would do and where they would go during the seven days they would have free.

'My parents live in Cali,' explained Claudia, 'but our finca is further south, near Popayán. It's been in the family for generations. I normally go there to chill out, get the city out of my hair, go riding up into the mountains, that sort of thing. It is not the sort of place to party. I don't do anything much but rest, enjoy the scenery and soak in the peace and quiet. I don't

EL MONO

know if that appeals to you – it sounds boring now I mention
it – but I'd love to have you come and share the place with me.
How would you like that?'

'It sounds absolutely perfect to me! Life has been pretty
hectic here from the moment I arrived. I've met so many
people and seen so much of Bogotá; it seems as if I've been
working all day and partying all night. A complete break plus
a chance to see another part of this country would be lovely.
Are you sure your parents would be happy to have me?'

'Of course! They are quite used to me showing up with
friends. That's the way we do things here all the time. And they
will be staying in Cali anyway so will be very pleased that I've
got you to accompany me to the finca. Do you like horses?'

'I do when I get the chance. I used to ride a bit on weekends
when I was in school and then occasionally when I was at
home from Durham ... but I can guess from what you've said
that you're a real horsewoman. You will have to be patient
with me!'

'Don't worry. It's just for transport. We won't do anything
really testing but it's just that for getting around and seeing the
sights further afield we will need to ride.'

The farm was located above Popayán, its lands stretching from
fertile valleys up to the *páramo*, or high moorland. In an
earlier age it had generated income from breeding fighting bulls
for the corrida, but now the family used it mainly for vacations
and recreation. It was set among impressive mountain scenery
close to the Puracé National Park – an area that had once had
the reputation for harbouring guerrillas but which now, thanks
to the army having cleared the area, was the perfect place for
Claudia and Karin to go riding and exploring.

Claudia introduced Karin to Alfonso and his wife María
who lived on site and were employed to look after the farm
and its horses. Of indigenous extract, they were related to
what seemed like half the local population and could trace

42

their origins in the area further back than the farm itself.

'Karin's never been here before,' explained Claudia, 'so she really ought to ride Bella, our mare, Alfonso. You know, the one who is so good with visitors.'

'I'm sorry, Señorita,' apologised Alfonso, 'she's not here today.'

'Why ever not?'

'She was not too well last week. I think she needed some special love and attention so I asked El Mono to take a look at her. But we have another horse that will be just as good for the Señorita Karin, I assure you. Just wait a moment.'

Alfonso doffed his cap at the two girls, bowed and went off to saddle up two horses that he judged would suit them both.

Karin meanwhile asked, 'Who is El Mono?'

Claudia shook her head. 'I've never met him. He's a complete enigma so far as I am concerned. But they all talk of him and he lives high up around here someplace. Like all the *indígenas*, the mountain seems to be in his blood but Alfonso says he is not one of them. He is El Mono – the fair one. They say he speaks not only the language of the tribes but also the language of the animals and birds. How about that? I always thought that Alfonso knew everything about horses but you heard him just now: if one of ours needs sorting out, he defers to El Mono.'

'What is he like? Some old mountain man?'

'Not so old, apparently. But whatever his age, he has had some impact on everyone around here. Let's ask Alfonso ...'

Two horses, fit and ready to go, were being led towards them by the farmhand. Karin took the initiative:

'Alfonso, you mentioned El Mono just now. Can you tell me who he is? Is he your horse doctor?'

'El Mono? He is a wonder, this young man. El Mono lives among the animals and birds on the mountain and they do his bidding. I have lived with horses all my life but I cannot talk to them as he does. They love him. And not just the horses, I have

seen him conjure birds out of the sky. Some of us call him El
Mago – the magician; others – the linguist. He talks all the
languages.'

'They do his bidding? How romantic! ... Does he live near
here?'

'No one knows where he lives or where he is from. We see
him some days but not very often. People say he has been
raised by the animals and birds themselves. He is one of them
and not one of us.'

'And he has our mare?' asked Claudia. 'When will we get
her back?'

'Have no fear, Señorita Claudia. El Mono will return your
horse better than ever. He always does. If you ride up high
today, maybe you will meet him on his way down here – bringing her back to me.'

The two friends looked at each other and grinned. They
both knew what the other was thinking: this was a chance that
should not go begging – to search out the enigmatic El Mono.

They both mounted and Claudia led the way across the
fields from the stables until they reached the surrounding
woods. A narrow path led up between the trees which the
horses knew well and Karin had little to do but accustom
herself to her horse and follow the route taken by her friend.
As they rode higher, the air became cooler, the size of the trees
diminished and the mountain slope slowly steepened. During
the next hours the vegetation around them changed from
woodland to scrubland to high moorland – the *páramo*. With
no sizeable trees now blocking their vision, the two friends
could see a fair distance in front of them and there, some
hundred metres to the side and at the same altitude as themselves, they could see a horse grazing on the meagre grasses
that sprouted through the stony terrain.

'It's Bella!' cried Claudia. 'Come on, Karin. Let's go to her.'

With that, Claudia turned her own horse to the right and
cantered over to the waiting mare. Karin endeavoured to

follow, a little more clumsily than her friend. Her mount stumbled among the giant rosette plants, or frailejones – native to the *páramo* – until she reached the other horses.

'What is she doing here, all alone?' grumbled Claudia. 'Alfonso said she was with El Mono …'

She was interrupted by a flash of grey and brown as a falcon darted between them, its wings seemingly spinning as it banked sharply once, twice and then flew towards some boulders scattered above them.

'She's not alone,' said a voice.

Both girls jumped in shock. Their mounts backed off a little, trampling yet more plants below them. Karin looked round to see the falcon sitting on the arm of a man hunched motionless, partly hidden among the boulders.

'And she is not destroying the frailejones around here either,' said their observer. 'You shouldn't ride this way if you can't be more careful with all those that share the mountain with you.'

Conscious as she was of her limitations as a novice horse-woman in this totally new environment, Karin did not take too kindly to this criticism launched at her from a stranger.

'I suppose this must be El Mono,' she confided to her friend in English. 'He's a lot of help, talking to us in this way.'

'People do call me that, and I am trying to help – you, as well as the environment,' replied El Mono in the same language.

Karin looked at him closer, surprised again.

'You speak English as well as Spanish?'

'The same as you. Is it so rare?'

He was quite combative, Karin surmised. 'OK, I suppose it isn't, but I didn't expect to find it up here, nonetheless.'

'Well, you two are here. Why so unexpected to find another?'

Karin found herself getting annoyed. This was getting nowhere – time to change the subject. 'OK, OK. We came looking for the mare. We heard that she wasn't well.'

45

El Mono stood up. He walked a few paces down towards them, launching the falcon into the air as he did so. Three horses, the mare and the two that the girls were riding, all moved as one towards the man approaching them. Karin, who was a little upslope from Claudia, looked round at her companion and raised her hands as if to indicate that she was not in control of her mount any longer. Claudia urged her own horse forward as if to draw level with Karin but found, equally, that her charge was of a mind of its own. The three horses all closed around El Mono, who fondled their heads, each in turn.

When he finished addressing the horses, El Mono looked up. He continued in English: 'Bella was pining for my company, I think, that and a bit of fever. She is a sensitive one and needs a little more attention than the others. Alfonso understands. She needs a day or two more, however, before she's ready to go back to the stables. Are you from there?'

'The stables are part of the estate of my family,' replied Claudia, in rather haughty Spanish. 'That is, the Fernández estate. I am Claudia Fernández; who are you?' She, like Karin, did not take too kindly to being talked to rather brusquely by this interloper.

'You know well enough.'

'We know only that Claudia's mare is with "El Mono" but we know nothing of you and why you are involved with her stables,' interposed Karin in English. 'My name is Karin Roth and, as you can tell, I'm new here – to these horses, this place, this country. Can't you tell us more about yourself?'

'Not much to say. I live in these parts and help out with the stables when asked. I'll bring Bella back down in a day or two when she is ready, that's all.' Clearly, this man did not want to say anything more about himself than the girls already knew.

'Oh please don't bring Bella down. I'd much rather come up and meet her with you here.' Karin smiled at him. 'This is such a lovely place and I need the practice to ride more carefully,

46

don't I? Will you agree to meet me here?'

Faced with such a polite request, El Mono could not refuse without being obnoxiously stubborn. He decided not to be. With as few words as possible, he agreed to meet Karin at the same time, same place, two days hence. The girls thanked him, said their goodbyes, turned their horses round and made their way back down the same path that had brought them so far.

Karin glanced back to see if they were still being watched. They were.

'Not exactly sociable, is he?' commented Claudia as they reached the cover of woodland. 'Did you really want to come back here the day after tomorrow? Why not let him bring the mare down to Alfonso?'

'If he took Bella direct to the stables, we would never see him again. And he is quite the enigma, isn't he? I'm dying to find out more about him.'

'You'll be lucky to get any more than a couple of sentences out of him, in whatever language you choose!'

'Do you mind if I come up alone, Claudia? Perhaps he will talk more if we don't outnumber him.'

Claudia laughed. 'If you want to see more of him alone, that doesn't bother me! Good luck to you – he's all yours. I'm not at all sure that I like him, myself.'

'It's not that I fancy him – though he is sort of attractive in an unconventional way. It's just that he is fascinating; surely you agree. He is clearly an educated person: just listen to him. And look at him – fair hair, blue eyes – where is he from? And where is his home now? He lives like some wild man of the mountains.'

'Maybe he's just a recluse that prefers the company of animals to people. Did you see how that bird flew to him – and the horses? Fascinating in its way but, if he wants the life of a hermit, then we should let him be.' Claudia finished the conversation by encouraging her mount to go down a little faster. She was eager to return to the comforts of civilisation –

47

to a warm and cosy house and a hearty meal and welcome. She had had enough of the discomforts of the high moorlands and nature in the raw.

3

The Corporate Executive

Morten Fields, the new manager of Triple F in Colombia, was not a happy man. He was sitting in his recently refurbished Bogotá office and fuming. His thoughts went back over the last few weeks – how he had been so successful in his post in the United States; how he had flown to corporate headquarters in Geneva, expecting a promotion to join the senior management team in Switzerland; only to be told he was going instead to Colombia – a dead-end job in an impossible country but dressed up as if it was some great honour. He, they told him, was the 'only man in the corporation that could sort the business out' there. What a joke! He could see right through the smug, smiling faces of the Board. They were out to get him. No doubt about it. This was a ploy to move him out of their sight, out of their hierarchy, a sideways move so sideways that it was more akin to walking the plank on a pirate ship. Most people in the corporation couldn't even spell Colombia, let alone know where it was and what was going on there. They knew only of the company's banana plantations, taken over decades ago, their boringly regular income stream, and the country's turbulent history of internal political conflict.

And why was Triple F venturing not only into dangerous territory but also into difficult business? Rather than stick to its core activities of farming, fishing and forestry in a country

49

that had all three in abundance, Triple F was now chasing El Dorado – the hunt for gold that had cost uncounted European lives in the past and was sure to go on doing this in the fore-seeable future if the Board did not rethink its doomed strategy. Why the change of direction? With property in the USA and Europe in a slump; financial crises that spread like a disease from one country to another; with central banks printing more and more money, gold was the inevitable last resort of the nervous. Add to this the fact that the Asians were buying up gold to flaunt their new-found wealth like never before and the result was that the price of gold had gone up through the stratosphere.

But Fields guessed that the official line of the Board – to make profits out of mining – was really only a cover for the true reason why Triple F had started on this folly. At root was the desire not to let the Transnational Mining Group run rings around Triple F wherever the two corporations bumped into one another. Getting involved in the Colombian mines was just a way of retaliating against its historic rival; it had nothing to do with sound business sense. The fact that Triple F's mining start-up in Colombia had experienced difficulties and lost labour and capital steadily since its inception was never going to make the Board reverse its decision. Better to use the black hole of this ill-considered venture to swallow up people and projects that they had tired of, or had no further use for, or were embarrassments that simply did not fit their chosen vision. Well, Fields was damned if he would go quietly. If they thought they had given him a posting that would gulp him down and silently swallow him, then they were all mightily mistaken. Fields would fight mercilessly, as he had done all his life. He would cripple all his competitors, inside the business and out; turn round the balance sheet from red to black; and force all those smarmy, self-satisfied board members to take note of this dynamo that would one day heave them overboard.

Fields rose from his desk and paced the floor. One day he was going to be the master of the entire corporate vessel and it would be the board members themselves that would have to walk the plank. Yessiree!

Fields's personal assistant, Patricia, knocked discreetly and came in. 'The officers you wanted to see have arrived now. Shall I direct them in?'

'Do they both speak English?'

'Yes, certainly.'

'Then I'll not need you to translate for me. Send them in.'

Fields wanted to get to the bottom of the incident in Cauca where Triple F had lost three of its men and a couple of vehicles in what looked like a deliberate attack on their facilities. This was to be his first test: could he stop the corporation from bleeding resources in its most remote locations? He had ordered that all activity on and around the location of the attack should cease immediately and that the area be secured. He had then flown the two operatives who knew most about what had happened directly to see him. That very fact alone would send an important message around the business: the new chief of Triple F Colombia would not accept failure at any level.

Miguel Cortés, head of security in the Cauca region, and Alejandro González, chief of the Popayán office, came in. Ever since they had received their summons to head office, the two had been nervously checking and double-checking all the details of what had happened. Now was the time they had to face their new and formidable boss. Fields's expression gave nothing away as he shook hands with his guests. Instead of making any comment, he straight away invited them to air their views on the incident.

Cortés was first to speak. 'We sent in an armed security team before the attack and immediately after it. We combed the area thoroughly and particularly swept the road for any explosives the day before the Toyota was blown up. We found nothing.

51

Either it was a sophisticated, non-metallic form of device that was undetected, or it was planted the night after our sweep. I grilled the men in charge of the operation, and threatened dire consequences if they were covering anything up, but what I've just said is the result. There were no cock-ups. Our men did a good job.'

Fields sniffed and said nothing. Cortés was bound to cover his back, he thought. He would be the first to be axed if there had been any security lapses. He looked at González and waited to hear what he had to say.

'It looks like it was a trap, deliberately set to lure in and kill defenceless staff. One of our machines was sabotaged earlier, so I asked Miguel to investigate. As soon as the armed security unit had left the scene and the jeep arrived, someone detonated the explosion. Clever bastards! They waited until they could kill undetected. None of our personnel, apart from those caught in the explosion, were anywhere near the place so they saw nothing. This must have been planned in advance and the materials used were professionally deployed.' González stuck to the facts so far as possible. He did not want to conjecture any further until invited to do so.

'OK ... so who do you think was responsible?' Fields had his own ideas but wanted to hear what his subordinates thought first.

'The most likely candidates are political extremists like the FARC or some similar splinter group,' González said. 'They claim to be at war against international businesses. The FARC have the most resources at their disposal and are the likeliest candidates. Other, smaller extremist groups can be just as ruthless but probably don't have the means to carry out this particular attack against us. An entirely different possibility is that it's down to local indigenous or displaced peoples. We regularly have trouble with them. They have no political ideology as such – they just want us out. However, I don't think they are blood-thirsty enough to perpetrate this kind of atrocity.'

Cortés voiced his opinion next. 'The trouble is that the FARC, or ELN, or whatever extremist group is involved usually claims responsibility straight away. These attacks are propaganda coups for them. That is their whole justification. They either promise more or typically ask for protection money if they want the attacks to stop. But no one has said anything. So we can't really be sure who is responsible just yet.'

'Do you think it could be TMG?' Fields asked.

The two Colombians looked at each other. 'We thought of that,' said Cortés. 'We've been fighting a low-level dirty war against them for ages. It started with competition in bidding for mining licences. They didn't like us getting a foothold in the region and, since we set up, there has been some deliberate obstructionism: hampering lines of supply, cyber interference, that sort of thing. Attempts to steal our staff they have tried, but actually killing them would be a serious escalation if it is them behind it.'

Fields speculated aloud: 'What if TMG were behind this as paymasters but hired local terrorists to carry it out. What do you think of that?'

'It has to be people who know the terrain,' said González. 'They covered their tracks too well for it to be anyone else. The FARC fit the bill in that sense. Would they do it if they could make money out of it, working on behalf of TMG, one of their sworn enemies? Now I think about it, I suppose they might: it would suit their purposes to have two foreign enterprises slugging it out against each other and to get paid into the bargain. Yes. That does sound feasible for them. It just doesn't sound as if it is the sort of thing TMG would want to get into, though you'd know more about the politics of it than I.'

'Well, whatever is the case, I need more evidence to be able to decide. Cortés, I take it that the site of the attack has been cordoned off by us and no one, apart from your security unit, has been allowed access to our property there. Is that correct?'

'Yes sir. Absolutely!'

'Then you will have to send your men back into the site and search every inch of the ground around. I need something, anything, that could give us a better lead than what we've got so far. Understood?'

Cortés nodded. He took the opportunity to discuss the resources he needed and Fields promised that this operation would receive his greatest attention and support but that he wanted results as soon as possible and an update within the week. The conversation was brought to a swift close and both men were then dismissed.

When Miguel Cortés and Alejandro González got back to the regional office in Popayán a number of messages were waiting for them. Lifting gear to retrieve the Toyota from where it had come to rest had been ordered and now was ready to deploy. Cortés's deputy, Juan José Gómez, confirmed that an armed security team had been selected and he had already briefed them on their mission. And there was an e-mail from Human Resources in Bogotá to González saying they were sending out a new, bilingual trainee executive to join the office in Popayán: a certain Martín García. Could he be met at the airport straight away?

Cortés grumbled to his colleague. Had Fields decided to send a spy down to check on him and his operation? Or was this just a novice who needed training by González? Human Resources knew that, apart from himself, all of the security operatives in the region spoke next to no English and in a multinational organisation such as Triple F that was a weakness. Most of Cortés's men had been recruited from the armed forces and the first priority was that they be competent in their jobs and, most importantly, trustworthy. Linguistic ability did not come into it. Ironically, the one man who had the best command of English was Hugo Rosas, an ex-miner and sparkling talent that Cortés had really valued, but he had been lost in the attack. The arrival of a new bilingual individual to Popayán, he supposed, was Fields's way of putting pressure on him to raise his game. He discussed the implications of this message with González.

'If he is a spy, he has been detailed to be with me, not you,' said González gloomily. 'You wanted extra resources, however, and he just might have been sent now for that reason. Let's face it, we don't know what Fields's game is, we only know that investigating this terrorist attack is his top priority and he wants results pretty damn quickly. Given that, here's my suggestion: García will be an objective observer of how we run operations here. The most important operation now is to gather evidence of this attack. I'll send García out with your team so that he gets to know the region, what the land looks like and so he can watch how Triple F security shapes up in the field. How about that?'

Cortés thought about it. 'You are passing me the buck, aren't you?' he snorted. 'That's all I need, some ex-college boy with no field experience sitting in the back of one of our trucks taking notes on what we are doing.'

'Don't worry – he can't feed back any information to Bogotá without my authorisation. At the same time this will be an excellent opportunity for him to learn what goes on out here, what business is really like, far away from management text-books and the shining offices in the capital city. Just keep him out of the way from any possible trouble.'

'No fear of that. He'll be locked inside of one of our vehicles and told not to move. I'll send Juan José to go and fetch him from the airport and tell him to frighten García to death if he puts a foot out of line.'

Martín García was setting out on a great adventure with Triple F and he had been impressed by a number of things so far. They had flown him to Popayán, put him in the best hotel in the town and now he was seated in a convoy heading up into the Andes on a trip to investigate what he had heard was the most important event to impact on the corporation in years. The fact that he was thrown into the middle of this was a reassuring confirmation of how important they thought he was to the enterprise, though he was annoyed that the man in charge of this convoy, Juan José Gómez, clearly was an uneducated soldier who hadn't shown him the personal deference his executive status deserved. But he'd overlook that for now. Maybe he would mention it later to Gómez's superiors, depending on how things turned out during the rest of the day.

The convoy was certainly something that was turning heads as they passed by. A Chevrolet pick-up was in the van, stuffed with uniformed Triple F guards toting rifles. Then followed a motorised crane – heavy, eight huge wheels – with four men inside including an armed security guard posted as lookout next to the driver. His own vehicle came next, a long-wheel-base Land Rover Defender with Juan José Gómez positioned next to the driver, a security guard next to himself in the middle and two more seated at the back. Bringing up the rear was a truck-load of security men, most of them armed and all of whom, he gathered, had been briefed to get down on their knees and comb the area in and around their destination for anything that might provide evidence of those responsible for the attack. Gómez had given him some idea of what they were up to but had irritatingly refused to answer all his questions and insisted that he, Martín García, was not to leave the protection of his vehicle and was to confine himself only to observe all that was going on from the safety of his centre seat in the Land Rover. This had annoyed Martín, but he saw no point in arguing with his rather insolent attitude.

After a slow and tortuous journey, the crane and its attendant vehicles eventually arrived at the place where the Toyota had been blown off the road. With yet another terse warning to Martín to stay put, Gómez and all the men in the convoy spilled out on to the road with a number being especially detailed to bear arms and set up a security circle above and below the road and around the crash site.

The crane was slowly backed into position close to the place where the Toyota had gone over the edge. They had to manoeuvre the immense vehicle carefully so that it did not obstruct the hole in the road that had appeared thanks to the landmine. Men crawled all over the place, searching for any small trace of anything that might be useful as evidence. Some time then elapsed with nothing obvious happening. Martín guessed that below the road and out of his view there must be others searching the crash site, prior to attaching cables to the Toyota and lifting it up. Minutes ticked by. Martín was getting bored, stuck where he was alone.

Juan José Gómez was nowhere to be seen. Martín looked back along the road where it curved away and saw that, on the cliff cut out above it, there was a better vantage point to observe all that was going on. There were no guards around his vehicle to stop him getting out and he reckoned that if he circled around above his Land Rover he could reach the top of that cliff where he could sit undisturbed and watch the action. Looking all round to check once more, and seeing no one, he resolved to carry out his plan.

Climbing off the road and into the funny-looking scrubland above it was his first problem. He scrabbled on the loose earth, scratched himself on the nearest shrubs but hauled himself successfully up after a few seconds of clumsy indecision. He quickly moved round the slope, until he was back more or less parallel with the road, keeping his head down so as not to attract attention. Approaching the vantage point he was aiming for, he climbed a few steps upslope, then turned and scrambled up once more behind a collection of bushes that marked the way to the top of the road cliff.

Getting there at last, he was suddenly surprised to see another figure before him – lying down, peering over the edge with clearly the same intention that he had: to observe the proceedings below. This individual, who spun round to meet him, was not wearing the uniform of the Triple F security team, however. Nor was the man who appeared out of nowhere by his side and stuck an AK-47 in his ribs.

'*Buenos tardes, señor*' came the greeting. 'Now suppose you step back, sit down, and keep quiet. You don't want to cause us any trouble, do you?'

Back in Bogotá, when he heard the information relayed to him from the other end of the telephone line, Morten Fields went ballistic.

'What do you mean, García has been kidnapped? What was he doing anywhere near there? Are you guys crazy, or damn stupid, or what? Do I have to come down there myself to sort you people out?' The rest of Fields's comments descended into a tirade of expletives, insults and accusations that went on for a full minute and a half.

González waited for the tongue-lashing to blow itself out before he could answer. 'García disobeyed instructions, sir. He was given clear directions as to what he could and could not do, but he disobeyed them all and evaded our own guards to go off on his own. He was spotted some distance above the site by one of our own men before he disappeared.'

Fields was not impressed. Regaining his self-control, he spoke coldly to his junior. 'You did not answer my question,' he said. 'What was he doing on this excursion? I did not send him to you – he is just a new graduate trainee who ought to be sitting in some accountant's office someplace, not wandering around bandit country getting himself kidnapped. What on earth is going on with you?'

González stuck resolutely to his defence, hoping to minimise the personal damage that this latest upset was bound to call down upon his head. 'We didn't ask for him, sir. He was sent here by your offices and arrived here the same day as I did after meeting you in Bogotá. We assumed he was part of the men and resources that you approved for this operation ...'

'What? Do you think *I* am stupid now?' Fields erupted once more. 'Would I send some wet-behind-the-ears city boy down to you to go out and look for terrorists without any sort of training? What does Cortés have to say? Is he with you?'

'Yes, sir. Here he is now ...' González hastily passed the phone set across to his colleague standing nearby.

'Hello, sir, Cortés speaking ...'

'And what have you got to say, Cortés? You are the head of security in the region, up until now, that is. Why was García in any way involved in this expedition? Tell me!'

'It was as González said, sir. He was assigned to my security operation for reasons I cannot question and I had over twenty men surrounding him and the site of the original attack. But he proved to be trouble from the first moment to the last. He seemed to want to pull rank over the man in charge of the operation – one of my best men, sir – and when told to stay in his vehicle he escaped and went his own way. He brought it on himself, sir.'

'Come off it, Cortés. "Reasons I cannot question"! If you didn't want him on this trip, you have the authority to refuse his inclusion. You are, were, in charge of security, aren't you? Answer me: why was this man put on the investigation? I certainly did not send him down to you.'

'Sorry, sir, but Human Resource in your office sent him here, sir. We have the message from them in print, sir, dated the day before the operation. We thought you wanted him included on this excursion, sir.' Cortés had assumed military mode in his conduct with his chief: his back ram-rod straight, standing to attention at the phone, replying in staccato when spoken to.

'You don't think enough in this corporation. None of you!'

Fields was really mad. It seemed that even his people in Human Resources were half-witted, too. García should have been sent to some innocuous post in a banana plantation up north in the country – not south, where everyone knew there was a security alert.

'Leave this for a moment. What can you tell me now about the people behind all this?'

'Well, this confirms one thing, sir. The FARC have demanded ransom money to get your man back, sir. They contacted us immediately. On the ground at the time and confirmed by a phone call to this office a little later. They want ten thousand dollars delivered to them at the same place next week, sir. I'm guessing that that will be the first instalment of their demands.'

'I bet it is,' said Fields, thinking quickly. This is what you get when you delegate decisions to incompetents all round the organisation. Somewhere between the department of Human Resources in his own office building and those two clowns down in Popayán lay the responsibility for putting the wrong person in the wrong place at the wrong time. Martín García he knew vaguely – he was the son of a business acquaintance in the USA that he had taken on as a favour. He didn't think much of the man at the time and thought even less of him now, but nonetheless his recruitment into Triple F was his decision and no one else's. He accepted that. Where he went within his organisation and who directed him was another matter which he had to sort out in due course. Now his immediate problem was to get him free. He knew whom he would call on.

'Cortés, you still there?'

'Yessir!'

'I'm going to send someone down to you that will take charge of a rescue operation, is that clear?'

'Yessir.'

'You and González will both stay in post for the time being until such time I can conduct a proper review of all that has been happening. Clear?'

'Yessir!'

'The man you will meet as soon as I can get him to you – about three or four days I can guess – will bring ten thousand dollars with him and he will brief you on everything he needs to get García out unharmed. I can't be sure what he will ask for, but you will give him everything ... whatever it is ... down to the very last detail, understand? I'll cover all the necessary expenditures.'

'Yessir. I understand, sir. Can I ask who it will be, sir?'

'You can certainly ask, Cortés, but I'll not tell you. Not yet. Instead, I want you here as soon as the person I send for confirms his flight details. You and I will then meet this trouble-shooter in person the moment he steps off the plane in Bogotá. Got it?'

'Yessir.'

'That's all for now. Goodbye.'

Fields hung up without waiting for any comment. His mind was now focused on how to raise certain contacts of his in the USA. It took him an hour to locate the people he was looking for and to discuss the arrangements he would need in place to get the one he wanted into Colombia. This would have to be an entirely off-balance-sheet arrangement, not detectable by any party outside of those he was currently contacting and certainly not discernible to any in corporation headquarters in Geneva.

All things went smoothly, however, and in twenty-four hours he had received flight confirmation of an independent corporate jet from California to Bogotá scheduled to arrive, as he had estimated, in three days' time. His prize guest would go through Colombian immigration control as just another executive in a grey suit, courtesy of International Trade Solutions, a small Internet-based consultancy.

Cortés was summoned up from Popayán to meet Fields an hour before their man was due to fly in. The two sat just outside the airport in an unmarked limousine with blacked-out windows. It was time to brief Cortés a little more fully as to what was going on.

'The man you are about to meet is an expert security agent

61

whom I call for only in extreme cases,' said Fields. 'He is highly effective ... but his methods are not those that the corporation can officially condone. Do you follow my meaning?'

Cortés nodded without saying a word.

Fields continued: 'It is not just that we cannot approve of his way of operating; we cannot be seen in any way to be connected to him. He has to work independently from us with no paper trail, no e-mails, no phone calls from the office, nothing linking his operations to Triple F. Is that clear? The resources you will need that this man asks for will be hidden on the balance sheet by inflating the normal security budget for the region.'

Cortés nodded again. He was no fool. He could see perfectly well where all this was leading: an illegal, undercover operation that might possibly cause a great outcry somewhere if things went wrong. Or right.

'Have you had any further contact from the FARC regarding the cash handover?'

Cortés spoke this time: 'Yes – we received another call yesterday from an unknown location. The money is to be delivered by a lone agent from Triple F with no armed escort or they refuse to cooperate and the hostage will be harmed in some undisclosed way.'

'Do we have any means of contacting them before the rendezvous, to set out our side of the bargain?'

'Yessir. We are to use a market trader in Popayán as a go-between. He's known as El Ciego, the blind man. They are clever bastards, sir. It is all well thought out. If we want to speak to the FARC, or rather get them to phone us, then we have to tell El Ciego and he passes on this information to their contact on a Sunday afternoon. That's when the central plaza is packed and any stallholder will talk to scores of people every hour. If we watched El Ciego all day, we would still not know who the FARC contact was. Al Ciego, of course, would never be able to give us a description of the FARC person who approached him. Maybe what the person sounded like, male or female, young or old, but that's all. And one thing more – we have to pay El Ciego handsomely for the privilege of being our go-between. That way the FARC keep local people sweet and helpful and unlikely to give them away.'

'Well, two can play that game. Whatever amount the FARC say we should pay the blind man, we pay double and tell him to keep quiet about it if he wants more. We do need to contact the FARC, though. The cash drop is scheduled for next Tuesday, right? The only person who can make that drop is yourself – I'll need someone like you who can speak English and Spanish for reasons I'll explain later. But before the drop make it clear that we, that is you, need proof that the hostage is alive. You are not to hand over the cash until you can see García – at distance if needs be – and verify that he is OK. Gottit? No proof of life, no money. Simple as that. And nor is your own safety to be compromised or I'll send the army in. Reassure them that at present no Colombian authority knows they have one of our men and nor will they. We will give them money and cause no trouble if they keep to their side of the bargain. How does that sound?'

'It sounds a bit risky for me, sir.'

'Well, that's as maybe,' said Fields flatly. 'You helped get us into this mess so it's only right that you should shoulder some of the risks. But if all goes well, you will have partly restored your reputation in my eyes. Now let's go and meet Leopold Smith and get him into this limousine and out of sight.'

'Leopold Smith, sir? Holy shit!'

'What? Have you heard of him?'

'Heard? Yes, I have heard of him, sir, but I thought he was just part of someone's overworked imagination. A security chief I met Stateside once told me there was this guy they called "the nuclear option" and that, if I ever ran across him, I should keep well away.'

'The nuclear option, eh? The reason, I guess, is that he is the biggest, most destructive weapon I know of. Keeping that quiet is not easy. He is not to be associated with Triple F, however. You will not discuss his deployment here with anyone, anyone at all. Understand? He has to work with you since he speaks no Spanish but he should be kept in a plain business suit and out of sight so far as it is possible. If anyone else is to see him, say only that he is a security consultant, a desk man, who has been flown in to help you. That's actually not so far from the truth. One last thing: he is ... sort of different. He likes a lot of personal space. Don't touch him. Not even to shake hands. He doesn't like that ... and you wouldn't want him to not like something ...'

With that final cryptic comment, Fields broke off the conversation and got out of the car. It was time for their visitor to arrive.

Miguel Cortés had seen a lot of action in his time. Of dual US–Colombian nationality he had fought with the US Marines in the Gulf and later had worked with the Colombian military in fighting terrorists in their tropical jungle hideouts. He had had a couple of bullets taken out of his shoulder so wasn't fit for active duty anymore, and then, looking round for other employment, in his late thirties he found a good use of his services in security work for Triple F. He thought he had seen most military types over the years but Leopold Smith was special, even for Special Forces. The man was built large – no business suit could hide that – but he moved carefully, almost as if he was consciously controlling himself. His facial expression was continually flat, featureless, expressionless. Fields introduced him to Cortés, but the man said nothing and looked straight through him. He eased himself slowly, carefully into the back of the limousine and sat by himself, looking directly ahead, past both his hosts, like a statue. Cortés was at the wheel, Fields next to him.

Fields directed Cortés to his private apartment. This was at the top of a tower just a few blocks north of the city centre, set back in a secluded complex built into the side of the Andean hills. Their limousine entered the building via automatic doors that led into a spacious basement car park, and from there the elevator, accessed by a private security code, shot up undisturbed to open its doors directly into Fields's apartment. They saw no one else en route.

Shown inside the apartment, Smith placed an attaché case on the table in the lounge, snapped it open and took out five large photographs, which Cortés immediately recognised as aerial shots of the incident site, all at different scales.

Smith bent over the papers, traced a finger over one of them and, for the first time, Cortés heard him speak: 'No vehicle has been up this road since García was seized. Next time anyone goes this way will be the cash-drop.' He spoke monotonously with no inflection or emphasis and Cortés wasn't sure whether these comments were questions or statements or whether they were directed to himself or his boss.

'Correct.' Better to answer, whoever was being spoken to.

'I go in with Cortés who is taking the money but we set off to arrive half an hour earlier than agreed. I get out some way before the rendezvous point, here.' Smith pointed at the photomap where the road swung through some trees. 'The jeep will move slowly at this point and will not stop – I jump off with no delay – jeep continues. At the handover, Cortés will be in no hurry, insisting that he see García fit and well. This process must take time. Argue maybe … attract attention of FARC soldiers … so I have freedom to move. Time taken to be sure García is safe … is crucial. If satisfied, Cortés will turn the vehicle round and slowly drive away. Three miles back down the road, here, he stops … and awaits further instructions via the two-way radio. If there is no contact two hours after leaving the site, he should continue alone back to base. That's all.'

Smith stood up, fixed Cortés with a stare and said: 'Unless I think of more details to iron out, we meet next at 6 a.m. Tuesday, Popayán airport.'

Fields and Cortés looked at one another. Cortés was taken aback by how much this man already knew and had prepared. Did he have anything to say or add to what Smith had said? No. He couldn't think just yet; he was still somewhat stunned. Also surprised by this man's strange, halting English.

Fields spoke next. 'Excellent work, Leo. Very good indeed. Now move all your things into the spare bedroom behind you and we will talk later about anything else you may want. You've had a long flight and you should take a rest now.'

This was another surprise for Cortés – how pleasantly, almost fatherly, Fields was speaking to his guest, treating him with kid gloves. The impression was consolidated that Smith, 'the nuclear option', was indeed a very special weapon, which, if inadvertently detonated, would explode in ways that were unpredictable and likely to be very damaging for all concerned.

Cortés waited for Fields to finish fussing over his visitor, and then he confirmed their earlier arrangements. 'I'll get back to Popayán straight away, sir. We'll get a message on Sunday via El Ciego for the FARC to contact us and I'll wait for their call. I'll insist on proof of life as we have agreed and will phone you directly all this is settled. Is that all, sir?'

'Yes thank you, Cortés. Glad to see you're on top of all this. You can go now and take the limousine with you. *Adios!*'

Bright and early Tuesday morning, Leopold Smith appeared in Popayán in the same dull grey, executive outfit that he had worn on his arrival in Bogotá. He was met at the airport by Cortés in the long-wheel-base Land Rover Defender and Smith wordlessly seated himself inside, carrying an attaché case and a larger black bag. The attaché case was pushed across the front seat to Cortés.

'Ten thousand dollars,' said Smith.

Cortés steered the Triple F Land Rover away from the

airport, away from the town and off in the direction of the mountains. There was no conversation inside the vehicle; Cortés's questions about Smith's plan of action were ignored, though when they eventually turned off the public highway and on to the rough access road that led to their destination, most of his concerns were answered by observing Smith's deliberate and intensely focused activity.

First, Smith removed his shoes and stripped off his suit, shirt and tie and neatly, meticulously, folded them and placed them over the back on an adjoining seat. Beneath this outfit, Smith was wearing a dark-green sweatshirt and briefs. He then pulled out of his black bag a one-piece, camouflaged battledress, which he duly fitted over his huge frame. This was carefully adjusted in the same meticulous fashion that he did everything. A webbing belt came next. Cortés noted that a British Commando dagger hung from one side and a holstered pistol on the other. Smith tightened the webbing around his middle and then drew out the pistol, a snub-nose 0.38 Smith & Wesson revolver with internal hammer and integrated laser sight. He checked the five-shot chamber contained four bullets, the fifth empty chamber being at the top, and holstered the pistol again when he was sure everything was fine. Extra ammunition was already contained in the belt. He then unzipped a snug digital camera from the black bag and buttoned it into his breast pocket along with a penlight torch. He next lifted out a small, dark-green backpack and placed it beside him, and then unfurled an olive-green balaclava and dragged it down over his scalp. Last of all, he took out a large pair of lightweight, water-resistant combat boots, pulled them on and tightened their laces. All done, he was dressed and ready for action.

Smith lifted the empty black bag, turned, reached behind him and then transferred his business clothes from the adjoining seat and placed them into the bag, zipped it up, and returned it to where it belonged. He then lifted his small rucksack on to his lap. All this was done in the same, careful, methodical manner that Cortés had now got used to. He understood why this man didn't speak: he had his own routines, his own ordered way of doing things and he did not welcome any interruption.

The rucksack had clearly been prepared beforehand so needed no second check. Smith held it in one big hand on his left, sat back and took up a position of waiting, his right hand poised by the passenger door handle, his attention pointedly focused on the terrain ahead.

The Land Rover ate up the miles, hanging on to the bends as they motored onward. Cortés had been up this access road a number of times and knew it as well as anyone but he could not help but wonder at the amazing map-memory of his passenger, who had never been here before and knew this rough track only by an aerial photo. At the point near where Smith had earlier identified the place where he would dis-embark, he issued his one and only command.

'Start slowing down!'

As the Land Rover crawled around the next bend, with the drop on his left and trees overhanging on the right, Cortés got closer into the mountainside and watched as Smith quickly opened the door, swung out, slammed the door shut again and then crouched down against the earth bank, below the trees, as the vehicle slowly moved up-road and away in a cloud of dust.

Leopold Smith was once again a lone agent, on a deserted mountainside with a clear objective in his head and no other distraction – just the way he liked it. Looking round, there was little to see except a few yards of rough earth road either side of him, a small canopy of vegetation above and blue sky all across in front of him. Only the sound of the Land Rover diminishing into the distance disturbed this place; there was nothing and nobody that could see him where he stood at the moment. He guessed he had one hour remaining before the agreed meeting time between Cortés and the FARC: half an hour for the vehicle to get to its destination plus half an hour's waiting time. He had no need of a watch: it only snagged on clothing or branches and reflected light if ever he paused to look at it. No time to wait: he looked behind him to find a way to climb upwards.

If he was the FARC commander in charge in this operation, he would want to have his men high above the road to watch any incoming traffic. Smith was several shoulders of the mountain away from the rendezvous and the FARC would anyway most likely be moving into position down from where they had been based, so there was every likelihood that he would not be seen as they descended and he carefully gained altitude. That was the theory, anyway. No way to test this but to get going. Sixty minutes was not much to cover the difficult slopes above him.

Smith was no stranger to mountain exercises so he kept his weight forward and low, eagerly searching for some sort of animal trail that led in the direction he wanted to travel. Any sort of path would afford him much more rapid progress than trying to forge his own way through the low, tangled trees and shrubs of mountain rainforest. The cover was good and, providing he did not move too fast, too carelessly and did not cause too much movement of the bushes and dwarf trees in passing, he should be unobserved. If there were any FARC lookouts somewhere, they should anyway be scouring the land below and further round.

Smith was counting his paces and the passing minutes in his head as he travelled diagonally higher. Three-quarters of an hour into his excursion and he could risk gaining height no longer: he had to traverse round so that he could get a good view of the road and the rendezvous site. This was the potentially dangerous part where the objective was to see his enemy and where they might also be able to spot him. Crouching low, he scuttled across to the breast of the arête which soared downwards a little way in front of him. He sat himself as comfortably as he could under a bush that sprouted above him and examined the scene below. The road was clear to see – a reddish-brown line tenuously looping through the viridian tropical vegetation. Following it round to where he expected to see the Land Rover, he was frustrated to see that the exact site was covered by yet another curve in the mountain shoulder. He would have to traverse further across to find a better vantage point. Damn!

It was now approximately ten minutes before the deadline. Smith paused for several minutes more, absolutely stationary, searching the shoulder in front of him for any sign of movement. He looked higher up; then down. Nothing. Creeping carefully as he dared, he inched his way across to a bulge in the slope some twenty-five yards away. He prayed that this would give him the view he needed and also that no one would see his slow-moving bulk.

Ears pinned back he waited for any sound, dreading the crack of some firearm. But he made it safely. And the bulge offered the view he was hoping for. Smith settled down once more in dark shade below a tree and slowly, cautiously he removed his back pack and delved into it for his binoculars. These were matt black with long, tube-like shades that prevented any giveaway reflection. The Land Rover was still some distance across and further down from him but Smith's viewpoint afforded him an uninterrupted sight of above and below where it was parked. Cortés could just be seen behind the wheel inside; no other person was in view as yet. Further beyond the Land Rover, where the road descended a little way downslope, Smith could easily see the bright-yellow grader and leveller – the road-making machine that had been sabotaged in setting the trap for Triple F to fall into. Slowly sweeping the area with his binoculars, he could pick out the sorry strips of rubber tyres strewn across the clearing. Nothing moved.

Silence. The sun was slowly climbing higher, any shade still remaining was becoming shorter and blacker and it seemed as if the whole world was waiting. Again, Smith thought, if he was the FARC commander he would leave it a few minutes more to give time to check the terrain and to allow the tension to rise for the poor individual who had come to meet them. If Cortés was as experienced as his Triple F records showed, however, he ought to realise this also. That should help to calm his nerves.

More minutes passed. Close to the road and a little further ahead of the Land Rover a bush moved. Someone stepped out on to the road. Smith barely twitched a muscle – there must be no movement on his part to attract attention – but he refocused his glasses to examine the individual approaching Cortés. It was a young man with sunburned features under a brown baseball cap, a little stubbly growth on his chin, a dirty green T-shirt and grubby denims. He was carrying an AK-47 automatic assault rifle. Smith saw him approach the Land Rover; Cortés didn't move from inside. Clever man, he was not going to present himself as more of a target than he had to.

Some discussion took place between the two men through the open door window of the four-by-four. Smith knew what this was about and was meanwhile searching the surrounding vegetation to see if he could see anyone else. There was some fidgety movement directly above the point where the FARC soldier had first emerged on to the road. Scouring this place minutely, Smith could see evidence of another man there.

The conversation by the road was getting a little louder; so much so that Smith could pick out individual voices, though their language was indecipherable. The deeper notes were Cortés; the lighter ones his adversary. Training his binoculars back on to the two of them, the latter could be seen to pull out a walkie-talkie with the clear intention of passing a message to someone.

Moments passed. Then, higher up but still on the same line

above the point on the road where the first man appeared, there was more movement of bushes. Smith strained his eyes through the binoculars. Three people? It looked like it. Perhaps this was García being presented as proof of life? Slowly panning down to Cortés again, Smith could now see he had been given the walkie-talkie. No doubt he was being invited to talk to the hostage. So far, so good. He still could not be sure who the individuals were higher up in the bushes, perhaps they were better seen from below where Cortés was, but whether or not García was there, Smith at least knew they were his targets. It was Cortés's decision whether or not he had seen what he wanted.

Smith continued to scan the mountainside, up and down, left and right, taking his time to try and estimate how strong the FARC party was. While he was doing so, he heard the Land Rover start up and, sure enough, it seemed that Cortés had concluded the arrangements and was preparing to back his vehicle round and leave. Swinging down his glasses to the road once more, Smith saw the FARC soldier walking away from the Land Rover, slowly retreating with the attaché case in his hand. The drop had been achieved. All parties seemed happy.

Now it was getting interesting. Would the four or five people he had detected on the mountainside meet up and withdraw above? Smith hoped so. It would signify that only one FARC encampment existed and García would be with them. He sat tight and watched the proceedings.

Half an hour passed – the two he had identified by the road slowly made their way up slope, climbing towards the others. This was good news. As they did so, Smith continued to search the area. He had to ensure that there were no others, like him, just lying low and watching. He was anxious to move out upslope himself so that he could track behind his quarry and see where they were heading but he dare not take that risk just yet. Thinking it through, there were at least five persons he had confirmed in the FARC party with García probably handcuffed or some other way shackled among them. That would slow their movement down. He was probably three-quarters of an hour behind them from his current position – he figured it would take him that long to traverse round and up to the place where the three highest individuals had shown themselves. But he could very quickly make up that time as he would move fast and they could not, so there was no question he would lose them just yet. He could afford another twenty or thirty minutes just sitting here, quietly observing, making absolutely certain there was no other FARC agent out there, undetected so far.

Fifteen minutes passed and the persons he had seen had all come together and moved out, leaving the place seemingly deserted. Checking once more, there was no sign of any movement below. Smith very slowly stood up, stretched and then trained his binoculars once more to examine every point above him that had been obscured by the tree he was hiding beneath. He was glad he did so. There was a dwarf tree with branches twitching unnaturally that he could clearly pick out not a hundred yards directly above him. Examining the place with heightened interest, he watched as what seemed like one person left their place of concealment and headed off above.

Smith waited, watching for a few minutes more, then set off in pursuit. Moving unhurriedly vertically upward, he reached the dwarf tree with little difficulty. The path that was being made by the person he had just seen was not too difficult to follow, so he moved along without delay. The higher he reached the more the slope receded, until he could begin to see further and further in front. It was now mid-afternoon, however – the sun was burning brightly and a heat haze interfered with long-distant vision. Providing he made no obvious noise and did not catch up too fast with those in front, Smith was confident his stalking would go unnoticed.

The route the FARC had chosen continued to rise but also now trended back west in the direction from which the Land

Rover had come in. The party in front were moving away from the peaks behind them, towards a shoulder that would take them into the next valley and into which no motorised access was possible. Smith guessed that, once over the shoulder, they would swing back easterly once more and probably spend the rest of the afternoon descending into thicker and thicker vegetation.

He was now around one hundred and fifty yards behind the last of the party he had seen. Smith came to a halt and waited until the first among them reached more open ground at the top of the shoulder. Raising his binoculars he peered intently at everyone that passed over the horizon, unobstructed for a moment by any shrubs or bushes. The man in the lead carried an AK-47 and wore old combat fatigues and a lighter-coloured sunhat. Following him was a woman in similar fatigues, long black hair, no hat and with no obvious weapon that could be discerned from this distance. Then came a group: two men with rifles slung on their backs, one of whom was the man who had met Cortés on the road; the other was a larger, older guy with a grey jacket, black or dark brown breeches and long, lace-up combat boots. The two pulled ropes between them, on the other ends of which was García, stumbling along in a totally incongruous, screwed-up pinstriped suit and with body language that showed he was seriously unhappy. Last of all was another guy fully clothed in ex-army combat gear from his hat to his rubber boots, carrying the attaché case and what might have been a handgun or similar weapon tucked into his webbing. Smith guessed he might be the leader of the group, directing from the back, an experienced soldier who would keep the party closed up while they were following a pathway that was familiar to them. Five soldiers in all, moving along slowly but confidently with their hostage.

Smith reckoned it was time to call Cortés. He watched the party in front disappear over the bluff, out of sight and sound, then he removed his pack and found the two-way radio inside.

It took him a moment or two to raise his colleague who was parked three miles down the road and out of harm's way

'Cortés?'

'Yeah.'

'There are five of them, plus García. They are now in the next valley. They'll need to rest soon, so I hit them as soon as it's dark. Hopefully before they meet others. You leave now and come back tomorrow at daybreak. Same place as cash-drop. Savvy?'

'Yeah. Do you want me to tell Fields?'

'No. See you tomorrow. Out.'

Smith easily followed the party in front. García was unfit, ill-equipped, probably malnourished and clearly unable to move fast. Smith could hear voices snarling unsympathetically on occasions and he guessed they were García's captors encouraging him to keep moving. A few hours of this and the party was moving slower and slower. Now the sun had gone down, the jungle of low trees and bushes was covered in strange, eerie shadows of black and grey. Smith wondered when the party would stop. They were following a track through the forest that they obviously had carved out earlier and Smith had closed the distance between them as near as he dared, waiting for the opportunity to attack. His prime objective was to free García unharmed and secondly to gather as much evidence from them as he could to discover their motives in killing Triple F staff. But he couldn't see any way of achieving either just yet. He had to wait.

The evening advanced and still the party kept moving. They obviously had some destination in mind and were working towards it, slower than the FARC leader wanted, by the sound of the abuse that rose into the forest night. Then suddenly the path swung downslope and the group's noise level increased slightly. The air of anticipation increased with it. Smith could hear a stream cascading down somewhere in front and at last the FARC stopped. They had reached the place where they intended to bivouac overnight.

Smith ducked upslope, away from the jungle track his quarry had made, and hunched down. He had night-vision goggles in his backpack but he did not need them; all the FARC soldiers were now wearing head torches and they were creating enough light between them for him to make out what was going on. A small clearing opened out on some flatter ground near the stream. The FARC had probably done this earlier. Two men seemed to be tying García to some tree roots, giving him only enough space to lie down. His hands looked like they were chained somehow together in front of him. The leader of the party was preparing a sleeping space for himself; the long-haired woman appeared to be doing the same, next to him. The fifth one of the party, the one in a lighter-coloured hat that Smith had seen furthest ahead, seemed to be busying himself with several boxes and packets. This clearing was obviously a small base where a variety of equipment had been dropped: cooking and sleeping gear and a certain supply of food. Smith settled down to wait for his quarry to arrange all their affairs, eat something and then bed down for the night. He knew now what he would do.

García was clearly pleading for better treatment, more comfort, more food or whatever. Smith didn't understand a word of what was being said but García wasn't getting anywhere with his demands. The interplay this generated, however, was useful because Smith could more easily see how the group interrelated. The leader of the party issued all the orders and suffered no argument from any. The woman was his partner, second-in-command and clearly a favourite. The two men who had roped up García were detailed as his guards; the one in the sunhat was the smallest, possibly the youngest of the party and some sort of scout and general dogsbody who was sent to fetch water, help cook and run errands. So far as weapons were concerned, Smith had already established that the three men all carried AK-47s and the leader and his woman had handguns. Given the confined space they now inhabited, Smith estimated that the AK-47s were the least appropriate weapons to wield, while the two soldiers with handguns were the most dangerous, especially given their evident authority and likely initiative.

The older of the two guards was placed on watch while the others settled down to sleep. The leader and the woman got into sleeping bags. Excellent, Smith thought – that restricted their movement. The two other men wrapped themselves in blankets as well as they could to keep out the cold. García had also been given a blanket, though he continued complaining. The leader clearly told him to shut up and then one by one the head torches were switched off.

Half an hour passed in silence, broken only by the sound of the cascading stream and by García moaning and shifting in position. The older guard on watch moved a few paces away from the others and switched his head torch back on. He was preparing to have a pee. Smith silently rose and crept out on to the path where he could move quickly and without noise. He drew out his Commando dagger.

The guard stood by the stream, just where it broke through the undergrowth, chattering against stones and broken branches that blocked its way. As he silently approached his target, Smith couldn't help wondering why people urinating in the open seemed to want their waters to join with those from the earth. A bizarre question to ask, perhaps, as he snaked one huge hand around the man's face and mouth and, with the other, plunged the dagger deep into his throat. One swift movement sideways followed, with enough power to almost cut the man's head off. There was a horrible gurgle and Smith held the guard's weight as he collapsed. He dropped him carefully into the undergrowth. No unusual sound was audible above the splashing stream.

The next concern was to neutralise the other guard, nearest

to García, without giving any opportunity for the others to react. Smith decided to wipe his dagger clean, place it back in its scabbard and draw his revolver. He also unclipped the small pencil light from his breast pocket. It was pitch black now, but Smith had memorised the sleeping positions of the others. Speed and surprise was of the essence. He loped back to the clearing, picked out the shape of the other guard, and knelt over him. He decided to hit him hard enough to concuss him but not to kill him: a big man, Smith had to be careful with his strength. Crash! He brought the gun down on top of the sleeping man's cranium. As he guessed, this provoked alarm among all the others. García was calling out again; the two in sleeping bags struggled to sit up; the youngest soldier was probably trying to figure out who was doing what, where. Smith stood up, switched his penlight on to the two in sleeping bags, and fired one bullet into each of them from a distance of about four yards. He did not need to see their effect.

The noise of the revolver going off in the small space was deafening. The remaining soldier was clearly scared witless out of his sleep. He fumbled for his weapon, but before he had time to drag it round and aim, however, the penlight had caught him in its gaze and the red laser light on the revolver had caught him also. Another single deafening shot and it was all over.

Smith now returned to the soldier he had concussed, leaned across him and shone the light in his eyes. Vacant. He was not ready to speak as yet. Next García. The city boy was in a state of shock and clearly shivering in fright.

'Martín García, I've come to rescue you …' A simple monotonic statement in English but Smith could see it register in the frightened countenance of the poor man.

The rope tying García to the tree root like a dog on a lead was the first shackle to be removed. Smith thought of cutting the rope with his dagger, but his fingers were strong enough and agile enough to loosen the knots. García's hands were a separate problem. Smith found the concussed man's head torch and put it on so as to see better. A chain had been wound around and around García's wrists and it took some time before Smith could sort out the mess of knots and locks involved.

'Where's the key?' Smith asked the dazed captive. 'Which guard? This one?' Smith indicated the body lying next to him.

Martín García was shaking his head as if he was trying to come out of a nightmare. It was a truly horrific nightmare, but he found his voice.

'Yes, that one I think. He was the last to tie me up.' He watched like a stupefied, blank-eyed junkie as Smith rolled over the concussed guard and systematically searched his every pocket from top to bottom. A clip of keys was hanging from his belt on the side. Smith casually ripped this off and studied them closely in torch light to see if any of them looked like they might fit the padlock he needed to open. Moving across to García, he tried one then another and then he grunted in satisfaction as the second key turned and the chains were finally released.

The guard was now moving, moaning and beginning to revive. Smith hauled him up off the ground with one arm, held him standing in front of him and shook him from side to side. Smith's commandeered head torch burned into the man's eyes.

'What's your name?' he demanded. The guard was still half concussed and anyway did not understand English. Smith turned to look at García and told him to stand up, too.

'Ask him his name,' he ordered.

Martín had not been knocked on the head but he seemed almost as dazed as the other. He struggled to get up, wringing his hands, but then he staggered beside Smith and asked their prisoner, his ex-prison guard, what his name was in their common language.

'Diego Torres,' came the answer. The man was still very weak – his head was bruised and singing in his ears and he was

79

barely able to stand. Smith held him easily as if he weighed a feather.

'Tell Diego that, if he tells me what I want, I won't kill him.' Smith spoke as usual in a totally expressionless voice. García translated faithfully; the man nodded as if he understood.

'Ask him: who is he working for?'

García asked and gained the reply.

'He says he works for the FARC.'

'Not good enough. Who pays them? Who provided the equipment to blow up Triple F's Toyota and kill their staff?'

A lot of questioning and answering in Spanish followed that Smith couldn't follow.

García passed on the information. 'He says he doesn't know. His leader who is lying over there gets the gear and tells the team what to do. He has no idea what happens with the money. He sees precious little, he says.'

Smith was annoyed. His face was a mask as always but he lifted the guard bodily in the air and shook him like a dummy.

'He knows something. He must know something. Who did his leader meet when preparing for the attack? Where did the landmine come from? What sort of people made contact? Ask him which leg or arm he wants to lose first?'

García was almost as terrified of this monster as the guard who was now being shaken like a piece of paper.

A torrent of excited language flowed between the two native Spanish speakers. García spoke less and less and listened more and more as the threat of mutilation frightened the other into blurting out as much as he could to save himself.

'He says he honestly doesn't know who the people are. He said that the last contact he knows of was when they met a jeep with three men a couple of weeks ago on a road some way south from here. Packets of explosive were handed over. The leader said nothing to them, but he and the other guard reckoned the stuff came from a mining company. He heard them speaking English.'

'How does he know it was English if he doesn't understand it?'

Another pause while this was translated.

'Because it sounded then like his younger brother used to speak, and like we speak.'

'The jeep these men were in, did it have any company markings?'

The question was relayed to the other.

'He says he doesn't know; he didn't get close enough to see.'

Smith's left hand slid up to the man's neck. The right hand held his T-shirt, hauling the man up off the ground, his legs dangling like a puppet's.

'He's lying. If he saw the jeep, he can tell if it had any markings on it.' He started shaking the puppet, holding his left hand fast, releasing the right.

The guard's face was going blue, his eyes bulged. He tried to choke out a denial.

'Ask him again!'

Smith tightened his left hand and, with it, lifted the guard higher and shook him again. And again. The man did not answer. His lips didn't move. Not because he didn't want to. Not because he had nothing to say. But because he was dead.

Smith snorted in annoyance and dropped the lifeless body.

García was horrified. He had just seen a man strangled to death in front of him. He stood trembling in shock. Smith, on the other hand, looked around and reverted to plan. This meant checking on each of the bodies of his opponents, examining them carefully for any signs of life. He paced around the clearing, his head torch flicking from one corpse to another. He extracted two bodies from their sleeping bags, turned them over like he was playing with dolls and then tossed them aside into the shrubbery. He checked the youth with the AK-47 and, lastly, the older guard by the stream. He didn't need to look at the man he had just strangled. All eliminated, as he expected. He returned to the released

81

prisoner. Was he unharmed? Apart from chafed and raw wrists, he seemed to be.

Nothing more to do now until morning. He sat down in the space from where he had just cleared the bodies of the FARC leader and the woman, reached over for the least-damaged of the sleeping bags and prepared to bed down. He called over to Martín García, still standing dumbstruck.

'Nothing to do now. Go to sleep.' He switched off the head torch.

The personal mobile phone of Morten Fields rang, disturbing his breakfast. It was the call he was waiting for.

'Leo? Where are you?'

'Sixty-seven minutes out from the FARC camp. First place where there's a signal.'

'Tell me.'

'I have García unharmed. All five FARC soldiers eliminated last night. Ten thousand dollars in the bag. Photo evidence you want.'

'What evidence? Tell me.'

'Their camp contained bomb-making material. Packets of TMG explosives and detonators. Trade marks clearly photographed. Packets printed with: "TMG use only. Not for resale." Soldier interrogated admitted that English-speaking guys in a jeep delivered the stuff.'

'Excellent work, Leo. Well done. This is magnificent!' Fields's mind was racing. The materials could have been smuggled out of a TMG mine and sold on the black market to anyone, but the fact that English-speaking personnel had actually delivered the explosives to the FARC unit was really the information that was important. Just as he had guessed – the attack and killing of Triple F staff had obviously been planned by TMG and implemented by their paid stooges. But there was one remaining problem that had been worrying him all night.

'Leo, this is important. Has anyone alive seen you and García so far? You are not back at the Land Rover yet, are you?'

'No … and yes, I'm not.'

'Do you trust Cortés to keep his mouth shut over this operation?'

'Yes.'

'Do you trust García to keep quiet and not tell anyone either?'

'No.'

'I thought not. Leo, I have a new plan.'

Fields dare not tell his loyal lieutenant that he had changed his mind. That sort of thing provoked anger and unpredictable consequences. But García was a problem. The last thing he wanted was for the Colombian police or anti-terrorist units, or anyone else, hearing of what had happened and coming round and asking awkward questions. He did not want Leopold Smith, his most effective weapon compromised. He now had all the evidence that he wanted about the attack on Triple F. He didn't want García.

'Leo, I have to protect you. Your safety cannot be jeopardised. Do you understand?'

'Yes. I understand.' The reply came slowly, somewhat reluctantly.

'Tell García that you both have to go back and bring out some of the bomb-making material with you. Photos are not good enough. When you are back at the FARC's camp, use one of their weapons and silence García. Permanently. Understand?'

'Yes.'

'Do it.'

Fields waited for confirmation, then shut the phone.

4

The Mountain Man

·

It was early morning when Karin met Alfonso at the stables, saddled up the horse she had taken out before and then set off again, by herself, up the mountain path to find El Mono. She was a little earlier than the last time and so she wondered whether he would be at their agreed meeting place or whether she would have to wait. She rather hoped he would not be there so that it would give her time to ride around a little more, find another path or two, see a little more of the scenery. The mountain rainforest and, above that, the *páramo* were an environment completely new to her and, just like nearly everything else she had encountered in Colombia since her arrival, it was completely fascinating.

As she rode onwards, she thought about some of the friends she had left behind in university in Durham, in England. They were probably now preparing to return to lectures at the start of the academic year in their third and final year of studies – she would be doing the same if she had not chosen to take a year out on her language option. They would be returning to the same predictable world with its well-defined parameters – meeting the same faces, gossiping about who was going out with whom, worrying about their module marks, probably getting drunk on Friday night in the same college bars and pubs. Meanwhile, she was on the other side of the earth, encountering a totally foreign environment, taking on challenges she could never before had imagined. Amazing!

The sun was rising in a blue sky and the mist and low clouds that hung over the forests on all sides were beginning to disperse. The early-morning sounds of birdsong and the calling of whatever insects buzzed around here similarly faded. The sound of her horse plodding away uphill and its steady breathing were now the only music to accompany Karin's journey into new horizons. She felt alive, liberated, excited and, of course, intrigued about what sort of day and person she would find before her.

El Mono was an attractive individual, she ruefully admitted to herself. Fair-hair, a weathered, sun-burned face that only served to further emphasise shining, deep-blue eyes; she could hardly stop staring at him at first. When she had seen him, two days ago, he was wearing a thick woollen colourless sweater, probably locally made, grubby, well-worn denims, and tough leather boots. Nothing remotely fashionable or sexy, but they could not conceal a tall, slim frame, an athletic and effortlessly agile gait and an air of complete independence and self-confidence. There was nothing more attractive than a man who seemed to need nothing and no one, and who was so unhurried and comfortable in his own skin. She sighed. She really ought to stop thinking like this! He would probably turn out to be the biggest, most selfish bastard that she had ever met. Latin America was allegedly full of macho bastards, wasn't it?

Gaining altitude, the surrounding vegetation became shorter, less densely packed, with more scratchy shrubs, gorse bushes and dwarf trees. Now and again, at around 3,000 metres, frailejones started to appear, the native plants of the *páramo*. Karin stood as tall as she could in her saddle, looking ahead and over to the side, to see if she could pick out the place where Claudia and her had earlier broken out from the path and arrived at the jumble of boulders that marked the meeting place. Not there yet. Fifteen minutes more, a little higher, and she found it. She turned her horse to walk over towards the clearing she remembered, being especially careful this time not to trample plants underfoot. She didn't know whether she was pleased or disappointed to find the spot by the boulders unoccupied. Whatever, it gave her the opportunity to ride further forward, contouring round the mountainside until she found another track leading upward. This she took, her horse barely needing any encouragement to follow the easier, less troublesome route.

A flash of movement across the bright-blue sky in front caught her attention. Karin recognised the fluttering wing beats and the astonishingly rapid and subtle changes of direction that she had seen once before. The falcon soared and twinkled high above her and then, quicker than she could stop and hold her mount still, it reversed direction and dived almost vertically down, gathering speed to plummet out of sight over the ridge some distance ahead. Karin encouraged her horse to pick up speed in order to climb up a rise a little way in front of her. The ridge that marked the limit of the mountain slope she was currently climbing was still some way off but the rise before her would offer a better view.

Her horse clambered slowly up, panting rapidly; Karin could push it no faster. Having to stop, no longer swaying and bobbing about on the horse's back, she could now get a better idea of what the terrain looked like ahead. The land was clothed in a sweep of wiry, olive-green grasses, stretching away from the stony rise on which she had stopped, down to a small lake and then curving up again to the ridge that marked the horizon. The grassland was populated by a forest of rosette frailejones, regularly spaced, each one a metre or so distant from another as if they were a deliberate plantation. These formed a blanket of pale-green, almost white, velvety leaves hovering waist-high above the rough grass. Nothing moved over this picture-postcard landscape and, despite the altitude, there was not a breath of wind to disturb the view. Karin wished she had brought a camera to capture what seemed to be a dreamlike fantasy world. Then a figure broke across the distant horizon with a horse following. It had to be El Mono.

Karin could not help but admire what she saw. El Mono walked ahead of Bella, the mare, picking his way through the frailejones, scouting around the lake, moving towards her. Visible only from the waist up he seemed to be floating gracefully through a pale-green mist of leaves. He was wearing a striped poncho today and being looser and cloaking his upper body more it added to his grace of movement. Man and horse weaved their way as one, slowly closer and closer, looming larger and larger, until twenty-five yards away Karin caught sight of the hawk that had raced through the skies a little earlier now settled on Mono's shoulder. This party of three came right up close with no sign of any greeting. The falcon's eyes, and Mono's, were fixed on Karin as if piercing right through her. Why did she feel so naked and unsettled? She tried to hide her feelings with a bright welcome.

'Hello! I'm so pleased to see you.'

El Mono nodded. Was that a wry smile that played across his face?

'You came up early.'

'Yes, I couldn't wait. This is such a new world for me – nothing like I've ever seen before.'

This time there was no question. A smile transformed the otherwise guarded expression that she had grown accustomed to seeing on him until now.

'Well, there is a lot more to see up here – if you've got the time to look.' He reached up and coaxed the falcon on to his hand and then threw it up high into the air, gazing up after it as he did so. 'She can move here unrestricted and can get a better view than both of us. We are tied to the earth and fenced off from much of the land below the highest peaks ...' He turned and looked back at Karin. 'You've come for the mare? She's ready to take back down now.'

87

The guarded expression had returned and there was a gibe there about people, presumably like Claudia's family, owning and fencing off the land and restricting access to the mountain. Karin ignored it.

'I don't want to take Bella just yet, thank you. Please tell me more about that hawk of yours – have you been training it?'

'She's a peregrine falcon and no, I haven't been training her. She just seems to like me. When she's not hunting she comes to say hello, that's all.'

The bird was a falcon, not a hawk; and it was a 'she' not an 'it'.

'Well, it must be thrilling to have a falcon like that for a friend! How often does she come to you?'

'Now and again. Whenever she wants.'

'I've never see anyone else who has that effect on birds like you, Mono. I don't know how you do it!'

'I don't how I do it either.'

'But there must be something about you that she likes! The way you live and where you live, perhaps?'

Karin beamed him a smile and wished he would smile back in return. She was doing her best: he was such a difficult and distant person to draw out.

El Mono looked up in the sky at the falcon, now a tiny dot streaking away. Bella the mare pushed her nose into Mono's hand and drew his attention back to earth. There was that shadow of a wry smile again, directed at the horse, not Karin, as if he was apologising for his momentary absence.

'I've told you, I don't really know. Maybe because I'm content with them as they are and am not trying to hurt them, or capture them or control them in any way. Bella, of course, has been trained and she will follow you and do as she is told if you take her now.'

Karin could feel annoyance in her growing. He was refusing to be drawn and she felt as if he was trying to get rid of her.

'Well, I've told you – I don't want to take her back just yet.

Please don't push me away. Can't you help to show me more of this place, tell me more about your world? You live with falcons up here; I live with cars and exhaust fumes in the city and know nothing of this.' She decided to go on the attack: 'And I can't call you "Mono" anymore! I'm not used to such nicknames. I've told you I'm Karin. What's your real name?'

She had laid down the challenge. Either open up or continue being an unfriendly, detached, antisocial recluse. What was it going to be? Karin saw the struggle on his face. He was clearly a man comfortable in his own lonely environment, aloof from the contamination of others' demands and he did not want to be dragged down to the world of mere, fallible mortals like herself. Well, she wasn't having it!

Large, blue, impassive eyes looked up at her. 'I'm Daniel,' he said, capitulating. Then he recovered and came back fighting again: 'And you are right: there's all sorts of exhaust gases and poison in the cities, where people harm each other and themselves. That's why I live up here most of the time. You want to know more about my world – how much time have you got?'

'All day today, Thursday. Then I'm here until Sunday and I fly out that evening back to Bogotá. How long can you bear being with me, Daniel?' Karin grinned at him.

This time he smiled broadly and decided to stop fighting. 'OK. You're no worse than any other city girl I've met … and better than some. You want to see around here – let's start up on that ridge behind me!'

Success! Karin smiled in return. She felt like giving him a kiss, she was so happy at breaking down his reserve. On second thoughts, she dare not give him a kiss; she would not be responsible for her actions afterwards.

Daniel held Bella for an instant, spoke as if to warn her, then leapt up and settled himself on her bare, saddleless back. She didn't move until he was ready, then turned and moved back in the direction she had come, seemingly without any indication given by her rider. Karin followed, quietly impressed, bemused again at how he managed to direct her, like the falcon, without any visible means of control.

For the next couple of hours Daniel took Karin slowly along the ridge, on to pathways that criss-crossed the terrain, and up to vantage points where they could see the Andes stretching away south and east to the snowcapped Volcán Puracé. He told her of the *páramo*, the high moorland ecosystem almost unique to the Colombian Andes whose variety of flora and fauna were uniquely adapted to its characteristic climate of huge daily extremes of temperature, but inevitably vulnerable to the accelerating man-induced climate change. Daniel never tired of pointing out the destructive side of humankind's influence on the planet.

They chatted away, speaking sometimes Spanish, most times English. Karin listened attentively, questioned repeatedly, revealing all the attributes of the excellent student that she was. But she soon tired of this role and there was one area that she was desperate to know more about and which her guide had so far steered away from: Daniel himself.

Midday came and Karin asked if Daniel wasn't hungry; she was starving. He nodded and led the way down, back in the direction of Claudia's estate, back to the little clearing by the boulders where they had first met two days ago. Daniel slipped easily off the mare, knelt down by the back of one the rocks and drew out a plain canvas shoulder bag. From this he produced a single orange and two strange, dark-green packages.

'Would you like to share my lunch?' he asked Karin. 'Had I known you were staying I'd have brought more. These are *tamales*, have you tried them before?'

'I've seen them; never tried them,' she replied nervously. 'What exactly are they?'

Daniel laughed and went on to explain that they were food parcels common all over Colombia, although these were a Popayán version – filled with a mix of potatoes, minced beef, peanut butter and spices – all wrapped and tied tight in plantain leaves and cooked up that very morning. Karin said she would absolutely love to try one, thinking at the same time that he really ought to laugh more.

They both sat cross-legged on the stony ground and shared the food between them, Daniel peeling the orange, passing across half and carefully placing the discarded peel back in his shoulder bag. It was now early afternoon, the sun was beating down and Karin thought this was a warm, comfortable, perfectly convivial experience. She smiled at her companion and could hold her curiosity back no longer.

'Daniel – what are you doing here? I'm no expert on Colombia but even I can tell you do not look or sound like any of the people who live in the pueblos below … Yet at the same time your affinity with this environment is amazing. I've already told you who I am and where I'm from. Now it's your turn.'

Daniel looked down, wondering how much to give away. After a pause he raised his head and stared past Karin at the mountainside beyond. 'I was born and raised in Bogotá until I was twelve,' he said simply, seriously, 'but when both my parents were killed not far from here, I couldn't go back. I hated it there; loved it here. I've since stayed, lived and worked here in these mountains ever since.'

Karin put out a hand and touched his; the first personal contact between the two. 'I'm sorry, I didn't know.' She paused and watched to see his reaction. 'I don't want to pry and don't tell me if you don't want to … but what happened?'

'It's OK. It happened a long time ago. The official story is that they drove off the road on a particularly dangerous stretch and fell to their deaths. I didn't learn until I was much older that they hit a landmine and were blown up. No party ever admitted responsibility; no one was ever charged with their deaths. That is just the way that things happen here. People literally get away with murder …'

'Oh Daniel … How awful for you. Were you very angry?'

'Yes. There are times when I still am. First I was angry with the people who became my adopted parents. Why didn't they tell me what really happened right from the beginning? I found out later from others who accidently blurted out the truth. I went back and confronted my foster parents and shouted at them for lying to me. I left where I was living then and there and came to live in the mountains, with the creatures that I loved and trusted and where there was no one who would ever lie to me ever again. It took me several years before I could go back and apologise for my behaviour. I know they were only trying to protect me when I was so young, so I told them I understood and asked for their forgiveness. Things are better now between me and the villagers ... but I continued to live and roam around these mountains. After all, that was why I came here in the first place.

'And I found out that I could offer the pueblos some help. You've seen I'm good with all things up here – I was finding that out for myself all the time, learning how the animals and birds lived, how to care for the plants and crops, and so I could help the local farmers with their livestock, even increase their yields. And I found myself in doing that.'

Daniel looked back at Karin, the faraway look in his eyes gone now, a twinkling smile returning to them. 'That's enough about me. You say you've told me who you are but that's not completely true. Like you, I know nothing of your world so come on – let me into it ...'

So Karin launched into her own history, from her earliest, faintest memories of Munich and her father; to her growing up with her mother in Berkshire, near London; her delight at getting into Durham, postponing university to go to Madrid; then two years of study until she arrived in Colombia. She tried to paint a picture of what England was like and what it was like at university. She asked him about his own education.

'I dropped out of school in Bogotá when I was twelve,' replied Daniel. 'I sort of studied in local schools here for a bit but I was hopeless and couldn't settle. My life had turned upside down and, anyway, I was always a very poor student.' He looked almost shy. 'I ... I've always felt a little inferior to people like yourself who've studied and succeeded and gone on to greater things. I was a failure. I couldn't get away from school fast enough.'

What a sensitive, beautiful man! Karin reached out and held on to his hand this time.

'Oh, Daniel, you never cease to amaze me! You who are so confident and self-possessed and so much the master of the world you live in. You don't know how much people like me wish we could be like you. There are times when I don't know who I am and where I really belong. I rush around here and there, one end of the globe to the other, and continually wonder at the value of my life. You, on the other hand, understand the world perfectly. It is me who is inferior ... not you!'

Daniel smiled sheepishly. He left his hand in hers for a long, lovely moment before drawing it away. 'You're too kind. Are all English girls like you? You're certainly not like the Colombian city girls I've met and not at all like the *indígenas* of the pueblos.'

Karin laughed. 'I don't know who you've met, but I'm not so very different from my friend Claudia the *caleña*, with whom, incidentally, you were not very friendly when we were all together the other day.'

'Not so. I'm just very wary of wealthy urban people who seem to value possessions more than people ... and certainly more than the environment which they are busy tearing apart. You say you like it up here. I sometimes wonder how long it will stay this way when I see what some people are doing to it.'

'Such as?'

'Burning it, overgrazing it; draining it, digging it up and discarding all their poisonous chemicals upon it. I've travelled miles over the ridges and mountain tops over the years and seen men driving big machines, tearing up the vegetation, opening huge holes in the ground to extract what's underneath. Then there are the huge estates which push goats and cattle up on to the *páramo* where the plant life isn't good for them and they are not good for it. Both suffer, but it is all to make money in the short term, never mind what the long-term consequences are ... Don't get me started ... I'll go on and on and start getting angry again!'

'Daniel – if you feel this way, what can you do about it? You can't just stay here getting all bitter and hating the world and poisoning yourself!'

'You're right. I should do more. I do help the local *indígenas* make a living out of their farming – caring for livestock; promoting ways of harnessing the soil, not destroying it. And I have worked at times in the National Park of Puracé, acting as a sort of independent guide for tourists (ugh!) and trying to spread the word about respecting the environment up here.' Daniel stopped. 'My problem is I hate the people who have no respect for others, the plants, the animals and birds here; the sort, I guess, who killed my parents. People who want possessions – or other people's possessions. You now make me realise that getting angry about it is not good enough. I guess I have to confront them, not just stay away up here from them ... but I do hate the big city and all it represents!'

Daniel jumped up, stomped around and restlessly shook his head as if trying to rid himself of these thoughts, the conflict inside him unable to be contained. Karin looked at him in wonder. What passion and how quick he was to examine his own life and own up to his own failings! She could only watch speechless.

As quickly as he lost control, Daniel regained it again. He turned and helped Karin to her feet. His face was red and betrayed self-consciousness.

'I'm sorry about that. Please forgive me for being so foolish. But thank you, thank you for seeing some things clearer than I could.' He laughed scornfully at himself. 'You're right. I ought to do something other than just moan and complain. I've now got to go away and do a lot of thinking for myself. Do you mind if we say goodbye now? I'll go with you and Bella back to the Fernández estate but I'll have to leave you there. Come back tomorrow or perhaps the day after if you want to.' His face softened towards her. 'Karin, thank you again ... but you have really set me thinking.'

He looked at her again, half admiring, half shame-faced. 'Come on, let's go!' he said at last. 'Your rich friend will be wondering what's happened to you.'

On parting, Karin had agreed with Daniel to meet up again on Saturday, in two days' time. She owed that to Claudia, her host, whom she could not desert two days in a row – it would have been far too rude and inconsiderate. Besides, after such an intense exchange between the two of them in so little time, she needed space and at least another day to come to terms with it all herself. Yes – Saturday, same time, same place as before and let's try to play it a little cooler next time!

All day Friday, Karin could not stop talking about him. Lunch at the farmhouse was served by Alfonso's wife, the cook and housemaid, but Karin could barely concentrate on what she was eating. She told her friend where they had gone, how he had talked about the land, the wildlife, and particularly how he had shared his lunch with her and told her all about himself. Her face shone; her words came tumbling out in a non-stop flow. Claudia teased her wickedly.

'OK, so you say you don't fancy him. Then why are you talking about him all the time? Even when you were silent this morning, you were mooning around with your head someplace else every minute I tried to talk to you!'

'I don't think about him all the time. Lay off! All morning I've been thinking of how different it is here from Bogotá; what a great place you have; the mountains above; riding yesterday and ... and ...' Karin burst out laughing. '... And what a lovely man he is!'

Claudia joined in laughing, too. 'Well, he has certainly made an impact on you! The way you describe him, I've got to go see him again myself – if nothing else to try and hold you back from making a fool of yourself!'

'It's not just the way he seems to completely dominate the world up there; it's not even the magical hold he seems to have over animals, birds and so on, or the love and respect the people hereabouts have for him. It's none of that. You should have seen him yesterday talking about the life he has been through. He talks about really important issues, his feelings. He really isn't like all the other superficial, selfish men I've ever met. It's just that he's so honest, so open, so sensitive and so ... so ... so wonderful!'

'You are a hopeless case! And be careful, Karin. Be careful about your own feelings. You are reverting back to being a schoolgirl again – having a crush on the first dishy man you come across. And you know, we *both* know, that that is the quickest route to disappointment. Dishy men have feet of clay and hearts of stone. Take care!'

Karin sighed. 'You're right. I know you're right. I will be careful. Goodness knows I am old enough, seen enough and been hurt enough to know better. But let me have at least one day of dreaming before I confront reality! Let us both go up tomorrow, together, and you can keep the reins on me and tell me also afterwards what you think. Remember when we first met? How you wanted my impressions of Martín "the bastard" García? Well, it's the same again – forget all that I've told you of Daniel, El Mono. After we both have a day out with him tomorrow, make your own mind up and tell me your own opinion later in the evening. Agreed?'

Claudia laughed again. The two girls hugged. 'It's a deal. Agreed. Now for goodness' sake, stop talking about him and let's go out. We'll go shopping in Popayán and have a meal there together. The town is famous for its good eating. Come on!'

Popayán on a Friday afternoon was full of people, of shoppers, tourists and sightseers – as a traditional old market centre and regional capital, the town was a local hub of business and trade of all sorts. The two friends had a thoroughly enjoyable time, Claudia showing Karin around some of the beautiful white colonial buildings, the newer, Western chain stores and fashion shops, and the local cafés, restaurants and bars. By the time the sun had begun to set their feet were aching and a café in the central plaza had attracted their custom. As always, Karin was delighted with the experience and thanked her host profusely for the idea of coming down to town and away from the farm for the day.

'Well, I'm glad you enjoyed it,' said Claudia. 'I did too. With you, everything is such fun – and it's new for me in a way also, seeing things through your eyes. So thank you, too. That gives me an idea: tomorrow we will have a day out with a certain person that we are not going to talk about now. We will have most of the day after, Sunday, free – before flying back to Bogotá. How about if we come back here Sunday morning? The market in this plaza on that day is something special.'

'I'd love to. Are you sure we would have enough time?'

'Yes, if we pack up, take all our gear with us in the car, and have our driver take us down here to wait for us. Then we can spend lunchtime browsing around the stalls and then go straight off to the airport. Easy!'

Karin smiled and nodded her agreement. The lifestyle here for families with estates, horses, cars and employees to look after them was so easy. She had a sudden pang of conscience: she could imagine Daniel would not be quite so comfortable with all of it. But she really had to shake her head free of him for today.

They finished and paid up at the café. They were just about

to leave when Claudia caught sight of a newspaper discarded on the next table. Neither of them had kept up with any news during the week they were at the farm – that was one of the reasons for being there – but a headline in this paper caught Claudia's eye: 'Three men from Triple F killed and one missing, feared dead, in Cauca, not far from Popayán. FARC held responsible.'

Claudia began reading with interest – this was a tragedy that had apparently occurred not far from her own farm. Then she read the names of the victims involved and her blood ran cold. She burst into tears.

'Claudia! Whatever is it?' her friend was immediately concerned.

'Look! Read it!' Claudia couldn't speak. 'It's Martín!'

Karin hurriedly scanned the page offered. Three men from Triple F had been killed in their jeep by an explosion on a remote mountain road near Popayán, on their way to a new mining development. The names of the dead were given. Another vehicle, gone to investigate, had been stopped, and a certain Martín García, Triple F executive from Bogotá, had been kidnapped. A statement from the chief of Triple F in Colombia, a Mr Morten Fields, released today, Friday, had only now revealed all the details. The corporation had been keeping things quiet, it appeared, in the hope that negotiations to secure the release of their executive would be successful. The statement went on to say that ten thousand dollars had been paid last week to the FARC, who had admitted responsibility, and a second payment was due to be paid this week but that representatives of the terrorist organisation had broken off all communication and had apparently disappeared. Mr Morten Fields said he feared the worst, that Martín García had been a personal friend and that the family involved – owners of one of Colombia's more important and successful businesses – were frantically worried, as indeed he was. The statement finished by saying that the head of Human Resources for Triple F had resigned, accepting responsibility for placing Mr García – a recent recruit and trainee – in an area where there was a known security risk.

Karin put the paper down. She looked at the tear-streaked face of her friend. What could she say?

'I loved him, Karin! I once worshipped the ground he walked upon. I know he is a bastard, But ... but I also know that I still love him! And he's gone!' Claudia collapsed into tears once more.

'Don't say that, Claudia. You don't know. There's still a chance. The paper says he has been kidnapped, that's all.'

'You don't know the FARC. People disappear all the time thanks to them. Families end up paying for months, years, keeping their hopes alive – only finally to receive the dead bodies of their loved ones. In this case, the FARC have chosen not to receive any money – how nice of them. That means he must ... he must be ... already dead. There is no chance, no hope. It's all hopeless.' She wailed aloud.

Several café customers looked over in their direction. Karin moved her chair across to her friend and wrapped her arms around her. She wanted to let her know that she understood, that she was there for her, and that Claudia simply needed to release all her emotions.

'Go on, Claudia – cry it all out. Let go ...'

Minutes passed. At last, Claudia looked up into the worried face of her friend. She stopped weeping. Karin handed over a tissue.

'Thank you, Karin,' Claudia sniffed. 'I couldn't help it. It was such a shock ... Now what do I do? I still can't believe it ... It's like a bad dream ... but I've got to believe it ...' She was rambling.

Karin ordered another two coffees. Her friend was in no state to go anywhere just yet. The two of them sat together, silent for a moment, Karin holding her friend's hand in her lap, comforting her. An idea appeared to Karin.

'We still don't know enough about what has happened,' she said guardedly. 'But we do know that it was on a mountain road somewhere near here. And, Claudia, we know someone who knows these mountains better than anyone else around. Better even than the FARC, I'll bet. Claudia – we are going to see him tomorrow. Let's ask him if he can help? If he can find out anything; if Martín is alive or not. Let's ask him ... What do you say?'

Claudia looked at her. There was a glimmer of hope left. 'Thank you, thank you, Karin. You are such a friend! Yes – you are so right, that is a good idea. I don't know if it will help at all ... It may already be too late ... but we have to try. I don't know whether or not El Mono can find out anything, anything at all, and, if he can whether or not it will help. But as long as there might be just a chance that Martín is alive I'll try anything.'

Saturday morning the girls prepared their horses in a sombre mood – Claudia her own familiar mount, Karin this time with Bella. Alfonso's wife, María, had been asked to prepare packed lunches for them both, plus a bit extra as a present for Daniel, whose own lunch Karin had gratefully shared when they were together last. Karin also folded up a copy of the newspaper article to show Daniel – it gave them the only details they knew of what had happened.

Claudia was shivering with apprehension. She knew they were clutching at straws and she did not even know whether or not El Mono would help her. And if he agreed, whether he could offer any hope.

'Karin ... I'm so frightened,' she confessed.

'I know. I feel a bit the same. But it is all we can do.'

'I'm frightened that El Mono won't help – why should he? You said yourself he hates city folk, big business, all that sort of thing. And, if he does help, what if he finds out what I fear the most ... that the FARC have done their worst? Here I am, struggling to keep hope alive only to have it dashed once more.'

'Claudia … you have to be strong. Of course, you're frightened. But we have to go through with this. To know anything, even the worst that we fear, is better than not knowing, going on living in ignorance. And I am sure of one thing – that Daniel will help. You'll see. He really is the good man I think he is.'

'Good for you, Karin. At least one of us still has a man to dream about.' Claudia's eyes filled with tears again.

Karin went across between the horses and put her arms around her friend. 'C'mon, Claudia. Hold on. Don't think like that.'

'OK, OK. Let's get on with this.' Claudia shook her head, wiped her eyes and hauled herself up into the saddle. Karin returned to Bella and saddled up herself. It was time to set off.

It was a sad, solemn procession that took the path upward towards the *páramo* this time. At the boulders, Daniel was waiting. He had been restless, lost in thought walking over his old haunts for a day and a half and had returned to the boulders earlier than the agreed meeting time simply because he felt, for the first time in ages, that he had met someone who might be a sympathetic and objective audience for him and his ideas. One sight of the two horses approaching, however, and he could sense something was wrong. Both riders looked downcast, not at all the lively, irrepressible and somewhat carefree horsewomen that he had met a few days ago.

'What's the matter?' he asked Karin, who on this occasion was leading the way.

She smiled a welcome in return. 'Something pretty awful has happened. We wondered if there was a way you could help.' She dismounted, wondered if she should embrace Daniel as was customary when greeting a friend and, seeing he remained distant, turned instead to attend to Claudia's horse. Claudia dismounted also and the two girls stood together, looking at Daniel, apprehensively.

101

'What? Tell me?' The atmosphere between them was suddenly a little awkward. Daniel was not expecting Claudia to come and, as always, he held back when with people he was unsure of. Even with Karin, someone he admittedly felt a growing interest in, he felt there was something wrong about her that kept him wary.

'Daniel, there's a friend of Claudia's that's gone missing – the FARC have kidnapped him and may have killed him.' Karin fished in her saddlebag to find the newspaper article that they had read. She pulled it out, unfolded it and handed it over to Daniel. 'Read that – it tells you all we know.'

Not a good start. Daniel huffed, handed it back and turned away, hiding his face. 'Read it through yourself and tell me. I'm not good at reading.'

Karin blushed. She remembered now that he had dropped out of school early. Surely he could read and write? Perhaps not.

'I'm sorry. This is what concerns us: the article says that three men from Triple F have been killed and one captured by the FARC, not far from here. That is, in the mountains near a Triple F mine above Popayán. The one who has been captured is a friend of ours – Martín García, from Bogotá and he is a very important person to Claudia. Very important. Triple F say they fear the worst since the FARC have not come forward to claim the ransom money they originally demanded.'

'So what do you want me to do about it?'

'Is there some way you can find out more? His family are distraught. They own a big flower business in Bogotá. Triple F are distraught. Claudia is absolutely beside herself. Martín seems to have disappeared with the FARC into the mountains somewhere near here and we don't know if he is dead or alive. I thought that you were the one person more than anyone else who knows his way around here that might help … Can you help? … In any way at all? … Please.' Karin trailed off. Daniel's face did not look at all responsive.

'This is ironic,' retorted Daniel. 'I've spent over a day and more since seeing you thinking that I really ought to somehow organise opposition to all the foreign businesses like Triple F, big city enterprises like you say this García family run, and against people like Fernández who own huge estates and half the mountains around here. And now you ask me to help save the skin of one of them ...'

Claudia's emotions, which she had been struggling to keep in check, exploded.

'What's the use! He won't help. I knew it – for all we know he's in cahoots with the FARC himself! It's hopeless! Let's go back.' She remounted her horse.

Karin was utterly deflated. Disappointment marked her entire bearing. She had been counting on him and now her best friend was urging her to leave empty-handed. 'Daniel, please! If you can help, I'm sure there would be a reward ...'

Now it was Daniel's turn to explode. 'Have you come up here to insult me? What's this all about? I was really looking forward to seeing you, Karin, and now your friend accuses me of being one of the terrorists and you are trying to bribe me for something you think I don't want to do. How little you think of me!'

For a fraction of an angry second, Daniel was going to move forward and grab the reins of Claudia's horse to prevent her leaving, but of course her mount already knew it and so froze on the spot. Claudia, her face reddening and furious to get away, kicked her horse to try and leave but she was getting nowhere. Karin was covered in confusion. Two people she dearly respected were both losing control.

As before, Daniel quickly regained his equilibrium. 'Claudia – don't hurt your horse anymore. He knows I don't want you to leave so he won't take you. You're stuck with me, like it or not. Karin – you have so little faith in me. Offer a reward? I wouldn't touch any such money. You want me to see if I can find out what's happened to your friend? Since you want me to, then of course I'll do it. But it is ironic – you will, I hope, understand that. I've been wondering all night what I will do to stop Triple F and others from despoiling the Andes, here and elsewhere.'

Karin was now holding back her own tears. She had desperately wanted Daniel to help her dearest friend. She similarly desperately wanted Claudia to see in Daniel the lovely person she had believed him to be. For one awful moment he appeared not to be the person she wanted him to be. And now he was back, reproaching her for her own lack of belief. Her head spun.

'Oh Daniel. Forgive me ...'

Daniel nodded, stone-faced. 'Claudia, get off your poor horse. Let's talk about this.'

He led the way over by the boulders to the patch of stony ground where before he and Karin had shared lunch. Now he sat down, cross-legged again, and waited until the others did the same: two flush-faced women, both highly sensitive now and still apprehensive as to what was likely to happen.

Daniel sighed, looking annoyed. 'Karin, please read that article out aloud, all the way through, not missing anything, so that I know what you are talking about.'

She did so, apologising again before she started. Claudia sat down beside her, not saying a word, but Daniel could clearly see how upset she was about the article's contents. Karin came to the end and looked up at Daniel, almost pleading.

'OK, I get it now. I'll tell you what I know. The road to the Triple F mine is some way away from here. It is pretty obvious from the article which road it is – there is only one new Triple F mine hereabouts and I've crossed over that track several times. But we are talking maybe two days away if I walk there. Then there is the problem of whereabouts in that vicinity the kidnap took place. I guess it will be near the site where the explosion took place that killed the people in the jeep. I should be able to find that place after a bit of searching. But where the trail goes from there is anyone's guess. It will take months combing the mountains around there to find any trace of terrorists who do not want to be found. Do you understand? If I did then find the FARC, it might not be too easy for me to get the information you want. I mean I'm not frightened of them but I am of no use to them either. Why should they confide in me? They just wouldn't.'

'So it is hopeless!' Claudia was unmoved.

'No, I didn't say that. There is a quicker way to get some information, though how much I don't know yet.'

'How?' Karin was still pinning all her hopes on him.

'Tomorrow is Sunday. The midday market in Popayán is the place where all news in the region is exchanged and the man I know there is where all news eventually comes to. They call him "El Ciego" and he's a gold mine of information. I can simply ask him what more he can tell us. Even if it isn't much and I still have to go off searching the mountains, what news he has might help in narrowing down my field of operation.'

'Will you do it? Ask him, I mean? I don't think we can ask you to go off searching for a needle in a haystack, especially if that puts your own life at risk.'

'Of course I'll ask him. As to going off anywhere, we will see what El Ciego has to say first, OK?'

Karin sighed in relief. She turned to Claudia. 'I did say he would help, didn't I?'

Claudia nodded. Looking at Daniel, she blushed. 'I am sorry for insulting you, Mono. I can see now that you have nothing to do with the FARC. That was an inexcusable thing to say. Please forgive me – it's just I have been so upset. Martín is very special to me.'

'I understand. Apology accepted. And call me Daniel – I've got used to it now ...' He glanced with a twinkle in his eyes at Karin.

Karin looked back at him and felt her colour rising. 'Actually we were going to the marketplace in Popayán tomorrow anyway – wasn't that the plan, Claudia? We can meet you there briefly if you think it's possible. We have to fly out from the airport tomorrow evening, seven o'clock, though … '

'Fine. I can see you there in plenty of time before you have to leave. I don't always go to the marketplace but there are occasions when some of the village stallholders need a bit of my help in one way or another. You can usually find me in front of the big white cathedral, sitting under the trees to keep cool. Let's give El Ciego a little time to gather up the most recent news and then we'll meet. Say around four in the afternoon? How's that?'

After all the high emotion that morning, the two girls were really grateful. They felt like they had been thrown a lifeline. They knew, of course, that this was just a tiny step in the direction of lifting their general ignorance and that any information that could be discovered might not be what they wanted. But at least they felt they were doing something, not just passively, forlornly, waiting, consumed by hopelessness.

All three looked at one another. 'Do you want something to eat, Daniel?' Claudia asked. 'That is the least we can offer you.'

The Sunday market in Popayán takes a little time to get going – the stallholders need most of the early morning to set up before they are ready for custom. Those selling hot food start cooking at around eleven while others are still putting out their wares and organising their displays. *Indigenes* from the hill tribes tend to arrive late; many sell colourful clothing – sweaters, ponchos or ruanas, and hats in a variety of styles; others ply local foods – honey, goat's cheeses, yoghurt, potatoes and occasionally game.

El Ciego had friends or cousins who set out the various artefacts that his stall featured. He liked the early morning to go tap-tapping around with his white stick, meeting stall-holders, exchanging news and trading information. All the market was abuzz this day with news of the troubles visited upon Triple F. El Ciego took the opportunity to leave the plaza and go and find the regional office of the multinational organisation on the chance that some of the security men of that business might be outside, having a cigarette or otherwise passing the time. In fact, outside the building it was more frenetic than usual; a cordon was up keeping crowds away, a number of guards were checking all passers-by for anything unusual or suspicious. Certain important people were going in and out; other bystanders were just looking, speculating and swapping stories. El Ciego spent almost an hour chatting and listening to people, trying to get the most out of the situation. Then he returned to his own stall to open up for business. It turned midday.

Karin and Claudia were driven down to town in the farm's four-by-four. The driver parked some way from the plaza – it was impossible to get their rather large vehicle any closer, given the number of other small trucks, vans and pick-ups that had arrived earlier. The two girls walked in and joined the mêlée of customers, tourists and market folk that crowded the plaza. At one point, Karin left Claudia and stopped at one of the *viveros* – one of the larger market stalls selling plants and flowers. A wonderful array of colourful flowers would make a lovely photograph, she thought. She stepped back a little way to fit everything in the shot she was lining up. She took a fine picture and then turned her camera over to see the result. Suddenly a hand flew out, grabbed the camera and a quick figure darted away and around the narrow street at the corner. Karin gave a cry and started off after the thief. The crowd of shoppers parted for her but it was no use – after chasing past a number of buildings and rounding the corner of the next block she could catch no sight of him.

There was other trouble awaiting, however.

'Hey, gringa! Lost someone?'

'Come over here – I can help you!'

A group of youths and men idling outside a bar had seen her run round the corner, searching and looking lost, and the sudden appearance of this young, highly attractive and obviously foreign young women in their midst was an opportunity too good to be missed.

'Leave me alone, please, I'm looking for a thief.'

'Come here, pretty lady. I'm a thief – you can have me!' a tall negro called out. A lot of laughter followed.

A man dressed in a greasy vest and built somewhat larger than the others sidled up to Karin and ran a finger down her back. 'You stay with me, gringa. I can pay you well …' Another comment he made Karin could not understand but its meaning and his leering face was crystal clear.

'Get away from me, you pig!' she blurted out in English. Her control of Spanish deserted her.

The large man came forward, grabbing her arm and spurting out more filth. Karin struggled and cried out in fright. Other men closed around her, laughing and urging the fat one to take her into the bar. Karin panicked, fighting harder to stay in the street but the entrance to the darkened bar came relentlessly closer. She fought violently but this only led her assailant to use more force. He put a hand around her waist and lifted her up.

'You're going inside, gringa,' he said, 'and you are going to give me your lovely body whether you fight or not …'

Karin kicked and screamed in desperation.

'I'd let her go if I were you, Gordo!' a voice called out. 'Negro, tell him!'

'Fuck off and keep out of this, whoever you are' came the fat man's reply.

Negro spoke up. 'Hey, Gordo … that's El Mono. You'd better do as he says.'

There was an urgent buzzing from somewhere that accompanied that remark. A number of the men disappeared into the bar. Still struggling, Karin could now see round to glimpse

Daniel hurrying down the road towards her. She screamed again for help:

'DANIEL!'

The fat man spun her around, placing himself between her and Daniel, who had now reached them both. Facing Karin, he groped and pulled her forward, pressed his body against her softness, clearly enjoying the experience as he sidled her in the direction of his desire. He looked quickly over his shoulder at Daniel, judging that he was bigger and heavier than this light-weight who was seeking to spoil his fun.

'I just told you to fuck off,' he sneered, waving away a bee that now buzzed around his head.

'And I just told you to let her go,' replied Daniel.

The buzzing increased in intensity. Suddenly a swarm of bees descended upon the two men. Daniel didn't move. The fat man, however, leapt as if stung. He had been stung! And again and again and again. The fat man roared and swung his arms here, there and everywhere, but the bees kept coming.

Daniel watched coldly as the man ducked and weaved, swinging both arms to stave off the attack. Karin shrunk away, behind Daniel, and stared in awe at the unfolding drama. Bees were relentlessly assaulting the large man, zooming in from all angles and covering his partially clothed upper body. They could not be dissuaded by any wild waving that their target resorted to.

Daniel spoke calmly and clearly to the fat one who was becoming more and more frantic.

'Don't let a bee sting inside your ear or you'll go deaf. Don't let a bee sting you in the eyes or you will go blind. And most of all don't let a bee into your mouth or it will sting your tongue and you'll choke to death!'

The fat man roared in pain again, stumbling about under the ferocious bombardment. 'Hey, Gordo,' shouted Negro. 'For God's sake, keep your mouth shut!'

'Wise advice,' commented Daniel. He held up his arm.

Just as suddenly as the attack had begun, the bees stopped. They swarmed back to Daniel and settled on his arm. To Karin's amazement, the furious noise of the hundreds of wings all beating at the same time stopped as if they had been switched off and Daniel's arm was now covered in a shimmering black mist of insects that slowly moved and rippled as wave after wave of creatures shifted their bodies in unison as they clung to him.

Gordo, the fat man, was meanwhile lying on the floor. His face, neck, shoulders, arms and hands were covered in red welts where he had been stung. There was scarcely a square inch of bare flesh that had been spared. The poor man was semi-conscious and gasping in pain.

'Maybe soak him in beer?' said Negro, looking at Daniel. 'Will that help?'

'It might. I'm more concerned at the scores of bees that have sacrificed their lives in stopping him behaving like a beast. Look at all those poor creatures dying there,' he said mournfully. The fat man was lying in a carpet of insects that had stung him and were now crawling in their death throes.

Daniel looked at the number of people who had now reappeared from the bar and were gazing in astonishment at the scene in front of them. 'Bees are exceptional creatures,' he told them in a sad voice. 'Any one bee will thoughtlessly lay down its life to serve the will of the colony. When they sting, some part of their own body is ripped out and they must die as a result. What a sacrifice! How they must suffer. They are highly evolved, complex and social creatures that deserve our respect. Regrettably, I can't say that about Gordo lying here. Come on, Karin. Let's go!'

At that signal, the bees swarmed away as one, circling above Daniel for a moment, then they flew up and away over the rooftops back in the direction of the market. Daniel gently offered Karin his hand, now free of his marvellous visitors, and the two walked slowly away, leaving a stupefied crowd, and one very sick fat man, behind them.

Turning the corner, on the narrow street that led down to the *viveros* on the corner of the market, Karin sank exhausted against Daniel and he had to hold her up. She looked up at him, her eyes registering fear, relief, amazement and bewilderment all at the same time.

'I've never been so frightened in all my life,' she gasped. 'That was horrible, horrible.' Her whole body shook in disgust. 'And then ... I've never, ever seen anything like what you did, ever before.' She stopped, lifted both hands and held Daniel's face to hers, inches away, searching his eyes. 'Tell me how you do it. Don't, please don't fob me off with some noncommittal remark. I was going to be raped back there and what you did saved me. How do you do what you do?'

Daniel stooped and kissed her lightly on the forehead. 'I really don't know how it works. Really. I just know that what I feel, any creature around me feels. And what they feel, I feel. Equally, what I want, they seem to want, so they act as if I've ordered it. But I never do. People don't believe me when I say that I don't control them. But I don't. Look: I ran towards that bastard, really hating him. For an instant I wanted to kill him for laying his hands on you. The nearest creatures were those bees – from the *viveros*, I guess. They would have killed him had I not relented. I could see it was getting serious so I suddenly didn't want to hurt him anymore. And so the bees let him go. They came to me because they knew that I was upset about the loss of so many of their lives. I think they were trying to console me. They are quite accustomed to giving up their lives. I'm not. I was more upset than they were. Funny, isn't it?'

'Not funny at all. It's miraculous. Saving me and then you worrying about the bees ...' She laughed, then looked up at his eyes and saw that they were serious. Her voice dropped in wonder: 'But you really mean it, don't you? You were upset about their lives.'

Daniel shook her off and walked away. 'Of course I was. Don't make fun of me.'

Karin caught him up and held his arm. 'I wasn't making fun of you. How could I, Daniel, after what you have just done?' She stopped him again and made sure he was looking at her. 'Thank you, thank you, thank you. You're amazing!' Her eyes shone.

Daniel looked down, embarrassed, not sure what to say. Karin spoke for him, filling the awkward pause.

'Let's go and find Claudia. She must be wondering where I am.'

They returned to the throng of people circling the market. After a few minutes, Karin spotted Claudia trying on a wide-brimmed hat on the other side of a line of people pushing their way past the variety of stalls. She slipped through the crowd to join her friend who was now turning her head from one side to the other, looking at herself in a mirror that the kindly proprietor was holding up.

'Oh there you are,' she said. 'I've been wondering where you'd got to. How do I look?'

'Divine. Buy it if you like it … and it will make you feel better, too.'

Claudia smiled back at her friend gratefully. Her normally bubbly personality had been flattened over the last two days and Karin had been doing her best to raise her spirits. But catching a look at Karin's face, Claudia could see it was flushed and drawn and her friend was unusually agitated. She put down the hat at once.

'What's happened?' she enquired urgently.

Karin didn't answer but pulled her away, round the side of the stall and into the middle of the plaza where there was a little oasis of calm in the centre of the market place. She was meanwhile turning her head this way and that, searching to find Daniel. He had disappeared.

The two girls stopped together and in a breathless rush

Karin spilled out all that had just happened. Claudia's eyes widened first in horror, then in astonishment.

'I don't believe it ...' she said slowly, clearly believing her friend.

'I know ... unbelievable. But Claudia, it was awful. If it wasn't for Daniel and what he did, I don't want to think of where I'd be now ... *Where is Daniel?*'

They looked round. There was no sign of him.

'He said to meet up at four under the trees, over there,' said Claudia, pointing at the impressive white cathedral that fronted the plaza. 'But he's not there yet. What do you want to do?'

'Let's go to that café where we were before. I want to sit down before I fall down.'

'Of course. We can find Daniel later, you need a break.'

Daniel had found a stall of bright, painted pots and varnished wooden objects. A large bulldog sat behind with two men, one of whom had a white stick. The dog waddled forward as soon as he approached.

'Hello, Juan Sebastián, how's business?'

'Mono! ... This is an honour. What can I do for you? Look, I have a furry friend who comes and brings his master to see me every Sunday now.' El Ciego touched the dog with his stick. The dog grunted, looking up. If the wrinkled, punched-in look of a bulldog's face could be said to smile, that was what it was doing.

'Glad to see it, Juan Sebastián. Tell me, what's up?'

The blind man's expression became immensely sad. He shook his head.

'I've just lost a dear friend. I'd heard about it over a week back but it has been all the talk of the market here yesterday and today. He was in that jeep that was blown up recently ... He was one of the nicest, most considerate and generous people I've ever known.'

'Well, *amigo*, strangely it's that I've come to ask you about. I need to know what happened because the family of someone else involved wants to know more. Can you tell me what you know?'

'I owe you as much as I can tell you, and more. Come back here.' El Ciego stood aside, leaving the bulldog and the other man to mind the stall while he invited Daniel to enter.

El Ciego's stall was set up with a large, dark, curtained-off area at the back where he could sit among some of the artefacts that he had no room to display. Daniel was led into this and invited to sit on one of two wooden stools. El Ciego sat on the other.

'I know you cannot see too well in here,' grinned the stall-holder, 'but that's the point. It evens things up between us! Now, where shall I start?'

'What do you know about Martín García and what Triple F has been saying, and not been saying, about him?'

'García ... he's the one, eh? OK. Well, the word from contacts I trust is as follows: the Toyota jeep was blown up by persons unknown. Unknown, gottit? A second jeep goes in with a convoy of vehicles to investigate, including García. Triple F are crawling all over the attack site but García wanders off alone and gets captured by the FARC. Triple F security are mad about this but can do nothing. One of the FARC tells them to bring in ten thousand dollars in a week's time if they want to deal. Now, I'm approached by both sides to arrange the money transfer. A guy from the FARC whom I can't say I've met before asks me: do I have any messages for him from Triple F? Yes: Triple F had already contacted me, and paid me generously, to say that they want to see García alive and well at the transfer point if they are to hand over any cash. OK. The head of security, no less, goes in alone with the ransom money a week later, then again, oddly, the day after. The money is apparently handed over, though my informant isn't completely sure of that. Whatever, there are no more contacts with the FARC. Triple F goes strangely quiet. No one comes to see me. Neither side. That implies there's no negotiation possible. Then the newspapers break the story on Friday last. That's it.'

'Thanks, Juan Sebastián. Well ... you have a better nose for these things than I. What do you make of it all?'

'I'll tell you this. I don't trust Triple F. I don't mean the guys at the bottom – they are just the soldiers that do as they are told and most are good men. Like the friend I've lost. But I never believe official stories that come from the top. Secondly, the FARC never usually go quiet and disappear like they have on this occasion. They are always on the lookout to make money or gain some advantage by torturing someone – and if it's big business all the better.

'Maybe the Toyota was destroyed by someone else. The FARC never claimed responsibility for it. Maybe the FARC saw what happened and got lucky, capturing this García who wandered off. The fact that they have not been heard of since is odd. Why did the head of security go in, and not some junior as might be expected, and go in twice, not once for the cash handover? Maybe because he wanted no one else to know what was going on? Maybe the FARC went quiet because Triple F got them all? Why don't Triple F want to see me again to contact the FARC? I think it's because the hostage got killed in the process, there is no need for negotiation and they want to keep it under wraps. What is certain is that there is nothing, nothing going on out there now. Security have not been asked to go in since ... That seems to indicate there is nothing to go in *for* – they are not looking for García, or the FARC or anybody. Ominous!'

'What is actually, definitely known about García? Is he dead or alive? And where exactly did all this happen? Where was he seized?'

'On García we have only silence. That reeks! To me, it means he's dead. Sorry. Where he was captured is easy. Plenty of security men were there and can give a description of the area. Where he is now, or rather his body, no one can say, except perhaps for Triple F's head of security. I'm sorry I can't tell you anymore.'

'That's fine, Juan Sebastián. You've been great. Thank you very much and if I can help you in any way in return I will.'

'No problem. You've already done enough for me, Mono; you know I'm always in your debt. Of course, if you want to help you can always pass me over any information on anything at all, at any time …'

Daniel smiled and rose to take his leave. 'I will. Thanks again … I'll let you know.'

The news he was to take back to Karin and Claudia was not at all optimistic. Daniel left El Ciego's stall and walked along among the lines of market folk with his head down, wondering how he was going to tell them. It was not near four o'clock yet but he headed in the direction of the white cathedral.

Walking along lost in thought, the girls saw Daniel passing by as they were seated outside their café and so called him over. He went over and blanked his expression as he did so, concealing his thoughts and feelings. He listened politely as Karin sang his praises and recounted for the third or fourth time to Claudia how terrible her experience had been and what a saviour and miracle worker Daniel had proved to be.

Karin stopped. The adrenalin had worked its way out of her system and her enthusiasm had run its course. She looked at Daniel who remained silent. She looked at Claudia.

'You've met El Ciego, haven't you?' She addressed Daniel again; she could read his face.

He nodded.

'What? Tell us.'

Daniel looked at Claudia, how could he tell her gently?

'I'm afraid the signs are not good. It is mostly speculation but those closest in the know do not seem to hold out much

116

hope. I think you should prepare yourself for the worst. I'm very sorry.'

Claudia did not move but the colour drained from her face.

Karin interposed: 'Daniel, you talk of speculation. What do you know for sure? Is there anything that El Ciego told you that he is really certain of?'

'Yes, I can now find out exactly where Martín was captured. So I could go in and search the area more easily ... but El Ciego says he is sure that Martín is dead.'

That comment froze the atmosphere around them as he knew it would. Daniel looked at the two girls. Their silence and Claudia's ashen, despairing expression spoke volumes.

'OK, I'll go in. I'll find out for certain. It might take some time but then at least you'll know.'

Claudia looked down. 'Thank you,' she said in a tiny voice.

Karin reached a hand across to hold Daniel's for a second. 'Do take care. Please. Don't put yourself in any danger for us. How will we know what you find out?'

'I'll borrow one of Alfonso's horses ... sorry, Claudia's horses. I've done it before. That will make it easier and quicker for me to cover the ground. I'll return to Alfonso as soon as I have something and he can pass the message on to Claudia's family. Leave it to me. You've got a plane to catch.'

Daniel got up to leave. He did not want to intrude on their silence any longer and he was anyway uncomfortable in this urban environment. He needed to get back into the mountains where he could breathe.

Karin called out as he departed. 'Wait. Don't go!' She left her seat and rushed over to embrace him.

Daniel stiffened but she wouldn't let go. 'When am I going to see you again?' she pleaded.

Daniel yearned to be free. He resumed his default expression – blankness and distance.

'Anytime you're in the mountains. Local people here know how to contact me.'

He extricated himself from Karin's embrace and backed away. His last glance towards them both before he finally disappeared showed him two girls, one seated, one standing – both forlorn, both filled with anguish.

5

Multinationals at War

The intercom buzzed and the voice of Patricia, Fields's assistant, came over the air: 'The two officers are here, sir.'

'Thank you. Send them in, and please block all other calls. We will not want to be disturbed.'

Morten Fields cleared his desk and welcomed Miguel Cortés and Alejandro González into his office again. He invited the two to sit down and then got straight to the point.

'Well, now it is confirmed that TMG were behind the attack on our staff. They set up a team of terrorists to do their dirty work. Before I decide what we do about this, I've called you in to grill you on what you know of the history of this sort of thing between us. You said, if I remember you correctly, that there's been a dirty war going on between us for years. Am I right? Well I'm the new boy here and you two have both been around in this region, this country, for a lot longer than I. So tell me what you know; hold nothing back. Understand?'

Cortés and González looked at one another again, like the last time they were in this office. Who was going to start?

González cleared his throat. 'You've been closer to the action than I,' he said, looking at Cortés. 'You start.'

'Thanks.' Passing the buck again, Cortés thought. 'Well, to be honest, sir, it's been going on longer than both of us have been in post. From even before we won any mining licence in this region, if what I've heard is right. I came in a little while after being wounded and pensioned off from my services in the military. When I got here things were pretty active but then Triple F's chief left and was replaced by your predecessor, who scaled everything back. It's been a lot quieter until now.'

'Yes, yes, very nice, I'm sure.' Fields was an impatient man. 'Now tell me what you're talking about. Don't worry, I'm unshockable. Give me the details, man. What do you mean by "pretty active"? What was scaled back?'

Cortés decided to go in the deep end. He looked straight at Fields and gave it to him. 'Well, killing each other's staff isn't new. I heard it as soon as I got here. Only a few knew about it then and none left now except us two. It was always dressed up as terrorist or paramilitary activity, but orders undoubtedly came from the top – that is this office here or, if rumours are correct and I don't doubt that they are, the equivalent national office for TMG. How far up the chain of command from here I don't know.'

'I was a junior executive in this building when TMG beat us to the mining licence for the entire Cauca region,' said González. 'That was way before Cortés was hired but I can tell you that the shock waves that went through here were pretty major. Triple F was supposed to open up a new mining enterprise, surveys had been undertaken, men and equipment hired, everything was being set up to start operations, when we heard that TMG were to have an exclusive contract. Nothing for us to do. I never knew the boss personally then, but apparently he went purple and said that we all had to do everything to get a foothold, a licence somehow. That's when the dirty war really got going, I gather.'

'Tell me more.' Fields was getting interested.

Cortés resumed the narrative. 'Neither of us was directly involved then, sir. But what happened was there was a concerted action to make some element of TMG's operation malfunction. If terrorist activity was seen to be excessive in one region or another, then they would cut their losses, maybe sell up and get out. That is precisely what happened. Lots of low-level sabotage and the occasional kidnap. Huge ransom demands that went on endlessly. TMG obviously cottoned on at one stage, or so the story goes, since they started retaliating. Then it was a sort of arms race – who could be more daring, destructive and ruthless. On our side, I heard there was a period of inaction when the top office here was having qualms of conscience ... but that only served to lure the opposition into a false sense of security. The key that turned it was the death of a senior TMG executive and his wife who were apparently out in Cauca on holiday. Soon after that we bought up the mineral rights to part of the region and we've been operating there ever since. Not that we've made much money out of it, I gather.'

'I was posted out to Cali as deputy regional chief as soon as we had a licence to start in the south,' said González. 'We used contacts with the paramilitaries to recruit our first security men. Cortés came in. It was a small office then and what one knew so did another. So naturally everyone knew what had been going on – local independent paramilitaries had before been hired direct from Bogotá and they had a tendency to brag about their exploits. But now they were Triple F employees and we had to put a stop to the gossip. Cortés called all his men together and as the new commander of security operations in the region he rammed the lid on tight. Whatever had or had not happened before the office was open was not to be mentioned again and no documentation of any dirty war was to exist.

'The head here who had been behind all this then went and had a heart attack. Despite all the rumours, we think it was genuine. No funny business. But the new man who came in didn't have a clue about what had been going on and we got the distinct message that everything had to calm down. It did. Regular business. TMG, meanwhile, were raking it in and we weren't. The Popayán office had been opened recently and I was transferred there since it was thought that a new mine near Puracé could turn things around for us. Maybe TMG think the same because that's the only motive I can think of for this recent escalation. Now you're here. Over to you.'

Fields leaned back. 'Thanks. Thanks to both of you. That is a very clear perspective on the whole mess that we are into. Now, first things first ...' Fields looked down at his hands and at his papers and then began.

'As a business, Triple F is making money here in Colombia only on its farming operations. Bananas and cut-flower exports; domestic supplies of market produce to Bogotá, Medellín and a few other cities. Steady profits but little growth potential. Losses on mining, however, have been steady ever since it started up and it is a major embarrassment to the corporation. Headquarters in Geneva regard mining here as a black hole that swallows everything up and it can't be long before they decide to close it all down.'

Fields stopped and looked up. 'I'm here to prevent that outcome,' he said forcefully. He then leaned across his desk and concentrated his gaze on the two men sitting opposite; first Cortés, then González.

'I, we, will do everything in our power to turn Triple F mining in Colombia around and make it a star performer in the corporation so that we can all hold our heads up high and have everyone else gasp in wonder. As a result, your career prospects will soar, as will your salaries. And I will get a seat on the Board where I will be eternally grateful to that handful of individuals who helped me make it there.

'Let me make it clear. When I say we will do everything in our power to achieve that end, I mean *everything*. Gottit? No holds barred. Now, you have said that no one else to your knowledge besides you two knows what you have just told me. Is that true, or are you just hoping it's true?'

Cortés answered. 'I said that, sir, and I back what I said. To my knowledge, no one in Triple F Colombia or anyone outside knows the full story, as we've just told it. Inevitably, sir, there will be some that know some of the pieces of this jigsaw puzzle, but no one knows it all. And if I may say so, sir, if you are thinking of responding to this latest TMG attack, you should know that no one, not even González here, knows the whole story of what we know, sir.'

And you don't know it either, thought Fields. Still, I like the man. He is dead straight, not afraid to take up a challenge and he's even pushing me here to respond to this latest incident.

'Thank you again, Cortés. That is very reassuring. Given that, I think we should now go on to discuss how Triple F are going to react to TMG's outrageous provocation. And I do not need to emphasise, do I, that all our conversation is strictly confidential? In due course, specific orders will be given to certain named individuals within our organisation, but you will understand when I insist that no one outside of ourselves and those we identify should know anything about what we are about to decide. You do understand that, don't you?'

'Yessir!' both replied in unison.

'Right. Let's get down to business.' Fields walked over to the wall where he had hung a large map of the area around Popayán stretching eastwards to the Volcán Puracé, including the national park, the main public roads and the two access roads built by the mining corporations to their respective developments. He pointed at the map, tapping his fingers meaningfully at the various locations as he developed his argument.

'Here's the main highway 24 running east from Popayán. It rises up, passes north of Volcán Puracé and continues on into the next Department. We have constructed our own track that leaves that road here, comes down south for approximately ten kilometres and then turns round east climbing up to our new development at almost 4,000 metres altitude here.' He placed a finger at a spot on the western flank of the dormant volcano.

'Now, on the other side of the mountain, the TMG access road leaves highway 24 close to the departmental border and runs due south-south-west to reach their mine here, altitude around 3,300 metres.'

'First, we ensure that our own access road is completely safe. Cortés – we don't want any more disruption to that route in. We have eliminated the most recent threat but that doesn't mean that TMG won't try anything else. You put your men all over the route, twenty-four hours a day.

'Secondly, González, you resupply our pitiful little operation at around 4,000 metres. That mine opens for business again, got it? Again, Cortés, you will ensure that our own property here is secure from any outside interference.

'Now as I understand it, the volcano has been pretty active in the past. Correct? Well, we shall equip a demolition team at our base up here in the mine – all of whom must look as if they are some terrorist outfit and nothing to do with us – and they will go circling round the mountain in complete secrecy, descending to the mouth of the TMG mine and they will engineer a sudden and catastrophic local volcanic explosion which buries all evidence and brings an immediate halt to TMG operations. Cortés, you and I alone will discuss the complement of this team. But all that I have just outlined will take place over the next seven to ten days, maximum. Understand? The quicker we get going the less time there will be for any TMG-sponsored outfit to try anything on; the less time there will be for our own people to talk, and the more impact it will have on those bastards in TMG head office who think they have recently got away with murder. Any comments?'

'How big a demolition team are you thinking of? That determines how much stuff they can haul around the mountain.' Cortés was on the ball straight away. Fields smiled. No squeamish protests, no attempt to place obstacles in the way – just how can we make this work effectively.

'You tell me. We have to trade off light weight, quick move-

124

ment of as few people as possible – two or three operatives, maybe – against installing maximum explosive force. I don't want a petty little bang. I want to bring down tons of stuff to block their mine and bury any evidence that we were there.'

González leaned back with his eyebrows raised. He needed a little more time to get used to the idea. This was escalation, big time. His own involvement, however, meant that he was responsible only for what would be regular mining operations. Organise a convoy of materials up the road; install men and machines to start work at altitude – all this had to happen sometime anyway. A certain amount of preparation had been going on for this which had recently been put on hold thanks to a sabotaged road machine and losing his Toyota in the TMG attack. The access road could be made passable for heavy equipment quickly with one, two days' work at most. He could start things up at the mine again with little time lost.

'OK with me,' González agreed. 'We will start ordering materials and organising men as soon as I leave this office. We won't actually be able to begin mining in ten days, but, as I understand, that is not important. We will have people up there, busying about, preparing to start operations. Your demolition outfit will have plenty of cover while all this is going on and any materials they want can go up in regular supplies.'

Fields looked at his colleagues with satisfaction. He returned to his desk. This was going to work out fine.

Leopold Smith thought out aloud. 'Operationally, easiest to locate explosives on mountain, outside, above entrance … But blast will go upwards … lose most of the impact. Better inside the entrance … deep inside as possible … in confined space for maximum effect. Ideally, in the roof. How to do that? Especially if the mine is in operation twenty-four hours a day? Difficult … Hmm.'

As they sat across the room from each other in his apartment, Fields looked at Smith, at his mind whirring as he contemplated the problem. Smith was at his best when given a fixed objective and limitless resources. Resources, however, were not limitless. They had little more than a week and, despite trying, they had no access to any plans of the TMG mine layout or its geological survey. The placement of the explosive device would determine how much damage it would do and that correlated to the size of the explosive charge needed.

Smith looked up. 'Best solution as follows. Two or three men only, no more. Night-time assault. Stop TMG personnel outside, steal their clothes, walk into mine in disguise. Two best, three maximum – any more, too suspicious. Carry as many explosives as possible. Go in as far as possible. Position of explosive charge to be decided as we go. No layout map so no possibility of knowing before. Place timer. Get out. Bang! Wait and see effect before coming back. Easy to get away in general chaos.'

'Leo, how are you going to find any TMG personnel with clothes to fit your size?'

'Black underclothes. It's dark. Have to fit what I can.'

Fields was worried – Smith was absolutely first rate at following any agreed plan of action; not at all good at making things up as he went along. Any hiccup, any change of schedule usually threw him and provoked unpredictable behaviour. And his suggested mode of entry to the mine was potentially full of hiccups. He looked to Cortés.

Triple F's head of security for the region was sitting behind the two others, keeping quiet and watching proceedings. He knew how Smith operated now so had not interrupted, but Fields's worried look put him on the spot.

'I suggest a variation. Correct – we have to get inside the mine to place the explosive device. OK. But rather than disguise Smith, which is close to damn impossible, make the fact that he is so different an asset. Make him stand out, say as a visiting safety inspector from the Canadian headquarters on a surprise visit. He asks the guards on the ground – not their bosses – which part of the mine looks least safe and they are most worried about. They can take him there to see. "Thank you very much, we won't trouble you any longer, give us a minute to inspect it closely," then place the explosive and retreat. Bang! Chaos. Get away, etc.'

Fields looked skyward. Thank goodness for Cortés! 'Leo, I'd be much happier with you following that plan of action. It covers us since any guards won't expect you and speaking English becomes an asset. All TMG bosses speak English. But we need an English speaker to go with him, Cortés. Who should go with Smith in the demolition team?'

Cortés was on top of that already: 'A munitions expert has to be in the party to place the device and set the timer. No question. That has to be a trusted Triple F operative, not some outside paramilitary. Maybe Alejandro can think of one who is reliable, got all the right technical qualifications and speaks good enough English. He will have to be briefed to keep his mouth shut – I'll do that. Do we need any more in the team? Maybe not if the explosive is to be placed in a known weak spot. But there's one problem I can see – finding the way round the mountain from our base to locate the TMG mine. It will have to be in daylight and even then it won't be easy. Getting back in the dark will possibly be even more difficult.'

Smith spoke. 'No trouble. I do it, no trouble.'

Cortés grimaced. He spoke to Fields: 'I've seen how effective Smith's map-memory is. Impressive. We could even take satellite GPS positioning systems with us. But it's not a problem of getting lost – it is a matter of what's on the ground that could throw us. It's a dormant volcano. The altitude is high. The terrain and weather conditions could be difficult, even dangerous. A local guide would help.'

'No! Can't afford the risk,' Smith was adamant. He was anyway only happy with as few as possible going with him.

127

Fields was well aware that there were a worrying number of unknowns involved in this exercise … but he would have to trust Smith to pull it off. He would somehow. It was just a matter of how far to limit the damage if things got out of hand.

'No guide!' He smiled at Smith, letting him know in no uncertain way that he had every confidence in him. He threw a fierce glance at Cortés to warn him off causing any disagreement.

Cortés got the message. 'OK. I'll go back to Popayán and find and brief the men necessary. I'll be back in touch as soon as things are ready my end.'

Adrián Cárdenas had been having it easy these last couple of weeks with operations at the Puracé mine suspended, but now his boss, Alejandro González, had called him into the Popayán office to meet the region's head of security. What was this about?

He was soon to find out. The conference room door he was waiting outside opened and Miguel Cortés beckoned him in.

'Come in Adrián,' he said. 'I'm pleased to meet you. Alejandro González tells me that you are just the man I am looking for.' Cortés shut the door behind him and indicated that Cárdenas should sit down.

'Am I? What have I done to deserve that recommendation?'

Cortés sat down at the conference table beside his guest and adopted a friendly, collegial tone. He raised his arm and patted his neighbour on the shoulder. 'You are a qualified mining engineer, aren't you?'

'Yes, sir. MA in Geotechnical Engineering and Mining, Universidad Nacional, Medellín. First-class honours. Research into gold mining: on-going with Triple F.'

'And you speak and understand English, don't you?'

'Yes. No problem.'

'Excellent! And you are having an affair with Alejandro's wife, aren't you?'

'WHAT!?' Adrián's composure vanished in a flash. His face went white. 'No! Where on earth did you hear that? Did Señor González tell you?'

'No, no. González doesn't know. Hasn't got a clue. But wives sometimes talk and it is my business in this corporation to pick up gossip, check facts and make sure that our security, especially the security of key personnel, is not compromised. We can't have our top people being blackmailed for example. Get the idea?'

'Yes … yes.' Adrián Cárdenas felt awful; he felt as if his career was going to end. Was he going to get the chop in order to keep González happy?

'The fact is', Cortés smiled, 'you are one of our brightest mining engineers. So you have the potential to be one of our top people. In which case, my job is to look after you. González says he wants you involved in our newest mining exploit and if that's his recommendation then I have to ensure that security around you is tight. Do you see?'

'Ye-e-e-s.' Cárdenas was not sure where this was going.

'Let me come at this another way. The corporation needs your help in a very delicate exercise, a security exercise, a technical mining operation where you have the expertise that I need. Now: what I am to tell you is classified. No one outside of this office is to be told of what you are about to hear, is that clear? *No one!*'

'OK, I understand.' Cárdenas now began to feel that maybe he was not going to get the chop after all. Indeed, he was going to be entrusted with some high-level secret. He'd tell no one, especially if he wanted his affair with González's wife to be kept quiet, too. Keep everything classified: that suited him.

Cortés fixed him with a glare. 'There is a dirty war going on between us and Triple F. You have heard, no doubt, of the loss of three of our men – my security men – plus the kidnapping and disappearance of one of our junior executives? Well, that was not the work of the FARC. It was the work of TMG.'

'What? I don't believe it!'

'You had better believe it. The evidence I have is damning. Not only that but, unless we do something, they are going to come at us again. We are mining in Puracé, which is an area that they want us out of and they will do all they can to kick us out. Are we going to lie down and let them kick us? No. So we need to stop them … and you are needed to help.'

'Me? What can I do?'

'This is what you will do. Go with one of the world's best men in the security business on a night raid to the TMG mine on the other side of the mountain. They think they can knock us around here; we are going to give them the biggest knock we can deliver on their patch. Get the idea?'

'Yes!' Cárdenas grinned. 'I'm up for it! Serve 'em right!'

'Good, good. González was right – he clearly knows his men. I'm pleased you're with us on this. Now, here's how it will work. You and your team leader will dress up as outside contracted safety officers. You will track round the volcano, locate the TMG mine and go in bold as brass and ask their security guards to show you where they are worried about the roof supports. Gettit?'

'Absolutely.' Cárdenas grinned again. This sounded like fun. 'Tell me more.'

Cortés turned his chair a little to face the younger man and emphasise his instructions. 'You are going to have to do the talking because the leader who is taking you there is a US or Canadian national who only speaks English. It is absolutely crucial that you convince the guard you approach that you and your leader must inspect the weak spots they identify. Tell your leader, in English, what the guard says. That will impress your fall-guy guard that you're with a top foreign expert on a surprise visit. The guard may want to check with some higher authority whether or not you have clearance to be let in. Stop that, OK? Your argument here is that of course no higher authority in the mine knows about you because you don't want them to cover anything up – you want to hear the opinion of people on the ground – that is, your fall-guy guard. See? Are you with me so far?'

Cárdenas was visualising all this as Cortés was speaking. Wow! This was an important responsibility. He was going to be out there on the edge, blagging his way into a foreign business. He hoped he wasn't going to foul it up.

'Yes yes, I'm with you. I just hope I can smooth my way in as you want ...' His attitude now became more serious. This game was still fun ... but it would not be that easy to play.

Cortés laughed. 'Hah! González said you were a good talker. I guess you must be if you can knock up his wife without him knowing! You'll do just fine, I'm sure.'

Cárdenas blushed to his roots. Cortés really had him sized up.

'Once you're in the mine, let the guard take you where he will. Thank him for his cooperation. You'll mention it your report, blah, blah. You get the idea? Now we get to the part that we really want you for. Your leader will be carrying the high explosives, detonator and timer. He is big and strong and can carry heavy loads so he will take in as much as can be done without raising suspicion. You will have to identify the best place to set it all up, where it will bring down the roof to the maximum extent. We want a really big blast to block the tunnel up tight with as much debris as possible. That is import-ant, understand? We need you to plant the explosives where it will do maximum damage and only you, the expert, can pick that spot. OK? Also bear in mind that we want no evidence that Triple F has been engaged in any way with this operation, and the more stuff you bring down in that mine, the more it will cover any evidence, any trace that we, or rather you, were there. Set the timer only for the delay necessary for you to get the hell out. Once you're out – bang! Wait until the smoke clears, and only if it's safe for you, check to see what damage you've done so that you can report back. That's it. All clear? How do you feel about this?'

Phew! How did he feel? What an operation! Never in his wildest dreams did Cárdenas think he would ever be getting into something like this. But the challenge was tremendous. The potential for being found out was high. But what a high! The adrenalin was kicking in now just thinking of it. What a mission to be entrusted with.

'OK. OK. This is big. I've got to go for it. Just one question … seriously, what happens if we get caught?'

'You won't. So long as you tell no one of this – both before the mission and after – you will be safe, of that I can assure you. In the field, your leader is just about the best in the world at this sort of operation and he will get you out of there, no matter what happens. Trust me. You'll meet him in due course and, although he might strike you as a bit different from anyone else you've ever met, that is because he is a highly specialised security agent. Your and his safety is his speciality. Setting the explosives in the right place to give TMG the biggest headache is your speciality. You make a good team. Do this, keep it secret, don't let your tongue slip on any account and you'll go far in this corporation. And you can then trust me to keep your own secrets, get it?' Cortés winked.

Cárdenas got it.

Nine days after Cortés's and González's discussion in Fields's office, the demolition team set out just before daybreak from their base in Triple F's Puracé mine. Two men on horses – Smith and Adrián Cárdenas – and a mule-load of explosive materials towed behind. They set themselves twelve hours to track round the mountain and arrive at the TMG site. Both Smith and Cárdenas wore similar dark-blue uniforms in the guise of safety inspectors, bureaucrats, from an unspecified organisation. Over these, both had pulled on and zipped up a one-piece padded battledress to provide cover in the open *páramo*, if it was needed, but more especially to keep them warm.

Cárdenas had to agree with the description of Smith – just about the oddest character he'd met. He was huge, impassive, and very deliberate in his preparation and he refused to be questioned or interrupted as he went through his checklist of materials for their excursion. No welcome, no explanations and, with his expressionless face, very difficult to read. Cárdenas nonetheless trusted him to know what he was doing – he inspired confidence from the outset as they pulled their horses up off the Puracé mine road and struck off across the mountainside.

Smith said next to nothing on their trip except the occasional, terse command: 'Keep up!' Finding their way safely across the landscape was not at all easy. There were stretches of the typical high moorland vegetation – tough grass and frailejones – interspersed occasionally with pools or small lakes of water, and then they crossed two vast rivers of solidified lava: dark grey, sterile, extremely rough and broken flows that, some time ago, must have come pouring down from on high. Among one of these stone rivers, plumes of steam were escaping and hot springs bubbled to the surface. In contrast, the air around them in early morning was very cold, just a few degrees above freezing.

They stopped briefly to eat packed lunches. Smith was pleased with progress and, though he spoke minimally, Cárdenas could see he was checking out how well the horses, and Cárdenas himself, were coping with the trek. No problems – they restarted their excursion after fifteen minutes.

The team kept going, now plodding through hummocky terrain and descending into a warmer and cloudier climate. By early evening, Cárdenas reckoned they must be close and he could see Smith in front peering ahead, looking for the TMG access road which must somewhere be climbing towards them.

Cárdenas was delighted and again his confidence in his leader was reinforced – there below them through the light mist and fading light a pencil-grey line was drawn looping up the mountain and leading to its goal off to their right: the TMG mine. Large arc lights were just coming on beside a couple of low, one-storey buildings, illuminating the entrance to a gaping tunnel.

Smith stopped and indicated that they should wait. Both men dismounted and led the horses and mule into a thicket of bushes to secure them. Smith sat down and gestured to his companion to do the same: there was no need to maintain absolute silence but his behaviour induced Cárdenas to do the same. They waited as the equatorial twilight quickly seesawed into night.

Both men unzipped and climbed out of their combat dress. From the mule, Smith loaded two carry-bags full of demolition equipment, stuffed a fake computer case over the top of one and lifted both as if he was carrying polystyrene. He handed over only the timer to Cárdenas to carry in his inside pocket. Now fully prepared to take on their new roles, the two carefully made their way down below the mine entrance, aiming for some deep shadows thrown by the arc lights behind the last bend in the road as it climbed upwards to its destination.

They stepped boldly out on to the road and walked deliberately up to the low buildings in front of them. Cárdenas chatted nervously to Smith in English, commenting blandly on the outlines of the buildings, the size of the mine entrance, whatever he could think of until the noise he was making caused a door to open.

A security guard in smart TMG uniform barred their way. '*Buenos noches, señores*,' he politely greeted them. 'And what business do you have here?'

Cárdenas took out of his pocket his wallet with his old ID card from Universidad Nacional, Faculty of Mines, and flashed it at the guard. It was a younger version of himself in the photo on the card but still a good likeness. He was pleased he had thought to prepare for this.

'*Buenos noches*. We have arrived to undertake a safety check on the roof supports of the mine. I understand from some of the labour force here that concerns have been expressed. I am from Universidad Nacional; let me introduce you to John Jones of Toronto Mines and Safety executive. We have come to do a snap inspection.' Cárdenas then told Smith in English all he had said.

Smith nodded. 'Very good.'

The guard took a step back, flummoxed by the unexpected appearance of these two senior inspectors. He fished out a two-way radio.

Cárdenas cut in quickly: 'Excuse me, if you are contacting your superiors, don't! We do not want any official cover-up, you understand. We have to send in a report based on what you men on the ground are concerned about. Not some official excuse. Could I ask you to escort us into the mine and show us the first place that you know of that you consider needs our attention?'

This was a change of standard procedure for the guard and he was somewhat nervous on hearing this request. The best way to cover his back, he adjudged, was to take these men in with another guard. He called into the building behind him to have his colleague come out and join them.

Cárdenas faithfully explained to Smith, in English, what was going on. 'Fine, very good' was the monotonic response. Smith set off, walking in front as if assuming there was no problem. A big man with an air of authority, Cárdenas grinned inwardly, and followed after. With that attitude, there was no problem.

Arc lights buzzed up in the roof of the entrance and a lot of noise of mining machinery issued forth from inside, deep below. With security guards hurrying after them, the two fake mining safety inspectors wandered on, examining the roof high above. Too high, it was clear, for their purposes. A hundred yards in and the guards were now beside them, guiding them on. The roof had lowered somewhat but still not enough to reach. Cárdenas started looking around for alternative bomb locations. He was not happy walking like a nervous fly too far into this spider's nest.

'Wait!' he called out. There was a substantial fissure in the side wall that ran up to the roof. 'There's no particular reinforcement here in what is potentially a geologically unstable area!' He knew what he was talking about. 'Has no one pointed this out to you before?'

The guards looked at each other blankly and shook their heads.

Cárdenas turned to Smith and spoke rapidly in his partner's language: 'We've gone a long way in and to get to the roof will be impossible for a long way yet. I'm not happy going any further and this is the best site I've seen so far. What do you think?'

'You're the expert.' Smith replied, expressionless as ever. 'You say here – here it is.' He put down his bags and peered at the fissure in the wall. 'OK, let's do it!' He picked up a big rock that had fallen from the wall below the crack and looked at it, turning it over in a large right hand. It just fitted.

Cárdenas spoke to the two guards. 'We have just seen this first site of concern. We shall have to examine it more closely ...'

While Cárdenas was holding the guards' attention, Smith had sauntered around behind them, looking preoccupied. Suddenly, moving incredibly rapidly, he cracked one a massive blow on the head with the rock he was holding, then grabbed the startled other man with his left hand around his throat and brought the rock viciously down again – bang – into his face. In the space of a single second, two guards were sprawled motionless on the floor.

Cárdenas nearly jumped in fright.

'What's going on?' he whispered urgently.

'Just plant the explosive and get on with it!' Smith opened the bag and looked up at Cárdenas. 'Come on!'

There was no time to waste now. So far they had seen no other personnel and Cárdenas, shaken up and nervous as he was, got to work as quickly as his fumbling hands would allow. He supposed that Smith was right to knock the two guards out – it would take an age for him to persuade them to leave them alone to their 'inspection'. Still, he did not like the look of spilt blood. Both men had been brutally flattened and it showed.

Smith helped stuff all the explosive into the deep crack in front of them while Cárdenas busied himself with the detonator and timer. Five minutes and he was ready. All the while he cast his eyes around to see if they had been seen yet. No. Yes! Horrors, what looked like a lone miner was walking out towards them, not taking especial notice of what these two suited individuals were doing – until Smith approached him. Bam! Another enormous blow around the head and Smith dragged the third body over to drop him with the others.

Cárdenas leapt again in shock. Another bloodied victim.

'Did you have to do that?' He was losing his nerve.

Smith swept aside his question. 'Set the time and we go. Now!'

He picked up the empty bags and started walking back. Cárdenas had already activated the timer, giving them ten minutes to escape, but he quickly caught Smith and protested.

'We can't leave those men there. They will be killed! It will be murder!'

Smith kept walking, ignoring the desperate pleas of his younger partner.

'First, orders are we have to bury evidence. They are evidence. Second, they are already dead.'

Cárdenas stumbled alongside the big man, absolutely stunned. He looked at his companion's face. Expressionless as ever. Not a hint of emotion. He realised in an awful moment that what he had just seen was absolutely routine for this individual. The world's best security agent had planned this all along. How stupid, how naïve he now realised he had been. He thought he was just going to bring the roof down, block the tunnel – give TMG a difficult problem to solve. Now he was a witness – no, an accomplice – to three brutal murders. His legs shivered like a fountain in the wind. He had wet himself.

Smith was in command of the situation at once. With a hand under his partner's arm he almost carried him along, out of the entrance, towards the two single-storey buildings, now empty of personnel, and behind them into the blackness that was created by the arc lights.

There were a couple of precious minutes left. Smith scrambled up the rough slope behind the buildings, hauling his enfeebled partner with him, and on to the mountainside proper. A few straggly bushes offered some help for hands; both men scrabbled and clambered higher, Smith leading the way in the darkness towards where he estimated he had left the horses.

An almighty explosion took place which sent shock waves through the earth all around. A mighty blast blew out of the mine entrance and down the road, carrying all sorts of debris with it and, up on the mountain slope where they were scrambling, stones, dirt and rubble came bouncing down towards them. Both men ducked as low as they could, keeping their heads covered. A couple of minutes passed. Rumblings carrying on deep below them indicated that there was still debris on the move, but the surface slope where they were sheltering was stable now. Smith checked round to see a gathering cloud of dust and debris billowing forth from the mine entrance, flickering yellow and orange in the arc lights. He grunted in satisfaction. Cárdenas was silent, still shivering. He now knew what sort of savage, slaughterous mission he was engaged in. The sudden realisation froze his every move-ment, as if he wanted to deny it all and be whisked away from here and into a parallel universe where this had not happened.

The earth seemed to give another heave. More rumblings and another puff of cloud emerged on to the road below. Cárdenas was shaken into thought, if not action. This was a dormant volcano after all and something was stirring below that their manufactured explosion had awoken. Smith did not need a postgraduate degree in geophysics to understand either. He beckoned Cárdenas to start moving upslope as quickly as possible.

Dark as it was on the open mountainside in the small hours of the night, there was still enough light for Smith to recognise where he had left the horses. As they climbed closer, searching from below, the horses' heads rose above the bushes, silhouetted against the starry heavens. The two men reached their quarry and immediately set about preparing for their retreat, one far more efficiently than the other. At last they finished packing, pulled on their combat outfits once more, saddled up and, dragging the mule behind again, they set off on the long trek back, circling round and up, retracing the route taken earlier that day.

Two hours later and higher up the mountain and Cárdenas was close to exhaustion. He had been almost continuously active for around twenty hours now. The whole exercise had been physically tiring, emotionally draining and the adrenalin high that had kept him going at first had been replaced by the torment and shame of being involved in the violent deaths of three men. He felt unable to continue – just as the first stretch of lava flow appeared before them. This time the steam that was gushing forth above from hot springs was not just water vapour. The distinct and dangerously unpleasant smell of sulphur was all around them.

'No, Smith. I can't make it across here,' he pleaded. 'I'll throw up and collapse if we go a step further.'

Smith looked back at the straggler behind him and growled in reply. 'No stopping. Too dangerous!'

Smith was correct in his analysis of the volcano. Operations out in the field he knew about. But always the loner, reading the condition and emotions of other men he was distinctly not good at.

It was dark, difficult to see where he was going and Cárdenas was not stable in his saddle. As his horse tried to clamber up and follow the one in front, his rider wobbled once, twice, was unable to regain his balance and so toppled off. He hit the ground like a sack of bones. Consciousness came and went in waves. And went.

Leopold Smith cursed loudly and impatiently. He hated it when things did not go the way he had planned it. Smith turned his own mount back and circled the horses and mule around the fallen body of his partner. What to do? The easiest would be to hit him again even harder and leave him there to die. Anyone finding him – if they ever did – would see the blow on the head and, just like the three other skulls he had already cracked open, they would assume he had suffered a fatal accident. That plan had a simplicity to it that he liked. He dismounted and went to carry out just this action. Something in his brain sparked and told him to wait. He hated this. His head ached. Maybe not as much as the one on the ground beneath him, but still he put both hands up and placed them over his ears, as if he didn't want to listen to the chaos in his head. He roared out into the night.

What to do? Maybe killing the stupid man would not solve the problem. He had evidence on him that would lead to Triple F if he was found. Strip the body? What would people think finding a naked man out on the mountainside? Aaargh! No idea. What if he put the man back on the horse, try and wake him up, maybe tie him on? Take him back that way? Think. Think. That way they would both get back to Triple F as planned. Yes. Follow the plan. Put the man back on his horse. Smith spent the next fifteen sulphur-filled minutes lifting and shaking his partner and trying to get him to regain consciousness. He was not the kindest, nor the most sensitive first-aider. Cárdenas was groaning with some semblance of returning to life, so that was good enough for Smith. He bundled his partner on to his mount and tied his feet together under the horse's belly. His body was bowed over and his hands were propped up against the horse's neck. Smith had been leading the mule; now he led the mule and Cárdenas, all linked together. By this time his own head was now aching even more; his nose and eyes were streaming, and waves of nausea were sweeping through his giant frame. But as daylight slowly returned they got going once again, with more difficulty, heading back the same general way they had come from. Or was it the same way? Smith's sense of direction had become hazier; the fumes above were making him sick, driving him crazy, and driving his route lower and lower on the mountain in the inevitable haste to escape the poisonous air. And then he saw another horse and rider below converging towards him. Damn, damn, damn! This was yet one more unplanned-for interruption.

6

The Puracé Mines

Daniel Mayor left the girls, the café, the plaza in Popayán and caught a ride with one of the *viveros'* wagons going back up the mountain to the pueblos. He needed time and the sense of liberation the wide-open spaces gave him to think. It was here, in the seclusion of his familiar haunts, that he came to the conclusion that he needed El Ciego's help once more before starting any search. If he was to look for Martín García, and especially if it was a body he was looking for, Daniel needed to know what he looked like, how he was dressed that last time he had been seen, and of course a description of the area where he was seized.

He put the question to the blind man the following Sunday.

'You'll need to question the security men who were with him last,' Juan Sebastián said. 'Here – stay and look after the stall. I'll go and find out for you.'

El Ciego was as good as his word. He emerged from under the curtaining at the back of his stall and set off, tap-tapping his way to Triple F's regional office a few blocks away. As before, the office was still at a heightened state of security alert so it was cordoned off and guards were letting no one go in without legitimate business. That was no problem to El Ciego. He didn't want to go in. He only wanted to chat to the first couple of guards he met; to say what a terrible business this was, having one of their executives kidnapped, and to invite their comments in return.

Most people are generally very helpful to blind people. What harm does it do to chat and answer their questions, after all? El Ciego found two guards not especially busy and quite ready to entertain him. Between the two, one fed off the other, answering his queries, enlarging on the details, speculating where there were any doubts.

'Sure, García had only recently arrived here. Young handsome-looking chap, fresh out of college. He didn't really belong on that trip up the mountain, especially in that pinstriped executive suit and black patent-leather shoes. What was he, and anyone else, thinking of – going like that? Then again, he was only supposed to sit in the Land Rover and come back down again – not go chasing off who knows where ... Where? Just above a big hole in the road where the Toyota had been blown up, not a stone's throw from where the grader and leveller had been stationed. Sabotaged, they say. Yes – a terrible business. Now the police had been informed, they were apparently going to investigate the crime scene. Not that we have any confidence in them finding anything we couldn't find. They're better off here stopping any thieving and drunken assaults in the town. Did you hear of the fight outside the bar last week? Gordo got his come-uppance, it appeared ...'

El Ciego thanked his informers, offered to keep a beer or two aside at his stall should they ever come round, and back he went, waving his white stick, to meet up with Daniel, El Mono, who had so kindly stood in for him in his absence.

There are a few people who are unfailingly reliable, thought Daniel. Others are all over you with compliments, promises and more honey than in a beehive – but fail to deliver. People wearing fancy city clothes were like that, he thought, whereas those who you can really trust are more like El Ciego, who didn't care what you, or he, looked like ... though, of course, he could barely see anyway.

143

Daniel now had all the information that he needed. Nothing yet remained but to carry out his promise. The very next morning, up at the Fernández estate, he asked if Alfonso wanted him to check on any more horses. Here was another man whose value could not be calculated by the richness of his possessions – only by the richness of his character. Alfonso knew immediately what the other was hinting at. He reckoned there were no horses that needed urgent attention ... but if Mono wanted to borrow a steed, he could take his pick – he was always welcome.

Daniel smiled and thanked his friend. The fact was, he wasn't really looking forward to the task he had set himself but at least he now had enough to go on and the means at his disposal, and so he was eager to get started. It was far from a pleasant task that lay before him, but a promise was a promise.

Daniel carried with him a small pack of food and sufficient clothing and bedding material to stay out two nights. That was more than sufficient – he didn't want any more weight to hold him back and he knew that there were pueblos below to which he could retreat for support if needed. He set off straight away for the Triple F access road that moved west–east, low to high, across his path as he headed north. He reckoned that since the Triple F mine was at high altitude then the ambush spot where García had been picked up was likely to be quite high also – more to the east.

They moved quickly – horse and rider in complete harmony and over terrain that they both knew well. The peregrine falcon buzzed Daniel a couple of times during the day but she realised her friend was preoccupied with serious matters that kept his attention focused on the distant horizon. She flew on and away.

The weather was stable, the wind light and visibility good. After eight hours' steady riding, by late afternoon they reached the Triple F road. This was an excellent achievement and

Daniel thanked his mount profusely. He had stayed quite high and so could now look down to cover a wide panorama. It was a scene of some activity. Several armed men in Triple F uniform could be detected, spaced out at intervals along the dirt road. There was a wide circle at the side of the road in one place where he could clearly see a large, yellow road-making machine. More guards were around this place and there were yet more stationed around a bend nearby where the road had obviously been partially destroyed. That's it, thought Daniel. X marks the spot.

In what direction would I move from there if I had just captured someone by the road? he wondered. Without knowing it he was thinking the same way that Leopold Smith had done almost two weeks earlier, with the advantage that Daniel was much higher and on the other side of the valley with a better view than from where Smith had approached the ambush spot. The answer, of course, was kidnappers would climb higher up the mountain flank above the road, where incoming traffic could be more easily watched. Scanning across the valley, Daniel's first problem was how to cross the access road when guards were patrolling it and thus enter the terrain he wished to search. He would have to wait until nightfall, then cross, then bed down for the night to resume searching the following day.

Daniel was much more comfortable moving around the mountain in the dark than the security guards who were detailed to be out on the road. He felt sorry for them – their job of patrolling a deserted road at night was nerve-wracking. They had probably not done this before and it was almost impossible to accomplish effectively without more staff and resources. On the other hand, spending nights out alone on the mountain was something Daniel had done for years. Crossing the narrow road, finding his way up the facing mountain slope and then selecting and making camp for the night without detection was, for Daniel, ridiculously easy.

145

Daybreak brought with it the serious business of combing the area higher up to see if he could find where Martín García might have been taken. Daniel needed to keep out of sight of any security personnel on the road below yet sweep parallel alongside, zigzagging in long lines at higher and higher altitudes, trying to pick up any trace of a recent path. It was a long, time-consuming and unrewarding business. Many times he thought a particular animal track might be what he was looking for, only to be disappointed when it led nowhere. Hours passed and he steadily searched higher and higher and further away from the road. He got to feeling this was a hopeless quest. Experienced as he was at tracking in this terrain, the area he had to cover was immense and his assumption that García and his captors had come this way was anyway questionable. Then just as he was thinking he would never find any trace of anyone's movement on this slope, he came across something: clearly a man-made route that led up, trending westward away from the peaks behind him and towards a ridge at some distance that marked the limit of this valley and the lip that defined the edge of a new one. Vegetation became more intermittent as he moved up to the ridge so, despite the increased gradient, Daniel and his horse did not slow. Then, crossing the stony divide, Daniel saw something that made his heart skip a beat. There, far across in the next valley, although the path he was following became lost in vegetation, there was the tell-tale sign of *chulos*, or black vultures, circling some way below and to the east. What were they doing there?

Daniel knew, of course. He didn't want to see but he had no choice but to go and look. It took him some time to descend but when he reached the area the *chulos* had indicated he found scores of the black birds gathering and arguing among themselves over a feast of carrion. The awful, gut-wrenching smell and one look was enough: it was human carrion. This was quite the last thing anyone would want to see, but nonetheless, with his mouth and nostrils covered, Daniel prompted

146

his horse closer and encouraged the birds to leave the site – he had to do what he really had little stomach for: to check the remains.

Guns were the first thing he clearly recognised. They were untouched. So, too, were packets of TMG explosive. Blankets and items of dirty and misshapen clothing were much more difficult to decipher, strewn around and mixed up with, ugh, human remains. Finally he saw one, then two grimy but unmistakably recognisable black patent-leather shoes. And wasn't some of that clothing lying about possibly the torn fragments of a dark business suit? Daniel turned away quickly and rode out, his eyes filling with tears, his heart sick in his stomach. Yes. That indeed was what he had seen. He couldn't bear to think of it but those were undoubtedly the remains of a number of bodies, Martín García, ex-student, ex-executive, included among them.

Daniel's first reaction was to put distance between himself and what many would have described as a nightmarish, horrific scene behind him. He forced himself to consider, however, that what he had just come across was in fact nothing other than nature's way of dealing with all death. The spark of life that fills us all had long gone from those remains he had seen. They were mere empty shells from which the vital electricity had vanished. Let nature's waste-disposal creatures clear away the worthless empties. He tried to console himself with that thought.

Night was falling quickly again and Daniel had no desire to rush back. His spirits were low – he knew that the message he was to carry back would be devastating, heartbreaking, for the family and friends involved – and he needed to rest and come to terms with it all himself. The path he had followed was now associated with depression and death so he chose to take to the high ground – find a new way up to the ridge and make camp for the night in the clear air.

As he was bedding down, Daniel felt an earth tremor

beneath him. His horse snorted too: they could both feel the volcano was breathing. They waited. Nothing more ... but the warning signs were there and Daniel readied himself for a quick evacuation in the night should it be necessary. No further tremors occurred, however, so Daniel could sleep until first light.

The following day man and horse set out with the rising sun in their faces, aiming to go high and track above and round behind the Triple F mine, rather than cross the access road below in daylight.

As they gained height, they entered a swirling low cloud with the distinct smell of sulphur. The volcano had been exhaling, thought Daniel. He hoped it would be no more than that. He was thinking of how he had not been above 4,000 metres on this mountain for some time and was actually looking forward to it, providing the view was not obscured, when he saw descending from the north, on a trajectory that would cross in front of him, what appeared to be two riders with a pack mule between them. It was an unusual sight so early in the day – clearly they must have been out all night. He was instantly wary – the FARC? Paramilitaries? Or just some oddball mountaineers or environmentalists like himself?

Daniel kept his eyes on the other party as they drew closer. Something about them didn't look right – the horses were stumbling slowly downhill; he was alarmed to see that their riders were wearing camouflaged outfits, and the second in the party looked decidedly worse for wear. Wounded maybe? The big one in front raised an arm in Daniel's direction but this was no friendly salute – he was holding a gun!

As the fearful recognition dawned on Daniel, so it did on others, too. The lead horse which carried the big man immediately reared up, neighing in alarm. It shook itself as if wanting to rid itself of some awful parasite. It achieved its objective: still clutching his gun but without firing a shot, the rider was ejected from his saddle and, large man that he was, he crashed heavily on to the ground below. If that was not enough, his horse was still stamping and rearing in distress and a back leg kicked out and knocked the man senseless. Crack! Daniel winced as he heard the sound of hoof on head.

Daniel's own horse, which had similarly backed away in fright, now calmed down and he was thus able to approach the others. His first concern was to dismount and check the animals, ignoring the fallen rider who lay crumpled and unconscious. All was well. Despite violently plunging around on an uneven surface, the lead horse had suffered no ill effects; the other horse and mule seemed tired and a little fretful, but OK. The second horse, however, was not at all happy with his own rider. Daniel was surprised to see that this individual was semi-conscious and tied on rather ruthlessly to his poor mount. He set to and loosened the straps that held man on, watching to see if he, too, would fall to the ground. Thankfully, no. He left the straps in place, ensuring that the horse was no longer discomfited.

What a sight! Two horses, a mule, one man unconscious; another nearly so – he was waving slowly in his saddle and now Daniel could hear him rambling quietly, semi-coherently, to himself:

'Murderous bastard … now you fall off … Keep going you said … Hah! Now you keep going! Howya going to get back to the Triple F mine now, eh?'

Daniel knelt down to examine the big man on the ground. There was a lump on the side of his head, but he was breathing and, checking his neck, arms and legs, all looked in working order. There was still a revolver in his hand, however. An ugly sight that he recollected had meant to do him harm.

The rider above was still rambling. 'Sssh! Ssh! Don't say anything. Don't tell anyone. We were nowhere near the TMG mine. Explosion? Never! Murder? Nothing to do with us. No … Ssh!'

Daniel did not like what he was hearing. These were bad

men. Paramilitaries, hired guns, paid to do someone's dirty work. He checked over the horses and the mule again. The mule was carrying almost empty bags but what they contained was incriminating enough: some packets that resembled others he had seen recently. Undoubtedly explosives – though, in this case, they were unmarked packages.

Daniel considered what to do. The big man was groaning but still not conscious. On his own territory with the animals around him, Daniel was not afraid of these gunmen but he wondered if it might not be wisest to leave this party as it was and retire some distance to watch and see what they did. He certainly had no incentive whatsoever to help the fallen rider or to offer any sort of assistance to either of them. Daniel quietly led his horse away, upslope and into the low cloud.

Smith came round slowly, trying to figure out what had happened. He remembered his horse rearing up and then not much else. How long had he been out? No idea. His head hurt and feeling around he understood why: a massive lump on the side! He had his Smith & Wesson in his hand. What was that doing there? Checking, he could see it had not been fired, so he put it back under his arm where it belonged. He looked around. The mountain stretched about on all sides, the sulphurous mist was still hanging in the air – maybe it had caused him to pass out? By the look of the day it was still early morning and so little time had been lost. Get back in the saddle and revert to plan: no point in doing anything else.

Cárdenas was burbling incoherently – obviously half dead from exhaustion and maybe also from inhaling the poisonous fumes. Time to move quickly on. Smith kicked his mount and the party headed on south, looking for the access road. He cast a good look around as he did so – it was always important to check – but he was certain they were alone. There was no sign of any other sentient being, no sign that a man and his horse were high, some way back and walking along, shadowing their every move.

Miguel Cortés and Juan José Gómez were waiting impatiently at the Triple F mine to hear any news of Smith and his excursion when the two-way radio Gómez was holding burst into life. It was a security guard on the road a little way below reporting that two men with horses and a mule had just appeared, had ignored his warning completely and were now on their way up towards them. Gómez thanked the messenger and told him not to worry – they were expecting them. The two colleagues agreed: it was typical of Smith to push past any security personnel, ignoring their admonition – but at least it was an improvement on silencing the poor guard. The good news was it would not be long now before they got the full story.

Smith soon came into view, leading Cárdenas and the mule. They all looked tired, which Cortés thought would be understandable for most people, though it was unusual for Smith to look anything more expressive than a rock. Cárdenas seemed completely out of it: his eyes were open but glazed over with exhaustion.

'How did it go?' Cortés was anxious for feedback. 'What's up with him?' he added, looking at Smith's companion.

'Mission accomplished,' replied Smith impassively. 'He fell on the way back. Not strong enough.'

That figured, thought Cortés. It would be close to impossible for most men to keep up with Smith on such an exercise. He indicated to Gómez to untie Cárdenas and help him down. The man looked in need of complete rest and maybe the attention of a medic before he could be debriefed.

'Get him into the Land Rover, Juan José,' Cortés said. 'We'll get him off the mountain as soon as possible.'

Smith had dismounted and was unloading what was left of the supplies from the horses and mule, dumping it all on the roadside. He looked at Cortés.

'We'll leave all that here – it can go back with the rest of the stuff we brought up from Popayán,' said Cortés, reading as best he could what Smith wanted. 'You need to come down, too – Fields will want to hear from you as soon as we can get a signal. Tell me: you set the explosives OK? Nobody tumbled you?'

'No one's left who saw us. All evidence buried. Big explosion. I mean, big!'

'Great. Well done. Get Cárdenas and climb aboard the Land Rover and we'll get out of here.'

Cortés left Gómez behind to cover everything up and play down any awkward questions from their own staff who might be wondering what these odd goings-on were all about. It was, of course, just a survey of volcanic activity; that was the agreed official story. Now it was important to disappear off the mountain and wait below for the repercussions of their mission. With Smith and Cárdenas aboard, he started up the Land Rover and headed down the road, eyes fixed on negotiating the crater in front caused by the original TMG assault. He assumed his own security patrols would have kept any prying eyes away – not that there would be any up here, so high, so far away from anywhere and so early in the day.

One hour later and they had reached the public highway and, in darkening skies, they were motoring steadily back towards the regional office in Popayán. Smith was sitting in front, stony-faced and focused as usual on the way ahead. Cárdenas was tilted over sideways on the bench seats behind them, sleeping. It started to rain.

Cortés thought to raise González, who he reckoned would be like he had been: anxious to hear of the outcome of the operation.

'Cortés, that you?' González answered. 'Are your men back OK?'

'Absolutely. All's well and the mission has been a success. We even felt a tremor or two at our mine. We'll be with you in a couple of hours, I guess. What's the story your end?'

152

'We've picked up news that TMG have got problems. Nothing definite yet. Meanwhile, Fields has been on the line, pestering for anything I've got.'

'Contact him now and tell him what I've just told you and say we'll be in touch as soon as we arrive. I don't want any interrogation from him while I'm driving. Bye!' Cortés switched his phone off.

True to his word, just over two hours later in driving rain the long-wheel-base Land Rover drove splashing down into the basement parking lot of the Triple F Popayán office with its driver feeling relieved and satisfied. Job done. Well, almost. Smith had removed his combat dress and was now back in a dark-blue, anonymous uniform but Cárdenas, still asleep, had to be similarly returned to anonymity before somehow getting him home. Cortés struggled to unzip the semi-comatose engineer and remove his outer garment, cursing and muttering under his breath all the while. Smith, of course, was impervious to the travails of his colleague and just stood back and watched.

Finally sorted, Cárdenas was left on the bench seat while Cortés and Smith took the elevator up to González's office. They entered an atmosphere of subdued elation. González had a big grin on his face.

'The news media have heard of some sort of mining disaster with TMG. Local television are sending a helicopter up to have a look. They've asked us if we have suffered anything on our side of the mountain but apart from a tremor or two I've said we are OK. They are guessing that the volcano may have burst into life ...'

'Well, what next? Dangerous places, volcanos ... Have you heard from Fields again?'

'Yes, but I told him to wait for you. You'd better get on the line.'

Cortés took the phone.

*

153

Fields buzzed his personal assistant on the intercom.

'Patricia, can you get me the head of TMG Colombia? He's here somewhere in Bogotá and probably under a lot of pressure. I'll need to know his name.'

He waited. Five minutes passed and then his assistant came back. 'Brian MacKay, chief of TMG Colombia, is on the phone, sir.'

'Thank you ... Hello? Brian MacKay? This is Morten Fields, the new man here in Triple F. Pleased to make your acquaintance. I've just heard the news that you've had a mine collapse in Puracé. Terrible business. I know things must be hectic right now but I thought we could offer some help. Yes. We're both in the area. Our people down there tell me they felt some tremors. Do you know what caused it? Nothing certain yet? Of course not. Are you sure it wasn't the FARC or some other such group? We've just lost three, maybe four or our own staff thanks to those bastards and I wouldn't put it past them to try something like this. We've had our security all over our property since and maybe they've gone looking for other targets? Yeah. Yeah.

'Look, if you want, we can get some trucks and heavy earth-moving equipment over to your mine in three or four hours, if not less. We are a lot closer than the rest of your people further south in Nariño and our resources can maybe help fill the gap until you get your own stuff in. No problem. Time is of the essence when people are trapped. We'd be pleased to help. We're all in the same business, after all. I'll send you the contact details of the head of our Popayán office, that's Alejandro González. He's a good man. I'll phone him in just a second and tell him to expect you. You can then contact him direct and discuss what you need and whether he has it on site. I'll tell him whatever he's got he should make it available to you. Yes. No thanks necessary. We're glad to help in any way we can. OK. Bye for now.'

Fields closed this call and then dialled the Popayán office direct.

'Hello, González? What's the latest you've heard on the extent of damage to the TMG mine? Is that so? I've just been speaking to my opposite number in TMG up here in Bogotá, Brian MacKay. He fears it might be worse. Says they've lost access to men and equipment deep in the mine and that poisonous fumes are issuing out over the place. Have we got anything with us down there that we can send round to the TMG site to help dig them out? I've told Mackay to contact you so you give him everything you can, gottit? Men, earth-moving equipment, trucks, whatever he asks for. Make sure you've got more explosive in the vehicles we send, OK? We are going to need it. Yes. TMG'll bring their own gear into position when they can, but all their other facilities are way further south in Nariño. We are the nearest who can help. Yes. Now listen carefully. I'm coming down myself as soon as I can get in the air. I'll need you and Leopold Smith to meet me at the airport soon as I land. I want Smith dressed as a Triple F miner or whatever because he is to be part of the rescue operation we are sending up. Understand? See to it all, can you? Good. I'll be down there directly we get clearance. Bye.'

Fields turned back to Patricia on the intercom. 'Can you get my plane ready for immediate departure, please? Get the pilot out on the tarmac and ensure that we have clearance to take off. I need to get to Popayán as soon as possible. Thanks.'

It was some two hours later when González met Fields off the corporate jet plane with a question mark written all over his face. Smith was meanwhile waiting patiently in the car.

'Has Mackay been on to you?' was the first thing Fields wanted to know.

'Yes. We are sending a convoy of JCBs and trucks to help shift whatever's up there. That's all we've got that he needs at present.'

'Have they all gone yet?'

'A couple of JCBs set off from our Puracé mine forty-five minutes ago. They will be slow. We sent five trucks from here a little later but they will probably all meet up before reaching TMG.'

'I want Smith up there.'

González shepherded his boss into the waiting car, took the wheel and set off towards the town. 'Oh? What's the plan?' he asked.

Fields turned to Smith in the back of the car. 'Leo, I want you to go up to the TMG mine and, amidst all the chaos I expect you to find, plant more explosive.' Fields turned his attention to González. 'You are sending more up in the trucks, aren't you?'

González whistled. 'Phew! So that's it. You want another explosion, don't you?'

'Yes. Their mine is unstable. We've got to convince them of how unsafe it is there. No better way than one disaster after another. Better still if some of our men and machines are caught up in it – our machines are all insured but it will look like we're victims just like TMG.'

Fields looked back at Smith. 'Leo, I want you out of the way when you detonate the blast. Anyone else but you can get hurt. Understand? Just make sure you set one off. This time you won't have anyone to help pick the spot to place the explosive. That is right, isn't it, González?' He cast a look at his driver.

'Correct, sir. Cárdenas is now in bed. Smith here wore him out. We've had one of our medics check him over and he says the poor guy is delirious and needs at least twenty-four hours rest.'

'OK, Leo. So you plant the explosive on your own, where you can, and repeat the same exercise as you did before. Bring the roof down, OK?' He waited for Smith's nod of assent and then returned to his briefing.

'If the media ask, we will be pretty upset. We could suggest that TMG's mine is unstable and we've sent our men into a death trap. Gottit? Depending on what it looks like, it could be that we can't blame an unsafe mine. We might have to say that the FARC must have infiltrated the rescue and done the damage. After all, we've got just cause to claim the region is crawling with terrorists. Either way, it's TMG's fault and the media should pick up that. The result we want is for TMG to suffer; their share price to suffer, and thus shake their head office's resolve to continue mining in the area. That way, they pull out and we move in.

'González – we need to get Leo here up on board a truck before they reach TMG's mine. Soon as you've dropped me off in your office, can you find someone to take him up and overtake your convoy?' Fields had it all worked out.

From a vantage point high on the mountain, Daniel saw what he assumed were two paramilitary gunmen and their mule-load of explosive cargo go up to the Triple F mine entrance where it looked like security men were waiting. The two gunmen transferred into a waiting vehicle and off it went, negotiating the partially destroyed part of the road in the process.

Daniel did not bother to stay around any longer and try to make sense of all this – that could wait until later. His priority now was to get back to the Fernández estate and pass on the bad news he had to Alfonso, whom he would ask to contact the Fernández family. With a long ride ahead of him he could not afford to delay.

The clouds lowered and, as the hours passed, it started to rain. Daniel pulled on his poncho and a wide-brimmed felt hat. The day matched his mood: the closer he got to his destination, it seemed, the gloomier everything became. At last, as the sun disappeared behind a black horizon in the west, he started down the familiar track to the stables where he would find Alfonso.

'*Hola amigo!*' his friend called out. 'Bring your horse in here, out of the rain, quickly. This is fine weather you've brought back with you!'

Daniel grimaced. 'Sorry, Alfonso, I tried to fix it but the mountain wouldn't listen. The poor horse is tired now. We both are, but when he's settled, can we go inside and talk?'

It took a little while for Daniel to remove his gear, lead his loyal companion into his own stable, wipe him down and make him content, Alfonso in attendance. Then the two men walked through to Alfonso's quarters where his wife had just started making up a hot chicken soup to feed them all. Alfonso directed Daniel to sit in his best chair. The family's long-haired dog came over and rested his head on Daniel's lap, big mournful eyes looking up at him. Daniel stroked his head.

Alfonso pulled another chair over. 'So tell me, my friend. You have a long face so I guess what you have to say is not good.'

'No, Alfonso. I went off to see if I could find anything about the *señorita* Claudia's friend, Martín García. He was the one who went missing, kidnapped by the FARC.'

'I heard about it,' Alfonso replied. 'And?'

'I found his body, Alfonso. Along with others, I guess, of the FARC.' Daniel looked down. 'It looked like a massacre.'

'*Ay dios mio*!' Alfonso exclaimed

'Can you contact Señor Fernández and give him the bad news?' Daniel asked. 'Of course it is unofficial until the authorities can confirm the death but I think he should know as soon as possible so that he can warn his daughter first. García's family will need to know as well, but Fernández can decide whether or not he gives them the news unofficially.'

'OK, Mono. I'll do that. Shall I contact the authorities in Popayán, too?'

'Can you? Thanks. Tell them, if the police or army want to visit the site where the bodies are, then I guess I shall have to take them.'

'OK, Mono. You want to stay with us until they come? Yes? María has just cooked a meal for us and you cannot leave afterwards – too dark, cold and wet!'

'You are too good to me, Alfonso,' Daniel smiled. 'But thank you. I'll stay tonight.'

Daniel went to help María, Alfonso's wife, finish preparing the table for their meal while Alfonso phoned first of all his boss, Fernández, in Cali. Then he next contacted the local police. He came back to the table to join Daniel as the evening meal was served.

'There's been some sort of disaster up at the TMG mine, the police say. They've taken note of what I said you've found but now they're waiting to see what's happened at the mine. So we will have to wait and see when they wish to follow up your information on García – until then they've got their hands full.'

Daniel wondered what had happened. He wondered if what he had seen on the mountain tied in with this mining disaster. He voiced his concerns to Alfonso and María and they discussed it all at some length.

'Mono, do you know my cousin Carlos Díaz?' Alfonso asked. 'He lives in the pueblo over near the TMG mine. Of course you do – he and his wife Valentina, they speak of you often. Well, he is something of a leader of the people in his pueblo now. Mostly farmers. They have nothing but trouble with the mine. They say it is poisoning the waters there. Some in the pueblo used to go panning for gold in the springs nearby but not now. Too dangerous. The women say they are even frightened to bathe in the water; they have to walk a long way just to wash. Then the paramilitaries come and warn them against causing any trouble. Stop complaining, they say, or we give you something to shut you up. As if poisoning their land is not enough!

'Carlos said they also have had visits from the FARC: trying to raise support to fight the mine. They usually come at night, wanting money or people to join them. The pueblo lost some men but Carlos put a stop to that. We stick together and only help ourselves, he said, not all these outsiders. Either one side or the other wants to cause trouble for the pueblo, he says.

159

They end up in the middle, trying to fight off both sides.'

'But do you think they might help someone to cause trouble in the mine?' Daniel asked. He was thinking of the men he had seen crossing the mountain on horse. 'What about stirring things up between TMG and Triple F? They are not so far away.'

'Go to talk to Carlos, if you want. He is right in the middle of everything and knows more than me. But I don't think they want anything to do with the paramilitaries, the FARC, or any of the mining companies. And I guess he won't like having the police or government forces up there now, either. The pueblo just wants to be left in peace.'

'Don't forget to talk to Valentina, also,' María added. 'Men don't know everything! She will have a different perspective from her husband.'

'Thank you both.' Daniel finished his meal. 'You've been so kind to me as always. I'll follow up what you suggest in the morning. But I guess I'll need another of your horses to go visit your cousin, Alfonso. Would you mind?'

Alfonso chuckled. 'They're not my horses, Mono. But they need exercising. As always – you are very welcome.'

Daniel retired to the bed his friends had made up for him, thinking as always that there were not enough folk like this around in the world.

The next morning Daniel was once again on the move north towards the TMG mine, though this time with the intention of visiting the nearby pueblo. He had had a difficult night, his head spinning with all sorts of possible explanations of what had happened.

The latest he had heard on the radio at Alfonso's before riding out was yet another twist – the TMG mine had apparently suffered a second collapse in the night. Triple F were quoted as saying that the TMG mine was not safe; they had lost a couple of men and machines and the rescue attempt had been badly organised. This comment put Daniel in mind of something El Ciego had once told him: that nothing the mining companies' public relations people said should ever be believed. They were all liars. OK: a piece of advice he needed to weigh up with all the other information he was struggling with.

As always, on the mountain in the clear air, Daniel felt happiest. There was lots to mull over and the long ride would help him fit the jigsaw puzzle together – hopefully without running across more loose pieces. The peregrine falcon came down again to visit him. She could see her friend was somewhat preoccupied, so she stayed on his shoulder to keep him company. Daniel put his hand up to ruffle the feathers of the bird. It helped.

Start at the beginning, he thought, and make the simplest, most obvious conclusions from what was known. OK, first there was Triple F's Toyota and its passengers blown up. No claim of responsibility straight away but then a Triple F executive is captured while investigating the site and a ransom demand made by the FARC. That does sound like the FARC set a trap.

Then the victim, García, and his FARC kidnappers are wiped out. That appeared like a paramilitary botched rescue attempt. Though what were the TMG explosives doing there?

Next, TMG's mine suffers a major disaster. Men are seen moving away from the area, one threatens him with a gun and the other deliriously implies his comrade is a murderer and that they are involved in the explosion. They both return to Triple F. Not an autonomous mining collapse, therefore – more like a Triple F-manufactured 'accident'?

Finally, a second mine disaster. Triple F are somehow involved in a rescue attempt but it goes wrong.

Two rescue attempts that go wrong? Does that sound familiar?

It would be interesting to hear what Alfonso's cousin,

Carlos, thought. He, his family and their pueblo must be a buzz with gossip just now. Daniel rode on eager to get there before the sun set too low.

The pueblo was a collection of simple, traditional one-storey farm buildings, with whitewashed walls and Spanish tiled roofs, that had existed at the foot of the mountain for not quite as many years as the volcano had been there, but it seemed like almost as long. Around seventeen or so families lived there and, with the passing of some older men, Carlos was the tallest, strongest and the one with the fiercest temper who remained. Only in his mid-thirties he was nonetheless the unspoken leader of the community. When he was younger he had attracted the attention of a number of local girls and as a result he had picked as his wife the most attractive of those who had teased and tossed their hair at him. This was Valentina, of olive skin and green eyes, who was the only one who had given him the run-around.. They now had a fifteen-year-old daughter Natalia who took after her mother and a four-year-old dynamo Luís, or Lucho, who everyone claimed was too much like his father.

The pueblo was connected to highway 24 in the north by a dirt track which ran parallel to the TMG company road some distance to the east. As Daniel rode into the pueblo, coming down the mountain, approaching from the south, he could see over to the TMG road, which was now alive with people, trucks and other heavy vehicles going to and from the mine. He called out as he approached Carlos and Valentina's house. A dog barked in reply.

A curtain was drawn back from a window. Then Carlos came out with Natalia, the latter looking at him with big round eyes as he dismounted. Daniel brushed the falcon off his shoulder; he had momentarily forgotten she was there. The bird immediately flew up to settle on the highest telegraph pole in the pueblo. In the front yard, Carlos's dog – a long-haired, bright-eyed mongrel – barked again at the sight of her.

'*Hola*, Mono,' said Carlos. 'Another one come to see the fun and games?' From just inside the front door to the house a little boy's voice echoed: '*Hola*, Mono! *Hola*, Mono!'

'Carlos, do you have to be so rude to our friend?' Valentina came to the door. 'Don't you mind him, Daniel. You are very welcome here. Come in.' She was one of the very few who insisted on calling Daniel by his proper name.

Daniel was grateful for the invitation to enter. He followed Carlos and ruffled the hair of the little boy who was standing, grinning up at him from the door.

A large wooden table dominated the room he entered. It was low-ceilinged, dark, simply decorated but with decades of use it had a warm, welcoming feel to it. Daniel walked around and waited by the far side of the table to see where the others would sit. He was anxious not to offend his hosts. Carlos waved a hand at a nearby stool. Daniel sat as bid. Natalia stood behind her father with big eyes, not saying a word. Carlos sat at the head of the table, frowning.

'So what brings you here, Mono?' he asked.

'I wanted your opinion, Carlos, if you wouldn't mind,' replied Daniel. 'Also any news you might have to add to what I know. I've just come from Alfonso, your cousin, and there have been people, friends, killed over that way. Paramilitaries have threatened me. Now there's a mining disaster here. I wondered what has been going on and if you knew anything.'

'Pah!' Carlos exploded. 'I've had my fill of 'em all. Two weeks back the paramilitaries came to see me. I've been causing too much trouble they say. Me? TMG are the ones causing trouble, I say – contaminating the waters; their heavy vehicles chewing up our lands. No, they say; I've got to stop complaining or else. So who is paying these guys with guns to threaten me, eh? TMG, who else? Well, now they've got something else to think about – a mine collapse. I and a few of us here went up yesterday to offer to help dig out the trapped miners. I've

163

got nothing against those ordinary workers trapped underground, but no – their security push us away. I get mad but they don't like us, we don't like them. Despite this, I went back again this morning because there's been another collapse. No, they still don't want our help and they look at me with suspicion, as if I caused it!'

'Have you heard anything about what has caused the mine collapse? An accident or someone up to no good?'

'No, I haven't heard. It's no secret that the people who farm the land here, and some of those who still pan for gold, none of us wants that mine open. But none of us has the time, or the resources, or the intention to do any real harm to the poor people who work there. If the explosion we heard was caused by someone, it was no one I know.'

'Do you think the FARC may have had a hand in it?' Daniel asked. 'You've had a visit from them, haven't you?'

'That's another bunch who have threatened us, yes,' Carlos said. 'They are just interested in exploiting our grievances. "Join us and we'll help you," they say. But what do they do? Demand a cut of our income for protection money. Or they will take over our land and grow and process coca leaves on it. They were going to come back here and force us to choose one of those options but then it all went quiet. I think TMG bought them off. It's possible, I guess, that the FARC might have detonated some explosion in the mine as a means of demanding their money ... but I wouldn't know how they could do that. The place is crawling with security.'

Valentina was standing by the door. 'What do the wives say in the pueblo?' Daniel asked.

'Like Carlos says, none of us wants the mine. We used to bathe in the spring above the pueblo but not now; we have to walk a across the fields to a tank that is fed by another stream. We hope that is safer but even then we are not sure.' Valentina stopped. 'But Daniel – that is not what really worries us. It's the men who come to threaten us – that is worse. I keep telling

Carlos not to provoke them, not to complain so much but he won't listen ...'

Carlos became angry. 'What do you want me to do, woman? Lie down and let them walk all over us? We have to stand up to all these people and tell them to stop. Stop poisoning our water; stop despoiling our fields; stop giving us orders, and stop threatening us.'

'And you will sacrifice your life in the process? Is that what you want?' It was Valentina's turn to become angry now. 'Because I don't want to lose you. A martyr is no good to me and your children!'

'And it's no good if we have nowhere to live!' Carlos retorted fiercely. 'All we have in the world is here, right here on these lands. These are our roots. They give us our livelihoods. They give us our identity; our freedom to be who we want to be. These lands are ours; they belonged to our parents before us and their parents before them. The mining companies want to push us off, tear it all up and dig out whatever minerals they find. Or, if we don't leave, they pay people to kill us. Or, if it's not them, we get terrorists demanding us to leave so they can harvest coca leaves. And they also threaten to kill us if we don't move. So what do we do? The only thing I can do is to protest; to shout loud; to complain to whoever will hear!'

Valentina stepped forward to glare at her husband.

'But what if the only ones who hear are those men with guns?' she demanded. 'I'd rather leave these lands with you than have to go without you. I don't want to wait here for you not to return one day. I don't ever want to go out and have to search for your dead body, do you hear? Don't you ever, ever do that to me!' She burst into tears and ran out.

Carlos just shouted after her. He didn't know if he was angrier with his wife, with himself or with the whole situation they were faced with.

Daniel went after her. He found her in the middle of the next room, the children's bedroom, with Lucho holding on tight around her legs, alarmed at his mother's reaction.

'What can we do?' Valentina's tearful face look up at his. 'We have so much to lose. We can't stay and be killed. But we can't run away somewhere else either and wait until we are pushed off again. Daniel ... can you help us? Carlos is too proud to ask but you see how it is here. I've been worried sick these last few weeks and Carlos just gets angrier and angrier. Daniel ... everyone here knows and respects you. You can do things that no one else can. But no one is going to ask you except me ... so please ... is there anything you can do to help?'

Daniel held Valentina to him and kissed the top of her head, his mind racing. He had to help ... but how?

'I'll do whatever I can. We have to stop the violence; the greed; the destruction of the lands. Why have I come here to see you? To tell you that there must be thousands of others all over the country like you – angry and suffering like you. You're not alone. If one person, one pueblo, complaining isn't enough to stop this, then we have to organise. You hold on to your man. I'll do it. I'll visit everyone who might join us. I'll even get the livestock, the animals, the birds, every living creature to protest. They will have to take notice. Valentina – you look after your family. I'll do all I can to look after the rest, you wait and see ...'

7

Christmas

Close to the end of the semester, Karin's spirits began to rise. Christmas was coming and that would surely be a time of celebration, of meeting people, and of yet more new and fascinating experiences. Even the weather in Bogotá seemed to perk up – days and days of non-stop sunshine.

October had been a terribly depressing time for Claudia, her best friend. First was the news that Martín's body had been found. Claudia's father, Manuel Fernández, had come up to visit her and tell her the bad news, unofficial at this stage, in person. Karin was introduced to him and, of course, they had both warmed to each other. Tall for a Colombian, he was dark-haired, greying at the temples, well-groomed and a very distinguished-looking gentleman. He kept thanking Karin for being such a supportive friend to his daughter; she in return kept complimenting him for having such a wonderful daughter who had made her stay in his country so welcoming.

Two weeks after Claudia's father's visit came the funeral of Martín García. This was in Bogotá and the surrounding details, as they emerged, were intensely sombre. Claudia shut her ears, her eyes, the door to her room in her aunt's apartment, and didn't want to see or talk to anyone about it for days. Karin had just held her hand through that period and had said little or nothing. The García family had paid for a helicopter to recover the body, or what remained of it, and had a DNA investigation carried out to confirm that it was, indeed, the body of Martín. As soon as this was confirmed, then relations and friends flew in from around Colombia and the USA to go to the funeral. Karin, Claudia and her parents attended, as did a large number of students and ex-students from Los Andes. The death of such a popular young man, with so much potential, cut off in his prime, and in such a horrific manner, meant that the delayed service, when it eventually took place, was an extremely sad and tearful affair.

In the shadow of that experience, it took some time in November for Karin to return to the routine of studying, getting on top of her subject, socialising with her fellow students, dining out and partying, and, particularly, getting Claudia out of her depression to partake in the various distractions of a big, vibrant city. Karin had insisted that the best way to feel a new person is to go and have a complete makeover: a new hairdo and manicure; buy a new outfit, with shoes and bag to match; to dress up, put on the best perfume and make-up, stand in front of a mirror looking a million dollars, smile, then go out and hit the town. This they did. It worked. They had the best night out possible in a salsa club – several young men competed over each girl on the dance floor and by the time they had retreated to a quiet table for drinks Claudia's face was wreathed in smiles. New boyfriends awaited her in the days that followed. The end of November thus finished on a high note.

December saw the close of studies in Los Andes and thoughts turned to the holiday.

'Karin – the long vacation starts soon. Would you like to spend Christmas with my family?' asked Claudia.

'Silly question!' Karin retorted. 'Who else would I rather spend Christmas with? It is a time to be with family, I adore your parents, and, if they are willing to have me, I'd be delighted.'

'Well, they would love to have you. I've told them already that I insist you come and of course they said yes. Anyway, my father took a real shine to you so he would be pleased to see you again.'

'And I took a shine to him, too. Quite a cultured gentleman. He must be quite disappointed to have such a philistine for a daughter ...'

'Pig! I hate you!' Claudia laughed.

Karin laughed, too. It was great to see the sparkle back in her friend's eyes.

They took the overnight bus to Cali soon after their university session finished. Claudia phoned ahead and the family's driver picked them up at the bus depot. He drove them straight to the Fernández home: a large, rambling, single-storey house in a suburb of similar properties on the outskirts of the city, with a low-pitched, overhanging roof, a patio, swimming pool and an extensive garden. Claudia's mother welcomed her daughter with a big hug. A similar welcome was bestowed upon Karin. All the while a maid stood politely by with a pitcher of iced fruit juice and two glasses.

Claudia was on a high and insisted on taking Karin in hand and showing her around.

'This will be your bedroom, K.,' she enthused. 'Look: right next to mine, with adjoining doors, so we can sit together on your bed or mine and natter all night if we are in the mood ... Here's the lounge – plenty of space – never mind the dog, he shouldn't be in here ... That's the dining room, lovely isn't it? ... And here we are back into the garden again. We have another bedroom I haven't shown you – it belongs to Andres, my brother who is currently in Australia; there's also my parents' room, and my father's study. He gets really annoyed if I so much as touch the furniture in there. But what do you think? Will you be happy staying with us?'

'I think it will be just fabulous ...' She made a bee-line for the pool and lowered herself into an easy chair. 'Aaaah! I love it already.'

The same question was put to Karin later that evening by Claudia's father while they were seated for dinner. By that time she had showered and changed and was feeling definitely in holiday spirits.

'This is a lovely place and I can't thank you enough for having me. This is so very kind of you. I am sure this will be a wonderful Christmas ... ' Karin laughed. 'But I have to say it seems so strange that it isn't cold. My first Christmas in the sunshine!'

'Well, of course this is normal for us, just as it is strange for you,' Claudia's father replied. 'In fact, I get quite tired of this heat, all day and every day here. By all means get your fill of this hot weather for the next couple of weeks while I'm at work, but just before Christmas, I think – if Claudia and her mother agree – I'd like to retire to our finca. Not quite a British winter, but it is a little cooler there, as you know. You will have a busy time at first – we'll invite lots of people round so that you may meet a number of our neighbours, friends and some of my work colleagues here in Cali – but then it would be nice to celebrate Christmas just by ourselves in the mountains. I could certainly do with the rest. How does that sound?'

Karin looked at Claudia, who looked at her mother, who looked back at Claudia, who looked back at Karin.

'You say, Claudia,' Karin said. The last time they were at the finca was when Martín was killed.

'I'm fine with that,' said Claudia, a little solemnly. Her mother breathed a sigh of relief.

'That's good then,' said Karin brightly.

'Of course, that will give you the chance to see a certain someone,' said Claudia. 'Only if you should wish to ...' she added wickedly.

'Not just me ...' said Karin defensively. 'We should both thank a certain someone for what he has done for us.'

Claudia coloured and lowered her eyes. She had forgotten. In all the trauma of the death being announced and the funeral being arranged, no one had said anything about who had initially found Martín's body – just that her father had un-officially heard from Alfonso and that the police later confirmed it. Thanks to Karin's prompting, she realised now that it must have been Daniel who had found the body and told Alfonso. Who else?

Claudia's parents did not quite follow what had passed between the two girls but they didn't pursue it. Best to let them sort it out, whatever it was.

Claudia's father picked up the conversation: 'Well, most likely I'll finish work on the twenty-first, maybe the twenty-second. The day following we will drive down to the finca. We ought to start early because it's a four- or five-hour drive. We'll let Alfonso and María know in good time and they can prepare all the rooms and get in plenty of provisions ready for us. I'll get the wine and lots of other goodies here to take down with us. I am sure, Claudia, you and your mother will think of everything that I am going to forget!' He smiled at both of them. Karin thought, yet again, that this was a lovely family and that she was so lucky to have been invited to stay with them

As promised, over the next twelve days the evenings at the Fernández house were full of introductions, conversations, cocktails, laughing, some social manoeuvring, and general promises to keep in touch – 'You must come round to our place'... that sort of thing: all very pleasant; some people absolutely delightful, others not quite so.

Daytimes were a welcome break, time to dip in the pool, relax and lounge around the house and, of course, to go shopping and look around Cali.

'Karin, you must come with me to a certain shopping mall in town,' said Claudia after lunch one day. 'It has a sort of reputation for the type of people who go there.'

'Are we going to add to its reputation? Are we the type of people who go there?'

'I'm not saying,' Claudia replied. 'Like I've told you many times before, I want you to make up your own mind. I don't want to influence your opinion beforehand.'

Karin laughed. She was itching with curiosity. Claudia was always doing this to her.

They called a taxi and set off. They arrived at the shopping centre Claudia had mentioned around mid-afternoon, entered and parked themselves by a table outside a small ice-cream and milkshake parlour. There was a sort of shoppers' walkway that passed in front of their table and then snaked around a number of cafes, fashion stores and miscellaneous shops and kiosks that spread out in front and beside them.

Claudia waited for Karin to comment on what, or rather who, they saw. There were lots of pretty girls, young women, walking round in twos, threes, or with partners. One or two pushing babies. Pretty girls ... but all with lots of make-up and skin-tight clothes – and surely they must have enhanced figures?

Karin looked at a number of these young women parading around in front of her and then she turned to look at Claudia. Neither said a word ... but both suddenly exploded in laughter.

'What is this, Claudia? Cali's answer to Silicon Valley?'

Claudia snorted in suppressed laughter again. 'Yes! More plastic here than at a Tupperware party!' she claimed.

Both girls tried not to look at the occasional passing poseur but at times it became simply too fascinating to resist. 'Look at that one in the white top,' whispered Claudia. 'They're pushed up so high she could be a frog, croaking for a mate!'

'And that one in the red jeans', said Karin. 'she's so round behind she probably can't sit still, just roll back and forth like a spring-back dummy!'

It was an entertaining hour's fun and Karin thanked her

friend for what she said was a titillating experience. Claudia guffawed again.

'I told you this place has a reputation. It's even in some tourist guide books now.'

'I can believe it,' said Karin. 'It is certainly worth the taxi ride.'

They returned home and exchanged their stories with Claudia's mother, who was interested to know what the two of them were laughing about.

'I suppose those girls see it as an investment,' she said, 'just the same as buying your best dress to attract a mate. It probably started like that and now the competition between them drives them to buy a better and better body shape ... or what they think is a better shape.'

Women in Colombia had no reservations about flaunting their femininity, Karin thought. All the emphasis on looks, figure, posture, fashion; all the pressure to conform to a stereotype model or ideal of beauty; all the values that back in the UK would be associated with a brainless bimbo were heartily indulged in here. Women loved being women and did not seek to compete with men.

Karin broached the subject with Claudia that night – sitting on her bed and exchanging views as was their ordained habit.

'I can't comment so much on UK or US society,' said Claudia, 'but here women are more accustomed and I guess more confident in using their femininity to get what they want, rather than compete head on with menfolk. I'm quite happy to have the boys shoot their mouths off first in seminars, for example. It doesn't threaten me. I can more than hold my own. Have you noticed that even the top academics and professionals of our gender look sexy and go out to turn the heads of their male colleagues? They are not content to just browbeat them in boardrooms.'

Karin resolved to look out for that. She retired for the night, not for the first time with a flood of thoughts, experiences and sensations all whirling around in her head.

The experience she was most looking forward to, however, was the long drive down to Popayan and then up to the Fernandez finca. The day soon came when Claudia's father brought out the family's capacious Toyota Land Cruiser from its garage and proceeded to fill it up with all sorts of supplies before finally he was ready and announced to his three accompanying women that, with their permission, they should be off on their way.

The evening they arrived at the finca, as Alfonso and María helped the family unpack and set up home in the farm, Karin found time to ask if El Mono had been seen around recently.

'He has been very active, journeying from one pueblo to another over a great distance,' said María, 'so there have been weeks when we haven't seen anything of him. But two days ago he brought me some rabbits to cook and he wanted a long talk with Alfonso, so, if you ride out tomorrow, maybe you will find him.'

Karin took her advice and the very next morning prepared to lead Bella out after breakfast. Claudia had refused to accompany her.

'No, Karin, you go without me,' she said. 'If you find him, it will be easier for him to talk to you than if I were there. You know how shy and distant he can be. As you have said, I do need to see him and say thank you for what he has done for me ... but you see him first. I hope you find him. If you get the chance, why not tell him that he is very welcome here? Why don't you ask him to come and share our Christmas meal with us tomorrow night? My parents ought to meet the famous Mono, after all, and I'm sure they would be intrigued by him as we were at first, and still are. Tomorrow night, OK? Be sure to invite him!' Claudia waved a goodbye to Karin as she mounted the mare and took the familiar path across the farm field, and up into the mountain rainforest.

And so Karin rode away from one world and into another. Material wealth, urban society, convenience and sophistication lay behind; rural simplicity, discomfort and a direct and immediate relationship with life, death and all that the natural environment offered lay in front. Being so accustomed to one it was not easy making the transition to the other but, as always, she was determined to be up to the challenge. There was one dominant reason to succeed in this, after all.

He saw her coming from a great distance away. The falcon set off to signal to her and lead her in the right direction. Karin saw her and her heart fluttered like the falcon's wings as she realised she had been sent the messenger. Daniel stood on the skyline, his poncho wrapped around his upper body, a bag or knapsack at his feet, waiting for her to ride up.

'Hello, Daniel … it's been a long time,' she smiled at him. 'How are you?' She spoke in English.

'Fine.'

It had been almost three months since they had seen each other; they came from different cultures, different worlds; it took a little while for the undoubted chemistry between them to close the distance.

Daniel was boiling up water to make coffee over a small fire. He helped Karin down from her horse and there was an awkward pause for a fraction of a second as the two of them greeted one another, not sure whether to embrace or not. In that space, the falcon dived down to perch on Daniel's shoulder as he invited Karin to sit down and share coffee. Karin looked around her as she tried to make herself comfortable. Everything here, especially the relationship between them, seemed so fragile.

'Daniel, where do you live here? Where do you spend the nights?'

Karin didn't know whether or not just leaping in and asking him the sorts of questions that she had often thought about was the best way to open a conversation between them, or whether it was the best way to close one.

Daniel opened up. He smiled ruefully. 'I move around a lot, especially recently, and call on friends. Then there are three places I gravitate between where I stay by myself – all disused cabins that in the past have been used by farmers, cattle and various stores – but I often spend nights with people I see and who invite me to stay over. Like Alfonso and María, for example.'

Karin loved his smile and the way it suddenly broke into his seriousness and distance, like the sun bursting through an overcast sky. She thanked him for the coffee, burning her lips as she drank from a battered metal cup he had produced from his bag. He carried a minimum of possessions with him.

'But you used to come from Bogotá, from a city lifestyle that I've just come from. Don't you miss it? Don't you want to go back sometimes? It must be hard living up here.'

'It was a long time ago and I can't go back now.' Daniel replied. 'I visit Popayán on occasions and see there what drives me away. So many people seem to chase such false idols; lead such shallow lives; want more and more things that they don't really need. It is not so hard here – it's just that life is much simpler, so much clearer here.'

'But we are not all shallow in the city. Don't be so hard on us. There are plenty of people who are leading important lives, working to create a better future. Didn't your own parents want that before you lost them?' Karin recognised this was a dangerous question but there was something about Daniel that always prompted serious discussion. There was never any way to pass the time with superficial chit-chat. He didn't live in such society.

Daniel struggled. His face contorted in reconciling buried feelings with what he had just said. 'You're right. They did want that. But I guess I lost them because that is what happens in the city. Life loses its direction. Good things get swallowed up or die out in the mad rush that goes on. There are good people down there – look at you – but it seems to me as if you are all caught up in a monstrous and destructive machine that is destroying the environment there as up here and chewing up people and discarding them as it moves along ...'

'Oh, Daniel, that is such an awful and pessimistic outlook on the world I live in.' Karin reached across to hold his hand, her eyes pleading him to reconsider. 'It really doesn't look like that from where I stand. So many lovely people, doing good things and looking out for one another. You've been up here so long and on your own ... Surely you can see that life doesn't always fit the stereotypes you've mentioned. Look, why don't you come down and meet some of my friends? Claudia has invited you to join us tomorrow night for Christmas dinner. Come and meet her parents, dine with us in their farm, spend the night with us like you do with others? You'll see what sort of people they are, *we* are. We're not so bad.'

A shy smile came out again. 'Thank you, that is very kind. Tell Claudia I'm very grateful ... but I can't. I know what it will be like. You'll all have a lovely time while Alfonso and María work in the background, preparing the meal, serving you at the table, seeing to it that their masters are well cared for first before they can relax and maybe return to the kitchen where they finish off the leftovers. I can't join you like that. I can't have them serve me. I share my own food with them; they share their lives with me. It would be a betrayal of our friendship to have them wait at table for me. I couldn't do it. I'm sorry.'

'But it's Christmas, Daniel. Who will you share it with?' She realised she knew so little about him, only that she wished he would share a little more of his life with her.

'I'll go and visit Carlos, Alfonso's cousin, and his wife and family. They are lovely people. I've had a lot of dealings with them recently and I know they'll be happy to have me.' He stopped. 'I'm going to need a horse to get me over there so I'll come back with you to see Alfonso. Do you understand now why I can't dine with you tomorrow? I'm going to need Alfonso to loan me a horse overnight. He will do me that favour since I will never betray him; I'll always help him and María in whatever way I can. Just as he will help me. So to sit at a table and have María serve me food alongside you and the Fernández family would, for me, be terribly wrong. Like an insult. I will never do that to them.'

Karin wanted to kiss him. He was a good man. He lived a simple life but with his own well-defined rules, customs and obligations. She understood perfectly and could not ask him to do what was against his nature – he was so eloquent in explaining his values and giving her an insight into his world. But how was she ever going to get closer to him? She decided to ask.

'I do understand. Thank you for explaining it to me. But I would have loved to share a meal with you tomorrow … so, if it can't be then, you have to come with me another time, OK? I won't put you in any situation with others that is uncomfortable for you. It might even be that we have a meal together with Alfonso and María, or with whomever else you are happy with, but I want you to come down and share time with me and join me anywhere but on the mountain. Will you do that for me? Please?'

Daniel laughed. 'OK, OK, I agree. I guess I have to if I want to see you again. Typical *gringa* – you can get away with doing things that would be difficult for us. María serving you one day, then you sitting alongside her the next. She would find that impossible with anyone else, but you are the different one, the *gringa*, and we have to expect the impossible with such people.'

Karin smiled. He said he wanted to see her again so she really did want to kiss him this time. She wasn't sure how to hold herself back. Quick, change the subject. She stopped grinning at him and suddenly turned serious.

'Daniel, the last time we saw you, you said you'd search for

Martín's body. The next thing we know was that Claudia heard from her father that his body had indeed been found. We have to thank you so much for that. Can you tell me about what happened?'

'Not an awful lot to say. It wasn't very pleasant. I found out after you left what your friend Martín had been wearing when he was taken, and also where he was captured. So I spent a day and a half crisscrossing the area and then suddenly came across his body and the bodies of those who I guess had kidnapped him. I told Alfonso, who told the police and army. We all had the impression that someone had tried to rescue him, or there had been some sort of argument among the captors. I guess we will never really know, but it looked like they were all killed. Not a nice sight.' He didn't mention the horrific details of vultures picking over the remains.

'It must have been horrible. It was so good of you to do that for Claudia. Traumatic as it was for her, finding out brought an end to the misery for her and for Martín's family. So thank you again and I know Claudia wants to see you to say that herself.'

'She needn't, that's OK. But I have to tell you that things have moved on up here since then. It has been a bit of a battlefield between the FARC, paramilitaries and the mining companies on either side of the mountain. Maybe Martín was just a bystander who got caught up in the violence, but there has been an increase in the fighting between all parties from that date on.'

'How's that? What's happening?'

'I told you I've seen a lot of Carlos, Alfonso's cousin, and his family recently. He lives some distance away, beyond the Triple F mine where Martín was killed, closer to the TMG mine on the other side of Volcán Puracé. Well, between here and there, the TMG mine has suffered from explosions where men have been killed. Paramilitaries may or may not have caused those deaths. Certainly, people have threatened Carlos, I guess like

Martín because he is in the wrong place at the wrong time. The FARC are also caught up in this; they've threatened Carlos, too. The mining companies, both of them, I reckon, are somehow feeding the conflict and paying one party or another to fight their battles for them. It has been getting dangerous.'

'Well, shouldn't you be careful then? You don't want to be in the wrong place at the wrong time either. If it's dangerous here, why are you not going in the opposite direction, away from where the trouble is?'

'Thank you but don't you remember what you said to me? You got me thinking that I can't just stay here or run away hating the big city and the big city businesses, that I should do something. Well, I am now. I'm visiting the pueblos, talking to local people, indigenous families that have lived and worked these lands since before the conquistadors. We are planning to make a lot of noise, hopefully to raise the attention of those who can help. I am organising a big protest for the start of the New Year when people go back to work after the holidays.'

Daniel stopped and smiled again. 'Well, you started me off on all this. I have you to thank for that.'

Karin was lost for words so Daniel continued: 'Would you like to help? You know city folk better than I. Can you get me the names and contact details of news media in Popayán and Bogotá? Bogotá would be especially useful since that's where the decision-makers all live. Will you do that for me?'

Karin gaped. 'Yes' was all she could say.

'Great,' said Daniel. 'Now let's go down the hill together. I need to see Alfonso, and you, Claudia and her family ...'

When they got to the stables, Karin darted inside the house to fetch Claudia, telling her that Daniel was outside talking to Alfonso and she had to go and see him. This she duly did, thanking him profusely for his services in finding Martín's body and trying to drag him inside to meet her parents. But Daniel pleaded to be left with the horses and his friend. He promised he would come and see them another time, but he really had to visit people a long way away and needed to be gone. And so Daniel escaped from the girls once more. He bid them farewell and a happy Christmas and then went with Alfonso to choose a horse, thanking him as ever for his loyal support. He walked quietly away at the back of the buildings, leading his mount until he was out of sight of eyes that he felt always seemed to follow him. It was time to join Carlos and his family and to discuss progress on what he had been doing.

By early evening, long after having crossed the company road to the Triple F mine, Daniel rode on into the valley just before Carlos's farm, and arrived at an old, unused cattle shed that he had been sweeping out and renovating. It was a little way above the stream that tumbled down and filled the tank where the women from the pueblo now came to bathe. He had mended the roof of the shed and stored one or two of the few things he possessed inside. The stallion he had borrowed from Alfonso he left patiently to graze outside as he stopped to make up a bed for the night on his journey to the pueblo to meet his friends.

On emerging from his hideaway the next morning, he saddled up and headed down towards the path that led to the pueblo. On second thoughts, he decided to keep a little higher than the path – it would not be very considerate for his horse to drop manure on the way that the women walked back along towards their houses. Women's shouts and laughter called out to him as he passed by. Looking over, he saw five or six women and girls, Valentina and Natalia among them, wreathed in towels and walking back after their morning bathe. One or two of them called out his name and waved. He waved back.

'*Hola*, Mono!' one shouted. 'You come and join us next time!' A fit of giggling followed this remark. The girl next to the one who had called out let slip her towel and showed an expanse of shoulder and a flash of breast as she did so. More giggles and shrieks of laughter. Daniel could hardly suppress a wide grin himself. He waved again and blew a kiss in their direction but thought it best to canter on ahead nonetheless.

He drew up outside Carlos's house, left the stallion by the front gate and greeted little Lucho who was outside waiting for his mother. 'Hi Carlos!' he called. He thanked his friend for the invitation to enter the house. He thought better than to mention what he had just seen on his way in – not being quite sure how such a fiery character would react to his wife and daughter being involved in such flirtatious behaviour. It was just as well, for at that moment Valentina and Natalia burst in, semi-wrapped in towels and baring a fair amount of flesh, sniggering and looking keenly at the two men to see if there was any reaction, then looking at each other and laughing again before they ran into the bedroom to get dressed.

'Cover yourselves up, women,' shouted Carlos after them, indignantly. 'What must our guest think finding you in a disgraceful state like that!'

More laughter emanated from the bedroom and Daniel tried not to smile in the presence of his disapproving companion. It was a good five minutes before Valentina reappeared with eyes that avoided her husband and twinkled at Daniel. Natalia followed shortly afterwards, her eyes more shyly looking away from both men.

From his knapsack, Daniel took out the bodies of three plump rabbits and handed them over to Valentina in the kitchen. It was a gift in part to say thank you for all the kind hospitality he had received from her and her husband. Natalia had asked him once, with big round eyes, how he could kill rabbits when he seemed to be the friend of all the animals and birds she had ever seen. Daniel had told her that he could never kill any creature that put its trust in him, rabbits included, but when he was out hunting, they knew it and would not come near. He was then just like any other predator on the hillside and he had to outwit his prey.

He was repeating much of this story to Natalia when he

heard the sound of a fierce bellowing from some distance away but which travelled into the pueblo on the morning breeze, sweeping up the valley. Daniel looked round with a question framed on his features.

Carlos anticipated the query. 'We have a new bull in the field below,' he said, 'thanks to the cooperative that the pueblo belongs to. He'll be with us for a couple of weeks or so to service the cows we have but I guess this morning he's getting a bit impatient for action. Come and have a look at him.'

But before the men could leave the house, there came the sound of a large motor and tyres turning on gravel. A big jeep pulled up outside and three men got out, wielding sticks and pickaxe handles. They did not look like they were coming to play games. One shouted: 'Hey, Díaz, where are you? We've heard of you!' It was an ugly, menacing demand.

Carlos rose, his face immediately colouring in anger. 'Stay in the house!' he commanded, looking at his wife and children. He strode out of the door, Daniel following.

'I'm Carlos Díaz,' he called out. He stooped to pick up one of the bigger logs that lay on top of a stack of firewood by the front door. 'And who the hell are you? Who wants to know me?'

'We've heard that you're causing trouble around here,' said the first of the three men walking towards him. 'So we've come to give you a little Christmas present ...'

The two other men fanned out on either side of Carlos, brandishing their heavy sticks. One added: 'We heard you're organising a big protest on the company road outside.'

The third added: 'And we think that's a very foolish idea, don't we, fellas?'

Daniel cut in. 'You've got it wrong, you three. I am the one who's organising the protest and you are the ones who are foolish.' He looked up and around and waved a hand in the air. Then he spoke very coldly and quietly: 'Now I suggest you get back into your motor and disappear before you regret it ...'

The three men turned their attention to Daniel. 'Oh look here, we've got ourselves a hero. You calling us foolish, eh? I think we are going to have to rearrange your opinion, and your features ...' the first man jeered, slapping his stick in his hands.

Daniel stepped wide of Carlos to draw the men away. He spoke again with ice in his voice. 'Have a good look at me. They call me El Mono. When you go back, be sure you tell those that sent you. You or anyone else who cause trouble here will be truly sorry. Remember that. Really, really sorry. Now go away and leave these people alone.'

The three men looked at one another. Who was this slight, insulting individual who thought he could threaten them? They angrily quickened their steps towards Daniel, not hearing at first a distant, wild snorting that came from behind them.

Suddenly, flashing out of the sky like an arrow into the face of the first man came the peregrine falcon. He never saw it coming or had time to cover his eyes but he fell back with a roar, blood splashing down his face. A rush of feathers and the falcon was gone, as quickly as she had come.

Then the road was shaking. A thunder of hooves hammering towards them and a deafening bellow as it hauled into sight and an enraged bull came crashing past the jeep. It was truly an awesome sight. An immense brute with fire in his eyes and half a ton of muscle on the move pounding towards them. Daniel held his ground, as two of the men who had come to threaten him jumped crazily out of the way. The man who had been blinded by the falcon, however, was unable to move. He caught the full force of the angry beast and flew into the air as if fired out of a cannon.

The bull bellowed again, tossed his head and, swirling his great body around in the road, made to repeat his charge. In an instant he lowered his horns, catapulted himself forward and swept his head viciously from side to side, aiming for the two men he had missed on his first onslaught. One of the two

184

screamed but both leapt as if their lives depended on it and they somehow avoided contact as the mighty animal thundered past them.

Again the bull slowed to a halt, turned and lowered his enormous head a third time and prepared to return, eyes blistering with hatred and searching for a target. Carlos had the sense to go to Daniel. The two frightened men who had been brandishing pickaxe handles ran behind the jeep. The bull pawed the earth, picked his target and charged. It was only a short distance to cover but the jeep caught the full force broadside. Doors buckled, windows crashed, glass spilt all over the ground and the vehicle tipped up crazily, hovered and then shuddered back on all four wheels, a good metre or so further across from where it had originally stood. It was too heavy to tip over with just a short charge.

Daniel didn't stop to see what had happened to the men who had sought cover; he was desperately concerned about the bull. He quickly covered the distance between them to reach out and grasp its sweating flanks, to bring his hands forward to stroke its mighty head. The bull backed up, snorted fiercely and tossed his head once more. But he allowed Daniel to stay with him. Daniel knelt in front, held the mighty head and searched it for whatever damage he had done to himself in that final charge.

Daniel almost cried in relief. Superficial cuts ran down the bull's face. His glorious horns were scraped and scratched but bore no cracks or breaks. Fortunately, the jeep had been hit amidships with only the empty cabin behind and not the heavy engine. It had crumpled and given way rather than resisted the charge.

'You crazy animal,' he rebuked the beast, 'you could have hurt yourself.'

The scene all around inevitably looked as if a bull had run amok. There was a broken body in the dirt a good distance away and a bent and battered jeep was slewed across the clearing and into the trees behind with two men warily and gingerly emerging from the back of it. They were now covered in dirt themselves having clearly been rolled in the road. Carlos had retreated to his front door and the bull still held centre stage, stamping and snorting and cooling his temper. At the sight of the two men, however, he bellowed once more and Daniel couldn't stop him from cantering forward, snorting crazily. The men whimpered and dived back around the jeep, fear lending speed to their limbs. Daniel ran forward and called the bull back. There was no space for the great creature to get between the jeep and the trees behind, so the bull eventually relented and decided to retreat as he had been asked. Anger still seemed to steam out of his nostrils nonetheless.

Daniel stood back. A flash of light and the falcon arrowed in once more to settle on his shoulder. Two very shaken men peered around at what lay about them – particularly at their colleague, still spread-eagled with who knew what broken bones inside him, and the bull whose eyes still glared venomously at them.

'I did warn you,' said Daniel in the same quiet and cold voice. 'Now while the bull is calming down, go pick up your friend and see if you can get that motor to start.'

The falcon suddenly flew at the men, swooped low over their heads as they both quickly ducked, and returned to Daniel's shoulder.

'And remember never to come back here. You two are the lucky ones this time.' Daniel still held on to the prize bull.

The jeep started. The injured man was lifted groaning into it, and his two very startled and nervous comrades somehow managed to steer the vehicle, limping crabwise, down the dirt track out of the pueblo and back to the main road, some distance below.

Daniel walked the bull down after them, towards the field from whence it had come. This animal was an enormous investment for the cooperative and, if he was hurt in any way

186

while in the pueblo, the poor farmers who had contracted him for the short time they needed would have to pay. Daniel was anxious that nothing like that would be necessary. For every step down the road, however, the bull's temper subsided and his body seemed to relax and release his tension.

When Daniel got back to the house and entered the door, Valentina rushed to give him a hug. Natalia overcame her shyness, too, and with eyes full of tears she held on tight to him. Carlos stood back, stiffly, until Daniel was free then shook his hand. Daniel nodded at him. He didn't want Carlos to have to say anything.

But Valentina gushed. 'Daniel, Daniel, thank you! Thank you! What can we say? Men like that keep coming and it's so frightening ... But you've saved us this time, you and your magic ways ... and hopefully, hopefully they won't come back, please God.'

'Don't thank me. I'm so sorry, I'm the one who is doing this to you ... I feel as if I have given you nothing but trouble.' Daniel was mortified. 'I'm trying to help but look what happens – the protest I've been working on brings those men to you, not me. Please forgive me. I should go away and take all this away from you too ...'

'Nonsense,' Carlos growled. 'Trouble comes here, whether you are with us or not. And what you are doing now is what we all want – every man here and in all the pueblos around. We have to stick together and turn out in force. So long as we do that, they can't intimidate everyone. The more they try, the more of us get angry.' Carlos's expression lightened. 'Mind, you've given them something to think about now! Maybe they won't come back here again after what they have just seen.'

'I really hope not. If they want to get angry and get back at us, then I hope they choose me, not you.' Daniel looked round at Carlos, his wife, his daughter and little boy who were all now crowded around the table that he had sat at before. 'You have so much to lose here; it's not fair that you should be in the firing line. It's much less risky for me. They won't know where to look if they come to get me and I can see and hear them coming from a mile away. Do take care here ...'

'OK. Enough! Please sit down, Mono.' Carlos decided to change the subject. 'It is about time we enjoyed ourselves and had something to feast upon. Whatever else may happen, all is well for now and it's Christmas! Natalia, go help your mother. Lucho, come here and sit on my lap. We have to celebrate. Can you serve us something to drink, my love?' The head of the house was beaming.

Valentina went into the kitchen.

8

The Mining Companies

In the Fernández finca, Claudia ran into the adjoining bedroom to find Karin. 'Come and look at the television, Quick!'

On the prime-time evening news for the nation a local journalist was reporting from the entrance of the access road to the TMG mine, Volcán Puracé, the Department of Cauca. Thousands of people were blocking the road with notices saying 'Stop the mine' and 'TMG out!' and 'You are destroying our lands, our people.'

Interviews with local people carried camera shots with various indignant farmers, miners and Andean Indians, all claiming that the mine was killing their livelihood and killing their lives. The local television reporter on the scene moved from one angry face to another. Moving among a group of *indígenas*, he eventually asked who had organised this resistance and several in the crowd pointed and called out: 'Mono! Mono!'

A blue-eyed, fair-haired young man stepped forward and in educated Spanish, addressed the camera. 'We have come today to stop the Transnational Mining Group from operating their Puracé mine. It is dangerous for the poor miners who are employed here and it is dangerous for all of us who live around. International mining companies like this are chasing as much profit as they can in the short run but they are poisoning

189

our water, tearing up our lands and displacing, and even killing, our people. We are calling on all Colombians to join us today and stop this mad rush for profits that is destroying our country, our people.'

The reporter could not believe his luck. Who was this eloquent individual? What was he doing here? Here was a story he couldn't wait to pursue.

'Excuse me, sir – do you live here? You are not one of the *indígenas*, are you?'

'Yes, I live here. I live with these people: they are my friends and relations. I speak their language and voice their fears. And it is time we all speak up together and stop this mine. This mine here and others elsewhere. They are too dangerous!'

'Dangerous? What evidence do you have for this?'

'The TMG mine recently collapsed, killing some of the poor miners. Where is the sense in digging into this mountain so quickly to extract as much as possible if it puts lives at risk? Also the mountain streams that water the pueblos around here are poisoned by the chemicals used in the mine. The quick profits made by TMG are offset by the long-term losses incurred by local pueblos. Where is the sense in that? And I and others here have been threatened to keep quiet and not protest against these crimes. It is dangerous living here. It is dangerous living in Colombia. Is that the news you want for our country?'

The local reporter was fed the line to finish with. He returned to the TV anchor-woman in Bogotá: 'And that is the news from Cauca. I am asked: is this the sort of thing we want to hear from around the country?'

Karin and Claudia whooped 'That's Daniel! On the national news! Oh well done!'

The same news broadcast brought a similar, though less emotional reaction from Morten Fields of Triple F Corporation in Bogotá. González had just phoned him from his home in

Popayán to ask if he had seen the television, but Fields, who had poor Spanish, said he had not. González then gave him the gist of what he had just seen reported.

'Excellent! "Close the mine! It's too dangerous." That's what I want to hear. And TMG are going to get sick of hearing that.' Fields was delighted. 'Can you contact Cortés. I want you both to come and see me here as soon as you can fly up? I think it is time we talked about how to crank up the pressure on TMG. Thanks for the call, González. See you as soon as possible.'

The next morning Fields called his head of Public Relations, Carolina Santos: 'Carolina, we need to distance ourselves from the bad news that TMG are attracting. Can you get out a press release saying that Triple F are committed to pursuing environmentally friendly ways of farming and mining Colombia's resources? Make no express comparison to what's going on in Cauca with TMG but concentrate on how well we treat our people and how we are helping to raise incomes and develop the country … blah, blah. You know what I mean. Oh, and Carolina, are we sponsoring any newsworthy cultural or environmental activities in the country? Time to raise our profile if we can. If there is anything coming up in the near future that we can support, let me know what budget you need. Gottit? Great. Thanks.'

His head of public relations was a bit slow off the mark sometimes, Fields thought. She ought to be phoning me, not the other way round: we can't afford to have all mining companies tarred with the same brush. Still, she was a pretty girl and had some good contacts in the city. Maybe she could come up with something.

Twenty-four hours later, at eight o'clock in the morning in Fields's head office, the three men met to discuss where they should go from here. TMG were looking under pressure and their share price had just taken a knock. Leopold Smith had been invited to attend the meeting but just sat outside the group, listening – not participating unless asked to do so.

'Well, gentlemen, the dirty war is now going to get a lot dirtier. We need to consider the most effective way to sap TMG morale and lower their share price even more. What other problem might we arrange for them – one that seriously questions the profitability of their operations here? Ideas?'

González was first up, the businessman thinking in terms of the bottom line on a balance sheet: 'The security costs of TMG operating there can easily be increased if we run a series of hit-and-run raids ... but so long as the value of mineral deposits in that mine is high then no cost increase is likely to shut them down. So first we need to know just what their margins are before we can know what target to attack.'

Cortés kept quiet. This was outside his field of operations.

Fields broke in. 'I like your approach. A bit of industrial espionage might be one thing we attempt in order to get at their survey results. Or, if not, break into their accountancy office where we can see their operation's income statement. Can we think around this for a moment?'

'TMG undertake their own surveys, just as we do,' said González. 'And their results would be closely guarded industrial secrets. If we found out what those surveys reveal, we would still need to know how whatever mineral reserves they have translate into likely annual revenues, and then how far their revenues exceed their costs. It would be probably easier to raid their headquarters in Bogotá and go for the accounts, rather than their mine's geological surveys.'

Cortés now contributed to the conversation. 'OK, breaking in and stealing records from the Bogotá office might not be too difficult, but we'd have to steal other stuff or do a lot of collateral damage to cover up what we are hunting for. Then once you guys have deciphered what we've found, what the figures reveal, then we decide what to do next – is that it?'

'Yes, that sounds about right,' Fields said, 'and we have just the man here to undertake the first part of that operation, don't we?' He looked at Smith, who nodded impassively.

González was thinking it through. 'Their accounts will all be locked away on computer files so that no one can read them. We will have to get some computer whizz-kid to break into those files.'

'Or find some TMG accountant who's arm can be twisted to give us the access codes,' said Fields. 'The latter might be easier. In fact, that might mean we don't need to trash the finance office and steal computers at all. We just kidnap their chief accountant and persuade him to cooperate. Hmm ...'

Fields was thinking how it might work. Kidnapping the accountant would have to take place quickly and efficiently and made to look as if it were undertaken by a terrorist outfit. The trouble was that, once this person was persuaded to give up the computer codes and release the financial information they needed, he would know what his captors were up to: only a rival mining company would be interested in those accounts. The accountant would have to be persuaded not to talk ...

'Karin, in four or five days now we will be going back to Cali and then shortly after that we have to return to university in Bogotá. If you want to see Daniel again, it had better be quick,' Claudia warned her friend.

'He promised to meet up with me and share a meal any-where but on the mountain,' said Karin. 'Let's invite him down to join us in a restaurant in Popayán. Maybe your parents will come and we can introduce them and at the same time congratulate him on becoming a television star!'

It was agreed. The only problem was how to contact him. They were so used to organising every detail of their social life via mobile phones and here was a man who did not carry anything so useful as this indispensable modern, urban accoutrement. They had to go up and look for him on the mountain.

They spent a day riding up on the *páramo* together, enjoying the views but achieving little else. No tell-tale flight of a falcon was seen; no man with or without horse was spotted. There was nothing for it but to return, hungry, frustrated and annoyed before the sun went down.

Both girls complained to Alfonso as they led their horses into the stables.

'What can we do, Alfonso? We can't afford to waste days on end trying to find him,' said Karin.

'Unlike him, we have a tight timetable that we have to stick to,' added Claudia, 'and if there's no way of getting in touch we won't see him again!'

'I understand, Señorita Claudia,' replied Alfonso, 'but there is little you can do. He just lives his life differently from you.' He looked at Karin who he realised was the one who was most upset. 'The ways of the world that El Mono lives by do not easily cross the ways of the world that you lead ...'

Karin knew that well enough. 'Thank you, Alfonso. I won't be going out again in the time we have left here but if he comes down, or if there is some way of getting a message to him before I leave, do let me know.' She left her horse and went inside the house, deflated.

Her mood did not change much over the next day, but the morning after, during breakfast, María came to see her at the table and in a low voice mentioned that El Mono was outside in the stables. Karin left her breakfast immediately and went out to see him.

'Daniel, I have been looking for you but it's impossible – I can't search all the Andes. Where have you been?'

The default distance and reticence returned. 'Moving here and there, seeing people; getting around.' He was somewhat discomfited at being confronted alongside Alfonso, especially when enclosed in the restricted space of the stables.

'Don't try to get away, Daniel. I've got you now and you promised to meet me anywhere that was not on the mountain. So come inside and have breakfast with us and meet Claudia's parents!'

'No ... no ... I couldn't join you ...' He looked at Alfonso for support.

He wasn't getting any. Alfonso whispered to him: 'Go on inside my friend. María will be pleased to serve you whatever you want. Go in and join them for breakfast ...'

'Daniel, you promised. You have to come with me now ...' Karin dragged him indoors. Daniel shot a look of alarm at María as he was marched into the house, past the kitchen and directed to sit down with Manuel Fernández, his wife Constanza and their daughter Claudia. He sat reluctantly and turned his head first one way and then the other, looking in all the world like a trapped animal.

Claudia clapped her hands at the sight of him. 'At last, the famous Mono, come to visit us!'

Claudia's father and mother were both delighted to meet him and rose to welcome him to their table, indicating that he should eat whatever he wanted that was in front of him. María then came bustling in, bearing a plate of scrambled eggs and mushrooms, and with a huge smile from ear to ear. Daniel was surrounded and had to capitulate. Karin watched all this with amusement, matched with concern. She had no idea how Daniel was going to react.

Daniel first apologised profusely to his hosts for his dirty boots and unkempt appearance. He had just come in from the mountain and through the stables and was not expecting to be seated in their house. He ate little and was terribly subdued. Claudia's mother, Constanza wanted to know more about him.

'You were on the television news recently, Claudia tells me. Involved in a protest against one of the mines. What was that like?'

'There were lots of people blocking the road. I was pleased with that – we wanted to make a point.' Daniel looked down shyly, uncomfortable talking about himself.

'You wanted me to find news media contacts for you, Daniel,' Karin interposed, 'but it seems you don't need that

now. You did it all by yourself – on the national TV. Congratulations!'

Daniel glanced across and thanked her but wouldn't be
drawn. He really was infuriatingly distant. He finished a small
breakfast and waited for the others to do likewise. He followed
their general conversation around the table but did not
contribute much. Claudia's parents rose from the table, said
again how pleased they were to meet Daniel, then moved
across into the lounge, leaving the three others behind.

Karin seized her chance. 'Don't think we are letting you go,
Daniel. Claudia and I are going into Popayán shortly and we
want you to come with us. You must. Visit us in our world in
town, on a busy weekday, just like we visit you in your world
on an empty mountainside. You have to stay and have lunch
with us before we let you go. OK? We will be leaving and
going back to Bogotá soon and this will be our last meeting
until I don't know when. So – do you think you can survive
coming out with us today?'

Daniel blustered but could not escape. The girls took him
out to the family's Land Cruiser, dusted him down, ensured
that he cleaned the mud off his boots, made himself presentable and then bundled him into the car. Their driver took them
the long drive into town and deposited them in the central
plaza. But this was no visit to familiar faces on market stalls.
The girls steered him into a shopping mall.

Karin said, 'I want to buy you a present before we leave.
Something practical for you to wear; something so you won't
look scruffy all the time, something really nice.' She was
chattering in English to him, really pleased that at last she had
got him on her own turf and could show him around, just as
he had always done for her before.

There were a variety of small fashion shops in a row and
Karin busied about, going into one, laughing with the assistant, coming out, going into another, laughing again, shooting a
glance or two back out at Claudia who was holding on to

Daniel as if trying to stop him escaping. Having wandered to and fro for a while, they eventually came to a halt. They stopped outside a particularly elegant menswear store and looked in the window.

'Look at those jeans, K.,' said Claudia. 'Divine! He'd look great in those!'

Daniel spluttered. He had been pushed into the Fernández house without expecting it; he had been cleaned up and fussed over as if he was a doll; bundled into a chauffeur-driven car and brought into town against his will, and now he was being sized up to be fitted out with fashion wear ...

Karin wondered about the jeans. 'I was thinking more in the line of a waterproof jacket for him ... but those jeans do look good ... Let's take him in.'

Daniel erupted. 'Enough! What do you think you are doing? I won't wear any of this ... this stuff! I won't go into this shop. I hate these shopping malls, these ... these temples to material-ism. Leave me alone – you know I hate all these city clothes and the shallow lifestyle that goes with them.'

Karin spun round and faced him. 'Enough you say. So I've had enough too! I just wanted to buy you a present, OK? I'm not forcing you to fall in love with everything about city life but it's not all bad here. Temples of materialism? What do you think of us? That we worship these things and nothing else? It's not all superficial the way Claudia and I live. But you are so black and white! Don't be so dismissive of our world. I'm trying to do you a favour and your throw it back in my face!' She was really angry.

Daniel was still steamed up. He had been holding it all in all morning while he had let Karin have her way, and now that she was really going for him, he lost his temper in turn.

'But you know I don't like these places. You drag me down here to torture me – is that your idea of a present? You've been treating me as if I'm some sort of clothes horse. Am I supposed to thank you for that? I don't like the materialistic lifestyle I see here. You know I don't – shop-loads and shop-loads of stuff that you don't really need but people are desperate to sell you. What a value-less society!'

'Aaagh!' Karin wasn't getting through to him. 'How can you be so stubborn, so prejudiced, so short-sighted? It's just a clothes shop. Nothing more. It is not some awful temple of materialism trying to undermine your values, or change your religion. I'm sure the shop assistants inside are quite nice people. Really! See through the fancy colours and the fancy clothes and look at the people behind it all. They are just like me. Daniel, please! I'm not trying to torture you. I was trying to buy you something nice. But have it your own way. I'm sorry I got it all wrong!'

Karin turned and stormed off towards the exit of the mall, trying to hold back the tears in her eyes.

Claudia looked daggers at Daniel. 'You ungrateful beast!' was all she could say. She ran after her friend.

Daniel stayed marooned behind in the shopping mall. Karin was hurrying away as fast as she could. Claudia caught up with her as she was going out of the exit, security guards holding the big glass doors open for them.

'It's no good, Claudia. We are worlds apart; *too* far apart. I'm so stupid to think that we could ever get closer … What do I think I'm doing?' Karin was trying to stop herself from weeping.

'Don't, Karin … Don't beat yourself up about him. You've tried. Now leave him alone … Leave him behind. Either he comes in your direction now or he's a lost cause. Let's go to that café in the plaza and have a coffee.'

Claudia led the way towards the centre of town, her arm around her friend. From behind the doors to the shopping mall, from behind the security men standing on guard, way back beyond from where the girls were walking away stood one very forlorn young man, watching through the glass, lost in thought.

*

One hour later Karin sat holding on to a large cup of tea, a small biscuit in front of her untouched. She was blank-faced, not tearful now but still close to it. She was thinking of where she was going, what she would do in the next semester, of her future back in Durham, and beyond. What had she been thinking of, making friends with a man who wouldn't move off his mountain?

Claudia was sharing the same thoughts. They'd talked about it, in a roundabout sort of way, a number of times and this latest incident had brought it all to the fore.

Claudia sighed and looked at her watch. 'Perhaps we'd better finish here and I'll call the driver to come and pick us up.' She looked at Karin to see if she was thinking the same: it was a way of finishing everything, not just tea and coffee.

She was. Tears reappeared in her eyes. 'What am I going to do, Claudia?' she asked.

Karin did not want to move just yet – but what was the point of staying any longer? She slowly gathered her things together on the café table and was about to call for the bill, but before she could do so, someone was standing beside her.

'I'm sorry,' Daniel said. Big, blue, sad eyes looked down upon Karin. 'I've brought you these …' He held out a small bunch of flowers. 'They're local flowers from the mountain which one of the *vivero* holders has given me. Please forgive me.'

Karin held on tight to her tears. She would not let him see her face but she jumped up and hugged him. 'Thank you!' she whispered.

Daniel was covered in confusion – as always surprised and unable to cope with the reactions of this woman. But he sat down with them. He wanted to apologise.

'I've been thinking,' he said. 'I was very rude to you. I'm sorry. I understand now what you were trying to do for me but I suppose I was just unable to understand it at the time.' He

199

looked down and then up at Claudia. He was unable to look at Karin.

'Damn right, you didn't understand,' snorted Claudia. 'I don't know about Karin, but I could have killed you!'

'Me too,' said Karin more quietly, though her face was smiling through tearful eyes now.

'I need to explain ... I've been busy recently visiting the pueblos, the local people, the indigenous tribes ... all the people who don't come into places like Popayán except on market day. In money terms, they are very poor ... though I can't help but see the richness of their lives. The difference between them and people like you, and the people of the shopping mall ... is so ... so different.'

Daniel continued. 'I'm sorry. You are right. I am prejudiced against the way of life down here. That's because the people I know cannot afford it. Nor can I. I don't carry wads of money around with me like I see people here do. I could never buy the sorts of clothes you were looking at. How can I accept them from you? The flowers I've brought you – they were given to me by a man I know and whom I can pay in my own way, by helping him as he helps me. But I can never pay for the sort of life you live down here. That's why I don't live here.'

It was a heartfelt confession. He was opening up to his own, embarrassing poverty. He looked at Karin now, hoping she would understand.

Of course she did. 'Daniel, I know you cannot have any money, but in your own words you have a richness that so many, many people don't have. Like me. So giving you some clothes that cost a bit of money is one of the few things that I can give you. There is precious little else that I can offer you. You don't like anything from my world, it seems.' She was challenging him again.

'What can I say? Again you're right. I've been seeing people, listening to their complaints and organising protests against the mining companies. Well, against TMG at any rate. But they are just one particular aspect of urban life, I can see that now – not all city people are involved in ruining lives and despoiling the environment. I shouldn't be so critical; there are things down here that I should come to appreciate, I suppose.'

'And even the mining companies are not all bad, Daniel,' broke in Claudia. 'I'm sure that many good people work for them also. But maybe they just don't see the damage they are doing where you are.'

'It's all a question of looking to see what is there, good as well as bad, and not shutting your eyes and making up your mind to hate things, and us, without giving us a chance. A chance to buy you a present, for example ...' Karin was pushing him again. 'Will you let me do that for you now?'

'Yes. Thank you. Please forgive me ... and I'll try to like even the mining companies ... Well, I'll try ... so long as they don't kill me first.'

Daniel got up. The girls settled the bill and the three went back towards the shopping mall. Claudia wondered if they might try looking somewhere else, since the mall had provoked such a negative reaction from their guest. She suggested they went a different way.

As they changed direction, Karin asked: 'Daniel – what do you mean, if the mining companies don't kill you first? Are they really killing people like you said?'

'Not directly,' Daniel replied, 'but who else is paying paramilitaries to stop me and others from complaining about the damage they do? You say you heard what I was saying on the TV. That was all true.' He went on to tell her about the incident the day before Christmas with three men who had come to assault Carlos.

Karin's eyes opened wide. 'You managed to stop them?' she asked.

'Well, the local bull did. He went berserk.'

Claudia and Karin both stopped and looked at him.

'No!'

201

'You did that, didn't you?'

'I keep saying ... it's not me. I don't actually do anything. It's what I feel. They know. All creatures know. In this case, the bull picked up on my anger and I could feel him coming as my own anger rose within me. Of course, once he had got going it was near impossible to cool him down. A mad bull is a frightening force to see. He was magnificent ... but a danger to himself as well as to others. I got hold of him in the end and I'm glad to say that he was unhurt. Unlike the three men and the jeep they came in.'

'They were gored by the bull? Were they killed?'

'One was hurt. Seriously, I think. The others were badly shaken but OK.'

'So they went away? Carlos and his family were unharmed?' Karin asked.

'Does Alfonso know?' Claudia asked

'Yes, Carlos and family are fine. Yes, of course Alfonso knows. We all hope that those men do not come back. The problem is that people who have lands and families here have a lot to lose. Not like me. I feel very responsible for what happens now – I really hope that no one gets hurt because of the protests I'm stirring up. If they do, I will feel absolutely awful. That is why I should make myself more visible, go on the TV for example, and attract any trouble away from anyone else. I don't have anything to lose like them.'

'Only your life!' Claudia said. She led the way to an outdoor clothing shop just off the central plaza.

Geoffrey Scott was one of a small team of Canadian expatriates who headed up the TMG offices in Bogotá. As finance director he was a key member of the senior management team and was consulted by his overall boss, Brian MacKay, on all matters of strategic importance. The recent protests in Cauca Department had had their cost implications but were not overworrying, providing they did not escalate. More investment in improving safety and security at their Puracé mine and also in containing any pollution should help reassure their workforce and placate the locals.

He was thinking over these things as he drove out of the basement car park of his office building in central Bogotá. At the top of the ramp by the road outside, a big man in a TMG peaked cap beckoned him to wind down the passenger window of his car and, in English with a Canadian accent like his own, he asked politely if he might be given a short ride home.

'Sure, hop in,' Scott answered pleasantly.

As Scott passed the next set of traffic lights and began to pick up speed, he asked his companion where he wanted to be dropped off.

'Actually,' said Smith, taking off the peaked cap, 'I'm going a long way ...' His large hand pulled out a Smith & Wesson revolver. '... And you're coming with me.'

Twenty-four hours later, Cortés called the TMG head office using a stolen mobile phone and said to the operator that Geoffrey Scott was now a distinguished guest of the *Fuerzas Armadas Revolucionarias de Colombia* and that a first ransom payment of ten thousand dollars should be paid in a week's time at a destination to be later disclosed.

Cortés put the phone down with a smile on his face. There was a neat symmetry in what he had just done that appealed to him. TMG had used the cover of the FARC to open the first salvo against Triple F in the current dirty war. Now he was using the same cover to fire back at them. Serve them right! Now for the interrogation.

Geoffrey Scott had been brought to a disused factory building in a run-down industrial estate an hour's drive north of Bogotá. He was sat in a windowless basement on a plastic chair alongside a grubby-looking single mattress. Handcuffs immobilised his hands behind his back; his legs were roped to the legs of the chair. Cortés unlocked the door, came in and phoned a number. He grinned at Scott and then spoke on the phone: 'You got her there?'

'Yes.'

'Put her on.'

Cortés put the phone next to Scott's ear. He heard a woman's voice on the other end of the phone call. It was his wife.

'Geoffrey, Geoffrey, are you all right? Where are you?' She sounded frantic with worry.

Scott replied, looking up desperately into the face of Cortés. 'Yes, I'm fine. Don't worry. I'll be OK they tell me so long as we do as they say ...'

Cortés switched the phone off.

'Well done, Mr Scott. You behaved perfectly. So now your wife knows you are well and she will no doubt be immensely relieved. What she does not know is that the person she is now with is not a man from TMG but in fact the same person who kidnapped you. And as you are undoubtedly aware he is a very dangerous individual. Very dangerous indeed. So it is not you whose life is threatened any more. It is your wife.'

Scott cried out: 'What are you doing? What is happening to my wife? Don't, please don't hurt her in anyway ... What do you want from me?'

'Nothing is happening to your wife ... yet. But you know now that we know where she is, that she has the trust of our most skilled and ruthless operative, who she believes is a friend of yours, and should you not cooperate then you might not see her again ... or rather you might not recognise her again. Am I making myself clear?'

Scott was trembling all over with fear. 'Yes, yes, please don't hurt her. I'll do whatever you want.'

'What we want is something very easy for you to provide us with,' said Cortés very amicably. 'We just need some financial information from your company records. You might actually

204

be able to get that information right now from the laptop I give you. OK?'

Cortés went out and returned with a very new, lightweight tablet computer. He took out a key from his pocket and unlocked Scott's handcuffs. Then he placed the computer into his captive's lap.

'You will do the following. Log into your company's financial files. Do it in a way that is perfectly normal for you and does not alert any security alarm – understand? What we want to see are the cost and revenue streams attributable to the Puracé mine over the last couple of years and projections for the future, got it? Download this information on to the machine you have in front of you – again, without arousing any sort of suspicion. I'll then e-mail that data straight to the people who want it and ask them if this is the information they need. It should not take long for them to say yes or no. If no, and if the information you have given us is not satisfactory for their needs, then your wife is going to suffer … badly. So better if the information you download is quite comprehensive and doesn't upset us in any way. Don't you agree? Incidentally, if in the future we find out that you have not cooperated with us fully; if the information turns out to be incorrect, or if you have alerted the authorities, then my ruthless friend will pay you and your wife another visit. You should know that he is something of an independent operator and I'm afraid that neither I nor anyone else can control him properly. What he will do I cannot predict other than that it will be indescribably painful … if not terminal. Now, get to work!'

It took fifteen minutes for a distressed and anxious Scott to find and download the information that he had been asked for, and another five minutes for Cortés to dispatch this data. The time needed for the confirmation that this was, or was not, what was needed by parties unknown seemed to crawl by. Scott was a nervous wreck, praying that there would be no problem and that he and particularly his wife would not need to pay the price for anyone's dissatisfaction with his work.

Cortés's phone buzzed and Scott would have jumped in the air if his feet had not still been tied to his chair.

'OK, good. Send me it through when you can!' Cortés smiled at the accountant and closed his phone.

'Well, it appears what you have got for us is just what was needed,' Cortés remarked. 'However, it is not quite enough yet.' He frowned.

Scott's heart leapt and then almost immediately collapsed in this body. Oh my God ... what now? he thought.

'The accountants on the other end of the line think that your balance sheet shows far too optimistic a projection for the future and they think it needs revising. So they are doing that now. In a little while they will e-mail back the document that they think is a better projection and you are to upload that in the place of the original you have just produced. Understand? Again, this must be done without alerting any security concerns in TMG.' Cortés was all smiles and friendship. 'Do all this and I will be happy and my colleague will be happy, too ...'

It was a heartbreaking, strength-sapping hour that then passed before the e-mail arrived with the attached revised balance sheet. Scott immediately set to work and uploaded this through all the various security routes needed to revise the company's financial records. Finally it was done and he sank back into his chair, handing over the tablet computer back to Cortés with exhaustion marking his features.

Cortés phoned Smith.

'Where are you? OK. Get back here now as quickly as you can.'

Cortés turned to his captive. 'Just a little while to wait now and it's all over. Well done!'

A little over three-quarters of an hour went by and then the door opened and Smith came in. Cortés had a quiet word with him first out of earshot before returning to Scott.

'Good, good. All's well that ends well.' Cortés was pleased. 'Your wife is fine, Mr Scott. My friend here is happy and, so far as I can tell now, you have done all that we wanted. No further business! Thank you.'

With that, Smith took out his revolver and shot Geoffrey Scott through the head.

The day was overcast and light rain was sweeping down off the Andes to smother Bogotá in a dull grey mist. The atmosphere was heavy and the general mood in the city centre offices was depressed. The news that a senior executive from an international mining company had been kidnapped and later found dead on the outskirts of town was in all the papers that morning and shock waves had passed through a number of company headquarters as a result. Gossip was rife in Triple F's main building like in any other, though this did not cloud the perspective of the people on the topmost floor.

Leopold Smith walked directly to the door of Morton Fields's office. His personal assistant, Patricia, knew better than to try and stop him.

'Oh good to see you, Leo,' Fields remarked, looking up from his desk. 'Come in and sit down.' Smith was doing that anyway. 'How's your accommodation now, comfortable?'

Smith had been booked into a large suite of rooms charged to the fictitious International Trade Solutions. He had been in a standard hotel room before but could not rest and the last thing Fields wanted was for this powder keg of a man to be unoccupied, uncomfortable and about to explode.

'I think it is time now to set you loose on the TMG mine at Puracé. A series of attacks to undermine their security I think would be best. Ready for that?'

Smith grunted in agreement.

Fields was never quite sure what his personal bodyguard and hitman thought of the missions he kept giving him, what he thought about all the death and destruction he was dishing out. Fields knew that Smith's capacity to empathise with his victims was minimal but even so he must have some understanding of right and wrong. 'God knows what goes on in his mind,' thought Fields, 'but let's put something in there for him to chew over, if he ever did have times when he thought of these things.

'These TMG people are bad people, Leo. They are poisoning all the land around their mine, killing off all sorts of birds and animals and they don't care. The local people are up in arms about it – it was on the news in the papers and on the television – so it's time to put a stop to it. The mine explosion was a start. That bad man you just eliminated was well done. Now we have to step up the pressure. It is time for you to go back to Popayán.'

Fields was pleased he put that comment in about birds and animals being killed. For some reason, Smith was capable of expressing some sort of concern for dumb creatures and what he imagined were their feelings that he never could with people. Bad people were not especially bad for killing people, but they were for killing animals. An odd value-system.

Patricia buzzed from outside and asked if Miguel Cortés should enter. Fields said yes – he had been in regular contact with him over the past few days since Cortés was the one man he most trusted to clear things out of the way for Smith to operate.

'Congratulations on getting all the financial information sorted, Miguel,' Fields welcomed the man as soon as he entered the office. 'You've done an excellent job. TMG are going to have their work cut out to replace their chief accountant, and when they eventually get round to reviewing their Puracé mine's financial situation they are going to have a shock. Add to that some steeply rising costs on their security there that are going to take place and we should see some interesting reactions.'

'You want me to arrange some security problems for them

now?' Cortés asked. 'Something that looks like an attack by the FARC?'

'That sounds good to me. We'll have Leo here go in first to shake them up. Then a bit later another assault. As before, whatever you do make it look like it's nothing to do with us. I'll pick up the reactions here and will get back to you to say whether to crank it up even further, or scale it back and let it go quiet. I'll let you know.' He turned to Smith. 'Leo, go with Cortés now and organise your next visit to the TMG mine. Good luck to you both.'

It was the same trip as before, only Smith insisted on going alone this time. A horse and warm clothing was all he needed. He had it all planned. Travelling light and with no other person or luggage to slow him down, he could go much faster. He would also take a lower trajectory around the mountain to avoid any sulphurous fumes. He checked his horse – a stronger stallion that could take his weight without tiring – and in the early evening he set off, leaving the Triple F mine like before and heading north.

Smith was dressed in his camouflaged battledress with matching gloves and a cap this time. No need to adopt the attire of a visiting bureaucrat or businessman. If anyone caught sight of him and lived to tell the tale, then he was a lone terrorist. He was offered a Kalashnikov AK-47 assault rifle to fit the stereotype but he had no use for such a cumbersome, inaccurate weapon. He wanted to act like a rapier, not a blunderbuss.

The long ride over to the TMG mine was uneventful. Smith was soon dismounting and leading his stallion down to the clump of bushes to be tethered. Below, the entrance to the mine had been transformed. Two tunnel collapses had been dug out and the access road bore the evidence. It was wider, its surface was badly chewed up and a number of earth moving machines still remained on site. Also the one guard house that had been seen on the earlier visit had now spawned a neighbour. Smith's first task was to watch the gaping entrance to the mine, illuminated by arc lights, and make out what was the easiest and most anonymous way to get in. It was half past one in the morning, the sky was overcast and starless, and he couldn't see any cameras. A short scramble down the hillside, dropping down behind one of the guard buildings was, he reckoned, the best way to go.

The last jump down on to the road behind the guardhouses made little noise but a small ginger-and-white cat ran out to investigate nonetheless. Smith bent down to stroke it as it mewed at him. The cat mewed again a little louder and wound around his feet. Then a door opened, light streamed out across the road and a security guard wandered out of the first cabin to have a look around. Smith straightened and hit him on the side of the neck with all the force he could muster. There was a crack and the guard toppled over. The cat ran away.

Smith reached down and unholstered the handgun the stricken man wore around his waist. He examined it briefly, flipped the catch and then walked into the second guard house to see if anyone else was inside. Another guard was on his way out when Smith met him in the doorway. At point blank range, Smith shot him in the chest. One bullet, but a tremendous noise in the small room. The man was thrown violently back against the wall opposite and collapsed in a heap. With his ears ringing, Smith again stooped and withdrew the second guard's pistol. He turned and walked back out on to the road, stepping over the body of the first one he had felled. He paused and looked closely at him for a moment to see if there was any sign of life. No – the guard's neck was broken.

Which way now? He looked to see if anyone in the tunnel entrance was coming his way. Not as yet. Would any security guards be inside the mine? Possibly ... he walked in sixty or seventy yards or so, swinging his arms with a gun held, partially smothered, in each giant hand. There was one man in uniform coming towards him, clearly bothered by the fact that he was approaching an unidentified alien. Smith saw him reaching for the holster at his waist, so he quickly raised the gun he had already fired once, took aim and fired it again at this newcomer. Hit amidships at twenty yards, the poor man staggered backwards and rolled over. Three down.

The noise of this last shot would have echoed down into the mine and also would sound enormous on the road outside the tunnel as if magnified by a megaphone. Smith quickly spun on his heels and retraced his steps. He reached the first body outside the guardhouse and ducked into the deep shadow cast by the arc lights beside it just as two men came running around the first bend in the road leading up to the mine. Confident he had not been seen, Smith waited and checked his weapons. Only two shots fired from the first – it looked a well-maintained pistol and had proven reliable so far, Smith thought. Stay with it.

The two men came running up, guns drawn and looking alarmed when they saw the body of a colleague sprawled in the dirt. One man bent over him while the other crouched a little further ahead, searching, pointing his weapon first one way then the other. As the gun swung away from him, Smith stepped out and fired once at the man who was crouching in the lead and then once again at the other who had stopped to check the body of the first guard brought down. Both bullets hit their targets with the desired effect.

Smith checked first to see if any others were coming and when assured not he crept out to examine his handiwork. All efficiently killed. He congratulated himself on his master crafts-manship. His thought now was to retreat up into *páramo* behind him. His main objective of carrying out a lethal and unidentified assault was achieved. Should he go for any more? No. Not worth the risk. A number of gunshots would be sure to attract who knows how many more people plus a combination of weapons. He couldn't be sure of a clean outcome if a messy fire fight ensued. Besides, five dead bodies carried the same impact as six or seven. He threw the two guns he had been holding on to the road by the three bodies. They were not needed now. Let whoever finds them figure out what had happened – it would be a difficult puzzle to unravel. He would disappear and leave them to it.

9

Turning the Page

Karin had reached a point where she was measuring out her life in semesters and vacations. She would study at Los Andes and live in Bogotá until Easter. There was then the possibility of spending two weeks on the finca with Claudia and getting in as many days as possible with Daniel, then her academic year finished shortly afterwards at the beginning of May. Either she would go back to the UK or, if she was lucky, she might be able to get some form of employment over the next few months to keep her in Colombia before her final university year in Durham started in October.

Was that the way she really wanted to organise her life? She knew she was basing it around a relationship that really could not go anywhere. Could it? It was a topic of conversation that Claudia and she talked about frequently in bars and cafés, on and off, over weeks during her second semester at Los Andes.

'Who knows where things lead, Claudia? I just know at the moment that the few days I get with him are magical. I know, deep down that I must move on. We are both, you and I, on the career treadmill that leads elsewhere – just like all the students around us. So I haven't much time left to see him.'

'No, you haven't,' Claudia agreed. 'Life doesn't always present you with easy choices. But I think that, if you are honest with yourself, you are going to have to leave him behind sometime soon enough. Your future won't wait too long.'

Karin was thinking out loud: 'I'm here on an exchange that is part and parcel of an education that will give me a professional future – an international career, if I'm lucky. It is also at present enriching my life in ways I could never have dreamed of. Getting to know you, this country and an amazing man who conjures birds and insects out of the skies and animals out of the countryside. A few more days with him at Easter, I suppose, is all I will get now … But if that is going to be all, then I can't imagine spending that time anywhere else, with anyone else. He *is* magical, isn't he?'

Claudia looked at her friend and smiled a sad smile. 'Yes … undoubtedly.'

'But I can't stay any longer with him, can I?'

'No. Absolutely not. If nothing else, his reticence, his distance and his lack of commitment to you and everything you represent would drive you absolutely crazy. If you waited for him to come a little closer, you'd wait a lifetime. And you are such an active, talented and passionate individual; you can't waste your life waiting in the back of beyond. You and I – we have to move on, get careers, get busy changing the world!'

Karin laughed. 'I'm sure you are more active and talented than I am! But let's talk about that. Where are you headed after this year?'

'One more year for me at Los Andes and then, I guess, like you I'd love an international career. But it's no use dreaming about that – we ought to be making plans. If you were in England now, what would you be doing?'

'I guess I'd be applying for internships for the vacation – it's not always possible, of course.'

'But you could try that here. We both could, couldn't we?' suggested Claudia.

'Well, you'd know the possibilities here better than me.

214

Whatever, it would do no harm to try and put ourselves about – socialising with people in international companies. Does your family have any contacts?'

'I can ask. But I like the idea: "putting ourselves about and socialising with international companies". Let's keep our eyes open …'

'Carolina Santos is outside, sir,' Fields's personal assistant called.

'Show her in, Patricia, thank you.'

Fields opened the door to welcome his attractive head of public relations. All smooth charm, he directed her to the sofa in his office and pulled up a nearby chair to sit facing her.

'What can I do for you, Carolina?' he inquired.

'You wanted us to sponsor some high-profile events in the city so I have been looking over a number of possibilities. Here's one that I think you should support, personally. Universidad de Los Andes are running an arts festival to showcase local dance and drama. We have agreed to sponsor this and the opening night comes up soon with a VIP gala opening which the Minister of Culture is attending. Naturally, as lead sponsor, you are also invited. I asked that someone from Triple F, ideally you, should give the opening address – saying how much we support this sort of thing. The press will all be there so it will carry some sort of splash in the media …'

'I'll be doing this in English?'

'To this audience, sir, that is perfectly fine. But do let me have an advance copy of your speech so that I can release it to the gathered press and Los Andes can put the title in their programme.'

'Saying nice things about Triple F and how we are supporting the arts and what not and what a good influence we are on the country. Yes, I see. Excellent! Well done, Carolina – that is just the sort of thing we need to do and this is the time we need to do it. I hear that there is more and more trouble impacting on TMG just now and we cannot have ourselves associated in the public mind with nasty goings-on over there. So this is a great idea. Really good! I'll get this in my diary as high priority. Congratulations again.'

Fields showed her to the door like the perfect gentleman and then went back to his desk. He picked up the phone.

'Patricia, has Carolina gone? Yes. Good. I've asked her to send through all the details of this arts event that she wants me to attend. Make sure you get that down in my diary as top priority, right? Good. Now can you get me González in Popayán? Thank you.'

It was a few moments until the phone connection was made. Fields was getting impatient.

'González? Hello. Tell me what has been happening down your way … Just remember this is an open line.' Fields had earlier warned González and Cortés that no incriminating information should be communicated over company phones in this way. All previous briefings had been on a face-to-face basis with no records kept.

'Hello, Mr Fields. Well, it seems the TMG mine near here has been having all sorts of problems. First, an unidentified attack on their security staff about a week ago – a number were killed. I think you've heard about that. As a result, their security has been considerably beefed up and just as well since rumour has it that another serious terrorist attack has just taken place. There have been reports of guns blazing out all over the mountainside. No reports of any terrorists captured or injured but two security guards were killed and perhaps some others hurt, I'm not sure. We are looking into it. Meanwhile, our own security staff have been doubled and we are all keeping our eyes open but nothing has come our way as yet …'

'Thanks, González. Keep up the good work. Tell Cortés to give me a call when you can, OK? Things sound serious. I'll be in touch again later.'

Fields put the phone down, reasonably satisfied. From what

he had just heard it seemed that Cortés must have hired some paramilitaries to go out and spray the TNG road with bullets. Certainly the rattle of gunfire being heard all around sounded like the work of a bunch of hired cowboys rather than the quiet and deadly assault of professionals like Leo Smith. Time to let things go quiet for a while, he thought. Let TMG pay for increased security for the next month or so before he tried something else.

It was three weeks later when Carolina's sponsored Arts Festival was due to begin. On the opening night, Fields and Carolina were ushered into a large, packed university auditorium and given places of honour to sit on stage along-side the government's Minister of Culture and the Arts and the university's President, who was acting as master of ceremonies for the evening. Various dignitaries of the government, the university and the Bogotá artistic scene were in the front rows and the rest of the theatre was full of students, friends and relations. Members of the press were also there and television cameras were at the back and in the centre aisle.

The President welcomed all and sundry, said encouraging things about the wealth of artistic talent shortly to be on show and then introduced the government minister. The Minister smiled broadly for the cameras, and said what a great job the university and Triple F were doing in supporting private artistic enterprise and how the government planned to spend pots of money in promoting arts charities and community centres around the country.

Fields didn't believe a word of it. How big a budget would this ministry be given to devote to the arts when there was still enormous work to be done in building roads, schools, and hospitals, let alone equipping the armed services and police to catch terrorists? Trust a politician to flannel the audience and the media: he was just building up his job. Fields wondered whether he was soon for the chop.

Then Carolina got up, said who she was and how proud she was to be there before introducing the keynote speaker for the evening – Mr Morten Fields, chief executive officer for Triple F Colombia.

Fields did the polite, gentlemanly thing – thanking the previous speakers, saying what an honour it was, apologising for speaking in English, etc. etc. – before warming to his theme of how Triple F were investing in Colombia. How they were involved in farming and mining as a way to raise incomes for their employees and exports for the country; how profits the corporation made were being ploughed back into research and education and into all sorts of environmentally friendly practices, and how Triple F were interested in supporting the arts as a means of sharing in the country's notable artistic and cultural development and identity.

That went down well – a ripple of applause went round the auditorium.

Fields next emphasised that many multinational enterprises were interested in doing business in Colombia as indeed was Triple F but how many others like he were interested in the business of encouraging ordinary people's artistic endeavours? Another ripple of applause.

Then came his final contribution to the evening. Speaking slowly and solemnly he said that, in closing, he must now make mention of a particularly painful topic: 'With our partners tonight, the Universidad de los Andes, we would like to share one final thought. Not so long ago we tragically lost the services of one of our most recent employees. He was a graduate from this university who came to us with great potential but had little time with us before he was kidnapped and killed by terrorists in the Department of Cauca. There will be many of you here tonight who will have known that young man personally, as I did, and you will agree with me that he is an irretrievable loss to any institution that had the benefit of knowing him. So, if I may, I would like to dedicate this evening's performances to the memory of that fine young graduate of this university, that most talented of Triple F executives, who was taken from us in his prime: the late Mr Martín García. Thank you.'

The audience, particularly those students at the back of the auditorium, leapt to their feet and applauded like crazy.

Good finish, thought Fields. Get them in their hearts ... They'll love us, now.

Fields and the others on the stage then took their leave and sat down at the front of the audience to watch the dance programme on offer. The Minister from the government and the President of the university both congratulated him on the sentiment expressed in his speech. As he sat down next to Carolina, she touched him on the knee and whispered in his ear saying how impressive he had been. Fields liked that. Especially the touch on the knee.

At the interval in the dance programme the audience had a chance to move, enjoy some refreshments and circulate. Fields went outside the auditorium to the foyer where he was served with a glass of wine and a sample of bites to eat. He nodded politely and said nice things to one or two of the audience who came to see him, and then he noticed two gorgeous young women who were clearly making their way towards him. He liked the look of this – he put his food to one side and smiled a welcome.

The first beauty smiled at him in return: 'Mr Fields, we just wanted to say first of all that we loved your opening speech this evening.' She spoke with a captivating English accent.

The second added, a little more seriously: 'And especially your dedication to Martín García. He was a close friend. There are many of us who miss him terribly ...'

'I guess from what you say that you are students or ex-students of this university? I did not have so much time to get to know this special young man but from what I know his loss must have been an awful shock.'

Claudia replied with delightful shudder. 'Awful is right. I still haven't got over it.'

'So we did appreciate your dedication of the festival to his memory,' Karin interposed, 'but we also appreciated your reference to what your corporation is doing for this country. Multinational corporations have some work to do, especially here, to improve their image, don't you think?'

Fields smiled broadly. Here was a challenging young woman who wanted to put him on the spot. 'I agree. That's why I'm here tonight and why we are making every effort to invest in the arts, in the environment and in the people of Colombia. But you are not from Colombia are you? I would guess you are guest in this nation like I am.'

'I'm an exchange student from England, but I love it here. I love the people I've met and I don't like what I've heard about some of the antics of certain mining companies,' said Karin.

'I am Colombian and we pride ourselves on making foreigners welcome here ... but some of the people who come, as Karin says, have not always treated us so well.' Claudia supported her friend.

'We sort of wondered what your corporation is like. What you are up to, so to speak ...'

'Up to?' Fields laughed aloud. He was beginning to enjoy this. A stunning young woman on either side of him trying to sound him about the ethics of multinationals in the developing world. This was his bread and butter. 'Well I am grateful for your interest in me and my corporation, as you put it. Karin, is it? And you are ...?' He looked at Claudia.

'Claudia Fernández. I'm nearing the end of my Economics degree here at Los Andes.'

'And I'm Karin Roth, coming to the end of my exchange year before I return to my final year of my degree in Economics in Durham. And as you can see – we are both interested in what Triple F are doing here.'

They both smiled winningly at Fields again.

Fields smiled back, though he actually felt like licking his lips: 'Well, Karin and Claudia, Triple F are doing all sorts of things here, as you have already heard me say this evening. Would you like to know more? Or is it that you'd like to see the proof of what I have said?'

'No, Mr Fields. Of course, we believe what you said. A distinguished business leader in your position – we don't need to see proof. But since you mention it ...' Karin smiled at Claudia, 'we would appreciate a closer look at your organis- ation ...' She took a deep breath and plunged in: 'Do you take on summer interns, by any chance?'

'Would a couple of lively student economists fit into Triple F for an internship, you mean? I guess they might. There is always room for bright talent to make their impact in any business. Back in the States I used to take on one or two interns a year in my offices. I haven't seen anybody I've liked here ... until now.'

'Mr Fields, we are very likable,' grinned Karen, 'and talented and hard-working and very easily bored in boring companies. Is yours a boring business?'

Fields laughed again. 'I certainly don't think so. But look here, young lady, everyone has to start at the bottom in any business and there is always an element of boredom at first ... so don't you get too pushy!'

'We don't push nice and interesting people,' said Claudia. 'Such people are interesting to work with, of course. So if your corporation has lots of such people ... would you like a couple more?'

Fields was thinking he might. He would actually like to see a lot more of these beauties, especially the English one. He was of the opinion that she in particular could have whatever she asked for and the more she pushed him the more he'd like it. And preferably he'd push down on her afterwards, he thought lewdly. How to take this further?

'All right, Karin and Claudia,' he said after a moment's

221

thought, 'come and meet Carolina, my head of public relations. Give all your details to her and we will see if we can find some interesting and definitely non-boring people for you to work with. Summer internships? I'll have to check with Human Resources to see what the legal situation would be for you in Bogotá, how much we'd pay, what sort of contracts we could give you. The situation here is bound to be different to that in the States. But yes – when your university term finishes ... what is it, around May sometime? Then we should be able to find an internship for you both. Come and say hello to Carolina.'

The two friends were almost bouncing up and down with glee as Fields turned away for a moment to find his colleague. They looked at another behind his back, grinning like cats.

'We did it!' Karin whispered.

'Fantastic!' echoed Claudia.

The two young women returned to their classes at Los Andes with an added spring in their step. Carolina Santos was the first to contact them just before Easter, confirming that Triple F would let them know some time at the end of April precisely what sort of temporary employment would be made available for the two friends, but could they come and see her in the next day or two to clarify some details?

Could they? They would be there the next morning, bright and early!

At eight in the morning the next day the two friends were waiting outside Carolina Santos's office. They did not have to wait long. Carolina came out and proceeded to give them a guided tour of the entire multi-storey building: Triple F's headquarters in Colombia. Either one or both of them would probably be working with her, she explained, and since in PR you needed to know about every facet of the corporation's business, she thought it would be a good idea for her two guests to have a quick look round. They would then have an informal chat together before she took them up to the top floor to see Morten Fields again.

Karin and Claudia were no fools. This was a sort of informal interview to size them up and to see how they might best fit into the organisation, if at all. The more formal session with the big boss upstairs would culminate the morning.

The three women got on famously. Within five minutes Karin could tell this was going to be a breeze. They looked into the different divisions of head office: Accounts, Human Resources; Farming; Mining and, of course, Public Relations. They chatted, asked questions, laughed a lot but did not duck any important issues. How far did women go in this organisation and were there any glass ceilings? What did Carolina, a Colombian, think of the operation of businesses like this in her country – were they just interested in sucking as much profit out of the lands and leaving precious little behind? Was their much movement of personnel in the business or did you have to leave in order to look for promotion? Carolina was very honest and open with them; they were very honest and forthright about their concerns.

Then came the time to meet Morten Fields in his own office. Carolina went in first for five minutes before the two friends were called in. Fields was, as ever, the perfect gentleman, welcoming them to his suite, guiding them to the sofa, pulling chairs round so that they could all face each other at the same level. Then he came straight to the point.

'Well, I have to say that I am taking a gamble on you two. I don't normally recruit personnel on the basis of a five-minute social occasion sandwiched in between dance programmes,' Fields said with a smile. 'However, I do on occasions back a hunch on the basis of first impressions and my first impressions of you, Karin and Claudia, were very positive. I'm pleased to say that Carolina here also had the same first impression. So: we start on a high note!'

'Thank you!' both chorused.

'But there is a long way to go yet. Looking at your back-grounds, Carolina will probably make a decision as to which of you could work with her over your university vacation and whether or not there are other divisions in this building that might be able to employ either of your talents. You might just have seen in your brief tour that it is a bit like working in the United Nations in this building. We have a number of US citizens like myself spread around the place; Colombians dominate the departments of Human Resources and Public Relations; we have a couple of your compatriots, Karin, in Accounting and Finance; we have a Dutchman, a Brazilian and a number of other Latinos in Farming; a Canadian and Australian in Mining and goodness knows how many other nationalities in total are all working here. We will see by the end of April where in this polyglot edifice we will place you.

'When you start work, however, I expect nothing short of excellence. Understand? There is no room for slackers, for pretty faces that want to use this place to socialise and enjoy themselves. I'm looking for excellence, initiative, efficiency and people who can deliver under pressure with no excuses for failure. Your first impressions are good; your second impressions are good; make sure you repay my faith in you by ensuring that your third and final impressions are not just good but outstanding. Gottit? You do that and we shall all be happy. You will convince me that my original hunch was correct and, in that case, I shan't want to lose you at the end of your short time with us. Triple F always looks after its employees. Show us how good you are and I shall want you both back here after you've finished you studies. Now: how does that sound?'

'Wow!' said Claudia.

'It sounds brilliant,' said Karin. 'Mind, if we turn out to be that outstanding maybe you will be lucky to get us back ...' she grinned at Fields.

He laughed. 'Attagirl! That's the spirit. Join us at the end of May and let's see where it leads. No promises, no commitments on either side until the end of your internship and then we can see what suits both parties before you leave us.' He turned to his head of PR. 'Carolina – do you want to say anything?'

'Only that I'm very pleased to meet you both again and that over the next couple of months I'll be looking for where we will have some sort of challenging work for you. As Mr Fields has just said, there are a variety of different possibilities but most of all we want to recruit young, energetic and positive people here who make a difference – and that is certainly what we see so far in you. I personally look forward to having you join us here as soon as possible.'

'Any questions, you two?' Fields asked.

The two girls looked at each other and then laughed.

'We are both a little dumbstruck at present ...' said Claudia.

'No questions just yet,' said Karin. 'I can't think now but I'm sure there'll be plenty nearer the time when we come!'

Fields rose, signalling the end of their meeting. 'Good, good. Like Carolina, I'm looking forward to seeing you both again, but, for now, thanks for coming in today. All best wishes for your studies in the meantime – Carolina, please see them out. Goodbye.'

The perfect gentleman chaperoned them to the door, shook their hands and bowed as they left his office.

The two friends walked on air all the way back to their university and didn't stop talking about that morning for the next day and a half. For Karin in particular this meant a big change in her plans. She telephoned her mother in the middle of her night in England to explain that she would not now be coming home at the end of May when the university semester finished; she would instead be staying on in Bogotá and working for a multinational corporation. She would then be earning sufficient money herself and would not be dependent on savings, scholarship funds and her mother's generosity. Yes, she was sorry that she wouldn't see her mother for another three months or so; yes she missed her terribly, but out here there was always the possibility that this temporary internship might provide a stepping stone to future full-time employment in a large and important international organisation and wouldn't her mother be proud of that?

Karin put down the phone and stared at the wall in her small student apartment. All sorts of things were going through her mind. How things change! A brief meeting in a dance interval had led to everything turning around and upside down. She felt as if she was on the point of opening a chapter in a whole new life. Her future was no longer a puzzle that was burning away unsolved deep within her. She would give everything to this internship and prove that she was worth taking on full time when her degree finished. Morten Fields and Carolina Santos had already impressed her on how open and amenable they were to two pushy students. No haughty indignation or patronising self-importance when faced with younger challengers to their realm. Not like some other businessmen and academics she had met. How exhilarating they were. She would show how adaptable, amenable and efficient she could be in return. Her final year in Durham did not seem so important now.

She would go to Claudia's finca at Easter, however. She would immerse herself in the mountain environment and see Daniel again. But her feelings towards him had suddenly changed. He was still an important and magical influence. How she would react to seeing him again she could not say – she knew how emotional she was – but she knew now that their worlds were not fundamentally compatible. When vacations and work allowed she would see him. But she would pursue her future first in Bogotá, go back to her studies in England with the determination to pursue an international career and then see if she could return to Triple F, or some other multinational corporation, after that. How things change!

226

For Claudia, this offer of an internship was similarly a great opportunity and achievement. It was also confirmation that her relatively recent relationship with this English friend of hers was a tremendously beneficial and horizon-opening partnership. Karin had kept thanking her for being so welcoming; Claudia had to thank Karin for causing the parameters of her own world to shift so remarkably. Suddenly she was on the verge of joining a version of the United Nations. Who knows where this would lead?

For Morten Fields there were changes too, but of a different sort. After his hearts-and-flowers interview with the girls, he had suddenly to switch to unrelenting toughness and aggression on another front. Having schmoozed these women and set them up for a closer relationship in the near future, it was time now to check on the status of TMG's share price and their future prospects at the Puracé mine. Was a further assault in their direction needed?

The share prices of both companies had been moving in opposite directions, Fields was pleased to see. Triple F's image had been rising slightly in the eyes of Colombian investors whereas the difficulties of TMG had caused doubts and concerns and a subsequent downward revision of their future profits. Not far enough yet, thought Fields. He asked Patricia to set up another meeting with Cortés and González.

It was a couple of days later before the two were able to fly in. As before, Fields blocked all incoming calls, shut the door and wanted to hear the latest from the Puracé area.

Cortés started. 'Smith's intervention a little while back really put the frighteners on TMG security. All their staff went around in twos and threes after his attack, armed to the teeth and clearly jumpy. Their problem is they have to guard a long stretch on the mountainside and they do not know from where they might be attacked next. You would have a better idea than me of the increased security costs that are involved, but given what happened I would expect that they have had difficulties in hiring staff and thus have to pay them danger money. Well, I left it around four weeks and then hired some paramilitaries to check along their road, pick a vantage point at night and then shoot whatever they saw going along. A jeep came driving up the road and, with its headlights full on, naturally enough, it was a sitting target. Our boys opened up with AK-47 fire and riddled it with bullets. Other TMG security staff arrived on foot, fanned out and fired back at where they saw our gunfire was coming from but by that time the damage was done and the paramilitaries had got out under cover of darkness. A week later I wanted to know what effect this had had, so we had someone ride over that way to take a look but he reported back now that they've got security guards with dogs on the mountainside and they're stringing up barbed wire and stuff some hundred metres or so on either side of the road.'

'And that's illegal,' butted in González. 'They've got a licence to mine there but they don't own the mountainside and can't fence it off.'

'Fat lot of good quoting the law does. No one is going to challenge them stringing barbed wire around the place. It'll restrict access to the mountain for the local folk but no one is going to listen to *them*,' said Fields. 'The issue now is, what sort of attack can we now mount, given these extra defences? Knock some of that out and they will have to think again, spend even more. They must run out of patience and money soon.'

'It's a bit like First World War tactics,' González said. 'Suppose we had someone close by, high up at night, watching for passing dog patrols. He would pick his moment, go down and cut the wire, run in quick, lay some landmines or something and then run out again. It's gotta work. They can't keep watch all the time over every inch of the whole mountainside, especially at night.'

Fields was thinking. Mine the mountainside in hope of blowing up a passing dog patrol? Sounds like using a sledge-hammer to strike a walnut. Nonetheless, he liked the idea of big explosions. The bigger the bang, the more publicity it got. That's what they want. Besides which – that was what had started this whole dirty war – TMG blowing up one of his vehicles. There's nothing as satisfying as a bit of sweet revenge.

'Yeah. We've got to try something like that,' said Fields. 'Terrorists blowing up their road would be great after they did the same to our road. If we could pull that off, it would really get them worried, especially with all that extra security. They'd have to put an army of people out there all the time after that. One more successful attack and we'd be close to finishing them off. But how to do it?'

'A one-man demolition squad would attract the least attention and have the highest chance of success. We all know who that might be,' said Cortés.

'Still getting to the road unnoticed would be near to damn impossible, given what you've just told me about the number of people patrolling the road and nearby mountainside,' said Fields. 'I can't risk the life of our best operative like that.'

'So create a diversion,' said Cortés. 'Same as before. Para-militaries can set up an assault say higher up the road. Lots of AK-47 fire. Attract all the heat up there and then Smith goes in on his belly and places a device on the road. Gets out. The paramilitaries disappear into the night; their security searches like mad and finds no one, goes back down the road, Boom!'

'Good idea!' Fields was impressed. 'That does sound a lot less risky. There is one concern, however – creating and priming the device needed to blow up the road. Smith is no explosives expert. What about the man we used before. Cárdenas, wasn't it?'

'He's a problem ...' said González.

'Oh! In what way?'

'Well, after the last mission he was on with Smith, he hasn't recovered,' said González. 'The man's a nervous wreck. He's been on sick leave just about ever since.'

'That's dangerous. Has he been talking?' asked Fields.

'No. Not to my knowledge. Cortés had been to see him a couple of times. What do you reckon, Miguel.'

'No, he hasn't talked – unless you count him rambling away at me and complaining about what I made him do. He says he would never have taken part in that raid if he had known what was to happen. I just told him to get used to the idea and snap out of it.'

'Trouble is the psychiatrists say he will never snap out of it unless he can talk everything out that is bothering him,' González said. 'Since he cannot, he is still a bumbling wreck on sick leave.'

'What a shame,' said Fields sarcastically. 'But keep a close eye on him since we don't want him spilling anything to doctors, nurses or anyone. He sounds a risk to me.'

'I'll keep visiting and putting the fear of God, or rather Smith, into him,' said Cortés. 'That'll work for the time being.'

'OK,' said Fields. 'I'll leave it to you. Go back to Popayán now and I'll make contact with Smith. We'll talk over the techniques of setting explosives. Maybe he will just have to learn to do it himself. If so, that may take time. Whatever, I'll send him down to you when he's ready and then, Miguel, I'll leave it up to you to coordinate the attack. Thank you, gentlemen. This all sounds fine so far. Before we finish, are there any other issues we need to touch upon?'

Cortés and González looked at one another and shook their heads.

'No, I think that's covered everything,' said González. 'We'll be in touch as things develop or if anything changes.'

The three men stood up. One last thought struck Cortés: 'There's one thing we haven't considered, now I think of it,' he said.

'Out with it,' said Fields.

'Well, we're rather assuming that TMG will just keep beefing up their defences in response to all these raids. Are they that dumb as to not be able to guess where they are all coming from? Are they going to keep swallowing the line that it is the FARC that are up and at 'em? I doubled our own security some time ago but we cannot rule out the possibility that some day they are going to take the fight to us, rather than just sit there and take what we throw at them.'

'Hmmm. You're right, Miguel. All the more reason to get in our next attack on them as soon as possible so as to weaken their arm. By all means, however, keep your eyes open and all your men on full alert. Keep me in the picture at all times.'

He bade both men goodbye. As he saw them out, he asked Patricia to call in Leo Smith for a breakfast meeting the next day. There was no time to waste.

Fields went home that night with Cortés's last comments mulling over in his mind. It was something to take seriously. Shame – he would prefer to go to bed thinking graphic thoughts about the women he had seen recently and what he'd like to do to them … but images of Triple F vehicles being blown off the road kept creeping into his head.

Just as he was preparing to turn off all the lights in his apartment, the phone rang. It was González.

'Sorry to bother you this late,' he said, 'but I thought you'd better know. I've just got here to my office after the flight back to find a letter of resignation on my desk. It's from Adrián Cárdenas.'

'Oh … so he has written a letter of resignation, has he?' said Fields. More like he's signed a death warrant, he thought. 'OK. Thanks for the information. You were quite right to tell me. Contact Cárdenas and tell him that we want him to continue until the end of the month under the same terms as always – that is keeping his mouth shut. Then we will pay him off. OK? I'll see to everything else.'

'Will do. Thanks. Goodnight.' González hung up.

'Well, Leopold Smith,' thought Fields. 'And now I have one more little bit of unfinished business for you, before the next mission. Triple F always looks after its employees and now we will have to look after Adrián Cárdenas.'

10

Saying Goodbye

Karin's second semester at Los Andes came to a close and, as she and Claudia had already discussed several times, this was likely to be the last opportunity for them to spend some time together in the Fernández finca and, particularly for Karin, probably the last chance to see Daniel. They had both agreed that their internships were the stepping stones to important careers, that they would devote themselves to the work whole-heartedly and that, in Karin's case, it would be most unlikely that she would retrace her steps to the mountain slopes above Popayán. Whether or not she was offered a future contract with Triple F, whether or not she would be able to return to Bogotá, this was likely to be the last occasion she would have to spend with the man who had fascinated her, on and off, for the last seven months.

It was a very subdued Karin Roth that rode up to meet Daniel on the *páramo* above the finca on the first day of the Easter vacation. It was cold, cloudy day with the mist hanging over the mountain in long, white motionless shrouds. She counted almost every pace Bella took on the familiar path upward, her heart in her mouth, half hoping, half afraid that Daniel would be there in the clearing where she had first seen him. Word had been sent to Alfonso some weeks earlier, and then sent again three days before they arrived, that Karin and

Claudia would be visiting and Karin hoped those messages would find their way through to the one she most wanted to see. Claudia had escorted her friend a little way on horseback and then returned to the fields below so not as to intrude on the meeting that both girls hoped would take place.

Daniel was there, waiting. He had lit a small fire in between the boulders to boil up some water, presumably for coffee or some other drink, and he stood up when he saw the horse and rider approaching.

'Hello, Karin.' He gave a shy smile. 'It's nice to see you again.'

Karin's heart leapt. She couldn't tell him. She didn't want to spoil whatever time she was to have left with him. 'Hello, Daniel,' was her tame reply. 'It's lovely to be here …'

As always, the first few minutes between them were a little awkward and disjointed but eventually the conversation began to flow and Karin especially wanted to spur him on to talk about the life he was leading, the places he had been, not the protests or his politics or the problems with mining companies, but his love of the environment, the plants, birds and animals that were part of his life and so far away from hers. This led naturally into her asking him to show her more of the mountain – to ride together, both on Bella, across pathways in the *páramo* that she had not seen before. He agreed.

He sat behind her on the mare, one arm around her waist, the other reaching in front to the share the reins, and it was the closest she had ever been to him, feeling his warmth, his body moving against hers in rhythm with the horse. He was shy and reserved at first but gradually he relaxed and was able to guide the horse, describe the terrain and enthuse about the landscape that began to reveal itself as the mist hovered and shifted about them.

Karin agreed that this was indeed a beautiful part of the world, but she was almost fainting as she felt his warm body against hers and the floods of competing emotions coursed through her veins. She asked to stop high on the ridge they were climbing and had to dismount alone, take in the view, and calm her hot blood for a moment while Daniel stood a little way back, stroking Bella's head and whispering to her, impervious to Karin, as if on a different planet.

The peregrine falcon appeared, fluttered around Daniel with first one sweep, then another, before she finally settled on his shoulder. Karin looked at him – the mare's head in his hands, the falcon apparently quite content a few inches from his face and him just standing there impassively. What was it with this man and females? He didn't seem to make any effort, give any sign of emotion, but they seemed to drool over him. She was in danger of doing the same. She *was* doing the same! Thank God his back was towards her and he couldn't see.

She had thought this before: there was nothing so attractive as a man totally independent, at peace with the world and at the same time with the entire world at his fingertips.

Her thoughts were broken in an instant. Daniel now was looking over the mountains stretching away into the distance and, following his gaze, she could see two large birds wheeling slowly in the skies way away from him. In a flash of yellow and brown, the falcon dived away. Of course: those two big birds were coming this way. Don't tell me, Karin thought, he has summoned those two giant eagles or vultures or whatever they were to come to him and the smaller bird was jealous.

Karin felt the same. Daniel had forgotten about her and was looking up at the sky as these two birds grew larger and larger. Huge wings, primary feathers spread out wide so you could almost count each one; tails fanned out ... these giant birds slowly, slowly wheeling in circles coming ever closer.

They were quite high on the ridge and now, as the sun rose into the sky, the mist about them dispersed and descended into the valleys on either side of them, covering the view. They seemed to be standing on a knife-edge at the end of the world – a solitary mountain rising up above a sea of white. One of these mighty creatures came sailing down and down and suddenly passed below the ridge to the left of them. Karin could clearly hear the hiss of air through its primary feathers as it glided by then slowly turned around to make a second pass. Its wings barely moved, just a slight change of angle: an amazing demonstration of aeronautic control.

Daniel turned to Karin, returning for a moment to her world, his eyes big and shining.

'Condors,' he whispered. 'Aren't they just fabulous?'

The second bird came down. It had glided one hundred yards or more to their right, had circled around and down, and was now zooming in towards them. There was no noise at first, just this enormous black glider closing rapidly in on them, head on; wings horizontal like two thick black lines in the sky, the only sign of movement being a slight rippling of primary feathers at its wingtips. At the last instant, this awesome aircraft banked slightly to one side and came hissing past. Karin saw its white-ruff-ringed head crane round to have a good look at them as it soared by. They were eye to eye, a stone's throw distant, the giant bird circling around and then down below them, down below the ridge and away.

Karin just gaped after them. 'Incredible ... magical ...'

'They're masters of the Andes. No fear. No predators. Monarchs of the air,' Daniel said, looking wistfully after them. 'They are mystical creatures and the *indígena*s revere them. You can see why. People's souls fly with them. Mine certainly does!'

'They are simply immense. No wonder they have no fear. How often do you see them?' Karin asked.

'Not often. They are quiet rare here but they grow in number the further south and more remote I go. I love it when they see me, however. They just come and have a look. They're quite curious.'

Daniel turned again and stood watching them, circling, swooping, riding the currents of air that rose over the ridge.

Karin stood and watched Daniel. His soul was flying with them: away over all the mountain tops; over the entire length of the Andes; into the wild, distant sierra. Away from her, if his soul had ever been close to hers anyway.

It was an even more subdued and silent Karin that returned to the finca that evening. She had promised to return and see Daniel again the day after tomorrow and could see that that was how things were going to be this vacation. Moments of intense emotion; moments of pure magic; floods of complex feelings; Daniel smiling gently, beautifully, distant and untouchable. She sighed and led Bella back to the stables.

'Well, Karin. Tell me: what happened. You've been out all day so obviously you've seen him!' Claudia was itching to hear everything.

'What happened? Oh Claudia – one moment I want to throw myself at him and have him make love to me on the mountainside. The next moment I seem to see him flying away from me on the wings of condors and I fear I'll never see him again. One minute he is close to me, warm and generous and I'm nearly fainting in his arms; the next minute he's as distant and unreachable as the tops of the Andes. It's driving me crazy!'

'Tell me something I don't know!' laughed Claudia. 'But did you tell him? Did you say that you are going away and maybe won't see him again? Did you tell him you were going to work for Triple F?'

'No! Not yet. I can't yet. I don't want to spoil the magic. Claudia, it *is* magic. He holds everything, every creature under his spell – me included. You should have seen him standing on the edge of the world, conducting everything about him. Moments of sheer enchantment. I want to get as much of it as I can before I have to go. I can't tell him yet. Am I being selfish?'

'Yes, you are, but then so would anybody be in your

situation. Enjoy him while you can until the spell is broken.'

The remaining days of the vacation floated by. Visits to Daniel were like a dream and it was if Karin was drifting half awake. She could see herself, talking with him, laughing, walking through clouds, on occasions holding his hand, but somehow it all wasn't real, it all had to end and she would wake up and find him, the mountain and everything else gone. Vanished.

The final day came. It had to. She walked up, looking at the thick, lush, green vegetation above the farm and how it slowly thinned out with altitude. Some of the frailejones were flowering with golden fingertips. The clouds were hanging over the mountain tops and a slight mist billowed down towards her. It grew colder and Karin hugged her dark-red sweater to herself, shivering a little and wondering how she was going to handle this last meeting.

He was waiting for her. He rose as if to lead her higher and she dutifully followed for some distance and then her resolve could not hold out any longer; she could not follow him any further.

'Daniel … wait! I … I've come to say goodbye.'

Daniel stopped in his tracks. He turned to face her: 'You're going? Already?'

'Not just going today, Daniel. I'm leaving for Bogotá and I don't know when, if ever, I'll be coming back …' Karin looked down and couldn't meet his eyes. 'I've been offered this amazing job, this internship. It starts as soon as my studies finish in a month or so. I don't think I can come back here again. This means … goodbye …'

'An amazing job?'

'Yes. I still can't quite believe it. I'll be working as an intern with the head of Triple F in Colombia, Morten Fields. He is the most wonderful man … and he wants to hire me. Claudia, too.'

'So you're not coming back? Where are you going ... and when?'

'If I'm working as an intern with Triple F then I'll be based in Bogota but ... that is just the start. If I do well, after I finish university in England, there's the possibility of a full-time career. And then who knows – it will be Colombia one day; Europe another; the USA or Asia after. It's ... it's like a dream.' She looked up at him. 'I leave for Bogotá tomorrow. I have to finish in Los Andes first and then report to Triple F's main offices in town and my induction will start almost straight away. This is it, Daniel – the chance of a wonderful career. Something that people like me can normally only read about in glossy magazines.'

His eyes flashed at her. 'Don't say that. You are miles better than all those false people posing in photographs. You're something special ... That's why they want you!'

Karin's spirit rose in return. 'Thank you but you don't know the competition. I'm just a hard-working girl who's studied a lot but up to now has had little experience of the league I'll now be entering. I've seen some of these sophisticated executives that fill the offices of Triple F. High-energy types. The best and the brightest recruited from all over the world. And all the languages they speak! Me – I'm just a girl from the back of nowhere and ... and ... I can't believe I'll be joining them!'

Daniel riled. The chemistry between them was still explosive. 'So this is *nowhere*, is it? Thanks very much. This is nowhere and I am nobody!' He rose up with his face flushed.

Karin caught his arm: he got upset so easily! 'I didn't mean it like that. You must know. This is not nowhere for me. And why have I come here? To see you.'

He tried to pull away but she wouldn't let him go. 'For everyone in Triple F this is just another mountain in the Andes, and South America is just another continent. For them, they know nothing of this place ... but I know that for you, and for me too, this is our world that we've shared ... Please, listen!'

Daniel pushed her away and turned to climb upslope, looking away from her. 'And now you're leaving. Well, thanks for telling me. You've known this all along, haven't you? These last few days we've been together, you've known you're leaving and you have said nothing. OK. I get it. So go. Go on ... goodbye.'

'Stop it, Daniel! Don't be so horrible ... I don't want it to be like this between us.'

'So what do you want it to be like? Oh ... Cheerio! Nice knowing you. I hope you have a pleasant journey ... Do give my love to Triple F.'

'Don't be sarcastic!' Now Karin was getting angry. 'That isn't you. We always fight but ... LOOK AT ME!' She caught up with him and demanded his attention. 'This ... this has to happen. You know I love coming up here in the mountains and spending time with you but it had to end someday. I've been thinking about it, looking for work for some time now and you must know what that means. I'm sorry I haven't told you before ... but how could I? Part of me didn't want this ever to end. But ... but it has to.'

Daniel struggled with his emotions. She was looking straight at him and he couldn't hide. His face creased and wrinkled as he tried to regain control but Karin reached for him again and held on. Suddenly she noticed his eyes were full of tears.

'Daniel, Daniel ...' She let go.

He turned his face away again but didn't move this time. His voice changed: 'OK. You're right. You always are. You have got to go to your amazing job and I guess I've always known it.'

He sighed deeply, collecting his thoughts, and when he had calmed down Karin saw a different expression and heard a different Daniel.

'We belong to different worlds, you and I, and always have done. My life is here and yet I can see that your destiny lies elsewhere. I guess that is why you are so ... so attractive to me.

You make me question everything. There are times when I hate where you come from and all that you stand for ... but I can't help myself. I find myself liking you, the way you do things, the way you talk to me, the way you move and react. You're ... you're lovely. How can I say that when the world you represent is so hateful?'

Karin was speechless. Who was this man? What was he saying?

'You made me realise that there is a big world out there and it's full of opportunity for you. I can see you want to throw yourself into it and let it take you where it will. That is your future, I know. I can understand that that is where you must go and at the same time I also know that that is not for me. I don't fit in there.'

Karin was still struck dumb; she could only stand and listen. Her thoughts were in a whirl but she focused on one thing: He said I was lovely ... Does he love me?

There was a jumble of rocks just behind them. Daniel sat down on one and shifted his gaze around to take in her, the rough, vegetated slope below, the *páramo* which stretched around them and the mist-shrouded summits above. He continued his soliloquy:

'You want to travel from one side of the world to the other. That's for you. Meanwhile, if I spent the next five years here on this one mountainside I would still not really know it well enough. What lives here, what the next day's weather will bring, where the falcon flies in the evening. And beyond that skyline,' he pointed upwards, 'the sierra stretches away for ever and I need to follow it. Where is my future? I want to see where the condor flies and where the big cats prowl ...'

He suddenly looked at Karin with the brightest eyes she had ever seen. 'I've never told you this before but over a year or so ago, some distance south from here, I was walking above the tree-line when just across the slope I was on I spotted a puma. For the first and probably the last time in my life. He was a

241

young male, I think, and their range, their territory is enormous. I just froze and looked at him. The most beautiful creature I had ever seen. So lithe, so graceful, yet so powerful and so confident in the way he moved. I ... I don't have the words to describe him well enough. He saw me. We looked at one another for an instant and then, somehow, he just melted away.'

Daniel's voice dropped and he smiled ruefully. 'That's all. Nothing important to people from the city like you ... but it meant everything to me. Everything. That is why I am here and what I am living for and why I can't leave ...'

Karin snapped out of her dream. 'Daniel, don't be so hard on me and on others like me. City life isn't all bad and nor is everyone who lives there. Using your language: we are just animals living in a different environment.'

Daniel sighed once more. 'Perhaps, but city people like you have evolved into something aggressive and terrifying. Amazingly skilled at tearing things apart, destroying places like this, killing everything and everyone that stands in the way and replacing them with concrete and glass, a vast supply of fancy but worthless goods, and money, money, money!'

Now it was Karin's turn for her eyes to fill with sorrow: 'I hate you when you say things like that! You are talking about me and the people I love. We are not all like that. And what about the people you know who live in the pueblos down below. Are they all like you describe? You make it sound as if we are all murderous philistines who value nothing and are greedy for everything. Answer me: Am I like that? Is that what you think of me?'

'I'm sorry, Karin. You're right again. You, and I guess many of those like you, are not the people I hate. I've already told you: I think you are lovely. But the world that TMG, Triple F and other big corporations have created terrifies me. When will they get here and destroy everything I love and live for?'

He said it again, Karin thought. Does he love me?

242

Daniel confirmed it a third time: 'Karin – if you are now to go and work for Triple F – don't let them change you. Don't turn into another selfish money-grubber. You're such a beautiful woman. It shines out of you. Don't become some hard, cold, efficient money-making machine like the cash dispensers in the plaza below!'

Karin didn't know whether to laugh or cry. How did he always do that? Such a torrent of different images and accusations, she thought. He gets under my skin all the time!

'Oh Daniel! You must be my best friend ... the one who I respect above all others ... but you have so little faith in me!'

'Not so. But why does it have to be Triple F you are going to? They're a monstrous organisation.'

'I know what you mean ... I know that is what you see when you are up here and their mines and trucks are tearing up the earth and taking it off somewhere else ... but honestly businesses like that are helping to create lots of good things that people need: clothes, houses, art galleries, museums and music. I went to an arts festival they put on in Bogotá – that's where I first met Morten Fields. It was wonderful. And he's such a nice man: no monster at all. Really. He made me laugh ...'

Daniel said nothing. It was a lifestyle he had left behind long ago. He just looked at her.

Karin stopped. She could not say any more for a moment. They both faced each other in silence. The mist above slowly sank down towards them, closer, colder.

Karin saw Daniel's eyes fill with tears again. He stood up.

'You've got to go ...'

'Oh Daniel, Daniel, please don't get upset. I'll be back again soon, you'll see. I'll always want to share this with you. It won't change, honest!'

'Mmm.'

This was wishful thinking, of course. They both knew it. Karin had to walk back down the mountainside and off into a

243

world away where who knew what adventures awaited her. Much as she felt for Daniel and everything around him, her new life was just about to begin and it was to lead her away from here – a long way away. She looked about her for the easiest path to take.

Daniel's intuition never failed. He stepped lightly past her and then turned to hold out his hand. She took it and followed: the first significant step downhill.

Daniel paused, held her hand lightly to his lips, kissed her fingers and then released her.

'Goodbye,' he said. His face was a mask.

'Goodbye!' Karin could not look back. She picked her way down past the low shrubs that tried to cling to her legs, sliding a little on loose stones, but ever downwards, zigzagging between boulders and gorse bushes, until the path opened out and became a little less steep. She dared to look up. He waved and she waved back, but she couldn't see him properly; her tears would not let her. Turning brusquely, she continued her descent a little faster now, her breath coming quickly in little sobs.

Daniel watched her go. Down the track they had climbed not so long ago together when he had shown her where the condors flew. Down, down to the clearing with the boulders where her horse had once waited so patiently for her. Above the frailejones he could still pick out her dark-red sweater that fitted her so snugly. He stood tall to catch the last fleeting glimpses: if this was the last time he was going to see her, he wanted to get the most out of it. Karin swayed further and further away, the line of her back curving round as she surmounted each obstacle in her path. So feminine, he thought. She moved so easily, fluently. The puma was not, after all, the most beautiful creature he had ever seen ...

Then she was gone.

Part Two

1

Working for Triple F

Karin gazed out of the window as the plane circled around El Dorado international airport, preparing to land in Bogotá. The last time she did this she was an excited exchange student about to arrive in Colombia for the first time and wondering what she would find here. What a difference a couple of years made. Now she was a graduate recruit about to join Triple F, one of the world's major multinational corporations involved in primary resource exploitation.

As her aircraft descended, through the wisps of cloud Karin could see large areas of the Bogotá savannah covered in a patchwork of what looked like glasshouses, but in reality were greenhouses of plastic sheeting, all devoted to market farming. Triple F owned large numbers of these: providing fresh fruit and vegetables for the city and, more profitably, cut flowers for export to North America and Europe.

Karin knew she would have to get to know more about this core activity for Triple F Colombia, though she gathered that there were other specialisms of the corporation that she would be more directly involved with. Her internship last year had been devoted to public relations and in particular with developing contacts to promote Triple F's environmental reputation. Her full-time employment that she had successfully secured at the end of her internship last September would allow her to develop this area but she had heard from Claudia that Morten Fields had other ideas for her as well.

Claudia had graduated from Universidad de los Andes last December and had been working at Triple F for five months already. The two friends had been in regular contact all the time they had been apart and Karin had felt a little jealous that Claudia was now deeply ensconced in her new employment, while Karin had been still engaged in her studies. But graduation at Durham had come at last, and Karin was now embarking on the next phase in her life, excited as before at flying into Bogotá, but this time with a totally different outlook and ambition.

Claudia was waiting in the arrivals bay at the airport and the two could hardly wait to be together. They waved excitedly through the glass at each other – the queue through immigration took ages but finally they met and hugged each other, both grinning enough to split their faces.

'Claudia – you look great! What an outfit!'

'Karin – lovely to have you here at last.'

After a long flight, Karin was tired but adrenalin kept her bouncing with delight at being back with her best friend. Two heavy bags were taken from her by a porter and Claudia led the way to her car. They had lots of gossip to catch up on and they started straight away as bags, handbags, presents and items from duty free were all stowed away in various locations.

'New car, power suit, you look a zillion dollars ... Claudia, this is just fantastic. Tell me you are as happy as you look!' Karin was wreathed in smiles.

'Yes I am! Things are working out fine and I'm particularly happy to have you back again. I've been looking at work for weeks now thinking: Karin would love this; Karin is going to do that; Karin would fit right in here; I haven't been able to rest this last week in particular. You are going to move in with me to my apartment, aren't you?'

'Of course! Where else am I going to go? We've talked about

it such a lot and I'm dying to see your place. *Our* place. Have you given me the best bedroom?'

Claudia swerved the car laughing. 'Hah! You've got some nerve! Well, actually there's no difference, so wait and see.'

It was early evening and the traffic was heavy going into the city from the airport. Karin was interested to see if there were any changes since she had been there last – some new tower blocks, a now completed road junction and flyover and a lot more traffic jams were her first impression. But what had been happening at Triple F? She quizzed Claudia all the way.

'Well, since we both finished our internships, all sorts of things have been happening,' Claudia said. 'First, of course, I was in and out of Carolina's office during my last semester at Los Andes, discussing work, sorting out a contract and generally keeping up with what was happening. I didn't start until the last week of January, as you know, but by that time Triple F Mining had gone from strength to strength. The TMG mine at Puracé – you know the one that was on the news with the demonstration that you-know-who was involved in – well, that ended up going bust and Morten made a bid for it. He bought up the mine and much of its machinery on the cheap since it was too much trouble to keep it working, so I understand. I don't think we have got it working again yet but we are undertaking surveys and bringing in staff and equipment apparently. People in the mining division at head office are all very upbeat about it, apparently. Carolina says Morten is really cock-a-hoop too.

'Well, that's all in the way of background ... The issue of environmental safeguards is going to be important in this takeover for us, so I guess you'll be straight into that. Except for the latest hot gossip, which might well have a big impact on you ...'

'What's that? Do tell!' Karin was all ears.

'Well, you know Patricia Ramírez, Morten's personal assistant?'

249

'Yes.'

'Well, she's just recently gone on maternity leave. She's now seven months pregnant.'

'No! But she's single, isn't she?' Karin didn't know much about her, only that she was the consummate professional: bilingual, efficient, always very well turned out and there were plenty of men in the corporation that loved to visit the top floor of the Triple F tower block just to go and see her and try their luck. She politely refused them all, up until recently, obviously. 'Who's the father, do we know?'

'Well, there have been plenty of rumours this last couple of weeks since all this has come out. The story, however, is that it is some lawyer outside the corporation that she has been seeing … but it seems he has dumped her now that she is having his baby.'

'What a bastard. Poor Patricia. How is she taking it?'

'She has had a tough pregnancy, apparently, which is why she cannot continue in work. High blood pressure, I gather. I guess her lawyer has probably caused much of that. Carolina has seen her and knows her better than most and says that Patricia was always determined to go ahead with the pregnancy and she is fine in that regard. Morten is keeping her on full pay, of course, and we will see how things turn out … but in the meantime I've got the definite feeling that Morten wants you in there as her replacement, or rather as his executive assistant.'

'No! It can't be. I don't believe it!'

'There's a part-timer in at the moment, holding the fort so to speak, but the fact that Morten has done nothing else to replace her and is clearly waiting for someone, makes me think, and Carolina think, that you might be the one he is waiting for! How about that?'

'C'mon, Claudia: it's only an impression of yours so far. It can't be more than that …'

'True, but I'm not the impressionable intern any longer. I'm well established now. Carolina and I work so well together and what with the various menfolk we knock around with we pick up an awful lot of what's going on in head office. Just wait and see if I'm right or wrong. You've got this weekend to recover and get yourself settled into Bogotá again and then Monday morning bright and early you have an interview with Morten Fields set up ... so we shall have to wait and see ... Karin – it's really lovely to have you back!'

Claudia shot her friend a warm smile, her eyes twinkling with pleasure as she finally eased her car into the entrance of the apartment block where they were both to live. Karin looked out at the big gates that were automatically opening to welcome the car she was riding in. There were butterflies in her stomach. This really was a new beginning.

Karin had three days to settle in before facing her new boss and her new future. The first day involved catching up on sleep, adjusting to jet lag and wandering around a little outside her apartment, getting her bearings and exploring her immediate neighbourhood. Claudia had found a comfortable two-bedroomed flat, high up in a tower facing east on to the forested walls of the Andes that bounded the metropolis. It was about twenty minutes north of the city centre on a good day with no traffic jams.

'Pleased with what you find?' asked her flatmate when she had returned from work on their first evening.

'Absolutely,' replied Karin. 'I'll take down a couple of your pictures and throw them out before I feel at home, though ...'

'Bitch! I'm going to hate living with you.'

'I know ... but we'll survive somehow.'

Both grinned. Both were looking forward to seeing how things were going to turn out, living and working together for the first time.

'Claudia, have you been back to your finca recently?' asked Karin.

251

'You mean, have I seen Daniel? No I haven't. It's like it used to be. I hear of him, from Alfonso mostly, but I haven't seen him. The same old stories about what a magician he is. Apparently, his cousin sees a lot of him – they've been organising demonstrations against environmentally damaging businesses. If Daniel has been down to the stables at all, it's been when I wasn't around. I met the one they call "El Ciego" in the marketplace one Sunday and asked after him and the story I got is that he visits from time to time, less often than before because he has been travelling a lot. Karin – he's going his way. Just as you are going yours. So let go!'

'I know. Thanks. I wondered, that's all …'

'Yes, well stop wondering about him and start wondering about what are you going to wear on Monday morning. You've got to go in with a big bang and impress the man. I'm taking you out tomorrow to see what we can fit you up with.'

'Steady on, Claudia. I've only just stopped being a student. I've got no cash to speak of and a big overdraft in my UK bank account.'

'Bank account! Yes – we have to open one for you. Don't worry about cash for the time being, I can loan you whatever is necessary. What is important is that we have got to get you dressed to kill …'

The two girls stopped, looked at each other and burst out laughing. They were both of the same opinion. If any job was going to work out, it had to be one where you dazzled the menfolk and didn't give them a chance to catch you up in your power suit and high heels. They hadn't actually talked about it in great detail, but over the last few months, in e-mails and on Skype, they had been discussing how Claudia had been turning heads, dating one or two and generally giving her male colleagues the run-around. Now they were going to get two femmes fatales zapping it to them – this new girl from England was arriving to turn up the heat and supercharge the atmosphere and the first in the firing line was going to be Morten

Fields. Starting a new job was all about making an impact – in whatever way you could.

Laughter was the default mode for the weekend. It took many visits to elegant womenswear shops in a number of shopping malls before the right drop-dead gorgeous business suit was found. Matching shoes and bag came next. The hairdo was easy – Karin had been to her favourite cutters in the UK before flying out so it was just a wash and blow-dry that was needed. Back in the apartment, turning in front of the mirror and spying herself from every different angle and asking Claudia's opinion took more time and more laughter before both were satisfied that, yes, tomorrow morning was going to be a knockout.

'I don't know about Morten Fields but before you get to him just about every floor on the way up will be talking about you, not to mention the men you'll leave swooning in the lift,' said Claudia.

'Well, if you haven't already finished them off before I get there,' said Karin.

Monday came. They drove in together, parked and went into reception. Claudia introduced her friend to the uniformed girl on the desk and was pleased to see that her male colleague could barely conceal his interest while dealing with someone else who had just come in off the street. They waited a moment outside the elevator, Claudia wished her friend good luck and got out at Public Relations. Alone with her heart in her mouth, Karin travelled the rest of the way to the top floor. The temporary personal assistant, Nancy, crossed over and met Karin as she emerged from the lift.

'Go straight in; he's waiting for you,' she said.

Putting her best high heel forward, Karin strode into his office.

Morten Fields rose from his desk, came straight forward and embraced her.

'Karin! I'm delighted to have you back with us. You look absolutely stunning!'

'Thank you, Mr Fields. I'm looking forward to a stunning job here.'

'And you will have one. That I guarantee. Take a seat, please.' He indicated the sofa, pulling round an easy chair to face her.

'Well, how was England? How have you been since I saw you last?'

'England is fine, not a lot of change there,' said Karin. 'As for me, I've been thinking of starting work here for ages. Now I've graduated I can't wait to begin.'

'Good, good. I've been thinking of you starting work here also. There are a number of things I want you to do – carrying on from where you left off last year, for example – but the post I now want you most to fill is that of my personal assistant. What would you think about that?'

'I'm not sure … I noticed a new girl outside as I came in. Won't she be staying? And what happened to Patricia?'

'Nancy outside is just a stopgap measure until you can take over. Patricia had to leave. She is going to have a baby.'

'I heard about that … but won't she be coming back afterwards? Do you want me as just another stopgap measure?'

'Certainly not. I want you there permanently. As for Patricia, I'm betting she won't return. Babies have a way of changing women's lives. If she does want to come back full time, which I doubt, then it will be in some other capacity. I am expecting you to take over outside here and make that job your own. That is – if you want it and if you can do it. You haven't said what you think yet. I might add, this is not the sort of offer I make to just anyone. Only to very special people who I think I might be able to work with.'

'Thank you for your confidence in me, Mr Fields. I'm very flattered and honoured to be offered the post.' Karin flashed her new boss a big smile. 'I have to say this has taken my breath away.' She crossed her legs and shifted back a little on the sofa, relaxing from her rather stiff and nervous posture that she had adopted until now. 'This is something I really was not expecting, but if you want me there I'm sure I will enjoy working with you.'

'Excellent!' beamed Fields. 'I'm sure this is going to work out fine. There are many ideas I want to take forward in this business and I need someone, particularly with an international perspective, with whom I can discuss some of these things and who can make them happen. Most importantly, you will be the focal point though whom all communication moves between me and the rest of this organisation. You will need your judgement to set priorities; push some people; put brakes on others; keep me informed about what's happening and pass on decisions to key personnel. Your initiative and efficiency impressed me last year. I'm expecting nothing less this year. Welcome aboard the top office! I'm delighted to have you here!'

Fields got up and walked around the sofa, smiling at Karin and giving her legs a covetous once-over. He was pleased with himself that he had waited for her – she was certainly the women he wanted in this position ... and in other positions as well ...

'Let's start right away.' He indicated that Karin should follow him outside. 'Come and meet Nancy. You'll work with her this week only and then take over from next Monday.'

He introduced his temporary assistant who was waiting patiently, standing outside Fields's office. Karin noted that she must have been warned that this new, foreign executive assistant was coming to take over since she was already a little deferential towards her.

'There are a number of meetings I want you to set up for me this week, Karin. That's just by way of organising my agenda – Nancy can show you the ropes on that – but there are a couple of things a little more important that I want you to work on.'

Fields thanked Nancy and then led the way back into his office, closing the door behind him and indicating that Karin should again make herself comfortable on the sofa. He walked slowly around his office, looking at her and spilling out his thoughts – at least some of them.

'Firstly, I'll need an environmental audit on both the Puracé mines we now have under our control. How do we develop these assets without too great an environmental risk? Who can advise us on this? What are the costs involved, the trade-offs we face, and thus how far is it worth our while? I am thinking of funding some university department which can do this for us. Some top researchers. Maybe from Durham? You know how things work there and you were working on this topic a year ago. Do some digging. Find some names for me. I don't want some private commercial concern that will rip us off. Start with some universities who are already working in this area. OK? Call around here, in the US and the UK, and tell me who is interested in coming here. We can tempt them with the promise of funding their research.

'Secondly, the next arts festival we sponsor here with Los Andes I want to be bigger and better. An international arts festival with some big names that will make news beyond these shores. Go with Carolina in Public Relations, who has the national contacts, and pull in some international events that will turn heads. Gottit? We can talk about budgets later – both for the environmental research and for the arts festival – when you can give me a feel for who might come here and when, and how much they would cost.

'How does all that sound? Something for you to get your teeth into?' He paused and looked down at her, smiling, he hoped, intriguingly.

'That sounds fascinating, demanding, challenging,' Karin said. And daunting, she thought. But she would not let him see how nervous she felt about it all. These were serious endeavours and would need a lot of work to put together. 'I'd love to do it!'

'Excellent! I'll be giving you all sorts of day-to-day business to attend to in the normal course of events but these two projects are to work on over the medium term. You'll find colleagues throughout this building who can help you, all with a variety of expertise and ideas, but you are the one driving it. Give me weekly updates on the progress you're making on those projects, OK? Good. Now I think we are finished. Join Nancy outside and the very first thing you can do is get me Alejandro González in Popayán on the phone. I need to talk to him. Thank you again, Karin, for joining us. This is going to work out great.'

He chaperoned her to the door, giving her one last desirous look as she swayed past him.

Within three minutes the phone rang for Fields. It was Alejandro González: Karin had started work.

Over the next months, Karin settled into her post and in doing so reassured Fields he had made the right decision for his personal assistant. She had a winning way with all the staff, shuffling appointments and arranging priorities in such a way as to keep everyone happy. She breezed in and out of his office looking absolutely gorgeous; she had a way of teasing him and challenging him that had him almost salivating; and she delivered on finding a unit to undertake environmental research in the Puracé mines.

She explained to Fields: 'There is a lot of pressure on UK universities to win research income from private sources. Just phoning around and suggesting we might be interested in funding a project here in Colombia meant that a number of academic departments were quick to phone us back and try and win our support. So I picked a department I know – Earth Sciences in Durham. They have a research unit which has been active in examining groundwater pollution among other environmental concerns, so when I asked one of them whether he would like us to sponsor his unit to audit gold mining in

Cauca he nearly jumped down the phone at me!'

'Well done, Karin!' said Fields. 'Let's fly this man out here and see what he looks like. We have to make sure he is up to the job. And I'd better contact González again; get him for me, will you?'

There were a number of things that attracted Fields to this suggestion. Karin said the man she spoke to knew no Spanish, so would be dependent on the corporation to point him in the right direction and feed him the information he needed and, of course, he would inevitably take time to investigate and make out a report on environmental recommendations. Time that would be useful to clear away some of the problems, and people, that Fields knew had to be dealt with – and he wanted to do so at least cost possible.

Karin buzzed through that González was on the line.

'Hello, Alejandro?' Fields was in a hurry. 'How are things looking in your new mine? Are we able to start up soon now?'

'Well, TMG were much further on – that is deeper – than we are in our original site. But, of course, they stopped work some time ago and so the place has filled up with groundwater. We haven't got started with draining that yet – what with moving a lot of the crap out of the way and bringing up our own equipment. And you know that shifting all the water is going to raise some concerns outside in the local pueblo. They're the ones who were demonstrating against TMG and I've had the news that they've just been waiting to see what we are going to do before they decide whether they are going to like us or not.'

'Do we know who are the trouble-makers who we have to … er … neutralise?'

'Yeah, it's no secret. The leader of the pueblo is well known for the weight he throws around – a guy named Díaz. But he is only one problem. There's another guy down here whom everyone seems to idolise. He travels around the different pueblos and drums up all sorts of support – from local indigenous people to the managers and staff of the National Park. They call him El Mono and apparently people worship him like he's the Second Coming. If he takes a disliking to us, we will have a big problem.'

'Well, I can't afford to wait long before we drain the mine. How quick can you dry it out and start up production? We are going to get some environmental wise guy out here soon and we don't want him to find out too many costly problems that need solving. Get rid of that water and any other waste we don't want before he comes – as soon and as cheaply as possible, OK?'

'I hear what you're saying. I'm just trying to figure out how we can do that without getting Díaz and El Mono in my face ...'

'Any chance of something happening to them?' He didn't want to be too specific over the phone but he wanted something untraceable to silence them. Permanently, if necessary.

'Dunno. I'll have to talk to Cortés. We know where to get to Díaz ... but TMG had major problems keeping him quiet in the past. You wouldn't believe the stories circulating down here. Apparently, El Mono protects him and the pueblo. So it is not going to be easy – trying to, um, pacify them might just kick up a major stink.'

'Well, it is precisely that we must avoid. Talk to Cortés and come back to me. As soon as possible, gottit?'

González groaned with his hand over the phone. He knew what was wanted. He just didn't know how it was going to be possible.

'Yeah – I've got it. I'll be back in touch. Bye.'

Fields was not happy. It did not sound as if it was going to be easy to clean up their new mining operation cheaply and quickly and at the same time present an environmentally green image. There had to be a way but he was unsure whether González was the man to find it. He was ruminating over this when Karin knocked and came in.

'Morten, I think there's something here that you need to attend to ...'

Fields loved it when she addressed him by his first name. He insisted she do so when they were alone.

'What's that?'

'I've had a call from the lawyers of Thelma Marshall. They insist you meet with their representative and their client.'

'I bet they do!' Fields angrily leapt to his feet, thoughts of how to solve the dilemma over the Puracé mines immediately forgotten. 'That woman wants more of my blood and her lawyers are the leeches!' He stormed around his office.

Always the gentleman in her presence, Karin hadn't seen him this side of Fields before. She wasn't sure how to respond to this outburst. Seeing her reaction, however, Fields suddenly cooled. He was quick to censor his own image so as she did not lose her faith in him.

'I'm sorry. That was impolite of me. You will perhaps understand when I say that Thelma Marshall used to be Mrs Thelma Fields and she has been hounding me ever since our divorce many years ago, to wheedle out as much money as she can from me. Every year her lawyers try something new. They are all liars and thieves and Ms Marshall, as she now calls herself, is someone who will say anything to get whatever she wants.'

'Do you want me to fix up a meeting?'

'Yes. As quickly as possible. I want her in here and out again as fast as possible. I hate seeing her so let's get it over with as soon as you can arrange it. Believe me, Karin, that woman is pure poison. How I made a mistake in marrying her in the first place I do not know but then ...' Here Fields struck an attitude of painful humility. '... I guess people make mistakes when they are young and too trusting. I'll be interested to hear your opinion of her when she arrives here with her legal advisor. But better contact our legal department and warn them. I will want Jonathan Fox to be with me at the meeting. Get him for me now, will you? Thanks.'

Fields returned to his chair, the wounded eagle. With pain in his eyes, he asked Karin to leave him alone and then watched her go out and close the door before he could sit up and swear silently at all four walls.

The phone rang. It was Fox. Fields had brought him with him from the USA, shortly after he had been appointed as CEO, since Fox was the man who had got him out of many a hole in the past and could be trusted to keep his mouth shut. Fields told him he would be needed soon once more to accompany him at the annual dispute with his ex-wife. Fox understood. No more was needed to be said, just the details of what day and when.

As Fields had instructed, the meeting was moved to the top of the agenda and set up for 9 a.m. the following morning. This suited Ms Marshall's lawyers – they had said that their client was not in the country for long so the sooner the better.

That morning Karin was surprised when she arrived at her desk to see Fox had already dropped anchor in Fields's office at least an hour earlier. Fields had left a note for all communication to be blocked and to be left alone with his counsel undisturbed, so they could prepare their brief before the opposition appeared.

Reception called. Ms Thelma Marshall and her companion were on their way up. Karin thanked the front desk and buzzed her boss, passing on the message. Then she waited for the elevator mechanism to stop whirring.

A tall, statuesque woman, expensively dressed in a tailored business two-piece, stepped out of the lift. Her lawyer, slightly smaller, came after.

'I have an appointment with Morten Fields,' Thelma Marshall said. He face was set in stone; her voice expressionless.

'Please go in, Ms Marshall. He's expecting you.' Karin knocked and opened the door for her and her lawyer. She closed it promptly as soon as they had entered – it was like closing a tomb, so cold and deathly was the silence within.

Almost immediately, Karin's phone rang. It was Claudia.

'What's going on up there?' said an insistent voice.

'I'm sure I don't know what you mean.'

'Oh come off it, Karin. Reception has just told me that Thelma Marshall has gone up. What's she like?'

'I'm not sure I should tell you anything, Claudia. I'm here to protect my boss, as you well know.'

'OK but either you tell me now or you tell me later when we are at home. So come on, what's she like? A fire-breathing dragon?'

'But, Claudia, I can't have half the office block talking about this. What will Morten think of me if I blurt out all he tells me in confidence?'

'But it's not half the building; it's just me and you.'

'And Reception ... and that means nearly every secretary in Bogotá.'

'I promise I won't tell Reception. Promise. There's only me. And Carolina.'

'Carolina?'

'Well, I have to protect my boss as well as you.'

'But why does she have to know?'

'Oh don't be deliberately dense, Karin. You know she's sweet on Fields. I promised I'd get as much of the lowdown on him as I could!'

'You're terrible. You really are. What if I said I'm sweet on him, too, and that I don't want the competition?'

'That's not true, is it? He must be at least fifteen years older than you. Possibly more. You can't fancy him surely? Even if you do, what's wrong with sharing a bit of information about his ex-wife? So come on – tell us what's happening!'

Karen relented. 'Well, she's no fire breather; more like an ice maiden. Morten told me that she is after her pound of flesh and keeps coming back every year for more. She certainly dresses very expensively ... but she has as much charm as a stone statue. Morten tells me not to talk to her and, if I do, not to believe a word she says. Anyway, how did you know she was his ex-wife?'

'Carolina told me. She's rather jealous so I'd better not tell her you are competition.'

'I'm not really. Don't tell her I'm after her man! Please. I'm not.'

'Don't worry. I'll protect her feelings like you try to protect his. But do tell me when she comes out and whatever else you pick up!'

'I might do. I might not. Bye.'

'Pig!'

The phone conversation ended but the meeting in Fields's office went on and on. It was near eleven o'clock when eventually the door clicked open and a very drawn and tight-lipped Thelma Marshall emerged, again with her counsel in tow. Karin stood up and asked if there was anything she wanted, directions to the rest room, maybe a coffee or any other refreshment? No. Thelma Marshall just wanted to get out and away.

Karin saw the elevator doors close on the two visitors and then went back to Fields's office. She asked the same – was there anything they wanted now the meeting had closed?

'Yes, please phone down for coffees, can you, Karin? Thanks. Maybe some snacks as well?' Fields looked across at his companion. 'Well, I suppose that went as well as can be expected. She'll be back again soon, I guess. When her sense of injustice gets her angry again. What do you think?'

'They put up a long fight but we held 'em off. Yep. They'll lick their wounds and come back for more. But so far so good. Yes, I will take a coffee now. If it wasn't so early, I'd go for something stronger!' Fox laughed.

The atmosphere in Fields's office was more relaxed than that Karin had registered for the outgoing pair. Morten Fields had obviously retained most, if not all, of his flesh. Karin withdrew, sharing their sense of relief and good humour.

The next business to attend to was the international arts festival. She called Claudia.

'This is not about Thelma Marshall,' said Karin straight away. 'There's not much more to report there other than she left looking distinctly stony-faced and there was no blood on the office carpet. They were in there for hours but got next to nothing, so far as I can tell. No, I want to know if you've made any progress on recruiting international stars for the arts festival. Morten will be asking about that next and I need to have something to give him.'

'No big names as yet, K,' Claudia replied. 'I'm working Carolina's contacts here at first and seeing if they can give me names in the USA or elsewhere. I've got the numbers of agents in Miami and Los Angeles but haven't got far with them yet. Have you got anyone in London?'

'I've been trying but no one has bitten yet. We just need one famous act to sign up and then we can fix dates and build the rest around that ... Are you sure there's nothing yet?'

'Nothing. But I'll keep going at this and let you know. Find something else to stall your boss in the meantime. Ciao!'

Karin was racking her brains about who next to contact when the phone rang – Miguel Cortés wanted to speak to her boss. She put him through straight away.

'I've heard from González, who I gather you've been talking to,' he said, 'about draining the TMG mine. Right?'

'Right,' said Fields. 'What's your take on this?'

'It depends on what causes the biggest reaction – certain protestors disappearing or pumping a lot of waste material out of the mine.'

'Well, if done properly, the former would not necessarily be blamed on us. The latter certainly would.'

'OK. Is Smith in the country?'

'He is now. I flew him in a week ago.'

'Fine. Can I come up and meet him with you to talk this over?'

'Certainly. Fly tonight and we meet tomorrow morning. Eight o'clock. OK?'

'Agreed.' Cortés hung up.

Fields was pleased. No beating about the bush. No problems. Cortés had a way of focusing on the essentials and moving quickly. He phoned Leopold Smith's mobile number direct and told him of the meeting. Then he buzzed Karin.

'Karin. I've just arranged another important meeting tomorrow at eight in the morning. Make sure we are not disturbed, OK? Fine. What are you doing for lunch?' He was now feeling in a good mood after a very productive morning and wanted to celebrate with the favourite feast for his eyes.

Karin's impression that the morning's meeting had gone well for her boss and badly for his ex-wife was confirmed over lunch. Morten Fields was on top form – taking her to a plush restaurant; ordering champagne; choosing the best food; complimenting the waitresses; laughing and joking with Karin; laying a hand on her knee when emphasising an anecdote. She let him. She was pleased the stresses of the morning had been overcome. She looked at him anew. He was a good-looking individual – all right, a mature man, but, because of that, experienced and on top of his game. She noted how staff here in the restaurant, like those in the office, all deferred to him and always tried to do their best to please him. He had the world in his pocket. There was nothing as attractive as a man totally independent, content and with the entire world at his fingertips. Yes … she could fancy this person.

The following morning Claudia and Karin were waiting for the elevator, discussing the arts festival, when a big man pushed in front of them, totally oblivious to their existence. The girls looked at one another. Who was he? There was a look of suppressed hostility about this individual that did not invite closeness or conversation. When the lift doors opened he entered, turned and glared at anyone who might have thought of joining him. He clearly travelled alone. The doors closed.

'Ouch! What a nasty piece of work,' said Claudia. 'I wonder what he is doing here?'

'There's something very threatening about him,' said Karin, 'apart from being simply huge. Security let him through, however.'

'Well, I for one wouldn't want to try and stop him,' said Claudia. 'I bet they didn't challenge him either! Come on, the next lift is here.'

They said their goodbyes and Karin went up to the top floor as usual. When she arrived at her workplace she noticed that Fields's early-morning meeting was already underway. She busied herself with clearing e-mails and sorting out the day's business while the top-office door was closed. No interruptions, the man had said.

Inside Fields's office, Cortés was summing up: 'As I understand it, you want an accident to happen to these two troublemakers. Something that cannot be attributable to Triple F?'

He turned to Smith: 'Maybe we get Díaz away from his pueblo and he breaks his neck falling from his horse. Something like that. You can maybe arrange for that to happen?'

Smith nodded. 'No problem.'

'The problem is not just Díaz, however,' said Fields. 'González tells me there's another agitator called El Mono. They say he travels all over the mountains, so just finding him will not be easy. Then we can't have him suffering from the same accident – it will look too much of a coincidence. Maybe we can have the FARC get him?'

Cortés suggested a change: 'The FARC would never go for El Mono. Why should they? From what they say he's more like one of them – few possessions and always on the move. The

FARC might go for the pueblo and Díaz, however, and that's where any protest about draining the mine will come from. We can leave El Mono for the time being and break his neck maybe later. Same plan; swap the victims.'

'I like that,' said Fields. 'Especially since those left behind in the pueblo are the ones who are likely to protest and this way you give them the FARC as fall guys who have to take the blame. That just leaves El Mono: all the better if he is to die on some mountain far away from us. Like you say – leave him for later.'

'We'll work on that,' said Cortés. 'First we have to set up a FARC group to get Díaz. Maybe some hired men to do the talking and Smith here to deliver the knockout? He looked at Smith again. 'How's that?'

Smith grunted. 'Fine with me.'

Fields wrapped it up. 'Sounds good to me, too. Leo, get yourself packed up and ready to go. Miguel, find somewhere for him to stay in Popayán until you need to use him. Keep González in the picture and I want regular evening updates to hear how things are going. Phone me at my apartment, not here. And ideally, I want this all done and cleared out of the way within a week or so – and then we can get on with draining the mine quickly, without opposition. Any other business? No? Good. Thank you.'

The meeting finished.

2

Two Worlds

First it was their dog barking. Valentina looked up. Then a falcon flashed by and landed on the tallest pole in the pueblo. Natalia glanced at her mother – they both knew who was coming.

Natalia ran to the door and nearly tripped over Lucho in so doing. She scolded him impatiently, upset that her greeting might be delayed. Little Lucho wasn't bothered. He picked himself up and ran in front of his sister.

'*Hola*, Mono! *Hola*, Mono!' A big grin cracked his face.

Daniel grinned in return, ruffled the little boy's hair and then climbed over him in the restricted space of the doorway to embrace both the teenager and her mother.

Valentina looked away from him as if to busy herself in the kitchen but she was not quite quick enough. Daniel caught a sight of her face. She had a dark bruise on her left cheekbone, just below the eye.

'Valentina – what happened?'

'It's nothing.'

'Valentina – tell me how you came by this …' He lifted his hand gently to the side of her face. 'That bruise was not here two days ago when I saw you last.'

'I bumped myself. It was an accident.'

Daniel looked across at Natalia. Her big eyes looked down –

she would not support her mother's lie.

'It was Carlos, wasn't it?' Daniel was still looking at Natalia. Fiery eyes raised and glared back at him.

'They had an argument ... He hit ...'

'You keep quiet, girl!' Valentina turned fiercely on her daughter. 'I'll tell you when you can speak!'

'Stop there! Don't you go and lose your temper with Natalia. She's only trying to protect you ...'

Daniel looked at them both. Both lovely women. Both obviously been bruised by what had happened. But what had happened?

'Valentina – tell me why he did it.'

Valentina said nothing. Tight-lipped she turned away but Daniel wouldn't let her go.

'I can understand anger ... and passion. What I cannot understand is violence. How anybody could hurt someone as lovely as you. It's beyond me.'

He drew her close and kissed the bruise on her cheek. She froze. Tears came to her eyes.

'D...don't,' she stammered. 'I love him. He can't help it.'

Big, blue eyes bored into her soul. He could see right down into her deepest feelings and she knew he knew and that there was nothing she could hide. She had been hurt. She turned away and tried to cover her emotions. But Daniel still wouldn't let her go.

'Tell me why,' he whispered gently.

Valentina shook her head. She was unable to speak.

Natalia watched all this with tears welling up in her own eyes.

Daniel persisted. He asked her again.

Suddenly Valentina blurted it out. 'He hit me because he was jealous. He hit me because he had been drinking. He hit me because I was looking at someone else and he didn't like the look on my face. Just don't ask me any more!'

Daniel didn't understand. What was Carlos jealous about –

he had the loveliest wife in the area who clearly doted on him, so why would he hit her? OK, he might have been drinking. He did have a violent temper but who was Valentina looking at and why should that provoke this reaction? He had to ask.

'Who were you looking at that would cause him to do this?'

Valentina struggled to get free from him. She cried out but refused to say any more. Daniel tried to stop her struggling but suddenly caught sight of Natalia. She had tears flooding down her face and was now crying uncontrollably as she watched the two of them. He and her mother. Daniel and Valentina. Suddenly he understood.

'Oh no! It can't be.'

He was here two days ago and he and Carlos had shared a beer or three, talking about changes in the nearby mine. Daniel didn't care much for beer but had sat with Carlos while he drunk quite a few. And when he left that night, Daniel remembered Valentina had been looking at him go …

'I think … I think I'd better leave. Perhaps I ought not to come round so often …'

'NO!' Both women shouted as one.

Lucho, who had not understood anything of what was going on but who nonetheless could feel the atmosphere in the house, ran up to Daniel and put his arms around one of his legs.

Daniel looked down and around at the three of them. A lovely family, he thought, but he had got too close for someone's liking. He had to go.

'I've come to see Carlos so I think I'll ask around below if they've seen him. I'm sorry I've intruded.'

Daniel bent down and released Lucho's hold on him, then backed out of the door. He waved goodbye as Natalia reached out to hold his hand and keep him back. He blew her a kiss and got out as quickly as he could.

Carlos's dog followed him out of the small yard and across the dirt track towards some other houses. Daniel thought it only reinforced how insensitive he had been. Of course, Carlos was jealous of him – this outsider who kept showing up and sharing his family uninvited.

Daniel had originally come to see Carlos and now spent most of the rest of the day looking for him – but to no avail. Two other men in the pueblo were also missing so he gathered they must be off somewhere together. People he met were pleased to see him as always – including some who knew him more by reputation and thus were surprised and a little in awe of him – but he missed his old friend. He couldn't go back to Carlos's house, of course, especially if the man was not there. Daniel decided he would have to come back another time – he would retire for the night to his little converted cattle shed in the next valley.

The next morning Daniel had barely risen from his straw-filled mattress when he heard someone frantically calling his name from a distance. He looked out and saw Natalia, running, half-stumbling up the stony path that led from the pueblo up to his abode.

'Daniel ... Daniel!' She was absolutely distraught.

He came running down to meet her and caught her in his arms: 'What is it?'

'It's father ... They've just brought him home,' she wailed. 'Those men, they've done it at last. They've killed him!'

Daniel was screaming inside as he held on to Natalia's hand and they both ran back towards the house. They careered along, Natalia weeping, Daniel trying to hold her up over the rough ground that was trying its best to trip them up. As they approached the pueblo, Daniel could see a small crowd gathered outside the house, which duly parted to let them through.

Carlos was laid out on the big table that filled the main room. He was dressed in his usual work clothes: a pair of tough blue overalls and well-worn boots, still muddy from

271

crossing the fields. There was blood on his chest, which some-one had done their best to clean up. Carlos's hair was all mussed up; his eyes were closed, his cheeks sunken, but he was in peace, as if sleeping. Valentina stood over him – her face red and all cried out. She now looked absolutely numb. Lucho was blank-faced, silent and hanging on to his mother. Two other women, Valentina's friends from the pueblo, stood close by, offering support.

Daniel's and Natalia's noisy arrival, crashing through the door and both panting, out of breath, disturbed the hushed room. Natalia let out another wail, seeing her father. Valentina, jolted out of her coma, turned to look at Daniel, an expression of utter wretchedness marking her features.

Daniel, still holding on to Natalia, drew in Valentina and Lucho with her and for the second time in twenty-four hours cast his eyes down and around at this lovely family, now deprived of its leader. He was desolate himself: he still felt as if he were to blame for the violence visited upon them.

'Who did this?' he struggled to speak.

Valentina shook her head and buried her face in his chest. Daniel looked towards one of the women in the room for an answer. She glanced at the door, as if to say: 'Ask the men outside.'

Daniel kissed the top of Valentina's head. Natalia looked up at him, her big round eyes still full of tears. He kissed her forehead, too.

'I'm so sorry,' he whispered. 'What can I say? I tried to keep them away from you. It's all my fault ...'

Valentina said nothing but let out a muffled cry and shook her head, still buried in his clothing. Feeling their pain, Daniel's mood began to change from horror and despair to one of silent anger. Who did this? Who was so callous and violent and so uncaring about the lives they were wasting and devastating? His arms still wrapped around them, Daniel slowly moved the family towards the woman closest to the door. He disentangled

272

himself, placing Valentina's hand into that of her friend so that he could go outside for a moment. There were a group of men gathered in the small yard, keeping a respectful distance from the inside of the house. Daniel recognised a couple of faces he had seen only the day before.

'What happened?' he asked. 'Who did this to Carlos?'

One of the men spoke up; one who Daniel knew was a close companion of Carlos, but who had been absent yesterday when he was looking around the pueblo.

'They said they were from the FARC. They said they had come to see us because it was time to pay up. They wanted protection money. Four of them it was, three with them big guns. They came down into our fields and surrounded us – three of us – and marched us up into the rainforest beyond. Kept pushing us to go higher. Carlos argued; he wasn't having any of this. One of them asked him who he was but he wouldn't say. They then threatened him and said they would come down and get his wife and family. Carlos then blew up and said that, if they touched his family, they would never get anything ever from the pueblo except trouble. He tried to threaten them. We told Carlos to calm down and be more care-ful – the FARC just listened to us for a bit, then this big fellow – he never said anything all the time they was with us; he was at the back just watching – steps forward pulls out a pistol and shoots Carlos at point-blank range. Just like that. We were terrified. Then the four of them just left us there and disappeared up into the woods.'

Another man joined in. 'It was Pepe and I, Mono. We were left there with Carlos lying on the ground in front of us. Horrible. Shot him just like that. Poor Carlos – at least you can tell Valentina he didn't suffer. He never knew what hit him. Big bastard came up, cool as you like and barely looked at him, as if killing a dog. Then he just walked off, the others following. Well, what could we do? Both of us were scared out of our wits. We eventually got down here just as it was getting light and found some of our mates to go back and help carry Carlos down.'

'Had you seen any of these four men before?' Daniel asked.

'No, Mono,' said Pepe. 'Never. And I don't want to see them again, either – especially that big one. Murderous bastard. No expression – looked as if he could have been switching off a light. But they seemed to know who we were. One of 'em had papers he kept looking at.'

Others in the group now started talking.

'Are they gonna come back? What we gonna do?'

'How we going to pay them?'

'They'll take whatever they want from us – not that there's much that we have.'

'We're lost without Carlos, Mono. What can we do?'

This was the question that kept coming up among them, that kept worrying everybody.

'I'll stay around,' replied Daniel. 'Tell them to come and see me if you see them again. I told that to the last ones who came looking for trouble ... though I don't think they were the FARC. Just tell them where I am and that I'll see them.'

Daniel thanked the men for their information. He shared their fears and kept repeating and repeating that, if ever there were others that came by to cause trouble, then they should send them to where he would now stay – in the old cattle shed in the next valley. Talking to the number of worried faces that were around him, Daniel realised that he could never call on these people again to organise protests or demonstrations. Whoever it was that had done this to Carlos, they had achieved one thing. He would never put anyone else's life at risk for a cause he believed in.

What comfort can you give to a family that has just lost its central prop, its main breadwinner, the life and soul of its existence? They were not his family – he had none – but Daniel had come to love them all as his own. Carlos was the volatile,

274

passionate and unpredictable friend who had so much energy, so loyal to those who loved him and who made things happen in the pueblo and far beyond. Daniel had always looked up to him – he represented all that he was not himself – a man clearly centred in his own community, part of the soil, who knew his own identity and destiny. He was not some quiet, reserved and wanderlust figure relentlessly on the move and unsure of where he belonged. Daniel could not think just yet as to how he would manage without his friend, this bulwark, so he could barely conceive of the magnitude of grief and loss his family must be going through. He went up to Valentina and Natalia and put his arms around them again. If nothing else, he would share the depth of their suffering.

There were practical things to attend to. After a while, with little conversation, people busied about. Carlos was such a figurehead in the pueblo that many now wanted to do something to help. Timber was found and men started making a coffin. The family were not overly religious but possessed a deep spirituality which many shared. A funeral in which all the pueblo could participate was discussed and plans made. Daniel asked that it be postponed until tomorrow so that someone could ride over to Carlos's cousin, Alfonso, and bring him and his wife, María, to attend; they were his closest relations besides Valentina, Natalia and Lucho. Daniel wanted to go himself but was torn between going and staying to lend support. Seeing his dilemma, Pepe volunteered to go with the bad news and promised to be back with Alfonso and María by nightfall.

Valentina and Natalia washed and prepared Carlos's body. They wept over him as Daniel helped lift and turn his unyielding weight. The single hole in Carlos's chest was the most awful and ugly thing that all of them had to confront. For the two women it was the final and cathartic experience that drained them of what emotion they had left and faced them with the awful truth of the life that Carlos had lost. Finally, however, when the body had been cleaned and dressed and stillness returned, there was a peace and resignation in the house that somehow transmitted itself to all those present. Carlos had gone. The shell that remained was a reminder but no more. His spirit was with the family; it existed in those he had loved and had left. Daniel felt this as well as the wife and daughter. They looked at each other and shared the same thought.

Friends brought food and drink around. Lucho had been dispatched to join the family next door where he regularly played, and Daniel, Valentina and Natalia joined him there for the meal. Later that evening Alfonso and María arrived with Pepe and there was a round of greetings and commiserations for all concerned. Men brought the coffin to the house and Daniel, Alfonso, Pepe and others helped place the body inside. The coffin stayed on the table.

Valentina and Natalia came to Daniel. They both looked exhausted.

'Will you stay with us tonight, Daniel?' asked the mother and widow. 'We don't want to be left alone now.'

'I can't Valentina.' He kissed her bruised cheek. 'I think you know why. I'd better return to my little place over the rise and I'll be back to see you in the morning. But you should ask Alfonso and María.'

Valentina nodded dumbly. Tears welled up again and Natalia put her arm around her. She took a moment to collect her thoughts and control her emotions.

'Yes. They can have my bed. I can't sleep in there alone tonight. I'll share with Natalia.' Then she stopped and looked at her daughter. Natalia nodded as if to say: Go on, tell him.

'Daniel, we wondered if you could say something at the funeral in the morning? They've organised a priest to come and he's a good man but we're not close. And Carlos wouldn't want anything too Catholic. But if he could tell us, he'd say you should give a speech. Natalia and I, we want you to say something. And Lucho would like that, too, we know. You're the only one who could do it and it would mean something to us. Something special. So please ...?'

Daniel was humbled by their faith in him.

'Thank you for asking me. Thank you for putting your trust in me. It would be an honour. I only hope I can do justice to the occasion.'

'I'm sure you will. We love you, Daniel.' Both Valentina and Natalia put their arms around him and kissed him, one after the other. Daniel blushed.

'Thank you again.' He backed out of the house. The falcon which had kept away throughout the day suddenly flew down and perched on his shoulder. She knew. It was time to go. Daniel waved goodbye, smiling shyly at the women who watched him retreat.

Everyone from the pueblo was waiting that morning. A grave had been dug by the two men who had been taken and then left by Carlos's killers. They felt it was their duty. They couldn't save him so they owed him this at the very least. They were helped in the last few spade strokes by any number of willing hands – men young and old, women and children, all anxious to show their respect. The small graveyard at the edge of the pueblo looked over the fields that swept across to the stream that flowed down from the mountain above – the same one that Carlos, Daniel and others had protested about since its waters had been polluted by the TMG mine. The bull that the pueblo had contracted had been kept in this field. Now there were cows that wandered over towards the graveyard, sensing that something was in the offing. Not just cows, there were horses that came over too. And dogs: Carlos's long-haired mongrel and a number of others he had fought with in the village joined the party by the graveside.

There were eight men including Alfonso and Daniel that brought Carlos's body from his house, across the rough tracks of the pueblo and into the graveyard. They slowly approached the small crowd gathered at the graveside; even the birds fell silent as they passed.

Valentina, Natalia and Lucho stood at the head of the grave and watched the coffin being lowered. They threw in flowers. Following their lead, many others did the same. The priest said a few words and then they all looked at Daniel.

Daniel began. He spoke of the man he knew; of the family that Carlos had raised and now must somehow live without him; of the pueblo he had given character to and which now had to learn to live without his lead.

Daniel spoke of the lands Carlos had farmed; of the generations that had preceded him and were buried alongside him in this small graveyard; and of the generations to come that belonged here and that Carlos had given his all for.

He drew his speech to a close: 'How do you take the measure of a man like Carlos? By the love he gave us. By the mark he leaves on all of us. By the example he gives us to follow. His body might sleep here but his spirit is within us. He will never grow old like the rest of us and nor will the ideals he lived for. We must all go on without him.'

There were many tears that accompanied his words. Daniel looked round at the sombre faces as he spoke – all honest, uncomplicated people leading simple lives tied to these lands. Most were of mixed blood – *mestizos* – part Spanish, part Indian, with a stronger attachment to the latter heritage. Poor in material terms, lacking in formal education, but with a strong sense of community, of family, of sharing and welcoming outsiders like himself. He felt honoured to be accepted by them.

The silence that stretched out after Daniel's homage to his friend was suddenly broken by a clump of earth that thumped brutally on top of the coffin. It was followed by others: a shower of brown tears that rained rapidly down, filling the dark oblong wound in the green of the graveyard. Then people slowly turned away. It was done: only a small gathering for a life that few outside the pueblo would ever know or care about.

Daniel was left thinking how he would go on. How could he make a stand against people who were capable of such violence – against people like Carlos and against the lands and mountain slopes that his soul inhabited? And if he could not stop it, what could he do to turn such violence away from these people and their world?

He was still standing there, thinking these thoughts when Alfonso came over to tear him away. Dear, kind Alfonso: as warm and considerate and predictable as Carlos was fierce, fiery and unpredictable.

'Come on, Mono. There's nothing else you can do just now. Let things rest and we talk about this later, OK? Come back to the house and we can have something to perk us all up.'

It was a brilliant, sunny day in Bogotá. Downtown, not far from the Universidad de los Andes, the big Triple F tower block dominated the skyline, dwarfing the surrounding competition of bank, hotel and business buildings.

Looking out of her top office window Karin noticed a couple of big black birds, *chulos*, circling nearby that must have strayed out over the city: idly wheeling in the blue, looking down on the streets full of cars, buses and people hurrying by. Those birds seemed to remind her of a different world, but she shook her head and returned her focus to the task she had set herself that morning. No time to be dreaming.

Karin was browsing through a stack of magazine and newspaper articles that had been downloaded from the Internet, plus several that she had had delivered direct to her office. They included numerous reports from Europe, North America and a few from countries as distant as India and Argentina. There were several ideas here. First, if the international arts festival she was pursuing was to have any media impact, it had to concentrate on quality, not quantity. Secondly, if quality and media coverage were the objective, then better to specialise in one art form only and focus on a contrast of styles from different nations and cultures.

What should that be? A big concert with singers and musicians from all quarters of the globe? Somehow a popular concert did not seem right. Maybe drama? From Shakespeare to modern theatre? Possible – though different languages from different cultures presented a complication. Film festivals were not such a good idea – there were so many others in the world to compete against.

Dance was Karin's preferred option; it had no obvious competition from any other event in the region and there was no language problem. Ideas started to snowball. There was a feature on Lovisa Berglund, choreographer of an avant-garde dance troupe from Stockholm that had just wowed the critics in New York. She started chasing numbers that might lead her to the Swedish group's agent. That led her to London. Yes, she learned, there was a possibility of fitting in a performance in Bogotá; they would call back and confirm later, but would this proposed international dance festival be interested in ballet as well? The Bolshoi had just been informed of a cancellation in Los Angeles, California, so, if the price was right, they might just consider a South American extension. It would not be the full company, just some key names – a prima donna and her partners. Would Bogotá be interested? Certainly!

It was now a matter of settling dates, discussing prices and confirming interest on both sides. Karin was certain that, once two famous dance performances were placed on the bill – one at the start of the festival, the other to close it – there would be absolutely no problem in getting others to participate: a modern dance troupe from New York; tango from Buenos Aires; salsa from Cali; maybe an Indian or Thai troupe to add an Asian flavour. She insisted with the agents in London that, if they could get them both, the Berglund and Bolshoi visits should be no more than a week apart; otherwise there was no deal.

Agreed. Karin thought she should warn her boss. No specific figure had been mentioned yet, but costs were bound to escalate. Then the phone rang. Just as she was thinking of him, so he called. And he was sounding particularly cheerful.

'Karin – can you come in, please?'

Fields held the door open for his personal assistant. He was beaming all over his face and he took her by the arm to sit her in front of him on the sofa. He had a lot he wanted to say.

'Karin, what's the name of this researcher you are going to fly out here to undertake our environmental audit?'

'Matthew Williams. Why?'

'Yes, he's the one. Well, he has apparently been saying nice things about us on the BBC World Service. I've just had an e-mail from corporate headquarters in Geneva to congratulate us.'

'Well, that's great, but he hasn't seen us yet. He's coming next month.' Karin looked puzzled. She leaned back a little and crossed her legs.

'No, but apparently you must have dazzled him because he has a favourable impression of our green agenda and has recently mentioned it in some televised debate. Headquarters picked it up and are saying well done. So – well done!' Fields reached across and tapped her on the knee to emphasise the point.

'Thank you, Morten. I'm pleased we are making them sit up and take notice. That was what you wanted, wasn't it?'

'Absolutely, I think you are doing a great job for me and I've now got a way to say thank you. They've asked me to attend their next board meeting in six weeks' time. Would you like to come with me to Switzerland?'

Karin's heart jumped. A trip to Switzerland! She sat up.

'I'd love to. That's simply brilliant. Are you sure you want me there?'

'Of course I am. You won't only be good company for me but I want you there for the impact you are going to have on the Chairman and his acolytes. As you say – we want them to sit up and take notice of us and one way or the other we are going to transform the image they have of Triple F Colombia!'

Fields got up smiling and walked around the sofa. It was a ploy he had often used before when he wanted to have a good look at her.

'The meeting will probably go over a couple of days and we will also need two days for flights there and back so we might as well take a week in all. I'll send you through the details. We will stay in the same hotel where the meeting is taking place. Book the best flights and rooms, please. This is going to be an important occasion.'

Fields paused and came back to sit in front of her. He looked serious.

'Karin, I want you to know what has been going on between me and the Board and why having you with me on this trip is important.' He paused again to ensure that he had her full attention. He need not have worried; she sat up on the edge of the sofa, staring at him.

'To be honest, the reason why I am the CEO of Triple F in Colombia is because the Board wanted me out of the way. I was perhaps a bit too successful in the USA and a bit too pushy for their taste, do you see? They thought they would give me the post here because they reckoned I would be in over my head. The farming side here was in a rut and the mining operation was losing money and going under. What with the news of terrorist attacks on us, there was no good news coming out of Triple F Colombia. Add to that the fact that my Spanish is almost non-existent, so they thought managing things out here would be too difficult, I'd make a mess of it and it would give them the excuse to get rid of me.'

Fields looked up. He bit his lip. 'Karin – they had it in for me. Maybe some on the Board thought I was too big for my boots and it was time to take me down a peg or two. All the years I was working to impress them in the States, they were thinking of ways to try and make my life impossible. They even promoted my wife – you've seen her – who was working with me then and that started the process that led eventually to my marriage falling apart. Moving me here to Bogotá was to be just another nail in my coffin.'

Fields shook his head and looked as if he had been through a tough time. Karin's eyes widened. This was an insight into his personal struggles that she had never guessed existed. Her heart went out to him.

'But thanks to you and others here, things are beginning to turn around. Managing in Bogotá with you has recently been a dream. The gold price has soared thanks to worldwide demand plus financial instability in the US and Europe, and taking over TMG's failing operation in Puracé gives us the chance to make mining here really profitable. Our share price has been rising. We have been able to borrow cheaply on the strength of that and more investment is thus on its way. We can afford to run arts festivals and sponsor research in the environment. The more we make news in those quarters, the more our image improves, the more our share price climbs and the more investments we can make. Our profits will inevitable catch up. It's a win-win situation now. I've been sending this sort of news through to Geneva regularly since you've been here and up until now I have heard nothing. Now there is a chink of light shining through the curtain they've put around me. I'm invited to the next board meeting.'

Here Fields took a deep breath and looked closely into Karin's eyes.

'You've got to understand what this means. They did not invite me last year ... but this year – yes – they want to see me. Either it is to say, "Thank you very much, we are closing you down ..." or "Thank you very much, you are doing a great job and we are going to back your expansion in future." Do you see? It is make or break time.'

Fields stood up and offered Karin a hand to stand next to him.

'I want you to help me make it in Geneva. Make them think they cannot close us down. Make them think that there is too much talent and too much potential out here. Make them think they cannot sack me and stop everything here. I need you to help me win them over in Geneva.'

Not for the first time, Morten Fields took her breath away. What a responsibility! She looked into Fields's eyes and saw that he meant every word. She trusted him. She took a step forward, put a hand on his shoulder and kissed him on the cheek. He tried to reach out to her but she stepped back and lowered her eyes.

'Thank you for telling me all this. Thank you for putting your trust in me. I never suspected any of this was going on and what a burden it must have been for you. Thank you again for saying this – I'll do all I can, everything, to help you. I only hope I can repay your faith in me.'

Karin looked absolutely sincere. And absolutely beautiful. Fields had to exercise all his self-control to hold himself back from throwing himself at her. For a second, he was lost for words. All he could do was to hold and squeeze her hand. The air between them was charged with electricity and both could feel it.

Then Fields stumbled back to his desk. When he found his voice he was surprised himself at the emotion that he could not quite disguise.

'Thank you, Karin. Every day I think appointing you was the best thing I've ever done here in Bogotá ... Can you go and book the flights and hotel, please? Then when you've done that I think we both need to go out and have lunch!'

They were both in high spirits when they went out for lunch. Karin was wearing some new stiletto shoes to match her power suit and nearly stumbled as she passed through the glass doors of the Triple F building and out on to the street. She had to laugh at herself as Fields rushed forward to hold her arm and steady her. Neither noticed a man with fair hair and deep-blue eyes who was staring at them as they passed him by on their way to the restaurant.

Lunch was in the same place as before. Fields was on top form and splashing out the champagne on his favourite companion as usual. The staff in the restaurant picked up on the mood and were hovering around catering for everything their wealthy client might wish for. Karin was all smiles, too. The more she got to know Fields and like him, the more relaxed she felt in his company. And, of course, this only spurred Fields's high spirits.

Karin brought up the subject of the arts festival.

'Morten, I think we are going to be able to take some more good news to the Board in Geneva.'

'How's that?' Fields was all ears.

'Well, I'm waiting to hear back from some agents in London. They are looking for a week to fix up a famous dance troupe from Sweden to visit us, plus a contingent from the Bolshoi ballet. They promised to call back soon and I'm sure they are going to charge us a high price. Of course, I'll need your go-ahead to confirm everything. But if it is OK with you, once that is set up I can pull in supporting acts from all over the world to the Triple F Bogotá Dance Festival. It will be big news. The critics will love it. It will be in all the international press.'

'Russian ballet! The Bogotá Dance Festival! I love it! I love you! Karin – if we can get this confirmed and out in the media before we fly to Geneva, it will be just the thing we need.'

'And we should have Matthew Williams with us here by that time. Maybe we can have a preliminary report from him as well?'

Fields held up his glass of champagne: 'Here's to my star

witness in Geneva. I'll let you tell them all that. There will be an evening reception before the start of the board meeting proper and I'll introduce you to the members of the Board then. It's a black-tie event where they like to wallow in their own importance. Get yourself fitted out and buy yourself the most beautiful ball gown in Bogotá. Charge it to me. If there's nothing suitable here, I'll fly you to the States to find one. We are going to make them sit up, remember? Your dance festival, our environmental audit, my profit projections ... add to that your beautiful looks and their stuffy old ways ... we are going to make them sit up, all right!

Karin smiled, her eyes twinkling. Fields gulped his champagne. God – he couldn't wait to get her to that hotel.

3

Intimate Liaisons

Six weeks flew by. In that time the Berglund and the Bolshoi dance groups had been signed up to arrive in January next and Public Relations had promoted the Bogotá Dance Festival far and wide. Matthew Williams had arrived in Colombia and been assigned to Alejandro González to establish his research base in Popayán. Karin had been measured up for a ball gown by a top dress designer flown in from Milan and was just days away from taking delivery. Fields had been locked away with his accountants for two weeks getting all the balance sheets in order and putting together investment plans, geological surveys and profit projections. Reservations had been made, tickets had arrived and both Fields and Karin were getting nervous about what was awaiting them in Geneva.

Claudia was almost as excited as her flatmate.

'I am so envious of you, shooting off to Europe like this, and Carolina is, too. But we both wish you every success. Just about everyone here now knows what's riding on this trip so make sure you knock 'em dead. The way you've been looking recently I'm sure you will. You've been positively glowing. Get those guys eating out of your hand!'

'Thank you, Claudia. You and Morten have both said the same but I really don't know if I can. This is such an important occasion and I only hope I am up to it.'

'Don't underestimate yourself. You're smart. You're not just a pretty face and they are going to realise that as soon as they talk to you. Men and women in their position might have money and power but they've probably not had an original thought, or met an original thinker, in decades. And don't forget to let some of those old men get a glance of your boobs!'

At the same time as these comments were being made, Morten Fields was thinking much along the same lines. His companion in Switzerland was going to be the surprise component in his appearance at the board meeting. They think they know what they are going to get in inviting me along, Fields said to himself, but I'm going to shake them up in ways they least expect. Karin Roth is going to be the living embodiment of that. I might not have changed from being the pushy thorn in their sides I've always been but, if I can pull profits and beauties like Karin out of Bogotá, then they will have to think again about their image of Triple F Colombia. He licked his lips as he lifted his suitcase on to his bed to start packing. Confronting the members of the Board at that first evening reception was going to be the site of his first victory and once momentum had been established he hoped he would be able to go on and win the war.

It was not too long before the big day arrived. A long flight from Bogotá, with a transfer in Madrid, brought them to Geneva. Then it was a taxi ride to the Hôtel d'Angleterre and two adjoining rooms for the tired travellers. They arrived in the evening and had a little less than twenty-four hours to prepare for the official reception and what would be the informal opening of business. The board meeting proper started at 10 a.m. the following day.

Karin loved the hotel. It was old fashioned but had been recently remodelled and perfectly equipped for business. The service was impeccable; the rooms and fittings comfortable and luxurious without being over the top. Fields was at his gentlemanly best, thanking his companion for getting all the arrangements right, kissing her on the cheek and trusting she would sleep well and be thoroughly rested before the start of proceedings the next day.

The next afternoon butterflies were flying in Karin's stomach. She had had her hair washed and dried: long, very dark brown, falling into waves over her shoulders. Make-up was simple – not overdone, just black eyeliner and red lipstick to match the ball gown. The long evening dress was beautifully cut, clung to her figure and swayed when she walked. She knocked on the adjoining door for Morten to come and see and check her over.

He came in and just goggled.

Karin grinned.

'Do you like it?'

'Do I like it? You look absolutely fabulous. Excuse me while I go back out and calm down – you know that this is really the red rag to the bull ...' He promptly did as he said, pausing in the doorway to look back and gaze again. He did not remember how much the corporation had paid for the dress designer to fly out and make up this outfit for her but whatever it was it was worth every penny. He took a deep breath and returned.

'Karin – I'll say it again. You look spectacular and this is going to be some night to remember. The reception starts in just over fifteen minutes but with you looking like that I don't think we should go down too early. I'll knock in three-quarters of an hour and then we will go – is that OK?'

'Fine, Morten. It's just that I'm so nervous if I don't hang on to you going in I'm sure I will trip over and faint. Look after me until I get my bearings, won't you?'

'If you can hang on to me all night, it won't be long enough, so far as I'm concerned,' smiled Fields, and he meant it. 'But I have a feeling there will be lots of others who will want to have your company tonight, so have no fear. In forty-five minutes, then.'

The reception room was thronging with people when they arrived but they parted like the Nile waters when Karin came in on the arm of Morten Fields. She, of course, knew no one, but a number of dinner-jacketed men made straight for Morten to say hello and be introduced. She lost count of most of the names but two stuck close by – a polite, rather formal Swiss gentleman with greying hair called Wilhelm and an over-familiar Australian named Brian who gave every impression of having hair sprouting all over his chest. Morten seemed to know these two quite well – he stopped to chat to Wilhelm while the Australian sidled up and wanted to know Karin as well and as quickly as possible.

'It's Karen, is it?' he said, getting her name wrong. 'And where did Morten dig you up from?'

'He didn't dig me up from anywhere,' said Karin sweetly. 'I'm not some mineral resource.' She noticed a waiter passing by. 'Could you get me a glass of white wine, please?'

As the Australian obliged, Karin said hello to the Swiss gentleman, trying out her German: '*Guten Abend, Wilhelm. Ich freue mich Sie zu treffen.*'

Both Morten and Wilhelm stopped to look at her. Brian the Australian stopped also, frozen out with two glasses of wine in his hand.

'*Guten Abend, Karin,*' said Wilhelm with a big smile and a bow.

'I didn't know you could speak German,' said Fields in surprise.

'Well, I don't really. I haven't used it in years but my father was German so I've always retained an interest. Excuse me, Wilhelm,' Karin returned the bow, 'if I do not continue this conversation in your own language.'

'Of no matter, my dear. Thank you for taking the trouble – very kind of you indeed. However, if we Swiss want to do business here we are accustomed to speaking English. You are with Morten, but you are not Colombian, I suspect?'

'No. I am English, but settled in Colombia. A beautiful country – do you know it?'

Wilhelm shook his head sadly. 'Regrettably not. These days I do not travel far from Geneva, though in my time I have seen many countries with Triple F. Latin America not included, I have to say.'

The conversation naturally flowed from here to a discussion of a number of international locations with Morten and Wilhelm comparing notes on where they had been. Karin took the opportunity of thanking the Australian for her wine but kept him at a distance until others arrived to break up the party and introduce themselves.

With a sideways glance and a wink, Morten introduced Karin to the Chairman of the Board, another grey-haired Swiss called Richard; an Englishman named George, and a rather obese American whom people referred to as John or sometimes Jack. Judging by the way others revolved around them, these three were clearly the more senior decision-makers on the Board. There were a number of other faces that came and went in the course of the next hour – only one woman of note, a tall American in her forties named Julie who was instantly friendly and a twinkly-eyed Spaniard from Madrid whom Karin immediately warmed to and could chatter away to enthusiastically, recovering her *madrileño* accent.

The reception room was full of mostly inconsequential small talk, fed by wine and canapés. but then a string quartet suddenly started playing. Karin was next to Julie and the Spaniard, Gustavo.

'How lovely!' said Karin. 'Something really nice to listen to at last.'

Gustavo nearly choked with laughter. Julie smiled at her.

'Yes, it can get a bit tiresome, can't it?' she said. 'So many male egos on display. Do excuse me, Gustavo, but you are as bad as the rest of them.'

Gustavo nearly choked again.

'*Gracias, señora.* You are so kind to me! But now that the music is playing, perhaps one of you dear ladies will be so kind as to take my ego with you on a quick waltz around the dance floor?'

Julie looked at Karin. Karin couldn't wait: she held out her hand to the Spaniard, curtsied and waited for him to lead her forward. This he did with panache. People stepped aside and the two of them – the black dinner-jacketed and very upright Castilian and his blazing red young English rose – waltzed out into the centre of the room.

Morten Fields was instantly jealous and came over to Julie, a compatriot, and insisted that they two must join the other couple. Julie did not demur. She was not exactly competitive but equally she was not going to let the younger woman have all the fun.

The string quartet were clearly pleased at the reaction they had produced and so played up and played along with what they hoped would keep the dancing going. They were not unsuccessful. Other couples slowly joined in: Geneva may not be Vienna and business receptions were not normally occasions for dancing but something was in the air that evening that persuaded some corporation executives to step forward and take their wives to the floor.

As soon as he could, Fields tapped Gustavo on the shoulder and demanded that they exchange partners. He wanted to get his arms around the woman he had brought here. Karin curtsied again, said goodbye to one partner and smiled up at the next. She was enjoying herself at last.

'Goodness, I am so glad that the music started,' she said. 'I couldn't keep going just nodding and smiling and saying sweet nothings all night!'

'You are doing just fine, Karin. More than fine. So many people keep asking me who you are and where I found you. I've said very little so you are going to tantalise them all week. One thing you can try, though, if you will. I'm going to deliver you up next to the Chairman of the Board so see if you can get him out here, will you?'

'OK. I'll do my duty,' Karin promised.

The two of them swirled around to finish their dance in front of the Chairman, his wife, and the two other important members of the Board that had greeted Karin earlier. Karin had not met the wives properly, so she politely introduced herself this time. She thought she had better not offend the ladies of such important men, especially if she was going to try and get one or two of them out on to the dance floor. She guessed, or rather hoped, that these elegant ladies were probably rather bored with men who were immersed in business and slow to involve their wives in something a little more diverting.

The usual niceties started the conversation and Karin waited for Morten to get Richard, the Chairman, pontificating on something or other before she broke in. She spoke first to his wife, making sure he could hear.

'Would you say that chairmen of large corporations like Triple F are entrepreneurs, decision-makers and risk-takers?' She posed the question with a teasing note to her voice.

'Of course!' Richard butted in. He wasn't going to let anyone answer for him – especially when the questioner was this highly attractive female who had just appeared at his elbow.

Karin grinned at his wife who could see she was up to something that her husband was walking right into.

'Well, I will risk my toes in the next waltz if he might decide to take me out on the dance floor ...' She turned and flashed him a smile. 'Will you risk a waltz with me?'

To Karin's relief, the elegant ladies all broke up, smirking and chuckling.

'Go on, Richard!' said one. 'You can't refuse such a charming request!

'Besides,' his wife chimed in, 'after all these years I want to

see if you can still cut it out there on the dance floor in front
of everybody!'

Karin curtsied decorously, bowing her head but letting her
cleavage show, and waited, smiling, for the Chairman to take
the lead. He blustered and coloured and was damned if he was
not going to rise to the challenge.

A buzz of conversation followed them out into the centre.
Richard was rather portly and not the most coordinated of
movers but he was determined to show his wife that he had
not entirely forgotten what dancing was all about. A much
travelled businessman and a proud Swiss, he was going to
show that it was not just Viennese who knew how to waltz.

Karin recognised his need to show how this business leader
could also lead on the dance floor in front of all these people,
so she did her best to show him off and place him in the spot-
light. Richard huffed and puffed and twirled, rising and falling
as best he could with the music. Karin swirled around him,
covering up any mistakes he made with her skirts and her
grace. They journeyed from one end of the floor and back
again just as the music came to an end. Karin dropped to the
floor, curtseying and showing her gratitude and a good part
of her cleavage again. The Chairman, in response, bowed and
walked stiffly back to his wife with the audience clapping and
cheering behind him. Karin looked at his wife. She quietly
nodded her thanks. Karin silently mouthed her thanks in
return – she was grateful she had not upset her.

The men around Richard congratulated him on his performance and welcomed Karin back to join them. In the time they
had been on the floor others had arrived – including Wilhelm
and Brian, the Australian.

'That was very well done, young lady,' said Wilhelm, 'you
dance very well.'

'Thank you but I'm nothing compared to my friends in
Bogotá. Have you heard of the Triple F Dance Festival we are
setting up there in just over a year?'

'A Triple F Dance Festival?' queried John, the American, who was listening. 'What are you doing organising that?'

'We are active in sponsoring the arts. Why? Don't you think that businesses like ours should be involved in such things?'

Brian, the Aussie, laughed condescendingly. 'We're in the business of natural resource exploitation,' he butted in, 'not entertainment.'

Karin looked at the two men – Australian and American – who had questioned her. She didn't like the expressions she saw.

'I do not think you appreciate how vulnerable multinational businesses like Triple F are in Latin America,' she said cuttingly. 'Europeans have been plundering resources from that continent since the fifteenth century and as a result we have an image problem that managers like you should be sensitive to. As it happens, Colombians will love Triple F for putting on a dance festival. They will certainly not love you for saying you are only interested in exploiting their natural resources. If Triple F wants to make a success of their business in Latin America, as I and Morten do, then we and you have to think long term. A focus on dig it up, ship it out and make a quick profit is a recipe for business disaster!' She stared pointedly at the two who had upset her, as if challenging them to respond.

There was a stunned silence that followed that outburst. Morten took the opportunity to break up the party.

'Excuse me, gentlemen,' he said, sliding between the menfolk and taking Karin's hand, 'but I'm taking this wonderful lady away – before she takes your jobs.' With that he guided her back to the dance floor.

Fields was absolutely beaming. As soon as people started thronging around and the focus of people's attention was diffused, he held her close.

'I think you are simply wonderful!' His eyes were shining at Karin. 'You could not have done that better. First capture the Chairman and then put down his attack dogs. You were beautiful, eloquent, perfect. You absolutely dazzled him and the rest of the auditorium, barring those two idiots.'

He put his arm around her and gave her kiss on the lips. Not too heavy, but something he had been dying to do for months.

'Thank you. Really, thank you. I don't know how I can thank you enough!' He looked deep into her eyes so that she could see how he felt about her. He wondered how she felt about him.

For a moment, Karin's head spun. She had gone from delight and enjoyment with the Chairman to annoyance and frustration with a couple of his acolytes. But that kiss was a surprise and it changed her whole outlook. And it awoke something inside her that was buried deep. She had not been with a man for a long time now and she realised she really missed that. And this man really appreciated her and all the subtle and not so subtle things she had been doing for him.

Karin had looked at Morten before a number of times and liked what she saw. Now, suddenly, her hormones were flowing like electricity coursing through her veins. She wanted to show him what she felt. It was time. She could see no one was looking particularly in their direction, so she reached for his hand and placed it on her breast, looking into his eyes as she did so.

A jolt of lightning surged through them both. Fields was at once intensely aroused. He had to confirm the signal she was sending him.

'I want to get you away from here and into my arms as soon as I can. Do you understand?'

'Yes. I want that too. But … but … you will have to decide when that is best for your reputation among all these people. You need to impress them still, don't you? We can't suddenly disappear.'

They stopped dancing and wandered over to the side of the reception room as if tired and looking for a rest. Karin leaned across and quickly kissed him.

'I'll wait,' she said. 'I'll do my duty first and you can give me my reward later!' She turned and looked back over her shoulder at him, coquettishly. She walked away, leaving him snorting though his nostrils like a bull in chains.

For the next couple of hours the two of them separately circulated the reception room, chatting with members of the Board and their partners. In Karin's case, she was busy making introductions, getting to know the various personnel and their different roles; in Fields's case, he wanted to demonstrate how relaxed and content he was with Triple F Colombia's progress and ensure that the people he met knew it. For both of them, their objective was to change the image of their business; to gently or not so gently emphasise that Triple F Colombia was not some dead-end backwater in this global enterprise but one of the brightest growth centres in an otherwise somewhat depressed world economy.

As Fields had calculated, their two-person, multi-dimensional offensive was having its effect. There was the takeover of a major competitor's asset – the TMG mine; the profit forecast was healthy; favourable news was coming out of Triple F's commitment to environmental safeguards while an international dance festival would be another step forward in transforming the corporation's image. Add to that was the impression created by an intelligent, attractive assistant to Colombia's CEO who possessed excellent interpersonal skills and who seemed to make Morten Fields a more relaxed, less abrasive and more acceptable individual, someone who just might be invited to join the Board on a permanent basis. Fields himself was as good as told how amenable he had become towards the end of the evening by the laconic George White, the English financial director and right-hand man to the Chairman. Colombia had obviously been good for Fields, he was informed. He swiftly rejoined that Colombia was good for Triple F.

Fields was under no illusion as to why the Board was looking more favourably upon him. He knew he had enemies among them and he also knew that all the most optimistic profit projections in the world were of no use against people who had personal objections to his progress in the corporation. Whatever business schools might preach, it was individual chemistry that determined whether or not you got on and in this case it was Karin's chemistry – promoting his case among some of his doubters – that was working to his distinct advantage.

Fields wanted to let his beautiful assistant know just what a good job she was doing and how much it meant to him. Not only did he mean it but it was the perfect opening move in a relationship that he hoped to develop all night. As the reception drew to a close, Karin was flushed with the success she had enjoyed but at the same time she still remembered with annoyance the Australian and American who had tried to belittle her in front of the Chairman. As they walked arm in arm towards the elevator, Fields was anxious to dispense with this distraction.

'Forget those two,' he said. 'Brian is based in Sydney and will not have any influence beyond there with an attitude like he has. Jack you made think twice. He is far from being a fan of mine, nor am I a fan of his, but he is no fool and you made him look like one. The fact is, you were right and he was wrong. So he will now have to take on board what you said. I guess he will. The two Swiss managers, Richard and Wilhelm, certainly like you and Jack won't want to be the odd one out. George White, meanwhile, will be impressed by the balance sheet and nothing else. He is one who thinks long term so there's no problem there. And after them, I had the impression that just about everyone you talked to absolutely loved you. George more or less said that I am a more presentable, more likely character for promotion thanks to you. You have done wonderfully tonight.' Fields picked up Karin's hand and kissed it. 'And you know how I feel about you, don't you?'

The doors to the escalator opened and they got in together.

As the doors closed again, Karin replied with a lingering kiss. Fields put one arm around her waist and for a moment toyed with the idea of stopping the lift with his other – a romantic but totally impractical gesture, he quickly realised. The lift arrived at their floor and so the romantic impulse turned instead to a fumbling for keys and a hurried movement to his room.

Inside, Karin turned to him with a serious expression. Much as she wanted him, she had to stop.

'Morten – we can't: I've got no protection.'

'You don't need it, beautiful!' Fields kissed her and looked deeply into her eyes. 'I have a very low sperm count. I can't get you or any woman pregnant.' He looked hurt, shy, embarrassed.

Not for the first time, Karin's heart went out to him. Here was another surprise at how vulnerable he was: beneath the image of an alpha male who had it all, Fields now shared with her an intimate secret that must for him seem to question his entire masculinity. She loved him for telling her. She flung her arms around his neck and pulled him down on to the bed. Now there was no holding back. Now passion could get hold of both of them and there was no need to delay any longer. For both of them this was a moment that they had been building up to for a very long time. At last they made love.

Switzerland is a beautiful, spectacular country and Geneva, particularly the old centre, is a likewise a highly attractive city. As a site for a developing romance, it has few equals ... but then for all lovers the place where their relationship starts is always very special. So it was for Karin and Morten. With each day's business finished, the evenings took on a magic all of their own. They went out alone together, avoiding all others, and found little restaurants or cafés where they could enjoy each other's company and ignore everyone and everything else. The fact that each business meeting seemed to bring better and better news for Morten and Karin only made each evening even more romantic. For Karin, especially, the days seemed to float by as if in a dream and she didn't want ever to wake up. Yes, Switzerland was special.

When Karin got back to her apartment in Bogotá after the week had finished, everything had changed. Claudia noticed it as soon as she opened the door and welcomed her friend home.

'Karin, what's happened? Tell me – how was it?'

Karin didn't know what to say. She bustled in clutching bags, her face a mix of emotions with her eyes shining and bursting to say something, but not knowing where to start.

'Karin – what is it? It's Morten, isn't it? It must be! Come on – what's been going on between you two?'

Karin dropped everything on the floor and had to sit down. Her flatmate grasped her hand and looked at her. The smile that she saw beaming over Karin's face spread across to her own.

'OK – I get it! You've fallen for him, haven't you?'

'Oh, Claudia, you have no idea. It's been fabulous. He's been fabulous. What a week! At the end of it he's been made Latin American chief of Triple F and he now has a seat on the Board. He says it's all down to me – a ridiculous exaggeration – but I love him for it. We've made love all week. Every night! I can't believe it …'

'*I* can't believe it! You did? All week? Wow – you and Morten Fields.' Claudia shook her head, grinning partly in disbelief, partly in happiness for her friend. 'I have to say that Carolina and I have been talking about you both all the time you've been away. Carolina has been saying that by the end of it all you'd either hate him or go to bed with him, or both … but I never guessed this! You look absolutely transported!'

'I never guessed this either. What a difference a week makes! Claudia, you should have seen him. He's been wonderful – sometimes a bag of nerves with me in private, asking my opinion, dependent on my support, and then in public I've seen him bursting with confidence and pride, win over the Board and then invite me to join him, praising my influence, pushing our agenda, defending what we've been doing against any critics. I've even had some of them thank me for what I've done for him. Me! As if I've been responsible for his success. But he *has* been successful; Morten is overjoyed about it and he never stopped thanking me, from the first day to the last.'

'Well, this is really going to have people talking at work. The place has been a hive of gossip all week, wondering what was going on. Now, by the sound of it, this should change all sorts of things – I'd love to hear what Morten says about where we are going in the future. And I wonder where you two will be going as well. Triple F boss for all of Latin America, eh? That certainly sounds like something big.'

'Well, we have been talking about it on the flight home. According to Morten, it won't change anything at first. He will be involved in decision-making for all major projects across the continent, but his first priority remains turning things around in Colombia. He says there is still lots to do here – and don't we know that. He may be called away on occasions to other centres, from Mexico City to Santiago de Chile, but they all have their local people in place and he reckons that, barring surprises, they will carry on much as before. The most important change is that we are going to get more investment, more people and more expansion here – our immediate future is one of the brightest in the Americas, North or South.'

Karin's bags were still on the floor where she had dropped them but she could not touch them yet. She and Claudia just looked at each other and laughed. How things change! The future for both of them suddenly looked more optimistic, more fun, more secure.

Then Karin's mobile rang. It was Morten Fields.

As soon as Fields arrived back at his apartment in Bogotá he phoned Alejandro González in Popayán.

'Tell me, Alejandro – how are things going in the new mine? Last time I spoke to you, you still hadn't got things up and working. What's the latest?'

'Well, at last it's dry in there now. We've been pumping the water out for weeks, as you know. The geological team have been down undertaking their survey since you've been away and they are still working at it. Some results are in, apparently, but they are waiting for more before they come back with their projections.'

'OK. What about this man Williams and his environmental audit; you've kept him away from all of this, haven't you?'

'Well, as you know we've spent as long as possible getting him set up here in Popayán and pointing him in the direction we want. I've got him to look at our original Puracé site first and that will keep him busy for some weeks yet. I've assured him we will do all we can to make his work easier and we are all fascinated to hear what he comes up with. As for our new TMG acquisition, he'll get to look at that only later – by which time we hope to have things a bit cleaner. We can expect some bad news when he gets looking at what we've got there, of course, and we'll let him know that TMG are an irresponsible outfit that have given us all sorts of problems, but it will be a little while before we see what he says on that score.'

'Right. Thanks, Alejandro. Our tactic for the time being is to welcome his efforts and agree with his recommendations. How much it will cost we will have to look at when he's gone. If much of it is too expensive – which I guess it will be – we will have to cover it up somehow, but we'll decide that later. In the meantime, has there been any noise from the locals about all the waste you've disposed of?'

'No. They've gone quiet without Díaz, thank God. Your man Smith certainly has an impact.'

'What about that other bastard, El Mono, you warned me about?'

'We've had people out looking for him but he's impossible to find. So long as it stays that way it suits me.'

'Fine. That's good. Let me know if the situation changes. I've some good news. Triple F headquarters in Geneva are delighted with us and we will be getting more investment coming our way as a result. Our profit projections are based, of course, on what we think we will produce from our TMG acquisition, so the sooner our geological team can confirm that the better. That's the one thing I want from you as soon as you can get it to me, understand?'

'Yeah. No problem. I'll let you know when we get all the results. There's one thing more you should know about. Cortés's men picked up a couple of guys from TMG snooping around outside their old mine. We asked them what they were up to and they came out with some line about wanting to know if there was any of their stuff left behind. Would you believe it! It just didn't sound right but that's what they said. Cortés told them to get the hell out and they would be shot if the ever came back. We thought you should know, however.'

'Damn right I should know. Thanks for telling me. Tell Cortés that it sounds like they are up to something, so keep your eyes open. Anything more?'

'No, nothing else. Cortés has already doubled security 'cos he is as suspicious as you. I'll get those geological survey results to you as soon as I can. Is that all?'

'For now, yes. I'll be in touch later. Bye.'

Fields hung up. He was irritated. There was always something to worry about with TMG – the latest news might be nothing or it might be something; no way to tell just yet. Whatever, he thought, it was time to put those concerns aside and to return to something much more satisfying: that other preoccupation in his life right now – Karin Roth. He dialled her mobile.

4

Baby Peter

A very different working relationship evolved between Karin and her boss during the first week that they were back from Switzerland – business-like one moment, fun and intimate the next. Karin nonetheless kept her lover at arm's length until Friday afternoon when he had promised to take her away for the weekend, to his finca. Fields had ordered his driver to bring round the Range Rover at 3 p.m. and the two of them then packed in their weekend bags and set off.

The finca, which Morten Fields had purchased shortly after he had arrived in Colombia, was a couple of hours north-west of the capital city, on the road heading down to the hot country and off the plateau that was called the Bogotá Savannah. The estate was an old hacienda with stables, extensive grounds and an impressive view of the immense, forested mountain slopes close by. It was Fields's usual weekend retreat, a place he could entertain guests, continue working or simply relax alone. Spending time with a beautiful woman there was his preferred occupation, and Karin was not the first he had brought there, but she was certainly the one he valued the most.

The Range Rover deposited the two of them in front of the main entrance to the finca where security guards and the resident housekeeper were already waiting. Fields directed his companion into the main building, leaving guards to fetch the bags. Karin was captivated by the old colonial style of the place – the stone walls, mahogany beams, Spanish-tiled roof and, inside, more mahogany, plush leather sofas and deep-pile carpets. She walked though, drinking in the utter luxury of all the fitments and came to large French windows that opened out on to a swimming pool and Jacuzzi and green fields that stretched way away in front of her.

'Do you like it here, Karin?' asked her host.

'It is very, very impressive,' she replied. 'So this is your week-end hideaway, is it? And all these fields that lead down and around – they are part of this as well?'

'Certainly. You can't see the stables from here but we can go out and ride tomorrow if you wish. After riding tonight, of course!'

Karin spun round and waved a finger at him. 'Morten! Behave yourself!' she cried out.

'Darlin', I always behave. Very professionally, I think were your words.'

Karin smiled at him. 'OK, I guess I asked for that. But give me a moment to get used to all this luxury. I do want to have a look round at first. Switzerland was something that we built up to over weeks. Coming here has been a bit of a rush and I still need time.'

She went out through the French windows and on to the stone patio beside the pool. She suddenly wanted to be alone. It was warm, early evening, the sun was beginning to set and the view of the mountains was calling to her. Looking at it all, she realised what it was that was unsettling her, and why she needed time to get used to this. The last time she looked at such a view was with a very different man and not at all surrounded by such luxury. Her eyes unexpectedly filled with tears. She was a very different woman now. She was living in a very different world. But was all this what she really wanted?

A footstep beside her broke her thoughts. Forget that, she told herself, just enjoy what you have for the time being and see where it takes you. She blinked away her tears and turned to face her host.

'Everything OK?' he enquired.

'I'm sorry ... this is all so new to me still. Yes – everything is fine. Let's go back in.'

The mood between them had subtly shifted as Karin's emotions had swung from initial delight to something much cooler. For the time being she wanted distance between them but an hour of busying about, unpacking and then preparing for the evening meal began to restore her fun-loving nature. By the time it came to sit down and dine she was ready again to resume the battle of the sexes that raged between them.

'Something to drink?' asked Fields, lifting a bottle of champagne out of its ice bucket.

'Champagne again, Morten? You are becoming boring. If there is nothing else you can offer me I shall have to seriously consider my position here.'

'Your position here, my beautiful one, will be something I will determine later. As for another wine, how does Napoleon's favourite burgundy appeal to you?'

'Mr Fields, you shock me. I shall accept your offer of burgundy, however, and consider your other demands later.' She proffered her glass.

As Fields went to fetch the red wine, a thought suddenly occurred to Karin – just how many other women had this man entertained in this fashion? She might as well ask him.

'Mr Fields, before we go any further I have a rather urgent request to make of you ...'

Fields returned to the table with an open bottle and a smile on his face. 'An urgent request? Please do not resist your urges. Ask away.' He began pouring the burgundy.

'I will. I want to know how many other women have you tempted to this hideaway before me?'

Fields stopped in surprise. 'My dear, on such a fine evening as this, that is a very impolite question!'

'Nonetheless, I refuse to go any further with this conversation until you have answered me,' Karin looked teasingly at him over the top of her wineglass. 'I do not suppose I am the first woman you have ensnared here, so: Am I one of very few or one of many?'

'My dearest Karin, if you must know then I confess you are not the very first but you are undoubtedly the very best I have ever seen grace this humble abode. And the very, very few that have been here before were here long before I met you and none of them were ever invited back again. That will not be the situation in your case, of course.' Fields put down the bottle, then lifted and tipped his own glass in Karin's direction. 'And now I have done you the honour of answering your question, I must ask mine: how many men have you entertained in your time in Colombia? I also wish to know if I am one of a few or one of many.'

Karin lowered her eyes demurely. 'You can ask but that is not only an impolite question, but also a forbidden question to ask of any lady. As a lady, I therefore refuse to answer you. But … but if you remember our first encounter in that hotel in Geneva I think there was a clue in what I said to you then that might satisfy your curiosity.'

Fields sighed at his companion: what a beautiful reply. She was absolutely bewitching. He stood up, leant across the table and reached for her hand.

'Goddammit, you're wonderful!' he said, kissing her hand and then sitting down again, mightily aroused. 'As soon as this meal is over, I'm taking you straight upstairs!'

The housekeeper came in with their meal while this exchange was going on but, not being an English speaker, she could not understand the repartee between them. She retired as soon as both had been served. Karin then replied to her host.

'Mr Fields, that is very impatient, not to say extremely forward of you. I shall take my time over this meal and give it its due respect. And you will do the same for me.' She lifted her knife and fork and flashed him another teasing smile. 'Bon appétit!'

Karin greatly enjoyed teasing Fields and his reactions consistently confirmed her impression of what a cultured gentleman he was and how she could thus relax and enjoy his company. And enjoy his company she did, all weekend: that night, the following day riding around his estate and Saturday night into the Sunday.

Karin had just finished packing up Sunday morning when she decided to take a final stroll around the main building and look across and down to the stables. While doing so she noticed a big man some distance away, stroking the horses and playing with one of the guard dogs that regularly patrolled the grounds. She recognised him as the man she had seen going to Fields's office a couple of times before. Claudia had once remarked what a frightening, nasty piece of work he was – yet here he was at Morten Fields's finca, playing with the dogs and horses.

She asked Fields who he was when they were out front, loading the Range Rover.

'Yes, don't you worry about him. That's Leopold Smith. I've known him for years and he comes here when I need him as a bodyguard. Not always necessary but you never know. If you ever meet him, don't take offence if he ignores you – that's just his way. The most important thing about him for my sake is that he is loyal and totally, utterly fearless. And for your sake also – if he knows you are with me, then you know you are safe, too.' Fields stowed the last bag in the Range Rover. 'That's it now. We will have a light lunch and then I think we are done. Ready to go?'

Karin nodded.

'Enjoyed your stay?'

Karin nodded again. 'Oh yes.'

'Want to come back again?'

'Does that mean I am more important than all those other women you've had here?'

Fields laughed. 'Oh yes, much better than all those others ... and the only one with a return invitation!'

'In which case, Mr Fields, I shall graciously accept your offer to return. Thank you.' Karin bowed ostentatiously.

'Come on in and have lunch!' Fields turned his back, waving away her play-acting, and walked smiling back into the building. He was pleased with himself: it had been a good, sexually satisfying and thoroughly enjoyable weekend.

The next weekend Karin wanted to spend with Claudia and attend to a hundred and one domestic issues that she had not had time to see to before. Fields was persistent about another liaison, however, so the weekend after that was the occasion for the much heralded return to his lair. So far as Fields was concerned, that occasion was ultimately as satisfying as the first they had shared there – but he had to wait longer and try harder to win her. She was poised, elegant, sensual and intelligent and refused to be taken for granted. If he wanted to satisfy his desire for her, he had somehow to rise to her challenges and outwit her first of all ... and the longer their relationship went on the more and more she made him work and suffer for it.

Time passed and it was well over a month since he had first bedded Karin, and Fields was becoming obsessed with her. Working with her outside his office, he began to wonder what she was doing during the day and had to keep finding reasons to go out and interrupt her. Meanwhile, his weekday nights were filled with dreams of her, some of them quite explicit and not at all lady-like. Weekends he was desperate to invite her to his finca – a third occasion away she kept putting off, much to his overwhelming frustration.

Karin, on the other hand, felt increasingly in control of their liaison and felt more and more content, confident and in possession of where this affair was going. She enjoyed this state of affairs for a couple more weeks until one fateful

Saturday morning at home with Claudia, after she had post-poned Fields's advances once more, she suddenly had to get out of bed very early and rush to the toilet, feeling terribly dizzy and sick. She threw up twice, feeling absolutely awful.

Both girls looked at each other meaningfully that morning. What was this? Karin was never sick.

'Is this what I think it is?' asked Claudia. She stared at Karin: they were both sitting on the floor, outside the bathroom.

'It can't be,' said Karin, white-faced. 'Morton is infertile; I've already told you.'

'So you have,' said Claudia. 'But maybe you are both wrong … When was your last period?'

'Oh shit!' swore Karin. 'Don't say that. This can't be morning sickness.'

'Then tell me what the fuck it is,' swore Claudia. 'You'd better check it out.'

'I'm not going to any Triple F medical centre,' said Karin. 'I'm not having anyone know within the corporation. I'm sure they've all been talking about us for ages.'

'Oh they sure have! I won't say it's been a flagrant affair but let's just say that Carolina is green with envy and has been looking daggers at you recently.'

'Oh Claudia, has she? Oh shit, shit, shit. I don't want to be pregnant. I really don't. He's a lovely man but she can have him now.' Karin burst into tears. She suddenly realised that deep down things were changing inside her. She feared the worst.

It took them an hour to get ready. Claudia had phoned around relations and found the clinic where her cousin worked and it was a place she hoped no friends and contacts would otherwise know about. The two of them took a taxi there. Then it was the routine tests that all girls of their age know about and either fear or get terribly excited about. They both sat outside in the waiting room, thankfully half empty, waiting for the medic to call them back in for the result. Still white-faced, Karin was feeling dreadful and at the same time almost resigned to hear what she now felt was inevitable. She knew her own body.

The doctor called them both in. He could read what was going on between them and understood that the news he was going to give was not going to be welcome. He looked at them both and saw Claudia holding on to her friend's hand.

He did his job as gently as he could: 'Miss Roth, I have to say you are going to have baby. There can be no mistake.'

He waited for the shock to wash over them. Claudia gave a gasp. Karin made not a sound but her eyes filled with tears.

'Thank you, Doctor. That's what we thought,' Karin said.

'I should advise you to fix up another appointment in a couple of weeks' time and we will make arrangements from there to look after you throughout your pregnancy.'

'Thank you very much, Doctor. We will do precisely that.'

The two girls walked out in a daze. Claudia sorted out the appointment and phoned for a taxi. Karin just wanted to go back home.

As soon as they got back, Karin stretched out on the sofa in their apartment and just lay there, trying to come to terms with the news. She couldn't move; she didn't know what to think; she just lay silent with tears running down her face.

Claudia felt terrible. Whatever pain her friend was going through was simultaneously being communicated to her. There were lots of insignificant things to do and tidy away in their flat but she flitted here and there not knowing what to do, visiting the same places, picking things up, putting them back, getting worked up and achieving nothing. At last after half an hour she sat down next to her friend and had to talk to her.

'What are you going to do, K?' she asked.

'I'll have the baby,' Karin replied. 'That's all I know at present. I know it with every fibre of my being.' She turned and looked at her friend, 'it is the only certainty I have at present.'

311

Claudia nodded. She could see the determination in her companion's eyes. 'When are you going to tell him?'

'Not yet. That is all I know at present. Not yet. Don't ask me why ... I don't know why. But I cannot tell him and don't want to tell him yet.' She was thinking out loud. 'But I'll tell my mother in England – when I have the strength to. Probably tomorrow: I'll see how I feel.'

She lay back again. Having said that there was now a sort of calmness that spread over her. It came from the centre of her womb and filtered into every part of her. Her baby had started dictating her life; she knew it and loved it even now. Claudia watched the peacefulness grow and the pain vanish and she understood. She put her arms across and gave her friend a kiss on the cheek.

'You look wonderful,' she whispered. 'And whatever happens we will see this out together.'

Karin turned her head and smiled; then she closed her eyes. 'Thank you' was all she said. It was time to sleep.

It took Karin a couple of days to get up the nerve to phone her mother. Before that she had to go to work and try to figure out how she was going to relate to the father of her unborn child. She tried to act as normally as possible. Fortunately, on Monday there was a lot of business for both her and her boss to attend to, so things were much easier than she expected.

It was Tuesday morning, bright and early in Colombia but a little after midday in England, when she got through. Her mother's reaction was as expected, and she said all the things she knew she would say and she guessed she deserved.

'What do you mean you're pregnant? How can that be? Why didn't you have any protection?' Mother was beside herself.

Karin tried to explain.

'Are you crazy or what? Do you believe everything a man tells you? Of course he's going to say all sorts of things like that. You're a grown woman, aren't you? When are you going to wake up? My God, Karin, I despair of you sometimes ...'

Yes, yes, yes. Karin sighed: mother distrusted all men and always had done. Ever since father had left her before Karin could walk.

'No, Mother, I haven't told him yet. Why? Because I'm not ready. Yes of course I'm going to tell him. Will he stand by me? I suppose he will. He's not all bad, you know. Really. Will he support me? I guess he will; he can certainly afford it. What? Yes, I have picked a rich one, as if that is important! Yes, Mother, I know these things are important ...'

And so it went on. Finally she hung up, promising to phone back or Skype on the following weekend. Karin relaxed, having done her duty, and accepted all that her mother had said. She was bound to be worried about her daughter: she knew next to nothing about the life she lived and the people she lived with in Colombia, so, looking at things from her mother's perspective, she must be intensely concerned.

Work that week was not so difficult. Having got through the first day, Karin simply kept going. Morten Fields was happy and busy attending to a number of problems that the new chief of Triple F Latin America was required to unravel. That was a relief. The only thing she was really wary about was when inevitably she was invited to stay with him for the weekend. She had to have her reply ready to resist the pressure he was going to exert on her. She did not have to wait long.

'Karin, can you come in, please?' Fields buzzed through.

'On my way!'

Karin opened the door and saw her boss rising behind his desk, on his way to greet her. She closed the door behind her and accepted his kiss.

'Karin, I have to be away this weekend, travelling to Lima and back. I'll see you here next Wednesday, most likely. And then will you come with me to my finca on the Friday evening following? It really is time to celebrate a third visit to my hide-away. I insist!'

'Morten, I can't. Not that weekend. I really can't. I'm very sorry but I have an important medical appointment that I must go to. No – listen to me: it's women's business and I'm not going to tell you any more but honestly I do not want to reschedule and I simply must sort this out. I promise to go with you another time after that. Promise. OK? But for the time being you are going to have to be patient with me.' She gave him a quick kiss. 'That's what relationships are all about, aren't they? Give and take? You give me that weekend and I'll give you another.'

Fields groaned. 'OK, OK. But I'll hold you to that promise. You have my agenda so make sure you fill it out with a date for us both: two weekends from now. Do it this instant!'

'Yes, Mr Fields. I will certainly do as you request.' Karin agreed with a mock salute ... and then added as an afterthought: 'But, Morten, if you are travelling to Peru this weekend, then you make sure you behave yourself. I'm very sorry you will have to wait for me – just make sure you *do* wait! How do I know what you businessmen get up to on your trips away?'

She spun on her heels and glanced back over her shoulder at him, giving him a very meaningful look as she left the office. Fields was left there beached on the carpet to mull over her last words – she heard him give a strangled roar as the door closed between them.

One week later and Fields was due back from his Peru trip. He was obsessed as always with seeing Karin and in his absence, as her pregnancy had progressed, she had started to glow with health and attractiveness. Fields, of course, did not know the reason for this, but from the moment he saw her on his return he was absolutely captivated by the way she looked. Karin welcomed him back at the airport – she had made all the travel arrangements so knew the flight he was on and it was typical of her to be there waiting for him, giving him a hug and a kiss on his arrival.

'My God, Karin, you are absolutely beautiful!' Fields blurted out as soon as he could find his voice. 'What have you been doing to yourself while I've been away?'

Karin blushed. She knew what would be coming next so sought to deflect it. 'That is exactly the question that I was going to ask you! So, have you been behaving yourself? Or have you been seeing any women in Lima?'

'With the way you look, darling, you have no fear of any competition whatsoever.' As if to emphasise that statement, Fields dumped his bags on the ground in the middle of the airport concourse. He took both her hands. 'But if you think I can wait another week and a half before I take you away with me you are very mistaken. This medical appointment of yours will have to wait!'

The medical appointment, of course, was Karin's first check-up on her pregnancy. There was no way was she giving in on this, but she was nonetheless bowled over by the passion in his advance so offered a compromise.

'Morten, please, I've told you I can't go this weekend. But, since you insist, I'll go back with you to your apartment and stay with you tonight.' She kissed him. He was the father of her child. Her feelings towards him were beginning to change. She would not tell him yet, but it would not be long now before she did and in the meantime her heart was telling her to draw him in closer. She put her arms around him and kissed him again.

Fields was ecstatic. He had been horny all weekend and, indeed, on a couple of occasions he had sought the services of one of the professional women that he had found in the Lima hotel bar, but, besotted as he was with the woman in front of him now, those liaisons had not satisfied him. What was promised this evening, however, was going to keep him warm for several days to come.

'Karin, you have made me very, very happy. Let's go straight away!' Fields picked up his bags again and followed Karin to the Triple F limousine that was waiting for them.

The Saturday morning following, Claudia accompanied Karin to her first check-up and ultrasound examination. The doctor was pleased to see how calm and prepared his patient had now become. Her blood pressure was fine; the baby's heart beat was strong and it was, he estimated, two months old now. Did that conform to the mother's experience?

Yes, Karin thought. That corresponds with the week in Geneva: she must have fallen pregnant almost straight away. With that information, she decided then and there that she would tell the father as soon as she saw him next. She wondered what his reaction would be.

On Monday morning Karin went to her office feeling more than a little nervous. Her boss's door was closed, however, indicating that he was already locked in a meeting and probably did not want to be disturbed. She nonetheless buzzed through on the intercom. He would not like that.

'Sorry to bother you, Mr Fields, but I'll need to see you as soon as you finish. Something important has come up.'

She heard an annoyed reaction. 'Yes! In a moment!'

Karin now felt even more nervous. She wondered who was in there with him – there was no meeting scheduled in the agenda for such an hour, so early in the week. There was nothing for it, however, but to wait, and wait, and wait … and become more and more agitated.

At last the door opened, then closed, and one big man came out alone. It was Leopold Smith, whom she had last seen at Fields's finca. Smith walked straight across to the elevator shaft and waited while Karin pressed for the lift. Expressionless as always, he looked round at Karin and then what he said took her totally by surprise:

'You look pregnant.'

Karin gasped. Where on earth had that comment come from? He didn't know her. But he'd got it completely right with just one glance. Karin was still speechless and amazed as this enormous enigma of a man got into the lift and, impassively, pressed the button to descend.

Karin went back to her desk and, still somewhat in shock, buzzed her boss again.

'Are you alone now? Can I come in?'

She got the go-ahead and went in. Fields was seated behind his desk lost in thought. Whatever Fields and Smith had been talking about in their meeting was clearly keeping her boss, the father of her child, in a world of his own for the moment. Karin walked forward and stood to attention directly in front of his desk. She couldn't sit down. Her stomach now was absolutely churning and at the same time she could feel the baby's centre of gravity dominating her body a little lower down. She couldn't help it but tears were welling up in her eyes.

'Morten … please.'

She waited.

Fields slowly came round. He was still with his head in another place. He groaned: 'What is it that is so important that it can't wait?'

Karin exploded. 'Me! I'm important! I can't wait! I've got something that I urgently need to tell you!' Her tears began to fall.

Fields sat up. 'I'm sorry. Forgive me. What's the matter?' He showed some concern at last.

'Morten … you know that first night together in Geneva when you told me that you couldn't get any woman pregnant … Well, you're wrong!'

Fields stood up. His first glance was to ensure that his office door was closed. His second was at the tear-stained face of his personal assistant.

'I don't believe it. You're not … not …?'

317

'Yes I am. I am going to have your baby!' Karin looked at him, tears now freely flowing, beseeching him to do something.

Fields came around from behind his desk to take hold of her. Karin almost fell into his embrace but he seemed just a little distant. In shock maybe.

'Tell me about it. How long have you known?' His voice was very calm.

'I've suspected it for a while but couldn't tell you. The appointment this weekend confirmed it, however. The baby is two months old. You made me pregnant that first week we were together in Geneva. Almost straight away. But Morten, you said you were infertile; that you had a very low sperm count; that you couldn't make any woman pregnant. Look at me: Was that the truth?' Karin's eyes were pleading with him.

'Of course it was, darling. Of course it's true! But somehow my sperm count must have soared – I guess it was you that did that to me – how about that? You've made me a father! Fantastic! Karin, that has been your effect on me!' Fields let her go and began to walk around his office. 'You're pregnant! Would you believe it! Amazing. I'm going to be a father!'

He stopped. 'You are going to have this baby, aren't you?' He looked pointedly at Karin.

'Of course I am!'

'Fantastic! Don't worry – I insist on you having the very best treatment. You will be well cared for. Come and sit down. Please! How are you feeling? Are you OK?' Fields suddenly switched into over-protective mode.

Karin wiped away her tears and began to smile. 'Don't be silly, Morten. I'm perfectly OK. I don't need to sit down. I'll just go back to work. Now I know you are fine with this then that makes everything better. But you will look after me, won't you?' She was still feeling very vulnerable after a highly emotional exchange between them.

'My darling, my beautiful one, of course I will. I've already said you will have the very best treatment and care from this moment on. Have no fear of that … Have you told anyone else yet?'

'My mother in England. And Claudia who was with me in the clinic. No one else knows.' Except for Leopold Smith, Karin suddenly thought. That was still a shock.

'Well, of course in time everyone will know. All in good time. Do you happen to know the sex of your child yet?' Fields was suddenly very interested.

'No, it is much too soon to tell. But do you want to know early, before the birth, or would you rather wait?'

'I want to know as soon as possible. Absolutely! This is so exciting! Yes, tell me as soon as you can – please. You are absolutely radiant! I haven't said this before but I've known it for some time: I love you with a passion and this only confirms it!'

Karin stepped forward and put her arms up to him. She really needed that. She kissed him tenderly. 'Thank you, Morten. I love you, too.'

The next milestone in the developing pregnancy came at just over three months. Karin had been attending her clinic every two weeks and had told Morten that she did not want any more fuss taken over her for the time being. Deciding on where she was going to have her baby and with which particular medical support would be something for later. Just for now she needed routine monitoring to ensure that all was proceeding smoothly. It was. With the result that, at just over three months, the news she took to the father next was that she was going to have a baby boy.

Fields was overjoyed. 'I have always wanted a son! Karin, Karin – you are wonderful. How do you feel about it all?'

'I'm fine now, Morten. Absolutely fine. Now that I have your support, I can look forward to the birth with equanimity. I am going to enjoy every day that passes.'

'I'm so glad you said that because there is one more thing

that I have to say to you.' Fields paused for dramatic effect. Karin looked at him quizzically: What now?

'Karin, will you marry me?'

That was a surprise. Karin supposed she should have guessed but she did not. Instead, she was dumbstruck.

'Well?'

'I ... I ... don't know. Morten ... I guess I will ...'

'You will?'

'Give me a moment. Morten ... let me think about it. Please.' She didn't know what to say – he was sitting beside her, looking for an answer, obviously, but she really did not want to be rushed into this. 'Morten, let me give you my answer tomorrow. Please. I have to phone my mother. This is such a surprise ...'

Fields laughed. 'I'm surprised you say it is a surprise. In the condition you are in I would have thought my question was going to be obvious. But I'll wait, beautiful one. Just don't keep me waiting for long.'

Karin reached up a hand to him. 'Thank you, Morten. You are so considerate, as always. I'll tell you tomorrow ...'

She told Claudia first. As soon as they were alone that evening she told Claudia what had happened: the test result; the boy he had always wanted; the marriage proposal.

Claudia went goggle-eyed. 'Would you believe it! The most important businessman in Colombia wants to marry my flatmate! Well? Are you going to have him?'

'What do you think?'

'You are going to have his baby. I guess this is the safest, most secure option. The thing is ... do you really love him?'

'I don't know. I really don't know. He is absolutely wonderful to me so I ought to. I guess I do ...'

Claudia harrumphed. 'I've never been too convinced by your guesswork. You guessed he was infertile, remember? You also said once that Carolina should have him. I'm not even sure that she would have him now and she was always more keen on him than you were ... but then ... but then you are going to have his baby.'

'Yes. Exactly. I'll ask my mother. If there is one person who will warn me off getting married it will be her – so talking to her will convince me one way or the other. It will be a good test of what I should do. It's in the night there now but I have to talk to her – get me the phone, can you?'

Karin's mother was half asleep when she came to the phone but the sound of her daughter's voice caught her attention immediately.

'Karin, what is it? What's the matter? Where are you?'

'Don't worry, Mother, I'm absolutely fine. I'm at home but I do need to talk to you. I'm so sorry it is in the middle of your night.'

'Never mind that. What is it?' she was still worried.

'Mother, Morten has proposed to me. He wants to marry me. I'm going to have his son.'

'A baby boy? Congratulations, my love. And he wants to do the honourable thing by you? So he should; so he should. I don't care who he is; he is lucky to have you. What have you said? Do you want him?'

'I've told him to wait. I wanted to talk to you first.'

'Good girl. Well, you've got that right, at least! The question is, of course, what do you want? Do you want to marry him?'

'I'm not sure ... that's what I wanted to talk to you about.'

'Hmmm. Does he love you? Is he going to love and look after you – now and in the future?'

'Now, yes. Undoubtedly. In the future? Who knows? Mother – you know better than I all about promises for the future.'

'My love, my only one, I struggled for years and years bringing you up alone and I would never want that for you, ever. If he is going to look after you for now – undoubtedly you say – then maybe you should go for it. As for the future, ask him yourself. Tell him that marriage is for keeps and does he want you for all time? Don't necessarily believe what he says, mind, but put him on the spot and see his reaction. Go with your instincts at that moment. Hah! Who can you trust? Which man in particular? But ask him and see what he says. When all is said and done, if he can give you financial security that is a big plus in his favour, believe me. But, my love, let your instincts tell you what to do. Trust yourself; no one else. I love you.'

'Mother, thank you so much. Really thank you! I love you and miss you terribly. But I'll phone back as soon as I can tell you what I decide. Thank you again!' She put down the phone.

Claudia wanted to know: 'What's the verdict?'

'Basically, there's a lot in his favour – financial security and all – but she told me to ask him how he really feels about me and then, according to what he says, to go with my instincts.'

'Yeah. Good advice. I like it. Well – let's get some sleep now and wait for what the morning brings.'

The next day, across town, saw Morten Fields rise from his bed with a distinct spring in his step. So far as his personal life was concerned he was a very happy man. He was going to get a beautiful trophy wife and something he had always wanted and dreamed about – an undoubtedly beautiful baby son. Daughters he knew about but the only approximation he had had for a son up until this moment was that weirdo Leopold Smith. Smith was certainly loyal and useful but he was a severely limited individual who Fields could hardly warm to. But now he was going to get the real thing: a chip off the old block, his own flesh and blood, a male heir. Given his parentage, his son was sure to be intelligent and good-looking and Fields was going to give him the very best start in life possible. He already had plans for his boy – the top, most exclusive schools and universities, then postgraduate studies, maybe an MBA, and after that a position following in his father's footsteps as the successful head of a global business. Yes, he was going to be the proudest of proud fathers.

So far as his business life was concerned Fields was delighted with his promotion to head up Latin America and his appointment as a permanent member of the Board of Triple F – but just as everything in his world seemed to be smiling at him an old enemy came back to bite. González had recently called him to tell him that a large delivery of fuel oil to their new acquisition had driven off the road and had polluted a whole swathe of the mountainside. This was the last thing they wanted – they had an environmental image to promote, after all. And guess what, the 'careless' driver had only recently been taken on. Oddly, the man had managed to leap from the driver's cabin in the nick of time. There was no evidence, of course but González was certain who was to blame. TMG had set it up.

Fields discussed with Smith the possibility of a reprisal of some sort, but who should he send Smith out to get and where? It was all unclear at present. At the same time just sitting, waiting and doing nothing was not in his character and would inevitably encourage TMG to come at them again. Something had to be done. He told Smith to get himself ready for a sudden deployment and would confirm what, where and when as soon as he could. Meanwhile, he contacted Cortés and asked him to put together a report on all the TMG facilities and activities in his area and, particularly, which might be vulnerable targets. The dirty war looked like it was going to start up once more.

But let that be for the time being. How was his intended wife getting on? Fields went to work that morning waiting to see what she had to tell him. Given what he had promised and the life he was offering her, he was confident she would accept, and so it proved. She made some play at being hard to get and wanting to know if he really wished to marry her and have her as his wife for all time, which of course she was bound to ask and he was bound to affirm. Then she accepted him. Fields was delighted. The next question was when? Fields wanted them to seal the knot as soon as possible but there were a few things to settle first. He would have to move out of his apartment and acquire a family house in the one of the most exclusive areas in Bogotá. A place suitable for the raising of his boy and for the comfort and convenience of his parents. He did not want a huge marriage ceremony – something elegant and prestigious, with close friends and relations only ... and brief. Karin's mother would have to be flown out from England but there was no one from his side that he wanted to come from the USA.

Fields had the finance department of Triple F find a suitable house and arrange the purchase for him – a big sprawling property surrounded by trees and an extensive garden, with a secure perimeter and other similar houses around in a closed, security patrolled neighbourhood at the back of Usaquén, some seven or so miles north of the Bogotá city centre. It was the sort of place that only the elite of Colombia could afford. He took Karin to inspect the house and area. She was duly impressed and happy with all his arrangements. Things were working out fine.

The marriage came next. Fields was not religious and Karin did not want a Catholic service, so the ceremony took place in their new home. Karin, he was surprised to see, was as nervous and highly strung as a kitten during the proceedings – she shook like a leaf as she said her vows – but then it was all over and everything went off to his satisfaction in the end, particularly the first night in their marriage bed. Fields did not want to be away from the office for very long so he suggested a brief honeymoon in the Caribbean before they returned to Bogotá.

At work, when they eventually got back, they received all sorts of gifts and congratulations and Karin's desk was festooned with banners, balloons and messages of good luck and best wishes. There were only four months left to her pregnancy and Fields insisted that she should not work right up until the end. He wanted no risks to the health of the mother and his as yet unborn son. For Karin, her main focus in life now was the rapidly advancing pregnancy.

Karin and Claudia were closer than ever. Their parting, the removal of all Karin's things from their apartment and their transfer to the marital home had been the occasion for a tearful celebration. They went out for a final meal together before the marriage ceremony and promises were made to always stay in touch and to keep each other informed of what each was doing. For Karin she wanted to talk about Claudia's role of maid of honour at her wedding the next day; for Claudia she wanted to talk about the new man in her life – Nelson Ferrer, someone thankfully unrelated to Triple F – a journalist who worked for one of Colombia's television channels.

Then it was all about phasing in the changes at work. All the arrangements and preparations for the Triple F International Dance Festival were passed over bit by bit to the Public Relations department, and the oversight of Matthew Williams and his environmental audit was now entirely in the hands of the Triple F office in Popayán. As a result, Karin was happy to have her husband reduce her workload even more and in the last month of work she was only in the office for half-days. Claudia was being groomed as her successor.

'For the next month we are going to share this workplace and then it will be the big B-day and you'll be gone!' said Claudia. 'How are you feeling?'

'Heavy! But otherwise I feel OK. It just seems this last month will never pass. I wish I could press a button and fast-forward everything now!'

'Don't worry, the days will go by just as quick as always – it's just you that's not moving so quickly now! How are all the preparations – if you can't get around as much as you want, do you need anything that I can get you?'

'Thank you, Claudia, but no. Morten has got me everything and more than I need. Peter's bedroom has got so much stuff in it that it looks like a baby supermarket.'

'Peter? When did you choose his name?'

'I've had his name in my head for months now but I finally decided only recently. Morten is happy with it.'

They chatted on until it was time for Karin to go, back to her new home and a rather boring, very slow final month. No matter what had been said, those final days really did drag by until, of course, Karin woke in the night to a wet bed. She pushed her husband: her waters had broken.

Then everything went extremely fast. Phone calls, pack everything (most was already ready), the race to the clinic and then the long hours of labour. Karin was not the screaming sort and never had been. She gritted her teeth and moaned a little, going with the pain, but not wanting to act the prima donna. The spasms came faster and faster and then never stopped. Nelson, the new and very special love in Claudia's life, was waiting and pacing outside the delivery room. Morten pulled strings and both he and Claudia were allowed to be with the mother that morning. Then at last, at one in the afternoon, Karin was safely delivered of a beautiful baby, Peter. Morten was fine; Karin was exhausted but in heaven; Claudia was in floods of tears, a nervous wreck.

5

Thelma Marshall

Three months later and life for all concerned had adjusted to the monumental arrival of baby Peter. The parade of visitors had stopped; comments on baby's resemblance to father and mother had all been made (verdict: facial expressions like his mother's; temper like his father's), and Morten had just about stopped walking around looking like he had won the lottery. Mother was breast-feeding with no difficulty and when caught on camera by her husband she looked an absolute picture of peace and contentment. Morten, of course, wanted to get near her in bed and was most often rejected with a plea to wait, but he had to admit she did look beautiful: tired much of the time, but a stunning young mother nonetheless.

This idyll of peace and contentment was disturbed one afternoon by a phone call from Morten Fields's new personal assistant.

'Karin, I've got something here that you might be interested in, something that will take you back to another time and place …' Claudia was being mysterious.

'What on earth are you talking about?'

'I've just had a call from Nelson. He tells me that there is a fascinating story scheduled to appear on the next news bulletin about an animal protest against Triple F in Cauca.'

'A what?'

327

'Yes, that's what I said. He said that it is all about a herd of animals involved in a demonstration in Cauca. There's someone called El Mono interviewed.'

Karin's stomach jumped. Daniel! She went hot and then cold. 'Something that will take you back to another time and place,' Claudia had said. That was certainly true. She didn't know what to feel about that, other than distinctly shaky.

'Are you still there?' Claudia asked.

'Yes. Thank you. Sorry, I didn't know what to say for a moment. But I'll certainly put the TV on. The next news bulletin, you said?'

'Yes, that's about ten minutes' time. I'm going down to the foyer to watch it myself.'

'Does Morten know?'

'Not yet. I phoned you first but I'll tell him now, then Carolina. It is a demonstration against Triple F apparently, so Public Relations will inevitably be involved. I'll get back to you after we have all seen the television report. Bye!'

Peter was sleeping so Karin had no distraction. She was suddenly desperate to know what this television report was all about. She switched the screen on.

National and international politics were always the first things on the news, so there was a little time to wait before the human interest stories were broadcast. Then an excited television commentator came on to the screen, reporting from Cauca and fronting an incredible sight of a crowd of farm animals apparently partaking in a sit-down protest. The commentator was clearly entertained by what he was seeing and did his best to communicate that to the viewers:

'This demonstration on the road up to Triple F's newly acquired gold mine we understand is designed to draw attention to the pollution of grazing lands of local cattle and horses. In this case, however, as you can see' – the TV cameras panned round to emphasise the point – 'the demonstration almost entirely consists of precisely these animals – cattle and horses – and there are no people protesting at all. The animals are not directed by anyone so far as we can see but they are blocking the road to all traffic for around two hundred metres. Most of the cattle are simply sitting down and will not be shifted. The horses seem to be doing likewise, though it looks as if they take it in turn to get up, move around and then sit down again – so there are always animals on the move. How this happens with no one person in charge is impossible to fathom. Indeed, all the animals blocking the road seem to ignore all attempts by anyone, truck drivers, pedestrians or Triple F staff, to direct their movements.'

The cameras cut away to show a queue of trucks, diggers and other vehicles all at a standstill. Engines are running, people are shouting, some horns are sounding, but no animal is taking any notice. There was one individual, however, who had agreed to be interviewed about this demonstration. The commentator put his arm out to bring forward to the cameras the man they had found. As he did so, Karin felt her insides turn to water.

'Let me introduce you to a person known locally as El Mono. He says he is willing to act as a voice for various landowners in the district and for the many animals that are out here making their peaceful protest on the road.

'Please, Mono, can you tell us first of all where all these animals come from?'

'Indeed. One or two animals from each smallholding, estate or hacienda in the district have been volunteered by their owners to join this demonstration since all are concerned that the health of livestock in the area must be safeguarded. Pollution by mining companies is a major concern. It is an interest that unites all local livestock farmers, from the smallest to the largest enterprises.'

'So it's you who have organised this protest, this animal roadblock?'

'Well, in each case the animals that were volunteered have

all followed me here. But I have not tried to tell them what to do. As you can see – they seem to know what to do by themselves and are taking orders from no one, me included.'

'So how is this animal protest to end?'

'Well, I would not advise any vehicle to try and drive through this herd. It may hurt some very valuable creatures and I do not think television viewers would find such a sight attractive. And as for Triple F, well spilling the blood of so-called dumb animals is not the best image for their business. When will the animals desert the road and go back to their various fields and stables? My guess is as good as anyone's ... but probably, like all of us, they will move on when they get hungry and want to go home. Maybe tomorrow morning?'

Cameras turned once more to look at the herd of animals on the road and then came back to the television reporter.

'There is no one from Triple F here on the roadside at the moment willing to talk to us, but we earlier received this quote from a spokesperson. They say: "The environmental integrity of the lands Triple F are mining is one of our top priorities and strenuous efforts have been made since we purchased this facility from TMG to minimise pollution and develop good relations with local inhabitants. We entirely sympathise with what we understand are the aims of this demonstration and urge all involved to bring it to an end as soon as possible." Well, thank you, Triple F, thank you Mono. That is all for now. We can assure viewers that we will continue to monitor the situation down here on the roadside with this first ever, this unique animal protest, but with that closing comment, I return you to the studio.'

After a few moments, the phone rang again.

'How about that?' said Claudia. 'El Mono organising another protest – this time against us. He hasn't changed, has he?'

Karin still didn't know what to say, what to feel. Claudia was right, however. After all this time, after all the changes she had been through, Daniel was just the same Daniel. It almost hurt to see him on the TV screen.

'No. He hasn't changed. Do you know any more?'

'Well, Morten isn't pleased, I can tell you that. Nelson is – he is delighted. He's sold the story all round the world – to CNN, National Geographic, to the BBC World Service and a couple of television companies in Spain. As you have seen, it is quite fascinating and very televisual. Unfortunately, this is not the best publicity for Triple F, though Carolina is working on how to turn this to our advantage.'

'Well, thanks for letting me know, Claudia. I'll see what mood Morten is in when he gets home. If anything else happens, do give me a call.'

'Of course. I'd better get back now. Talk to you later, bye!' She hung up.

Morten came back late that evening and didn't want to talk about it. Karin didn't really want to talk about it either, but it would have been remiss of her not to mention it at all. When she did ask her husband, the reaction she got was an angry comment that this stupid protest was totally unwarranted. She said nothing.

The next morning Claudia phoned back again.

'I'll be quick,' she said, 'because Morten is in a terrible mood next door, but this is for your ears only. Nelson has just come through to tell me that National Geographic have got a team out here in Colombia on some nature programme they are putting together and they are sending people down to Cauca to follow up on the story. They've been asking Nelson about which people to contact, so he might be going with them. I'm not telling anyone but you – but don't be surprised if this story starts to get bigger. Don't tell Morten!'

There was no need for the warning; Karin had no intention of raising the matter again at home. Besides, Peter seemed to have developed problems sleeping during the day and, at three months old, Karin was tired of getting up and down all the time seeing to his crying. But she did want to know what was happening down at the Triple F mine with Daniel. Floods of memories were coming back to her of her time there, and during the days that followed she found it difficult not to think about them – stuck as she was in the house with no one to talk to.

Fields was not in any sort of talkative mood at present. The birth had taken his wife's attention away from him when he was at home and conversation with what seemed like a permanently tired and preoccupied wife was boringly limited. He was almost incandescent at times at work, and this wasn't just down to the animal protest. Matthew Williams had produced an interim audit that showed just how expensive it was going to be to sort out the environmental problems at Puracé. Fields thus needed to play down the green image he had earlier been so eager to project and had to tell Carolina to go easy on the 'caring' press releases. That had sent his PR head off in a fit of pique. Another typical woman with more lofty ideals than practical business sense, he thought irritatingly.

Cortés had got back to him about likely TMG targets for a reprisal raid and Fields had approved of a hit on their oil pipeline further south, in the Department of Putumayo. That made him smile. It was an impossible target to defend for its entire length and even if the oil was shut off quickly after any explosion that would still give them a tidy mess to think about. The operation was a success, but then González came up with a piece of news that really set the seal on his temper. Did he know that TMG had sent out one of their bosses from the Canadian headquarters to have a look at what was going on? Brian MacKay had apparently been recalled and a certain Thelma Marshall had been seen visiting the TMG regional office in Popayán.

'Holy shit!' cursed Fields. 'That's all I need now. Thelma fucking Marshall out here in Colombia!'

The question González then asked was: Did Fields want an 'accident' to happen to her?

'Forget Smith. She has a hold over him that I cannot explain right now but he is likely to go off the wall if he even knows she is in the country. Smith is here on my finca outside Bogotá just now and he is definitely to be kept away from her, and her from him. You've never seen him when he goes absolutely nuts or you'll know why he's compared to a nuclear bomb. If you can get some local thug to put the frighteners on Thelma Marshall, then do so but nothing, absolutely nothing traceable to us. Gottit? That woman is too damn clever by half, remember that.'

'OK, boss. Don't worry, Cortés has lots of options. We'll see to it.'

At the root of Fields's ill-temper was the feedback from his own geological team, who were surveying the new Puracé acquisition. He had always known that their original mine, which had been the cause of the initial phase of the current dirty war when he had first got to Colombia, was basically unprofitable. But the TMG facility had always been a money-spinner for them, or so he thought, which was why he had led the onslaught to take it over. The irony was that the TMG financial projections which he had murdered to change were, after all, a monumental exaggeration. The revised figures which his financial department had cooked up to replace them were in fact not so very far from the truth. So, unless some miracle happened in the next survey undertaken, the gold retrievable from his hard-won conquest was unlikely to make Triple F fortunes turn around. That would make him appear a pretty dumb guy next time he had to report to the Board. And that must simply not be allowed to happen. He had to turn in big profits somehow.

El Mono was another thorn in his flesh. As always, the man was difficult to pin down and would be unlikely to fall victim to any attempted assault so long as he stayed on his own turf.

No sense funding a search and destroy mission just yet when the costs of doing so in financial terms and the risks to their public image were high. Let him go and see the oil pollution in Putumayo if he wanted to organise another protest.

What was next on his agenda? He'd ask Claudia. Unfortunately, after he had buzzed her, she only reminded him of another problem hanging over him – the upcoming Triple F International Dance Festival. This now appeared like a very costly albatross around their corporate necks, but there was no way to cut back at this late stage without losing face. He would just to have to make sure they made the best of it. Who should he take with him to see the opening ceremony? Not Karin: too tired. Not Claudia: she was another highly decorous assistant but she already had a boyfriend and was far too close to his wife. No fun there. He'd accompany Carolina – that would put him back in her favour and it would be interesting to see how far she would go in flirting with him, a newly married man. Yes, Carolina. He licked his lips at the challenge.

The Triple F International Dance Festival opened with a lot of fanfare and press coverage. Government ministers came. Various business chiefs and big-wigs wanted to be seen. Transnational Mining Group sent their PR chief, though thankfully, Thelma Marshall chose not to come. Arts editors from various national and overseas media companies tried to outdo each other in their praise for the whole exercise, and the performance of the Lovisa Berglund dance troupe was wildly applauded. Fields couldn't say he was overly impressed by this avant-garde stuff but his partner for the evening, Carolina Santos, loved it and was most appreciative. Fields was glad for that.

The rest of the week continued to make the headlines and the final evening performance of the Bolshoi stars made news around the world. Carolina said that Fields should be pleased about that. He was. He left for work on the following Monday morning with one woman at home behind him and another, with whom his relations were steadily improving, waiting for him at work.

Karin woke up. It was a bright morning, her husband had already left, the Triple F international Dance Festival had just closed after a highly successful week's run, and baby Peter was now four months old and well on his way to developing a strong personality. She was looking fully her old self these days – Peter had established a good routine and sleep was not so disturbed for either of them. Morten, the proud father, had provided every possible luxury for his new wife: the spacious house and gardens, a car in the driveway with a bored chauffeur and, indoors, a live-in maid and a nurse to make Karin's life in the role of mother as easy and stress-free as possible. As regards a return to work, however, Morten had said no; it was out of the question. Much as she had been successful as his executive assistant in Triple F, her place in the home in bringing up their child was far more important.

'Peter needs you here, my dear, and so do I,' he had insisted. 'My office at work will manage with Claudia now – much as we all miss you there.'

Morten was so considerate, and so right. The dance festival had once been Karin's pet project, but this last week she had taken only a modicum of interest in it. Little Peter was now the centre of Karin's world and she could not bear the thought of leaving him behind every day with her nurse, Ana María – good though she was – and going off to work at Triple F. Karin was happiest at home with her son, absolutely captivated by his daily progress and how rapidly he was growing.

The phone rang, disturbing Karin's thoughts. It was Claudia. 'Hi Karin, How are things?'

'Lovely to hear from you, Claudia. We're fine here. I've just fed Peter and now he is playing with me on the carpet. You really should see him, so big now – he's absolutely divine!'

'I'd love to see him. The reason I'm phoning is that Morten

has given me the day off today – he's just gone out with Carolina on some public relations exercise … so could I come round?'

'Please do! I'd love to see you, too. But wait – I haven't been out of the house for days and Peter ought to see a change of surroundings – can't we meet up somewhere?'

'Anywhere you like. Just say where.'

'How about just down the road from here in Hacienda Santa Barbara? It's close enough for me to push the buggy and Peter will enjoy it. He loves staring up at all the trees as we go under them. You can almost see his little brain ticking over, trying to work out what it is with these big green things and the flickering light above him. Wonderful!'

Hacienda Santa Barbara was a modern, upmarket shopping mall, tastefully built into and around a traditional Hispanic country house that dated back to when Usaquén had been a village on the outskirts of the city.

'Fine with me,' said Claudia. 'Shall we meet up in the café on the left-hand side as you come in from the main street?'

It was agreed.

It took a good fifteen minutes to get Peter cleaned up, nappy-changed, kitted out with a new suit of clothes and then strapped into his space-age, soft-suspension, best-that-money-could-buy baby walker. It took a further twenty minutes for Karin and nurse Ana María to cruise him downhill along the tree-lined avenue towards the shopping mall that awaited them on the busy thoroughfare below the gated community where they lived in quiet and isolated splendour.

Karin, the elegant, finely dressed mother, and Ana María, the dutiful and attentive employee, wheeled Peter in past the sliding doors of the shopping mall, where two smart security men saluted them, and crossed over to where they expected to find Claudia. It was still reasonably early in the day so there were not too many people about. Peter was gurgling at all the various colourful shop fronts that seemed to whizz by beside him.

A voice called out: 'Here I am!' Claudia was seated, perusing a menu at a café table a short distance away across the stone tiles of the old hacienda floor.

A ceremony of cooing, hugging and fussing over baby then took place before Peter was parked and happy. Ana María knelt down beside him to ensure that he was equipped with sufficient baby bottles and attractive plastic playthings to keep him busy while his mother could devote her attention to her friend.

They had a week's news to catch up on: what Peter had been doing; what clothes had recently been purchased; how his latest check-up with the paediatrician had gone; what film Claudia had just seen; how was Nelson; the trouble with maids and how unreliable they were these days ... lots to talk about. Claudia admired Karin's beautiful shoes that Morten didn't yet know he had paid for. A girl really couldn't have enough shoes and handbags these days, could she?

Karin asked: 'And how are things in Public Relations since you left, Claudia. Any recent changes?'

'Well, to be honest, K., it's all a bit bland. A couple of people have gone and been replaced. They circulated our response to some pollution at Transnational Mining Group ... the usual criticisms we voice, you know. Then there've been some protests from a local pueblo about water contamination in Puracé – though if you blinked you would have missed it, it was so briefly mentioned on the television news. We thought there might be some follow-up about the animal demonstration, but no. Rather disappointing.'

'Oh, what was the story Carolina circulated? I have to say I did catch something and mentioned it later to Morten but he pooh-poohed it as the television getting the wrong end of the stick; not understanding what was going on.'

'Our response was, as you can guess, that Triple F was engaged in developing the resources and raising the incomes of the country and we were keen to engage in a dialogue with all people locally affected so as to address their concerns, involve them in all decision-making and ensure that they did not miss out on participating in the eventual bonanza. The usual blah-blah.'

Karin nodded. 'Didn't they mention anything about our environmentally friendly practices – implementing the recommendations of the report from Matthew Williams?'

'Not this time. Morten thought it was not worth while making any fuss about it – not enough PR capital, he said.'

'Yes, but I still think we missed a trick there. It should have been an occasion to promote our image, no matter how low key the affair. I'll mention it to Morten.'

Claudia's mobile phone beeped. 'Excuse me, Karin. Let me get this ...'

A quizzical expression passed over Claudia's face during the phone conversation as she tried to work out the identity of the caller. A few moments later Claudia's eyes opened wide; she clapped the handset down into her lap and whispered to Karin: 'It's Thelma Marshall! She says she urgently needs to talk to you. What do I say?'

'Morten has absolutely forbidden me to speak with her. What is she doing talking to you?'

'She says she has no contact number for you but knows we are best friends and she wants my help to reach you. She says it's very important and it involves Peter! Karin – I don't want to give her your mobile number or anything but I could just pass over the phone. She has no idea that we are together right now.'

Karin hesitated. She knew nothing of this stony-faced woman other than what she had seen outside the lawyers' meeting over a year ago, plus the fact that her husband had never wanted to talk about her and had bluntly insisted that Thelma Marshall should never be trusted. But what was this about something involving Peter?

'Tell her you'll call back. I need time to think!' Karin was flustered by this sudden and unexpected interruption.

Claudia promptly assured her caller that she would be back in touch in a few minutes and then she cut the phone. The two women stared at one another in silence, eyebrows raised. What to do?

'I can't talk to her, Claudia. Morten would have a fit.'

'I know,' replied Claudia, 'but he needn't find out. No man ever wants his ex-wife and his new wife to exchange notes, but this is as good a chance as you'll ever have to find out what passed between them before you came on to the scene. Aren't you intrigued? I would be. And you have to know what she is talking about with regard to Peter. You know you have to.'

'But that might just be a ruse to get me hooked. I am hooked! She has said the one thing I cannot ignore ... but how can I trust her? Morten told me never to believe a thing she says ...'

'Well, you don't have to. But you've got to find out what she's up to. You'll die of curiosity if you don't. *I* will die of curiosity if you don't! Go on – let me call her back and pass you the phone.'

Karin took a deep breath and nodded. 'OK. Wait a bit while I ask Ana María to take Peter for a little ride around here and then let's do it! '

Ana María was suitably dispatched to entertain baby at some distance out of earshot and then Claudia dialled the number, established contact and, with a meaningful look in Karin's direction, promptly passed the phone across.

'Hello. This is Karin Roth ... Mrs Morten Fields, speaking. I understand you wanted to talk to me about something important?'

A cultured voice with a Canadian accent sounded on the line. 'Good morning, Karin. This is Thelma Marshall. I am very sorry to disturb you out of the blue like this but I am at present in Bogotá for a few days and I urgently need to speak with you.'

'I have to say that this is a total surprise, Ms Marshall. I don't know how or why you have contacted me ... You should know that Morten has warned me never to speak with you.'

'I bet he has. Nonetheless, I think you'll find that it is very much in our mutual interest to meet. The fact is that I have some important information that is vital to the welfare of your baby boy ... and,' – Thelma Marshall's voice lost an almost imperceptible degree of control – 'I believe you have some similarly important information vital to the interests of *my* baby boy. Will you agree to meet me? I think it is important to talk face to face ... and as soon as possible. I should add that this must be an entirely confidential encounter – your husband must not under any circumstances know about it.'

'Just a minute, please ...' Karin stalled, absolutely astonished. She covered the phone and repeated what she had just heard to her friend sitting across the table. Claudia's eyes grew as wide as saucers.

'You have got to see her! Karin, you must. I'll be with you if you want so that you'll be safe. Make it today, now I'm free ...'

Karin collected her thoughts. It had to be today and as soon as possible because she would never rest now until she found out what this was all about. Also, if it could be arranged before Morten got home, she would never have to try and explain where and who she was meeting. The last thing she wanted was to start living a married life hiding things from her husband. Yes, it had to be as soon as possible. And at the very least, if all this was a load of baloney, then there was no harm done. She picked up the phone.

'OK, Ms Marshall. I'll meet you. It has to be today and as soon as possible today since any other time will be impossible for me. Is that good for you?'

There came what sounded like a sigh of relief on the other end of the phone. Perhaps Thelma Marshall was not made of stone ... or else she was extremely devious and up to something dangerously Machiavellian. Karin was silently grateful that Claudia was beside her and offering hundred-per-cent support.

'Thank you, Karin. Today is very good indeed for me. Can I say I fully understand how alarming this must be for you, to receive this call from someone you cannot possible know and who you might think is some kind of a threat to you. So to respond so positively to my request is really very courageous of you ... yet, I can assure you, you will not regret this. I suggest we meet wherever you feel secure and comfortable. My only condition being that this must be confidential – away from prying eyes.'

'Well, my best friend Claudia knows already, as you may guess. And she will come with me to see you: I feel safest like that. Where are you in Bogotá just now?'

'I'm at the Hilton. Where are you?'

'A few miles north from you in Usaquén.' Karin decided to take the initiative: 'I know the Hilton well enough so I suggest we meet there, Claudia and I can be there in half an hour or so ...' She paused to look across to see her friend nodding furiously. 'How will that suit you?'

A note of surprise came down the phone. 'That is excellent! Thank you very, very much. I'll give instructions to reception to direct you to one of their corporate suites. I'll be waiting there alone in half an hour from now. I can't tell you how relieved I am about this. I have been worrying about this situation for ages now. Thank you again.'

'Thank you, Ms Marshall. I must say that hearing from you like this has been something of a shock to me ...' Karin was trying to sound as calm and professional as possible and to keep her voice flat and expressionless, 'but I nonetheless look forward to our meeting. Goodbye!' She shut the phone.

'WOW!' Claudia was the first to react. 'Well done, Karin! Talk about taking the plunge ... you are going straight in at the deep end. One way or the other we are going to find out about

Thelma Marshall and what is so dangerous about her. But don't worry – I'll be with you every step of the way.'

Karin was pensive and did not express any emotion at first. She was intrigued, worried, a little frightened all at the same time. She could not help wondering where this was all going to lead. Then she snapped out of it.

'Thanks, Claudia, for all your help in this. If I had been alone when she contacted me, I would never have agreed to meet her. But now the die is cast.' One of Daniel's mountain sayings suddenly came to her: 'We've chosen the pathway. Let's see where it leads …'

Ana María had been instructed to take Peter home, put him down to sleep and not to let anyone into the house until they had returned. Karin told her that she and Claudia were going to go shopping and hoped to be back in an hour or so; that they would call later to confirm.

Claudia's car was in the Hacienda's car park and it was only a short drive to the Hilton. Traffic midday between these two popular locations in town was never easy but they nonetheless arrived at their destination, parked and reached the reception desk in thirty-five minutes.

Security in Bogotá is a preoccupation in the upmarket apartment blocks, hotels, clubs and shopping precincts, so it took a little time for Karin and Claudia to get clearance and then a porter guided them to the second-floor suite of rooms where business meetings were normally hosted.

The doors to Room 205 were held open for them.

Inside, Thelma Marshall sat waiting behind a large, ebony-topped table surrounded by black leather executive chairs. She rose to greet them. She was dressed in a dark-blue business suit, nothing ostentatious, though Claudia noticed it was fabulously tailored and must have cost a small fortune. She was tall, with short dark hair, discreet make-up and possessed of a poise that comes from success, confidence and the knowledge that she was a force to be reckoned with. It made Claudia feel that her own fashionable casual wear was altogether overly colourful and lightweight. Karin, tense and boiling inside with mixed emotions, noticed only that Thelma Marshall was polite, elegant, composed, and was a mature, experienced lady of serious mien.

Then Thelma's face broke into a smile and she indicated that they should sit opposite her. 'I can't thank you enough for coming,' she began. 'I am sorry to unsettle you with what must be a really strange request from out of the blue, but I am truly very grateful that you have agreed to see me so quickly.'

'No trouble, Ms Marshall, but please do tell me what this is all about.'

'Call me Thelma, Karin. There is no need for excessive formalities here, and please believe me when I say that I am here to help you. I pose no threat whatsoever, whatever you might have heard to the contrary.'

Karin's mouth smiled, though her eyes did not. She was unconvinced.

'Let me start by saying that I've done my homework on you two. I know your nationalities, your educational background, your friendship, your experience at Triple F – both of you – and, of course, about your marriage to my ex-husband, Morten, and the birth of your son Peter, who must be now a little over four months old. Don't be concerned, Karin; I haven't been spying on you. Most of this information is readily available on the Triple F website, and on other sites of reputable standing. So now: I owe you an explanation as to who I am and what I am about.

'I am at present a senior executive of Transnational Mining Group Inc. I'm normally based in Canada, but let's say I have a special interest at present in our business in Colombia and in particular with the rivalry here between us and the Farming, Fishing and Forestry Corporation – Triple F. I've been at TMG some seventeen years now but before that I worked, like you, at Triple F where I first met and then married Morten Fields. Morten was not my first husband, however. I was married before, when I was foolishly young, to David, from Toronto, and with whom I had a son.

'Let me stop there a moment and ask you a quick question: Do either of you know a person called Leopold Smith?'

Another surprise. A sharp intake of breath from Claudia; Karin simply nodded.

Claudia spoke first. 'He is the most frightening person I have ever, ever encountered.'

Karin kept it simple and business-like: 'Nobody really knows him. He is seen by odd people at various times and a number of rumours circulate. I'm not at all sure of the nature of his relations with Triple F, but I do know that Morten sees him on occasions and tells me he is his bodyguard when he needs one.'

Thelma looked down, shook her head slowly, then looked up. Karin saw an indescribable sadness in her eyes. 'Leo is my son,' she said. 'He was my baby boy and David Smith is his father, my first husband. Morten, however, has basically dominated Leo's life and taken him away from me. I have had very little information about what Leo has been doing over the last few years, yet I suspect he has been following Morten's bidding. Karin, when was the last time to your knowledge that the two of them met?'

Karin felt more relaxed but deeply puzzled by this older woman who was unexpectedly showing a softer, more humane side to her personality. 'Leo Smith came to our house in the night some three weeks ago. I know it was all supposed to be secret, but I was up with Peter and I heard the two of them talking below. I'm sorry but I cannot tell you any more about it. I never asked.'

Thelma sighed. The sadness grew and shaking her head did not help. 'I feared as much. I really feared so but I could only guess. I had no proof until now. You don't have to know what they were talking about or what they were up to, I can figure that out as well. But Morten is such a terrible influence on my son and he has stolen him away from me. The tragedy is that over the last eighteen years he has done exactly the same for our daughter, too. She is also estranged from me, though I will not give up the fight. And I am here to warn you that, in the future, he might try the same with your son.'

The news hit Karin like a slap in the face. Her insides turned to ice.

'Morten has a daughter with you? He can't have!'

'Helena. She is twenty-one now and will not speak to me. From the day of her birth Morten showered her with attention, gifts, stories and all manner of poison and when Morten and I eventually separated for reasons I'll tell you later, he lied, paid lawyers and bent all the rules of the land to keep custody. It broke my heart. It still does. Helena has not yet become a twisted version of the child I initially raised – unlike her brother – and I'll fight tooth and nail to prevent that. But the fact is I have two children by two different men, yet Morten, who is the father of only one, has taken control of both.'

Karin's face flushed with emotion. She blurted out: 'This can't be true. Morten has no other children than Peter. He has always had a very low sperm count and that I became pregnant at all is something of a miracle!'

Thelma smiled ruefully. 'Is that what he has told you? I'm very sorry; I didn't know or I would have broken this to you more gently. But I am afraid it is Morten who has made up that story, not I. Helena is our daughter. He has one other daughter, too, that I know of – with Patricia Ramírez – so I guess that is news to you, too. He certainly has a very active sex drive and has bedded many women over the years, in and out of wedlock. Karin – I'm very sorry to be so blunt about this but I'm afraid that this really is the truth.'

Claudia's hand reached under the table and searched for that of her friend. Karin meanwhile became more and more agitated.

'No, Thelma. You can't be right. Morten told me not to trust anything you said. Obviously you hate him and are trying to get at him through me.'

Claudia drew her chair closer to Karin.

'Karin,' Thelma said quietly, 'you don't have to believe me. Patricia Ramírez now works in Cali with TMG. You could talk to her about her two-year-old. With regard to my and Morten's daughter, you can find her easily. Helena Fields is now a postgraduate mathematics student at Harvard; is listed on their website, and can be phoned direct if you want to hear her corroborate what I say. She won't answer any calls from me, however. Come to think of it, Morten has probably instructed her never to accept direct calls from Colombia unless it's from his own personal line. But you can look her up and I'm sure that, between the two of you, you will be able to find a way to speak to her. Try an indirect way to mention her father and see how she reacts. Sorry to sound so devious myself but I've learned how to fight him over the years. That's why he doesn't want us ever to meet.'

'It cannot be … it can't be true.' Karin was fighting back the tears. 'You get me here on the pretext that Peter is somehow involved and now you throw all this crap at me trying to undermine my marriage …'

Thelma continued, relentlessly pursuing her story like some soft-spoken juggernaut. 'Karin, you have to know what you and your baby are getting into. Morten is a very possessive, dominant individual. You must have seen that. Yes, he can be so charming, so generous, so winning in his ways … yet he manipulates people so skilfully to get exactly what he wants. If anyone stands in his way, he can be frighteningly vengeful. He has long lines of acolytes who faithfully follow him and deliver what he orders. It hurts me in ways I cannot describe to say that Leo is one. Leo is the reason we broke up. I wanted to get

346

Leo and Helena away from his evil influence as quickly and as far as possible. I failed!'

Now it was Thelma's turn to get emotional. The professional veneer began to slip; the collected exterior transformed slowly and steadily into that of an angry, devastated mother who had lost her one and only son and was desperately fighting to retain some hold over her daughter.

'You cannot believe what a beautiful little boy Leo was and how he has been turned into a terrifying machine to serve his master's orders. You said yourself, Claudia, what a frightening person he is now. You have no idea how such a comment hurts me to my very core. But ... but you are not the first one to say such things.' This usually stony-faced executive struggled to retain her composure. 'Give me a moment and I'll tell you his story ... my story ... and you can judge for yourself Karin whether or not this information is relevant to the welfare of your baby boy ...'

There was a cut-glass decanter of water and four tumblers on the table. Thelma poured water into one tumbler, took a sip and regained her self-control.

'David Smith and I met in our freshman year at the Massachusetts Institute of Technology. Would you believe that I fell pregnant with Leo when I was only seventeen? How dumb and innocent of the world I was then! Well, becoming a mother at such an age and trying to keep track of my degree programme while raising an infant soon made me grow up. And Leo was such a difficult child! Instead of things getting easier as he developed, things became steadily worse. He simply did not conform to any of the guidelines that parents and baby books lay down for young mothers. He wouldn't sleep! He was either feeding or crying. His appetite was ferocious: I blew up like a balloon breast-feeding him! Physically, he was healthy though hyperactive, and something was badly wrong with his behaviour. I ... I was a wreck, however. It was only thanks to my parents and some very supportive people at MIT that I could stay sane, postpone much of my studies and somehow keep in touch with what I was supposed to be doing at university.

'Leo became a very intense, uncommunicative little boy. Silent, he would shut out the rest of the world to concentrate rigidly on whatever caught his attention. He couldn't cope with even the slightest changes to his routines and would fly into uncontrollable fits if disturbed. David and I were living together, trying to share the burden of parenthood, but David couldn't cope with it anymore and after a couple of years I was on my own.

'When Leo first started school that, too, was a disaster. By their standards, he was a slow learner. He was certainly intelligent but the problem was he would only study what he wanted and could not be shifted to do anything else. As regards his relations to other children, they took him to be a freak. He was unable to socialise and as a result he was frequently and sometimes brutally bullied. I changed his school a number of times and each time I was struggling to understand what the problem was and what was I doing wrong as a mother. Leo was meanwhile growing up to be a highly introverted, sullen and aggressive individual. The way he learned to cope with bullying was to become a ferocious little fighter himself. That only served to increase his unpopularity and social isolation.

'Finally, some godsent psychologist – one of many who had been tried and found wanting – diagnosed him as having Asperger syndrome. I didn't know what it was then, but I soon found out and Leo fits the bill, though he's on the extreme edge, bordering autism.

Thelma stopped. 'Have you ever met people with Asperger before?' she asked.

Karin and Claudia looked at one another ... no.

'It is a psychological disability. It is permanent: part of your personality. People with Asperger simply cannot read others' emotions; they have no sense of empathy; cannot understand jokes; do not really understand why other people feel and react the way they do. It all made sense. When Leo was a tiny two-year-old I once smacked his bottom for being so naughty. He had no idea whatsoever why I did so. It was like bolt from the blue and it shocked him rigid. I never ever raised a finger against him after that since he simply would not have been able to understand it. Finding out so many years later why he could not read my feelings made an enormous difference to me, to my understanding of my son and to my self-confidence – not having to keep blaming myself all the time. Of course, it didn't mean too much to Leo: he was as difficult as ever.

'Leo is very wary of people he does not know. That means pretty much everybody. He doesn't trust people because for him they are totally unpredictable. Similarly, other people's pain is meaningless to him. It simply doesn't register. Strangely enough, having just said that, Leo is very good with animals: so gentle and kind. He wouldn't hurt a fly ... so long as it is a fly or some other dumb creature. Unlike humans, he does not have to read their expressions and try and figure out what they mean, or why they hate him as they do. Can you imagine someone so kind to animals but so distant with people?'

Claudia answered: 'Funnily enough we can. That reminds me of someone we knew a couple of years ago, though the one we know isn't hated ...'

'Well, somehow I finished my degree at MIT and I got myself my first job with Triple F as a trainee accountant. Balancing work with bringing up a difficult child became no easier. I was now in my mid-to-late twenties, having missed out almost entirely on a normal gregarious undergraduate life, with student debts up to my eyebrows to pay off and with Leo still demanding much of my attention, day in, day out. I wondered if I was ever going to get my head above the grind-stone. Then I met Morten.

'He was handsome, successful, talented, splashed money

around like water ... and I don't know what he saw in me. Well, I do: it was easy sex. I've always had a good figure, I'm not unattractive and, my God, with all the stress and running around in my life up to then I was certainly slim, physically fit and – as far as he was concerned – undemanding. He could have me when he wanted and, if he was out partying with others, I wouldn't complain. When I found out he was sleeping with other girls my only reaction was: OK ... so long as he stays with me. I didn't want to lose him and particularly the financial security he represented.

'He must have liked the arrangement because we got married. He knew all about Leo and yet still he wanted me. Can you imagine my relief? Was I in love with him? No. Not really. But I sure needed him.

'He was quick to learn how to handle Leo. Morten is no fool – he knew what he was doing and, unlike me at the time, he knew where he was going. He saw early on that Leo could be an asset to him. He could be moulded. You cannot touch Leo or crowd his personal space. He goes off the rails if you do. Routines are essential and cannot be changed. But he was amazingly single-minded at whatever he chose to do and always delivered results on a deadline, if not before. Deadlines he actually needs, in order to perform. In addition, by his late teens Leo had grown to be a big, very strong and physically imposing young man.

'It was around then that I saw what Morten was up to: paying for his weightlifting, martial arts and self-defence classes. Always supporting him, encouraging him, building up his ego as well as his physique. He began slowly and steadily poisoning his mind against me. He wanted a faithful acolyte. He wanted a bodyguard and, ultimately – to my utter dismay when I found out just recently – a ruthless soldier and hitman. From information I've received over this last year, and now just confirmed by yourself, Karin, I've found out that Leo is Morten's personal, loyal and highly effective assassin. They tell me that in Triple F security, he is informally known as "the nuclear option".'

Thelma stopped. Her face was blank. Karin and Claudia stared at her in utter amazement. Then Thelma's eyes filled with water.

'He was my beautiful baby boy ...' She dissolved in tears. 'And look what Morten has done to him.'

With a cry out loud, Karin exploded into tears as well. It was all too much to take in.

'No, no, NO! I can't ... I can't accept any of this. You are turning my husband into a monster. Why have you come to me with this story? Why are you trying to wreck my faith in the man I married? What is this all about? I should never have come. I shouldn't believe a word you say. Morten is right. Why are you telling me this? Go away – leave me, leave us both!'

Thelma Marshall nodded. Her face quickly adopted the serious, rather wooden expression that was almost second nature to her. She was a proud woman.

'I'm sorry. I understand. Since you ask, I can tell you that the real reason why I asked to see you was that I promised someone I would. However, that story is so unbelievable, if I had started with it you would have probably walked out right at the beginning.'

Thelma Marshall stood up, preparing to leave. Karin was now in floods of tears and Claudia had her arm around her shoulders. She looked daggers at the woman standing across the table from them.

'Try us. One more chance: Who did you promise that you would talk to us?'

'Someone I got to know in Popayán. Someone who saved me from being mugged, though you would never believe how. I spoke to him afterwards and, obviously, wanted to know all about him. When he heard who I was, he asked me to see you, Karin, and to tell you to take care ... He made me promise.'

351

Karin looked up. Tear-stained and devastated as she was, she had to ask: 'How did he save you? Tell me the truth!'

'By a swarm of bees. I told you you'd never believe me!'

Karin let out a wail. It came from deep inside her … Months and months of suppressed emotion were released in one awful, prolonged howl. She knew. Everything that Thelma Marshall had said was true. Her life was turned upside down in that instant. It meant the end of her marriage.

Thelma looked at Karin in shock but Claudia understood.

'You'd better sit down again, Thelma,' Claudia said. 'That is the one thing you could never have made up and it is the one thing you couldn't know we would believe. You were talking to Daniel, weren't you? El Mono.'

6

Confrontation

The three women stayed together for a further fifteen minutes, exchanging various phone numbers – how to reach Patricia Ramírez, the best way to contact Helena Fields and where to phone Thelma over the next few weeks. Karin was totally deflated but she was adamant that she would check out Thelma's story first and gather what evidence she could before she confronted her husband, as she knew she must, and as soon as possible.

Then it was time to return to baby Peter. Karin had promised Ana María she would be back home in an hour and that time had long since elapsed. Claudia and Karin stood up and thanked Thelma Marshall for contacting them. It was the most traumatic experience for Karin, and Thelma apologised for that; Karin and Claudia for their part apologised for their disbelief at first, but they agreed that no matter how shocking these revelations had been, it was better that it was done now and not any later. Karin grimaced at the thought of what she had to do next but thanked Thelma again and said she would be back in contact soon, probably within the next twenty-four hours.

Claudia drove Karin home. It was a short ride and when they arrived Peter was thankfully still asleep. Karin had to sit down first and try and calm her nerves but then she picked up her mobile and phoned Patricia Ramírez – Morten's personal assistant before her. It was the number of the TMG offices in Cali, two hours' flight away.

'Hello, Patricia, this is Karin Roth. Remember me?' She paused to let the message sink in. 'Yes – it's certainly been some time since we last saw each other, hasn't it? I was just an intern at Triple F then – but I guess you have heard what has happened to me since?'

Patricia Ramirez answered with a very non-committal expression: 'I heard. I gather I should offer congratulations.'

'Thank you, Patricia. I am not sure just at the moment if I deserve congratulations. But the reason I am contacting you is that I have heard some very disturbing news. Very disturbing ...' Karin could not keep the emotion out of her voice. She was still very upset after the morning's exchange with Thelma Marshall and she knew that the answer to her next question was going to make her even more upset, whatever the response would be.

'Patricia, since I think you know my situation now, you will perhaps excuse me if I ask a very personal question – something that I am desperate to know about. You have a baby daughter who must be now two years old?'

'Ye...e...s.' Patricia could guess precisely what the next question was going to be.

'Forgive me, but who was the father?'

'Morten Fields.'

Karin could hardly speak. She had to breathe deeply. 'Thank you for telling me. Patricia, I'm sorry to have bothered you. I owe you an explanation for this call: Morten told me he was infertile and had no other children ... You have now proven the lie.'

That little confession from Karin's side brought a rapid response from Patricia who instantly recognised another woman, a sister in kind, who had similarly been mistreated by the man she had fallen for.

'Karin, we should meet up sometime and I can tell you all about it if you wish. Yes, he fed me the same story and I fell for it, too. He was all over me like honey when I was pregnant but that changed after he found out I was expecting a baby girl. Then he dumped me. He paid me off. I let him pay for all my medical bills on the understanding I disappeared. Stupidly, I agreed. I still loved him. He spread all sorts of lies about me that everyone else believed. I could go on but I think you know now what you wanted to hear, haven't you?'

Karin had put her phone on loudspeaker so that both she and Claudia could listen. They both looked at each other. Karin was past tears now. She was angry and getting angrier by the second.

'Patricia, I cannot thank you enough for what you've told me. This is the second time today I have sat and listened to things that have shaken me to the core. The result will be the end of my marriage but at least I can start to rebuild my life. I do hope to see you sometime soon but first I have to confront Morten.'

'In that case, be very careful. He is a powerful man. But good luck with all that you have to do.'

The call ended. The two friends had heard it all together and now thought the same thought.

'The bastard!' Karin said.

She paused in thought. Thinking of her next move; how best to stack up the evidence for the prosecution.

'Claudia, can you do something for me. Go to Morten's office while he is out of the way and call Helena Fields. That way, she'll answer. The phone here is linked in with the head-quarters, so I can listen in from here and even talk to her directly. We can use some story about Triple F wanting to fund a research project at Harvard. I used exactly the same procedure in contacting Durham to get Matthew Williams out here so it's a valid introduction. Say anything actually that gets her to confirm who her father is.'

'Karin – you are evil. What a subterfuge: I love you!'

'Will you do that? You realise if Morten finds out he'll go crazy. You'll lose your job...'

'It's the least I can do. And after all, you're risking far more than me. Of course I'll do it. I can't wait now to hear what Miss Helena Fields has to say.'

It was an hour later when Karin's phone rang. She was breast-feeding Peter so it was a difficult act trying to place the phone against her ear, keep it in place and still give her baby all the attention he needed.

Karin heard a phone ringing and then a voice answering: 'Hello.'

Claudia sounded next: 'Could I speak to Helena Fields, please.'

'Speaking, who is this?'

'Good afternoon, Helena. This is Claudia Fernández, personal assistant to Mr Morten Fields, Triple F, Colombia. How are you?'

'I'm fine, thank you. But I only accept calls from my father directly. How come you are calling?'

Karin smiled. Well done, Claudia, she thought.

'Mr Fields is out of the office at present but we need to contact the Geology Department at Harvard and I wondered if you could do us a favour and represent Triple F for us? Will you help?'

'I'd rather talk to my father first, thank you.'

'Of course. Like I say he is not here at present but I can put you through to his house if you wish?'

'Er ... OK.'

Claudia then called out: 'Putting you through ...'

There was a pause and Karin thought she'd better say something. In order to prolong the deceit she opened in Spanish.

'*Hola. Buenos tardes. La casa de Morten Fields.*'

Helena Fields spoke up: 'Mr Fields, please.'

'Hello. This is Karin Roth, Mrs Morten Fields speaking. I'm

afraid that Morten is out of town at present – can I help?'

There was a click and the phone connection to the USA went dead. Claudia was still there, however.

'She rang off!' said Karin.

'Yes. She's clearly been warned not to talk to you!'

'But we got her to confirm who her father was, however! Well done, Claudia. That was all we needed!' Karin gritted her teeth. There was nothing more for Karin to do now but return to the routine of looking after Peter and wait for the confrontation that she knew she had to provoke. The longer the hours passed, the more she thought about it, the angrier she became. She no longer trusted anything that Morten had told her.

When the phone rang again, there came one final piece of information that seemed to confirm Karin's revised opinion of her husband. It was Claudia again.

'Karin – I've been doing some digging ...'

'Tell me.'

'I thought I'd check up with Matthew Williams in Popayan – you know, about the progress on the green agenda you were so keen on promoting.'

'And?'

'Well, Matthew was pleased to have someone to talk to about all this. He says he is somewhat isolated now and with very poor Spanish feels as if he has been forgotten. He says he sent an interim report off to Morten some time ago, received a lot of thanks but that's all. One of the first things he looked at was the disposal of waste water from the mine, the high levels of pollutant they contained and how this waste should not be allowed to contaminate the local farmlands. This was months ago, he said, and nothing has been done. The local demonstration at the mine site he only heard about when I told him of it just now. Like I say, he's cut off with no Spanish so when I told him the news he got really annoyed. He says he was grateful for the initial funding to come out here but the prospects for developing his research here look poor. He's fed up. When he heard who I was and from where I was phoning he perked up. He's hoping that I can help advance his cause. I tried not to raise his hopes too much! You can see what Morten's been doing, can't you? Everything on the surface looks just great ...'

'Too right. We were all inspired – none more than me. We've all been taken in. I'm married to him, for God's sake! Now we're digging deeper, it all looks rotten. There is one more dimension to all this, now I come to think of it, and that is what has he been using Leopold Smith for? You heard what Thelma Marshall had to say. She obviously fears all sorts of nasty work. Well, I'm going to have this out with him as soon as he puts his face around the door. I'm so angry! I'll let you know what happens.'

'Take care, Karin! If I don't hear from you I'll phone back tonight. Please be careful – you heard what Patricia said: he's a powerful man!'

'Don't worry, Claudia. I'll be OK. But the sparks are going to fly here, I can assure you of that!'

It was nine o'clock in the evening when Fields arrived back home. When he saw his wife she was just in the process of putting his baby boy to bed. He tiptoed into the nursery to see one sleepy little head being lowered into the luxurious cot in the fully equipped baby bedroom that he had provided for him. His wife was, as always, entirely focused on her child and seemed to ignore his presence completely. Something that was happening increasingly often, he thought with a pang of irritation.

When they had both retreated from the nursery, switched on the baby alarm and camera and closed the door, Fields thought he'd allude to this lack of attention on the way downstairs.

'Well, here I am, darling, aren't you going to welcome me back?'

The reaction Fields got was totally unexpected. Karin had

been waiting too long and now was at boiling point. She turned on him at the bottom of the stairs, almost spitting out her venom.

'Welcome? How dare you? Welcome back a liar to my home, to my son, to my bed? How could you? You've strung me along all this time – promising me you couldn't get me or any other woman pregnant. And you've got *two* daughters that I know of! Any more? How many other lies have you told me?'

Karin's voice was rising and rising through this outburst and she couldn't stand still. She paced across the lounge in front of her husband, flashing looks of pure animosity in his direction.

Fields didn't know what had hit him.

'What are you talking about? Are you crazy? Two daughters? Where has all this come from?'

He sounded so reasonable, so convincing. Karin almost wanted to believe she was wrong. Eyes glaring at him, she realised he was resorting to his usual technique of trying to reassure her that all was well. Except that it wasn't.

'Crazy? I suppose I must be crazy! I believed you. I married you on the strength of everything you told me. I hadn't talked to the mothers of your two daughters at that point. I have now. So tell me again, you liar. Have you or have you not got other children with other women?'

Now Fields got angry. 'You've been talking to Thelma Marshall? You bitch! I told you never to speak to her. Never to believe a word she said. How can you believe her and not me?'

'Don't you dare try it on with me! I called you a liar because it's true. It's not just Thelma I've spoken to; it's Helena as well and Patricia Ramírez too. And do you know what? It all stacks up. You've lied to me all along the line!'

'What the hell have you been doing behind my back? You devious little whore! Who have you been seeing? Who has put you up to all of this?'

Karin raged at him. 'How dare you! How low can you go? How many other awful names are you going to call me? I've done absolutely nothing – you are the one who's done everything so deviously. Get away from me!'

This last comment was made as Morten tried to get hold of her. Karin threw one of the plush cushions of the sofa at him and stormed out of the room, dodging an arm that swung round, trying to hit her. She was going to run off to one of the bedrooms but thought as she did so that most of all she needed to protect her son. She ran upstairs to his bedroom and locked the door behind her. Then she sank on to her knees beside the cot and tried as best as she could to keep herself from sobbing. The last thing she wanted to do was to wake up her precious child.

Fields tried to get into the room but couldn't. He tested the door. It was solid. Of course it was: it was the very best quality that money could buy. For a moment he toyed with the idea of breaking it down, dragging his wife out and giving her the thrashing she deserved. He was tempted. Very tempted. He had lawyers who would be sure to protect him ... Why not go ahead? But maybe the media attention would be a bit too much? The Board would never support him if any scandal like this hit the media, as it surely would, even if he got off scot-free. It was better to retreat and think of another gambit. Let the woman stay where she was – all night if necessary. He would sort her out eventually.

Fields realised he was hungry. He wished now he had taken Carolina out for a meal that evening but she had insisted that he go home to his wife. Hah! Bad decision that turned out to be! He went into the kitchen, found the maid and asked her to prepare a meal for him alone. His wife, he guessed, would not move for hours yet.

Karin's head, meanwhile, was reeling. Her emotions were beginning to subside and she told herself that now she had to let her head do the work and not move until she had proper control of herself and had thought through what she was doing.

Thelma, Patricia and Claudia had all said she should be careful; that her husband was a powerful man. Thelma had said he was terribly vengeful. She remembered, with a sob that she could not contain, that Thelma had met Daniel and his message to her was also that she should take care. Daniel – the one person who could see into the depths of anyone, certainly her, and always, always told the truth. But what should she do? She was undoubtedly not the only woman in the world to find out that her husband was a liar. She was also not the only wife to have been threatened or hit. Did she really want to finish with Morten – the man who offered her financial security, a fine home, all the luxuries and every possible material advantage for her son?

Did she love him? That was the crucial question. Respect – yes; sympathy even … up until now. Loyalty? Yes, but that had been her professional duty. Love? No. She didn't feel that. She knew that was so even at her wedding when she was asked to promise herself to him. She knew that because she knew what love was; she had felt that for someone else and she had never felt like that with him. There had been the fun of the chase but she had never intended to get caught, and the emotions that she had blurted out to Claudia, on the carpet in their flat when she had first discovered she was pregnant, those first reactions – they revealed her true feelings for him.

Claudia! Karin thankfully had her mobile with her. She phoned her friend and as soon as she answered, Karin whispered to her:

'Claudia, I'm going to need your help.'

'What's going on? Why are you whispering? You've now got me all worried about you.'

'I've locked myself in Peter's nursery. I'm going to make a bolt for it. I've got to get out! Can you get Nelson to drive you round and wait outside until I say I'm coming? I'm going to wait until Peter wakes for his feed. Hopefully, Morten will then be asleep … but I can't stay here. He's too dangerous.'

361

'Yes. Certainly. About what time do you think – so that we can be ready?'

'Peter will probably need feeding at 2 a.m. That's his usual time. So I'll next phone around 2.30. Please be here at that time. Can you do that?'

'Of course we can. I'll get on to Nelson right now and warn him. We'll be there before 2.30, don't you worry. We love you, Karin. Please, please be careful!'

'Don't worry. I will. Now I've seen what he is really like I'm getting out while I can. See you later, bye.'

Karin busied herself in the bedroom gathering all Peter's clothes together. There were a couple of bags that would hold most of his essentials. As for her own clothes and belongings she would simply have to run with what she was wearing. Having got everything ready, she turned off the baby alarm – there was no way she wanted that to wake her husband – stripped down to her underclothes and lay down on the single bed that stood beside the cot. Emotionally exhausted, she hoped she would quickly fall asleep.

It seemed like only five minutes later when Karin woke to the sounds of Peter snuffling and struggling in his cot. She must have fallen asleep immediately her head hit the pillow. Looking at her mobile she could see the time was 2.10 a.m.: the little darling was now as regular as a clock. She rose, turned on the dim baby light and held him to her. He latched on straight away and Karin was immediately at peace with the world. Amazing at how someone so small could communicate so much love and contentment to her and through her to calm the whole chaotic world about her. He sucked away happily with his little eyes half closed. Switching him over after a while, Karin reached for her mobile and called Claudia. She answered immediately.

'Hi Claudia. I'm halfway through feeding Peter,' she whispered. 'I'll call again when I'm about to leave, to tell you to get the engine running!'

'Fine, K., We are outside now. Nelson has already spoken to the security guard on the gate and said you will be coming out soon. He obviously wanted to know what we were doing here. We are all set. Just look after your end!'

'Will do. Speak to you soon. Bye.'

Peter finally finished feeding. Karin snuggled him down into the papoose cocoon that was easiest to carry him in and then finished dressing herself and packing the last bits and pieces. She picked up the phone.

'Right, Claudia. Start the engine!'

With Peter on one arm and two bags in the other she went to the door. The key turned, the door swung in, and out she went. As quietly as she could move, she made her way in the dark to the stairs and started creeping down. Karin could hear no noise whatsoever in the house and fervently prayed that Morten was asleep. There was a large hallway that led from the staircase to the front door. She was halfway across that when the hall light went on and Morten was there: coming out of the lounge. He had been waiting up.

'Where the hell do you think you are going?' he demanded.

Karin said nothing, just ran to the front door. She had to drop the bags to open it and one spilled out a large pack of nappies as she did so.

Morten surged forward to stop her but stumbled over the bags and nappies and meanwhile Karin was out. Clutching Peter to her, fear lent speed to her limbs and she ran like a hare for the gate and the car that was waiting outside.

Morten was shouting to the guard to stop her but was calling in English and the guard was confused. That confusion was all Karin needed to get through to the car and the arms of Claudia, reaching for her baby. Karin collapsed inside, the door slammed and Nelson put his foot down. They were away.

Karin thought her heart would burst out of her chest, it was beating so furiously. She was scared, triumphant, worried and high on adrenalin all at the same time.

She swore: 'That bastard was waiting for me downstairs. I had to drop everything to get out.'

'But you are out now and there's nothing he can do about it,' said Claudia. 'Relax, Karin. You've done it!' She handed Peter over to his mother.

'Where are you taking us?'

'Not back to my place. Not to where we used to live. Nelson and I were talking about that. Morten will probably look for you there first of all. So we are going to Nelson's place – we can all rest there tonight and you can stay for as long as it takes to figure out what to do next, without being worried about Morten finding you.'

'Thank you so much, you two. You've saved our lives. You have. Really, I don't know what I would have done without you.'

It was 3.00 a.m. and pitch dark as the car sped into the Bogotá night on deserted roads.

Arriving at Nelson's apartment, Karin found that he and Claudia had already made a bed up for her and Peter to spend the night. It was a little cramped – not at all like the spacious luxury she had just left – but it was safe and welcome and it was not long before she was sleeping with her baby curled up next to her.

When she awoke next, she and Peter were alone. Claudia had obviously decided to go into work early and Karin had no idea of the hours that Nelson worked but guessed he was in his office, too. First things first, Peter had to be fed, and then Karin wondered what to do. Last night had been a frightening experience and with no possibility of carrying anything with her in her flight, other than Peter; there were a hundred and one things she needed – but she could hardly go back to fetch them. Someone else would have to get them for her. Someone else: Ana María! Karin owed her faithful nurse an explanation. She decided to call her. It was an interesting conversation.

'Ana María – it's Karin.'

'Miss Karin! Mr Fields has forbidden me to talk to you. I'm supposed to call him straight away if you contact me!'

'We've had a terrible argument, Ana María, and I've run away with Peter. He must be furious!'

'He is, Miss Karin. He has his people out looking for you and everyone here – the guards on the gate, Juana the maid and myself – we are all warned not to talk to you and to let him know if you call.'

'Please don't tell him, Ana María. Please. I need your help.'

'Don't worry, Miss Karin. We all want to help you. Not him!'

'Thank you, Ana María, thank you so much. Can you do something for me? Can you pretend to go shopping? Smuggle out some clothes for Peter and myself in a bag or two and we will arrange to meet. Can you do that for me?'

'Yes, of course. Where do you want to meet? At the super-market where we usually do the shopping?'

'That's perfect. I'll come in a taxi and won't want to stop so if you are waiting outside when I arrive you can pass over the things directly to me in an instant. Shall we say an hour from now? Please don't breathe a word of this to anyone.'

It was agreed. The deal was done. A little discussion was necessary to clarify which particular items Karin needed most but the plan was set and Ana María was absolutely trust-worthy.

Karin was just about to call a taxi to put things into effect when Claudia arrived back.

'Guess what,' she said. 'I've got the sack! No explanation, as if any was necessary, but Morten just told me I was no longer required and could I go down to finance to settle up and sign off! Well, it solves one problem – I wasn't sure how I was ever going to work for that man again!'

'My goodness, Claudia. He acts fast! That's a warning if ever there was one!'

'Yes. It also gives me a problem – I need another job!'

'Well, we've both got contacts. You've got talent. You'll find somewhere soon, I'm sure. In fact, I've promised to phone Thelma Marshall today to tell her what's happening and she is someone we can now be sure will want to help you fight that man! Maybe you can work for TMG?'

'Great,' said Claudia. 'Serve him right if I could – all Triple F talent crossing over to the opposition!'

'Did you come home by taxi, or drive your car?'

'By car, why?'

'I need to go out and meet Ana María and pick up some of the clothes I had to leave behind. We've agreed to meet outside the supermarket in about forty-five minutes from now. Can we go in your car? It will be safer.'

'Yes, of course. We ought to leave in a quarter of an hour – the traffic is pretty bad.'

'Thanks. I'd better get ready.'

Karin sat in the back of Claudia's car holding on to Peter during the short drive to the supermarket. She had phoned Ana María to tell her of her imminent arrival in the car, not a taxi, and was looking out for her as they approached the lay-by at the side of the road where buses, taxis and short-stay cars could pull in. The supermarket was a located on a crossroads between two wide dual carriageways, both busy with traffic. Claudia was preoccupied with jockeying between two bright-yellow taxis – one pulling out, another pulling in – while Karin waved out of the car window at Ana María, who she could see standing by the lay-by, waiting for her. The car slowed to a halt, Karin opened the rear off-side door and was focused on picking up the two bags Ana María was proffering her. She did not at first see the large jeep that cruised up and double-parked on her left, nor the big man who emerged from it – until he appeared at the door just behind Ana María. It was Leopold Smith.

Smith looked as if he wanted to follow the two bags that Karin was pulling into the car. Karin screamed. Ana María struggled with Smith, trying to block his advance towards Karin and her baby. The jeep was immediately alongside Claudia's car and with a taxi stopped in front she was blocked and could not move. For what seemed an age, there was Smith with one hand inside the rear offside door, the other thrusting Ana María out of the way; Karin held Peter in her lap and had two bags on the rear seat between her and Smith; Claudia was gunning the engine but had nowhere to go. Then, miraculously, the taxi in front moved off. Claudia followed. Smith was an immensely strong man but with one hand not even he could stop the car from slowly pulling away.

'Go, go, go!' shouted Karin, terrified that Smith would come after them. The rear door was flapping as Claudia picked up speed. Smith initially ran after them but gave up and turned to get into the jeep. Then it became a race between the two vehicles. Fortunately, the jeep had to wait for Smith to climb aboard and in that time the smaller and nimbler car had pulled across into the traffic and was already some five or six car lengths in front.

Karin leaned over the top of her bags and closed the rear door, meanwhile urging Claudia to go faster. Peter was beginning to cry – thoroughly disturbed by the panic in his mother's voice.

The jeep chasing them was bigger, heavier and could easily knock them off the road if it could get closer and had a mind to. But the car could accelerate faster, brake faster and had a smaller turning circle. Neither had the advantage at first since the three lanes on the dual carriageway were all choc-a-bloc with traffic.

Claudia was scared but intensely focused on getting away from that monster pursuing them. There was a crossroads approaching and the traffic lights were just changing on their side from green to red. She dared not slow down. There was a bus in front which was applying its brakes, but Claudia pulled out on her left, ignoring the car that was forced to slow up, fiercely hitting its horn, then spun the wheel to her right and cut across in front of the bus, accelerating as fast as she could, just in front of the traffic released by the green light, crossing from left to right. The road in front of them was clear, so they could speed away while the jeep was left behind, stuck in the traffic behind the bus.

'Thank God!' said Claudia, still with her eyes glued on the road in front but now not quite so fearful of her pursuer. Karin was trying to pacify Peter, an impossible task since she was shaking with shock and fear herself.

'How did they find us?' Claudia shouted at the windscreen as she drove along, turning corners one way or another, not caring where they went so long as they were out of sight and on a route that no one could possible understand or follow.

Panic-struck as she was, and with her baby restless and whimpering, Karin was thinking exactly the same. 'Someone must have followed you to Nelson's place, thinking that you would lead them to me. Of course they couldn't get in, so waited to see if I would show. They knew what they were doing.'

'The bastard!' swore Claudia. 'Morten sacked me on the spot with people already set to follow me and I fell right into their trap. But where do we go now?'

'Thelma, at the Hilton. That is the only safe haven now. I'll phone her.'

It was another half-hour before they arrived at their new destination. But they made it safely with no further incident. Thelma had briefed the hotel that they were coming so that Claudia could drive directly into the underground car park, out of sight of any prying eyes. Karin, Peter and Claudia, with assorted bags, then took the elevator to Thelma's suite, high up in the hotel tower. She had the door open, waiting for them.

'They tried to get me or, rather, Peter,' Karin said. 'Now I've got nowhere to hide. They are going to keep looking for me, keep coming for me, until they can snatch Peter away.' She looked in desperation from Thelma to Claudia. She didn't want to say it but she was absolutely terrified of Thelma's son, Leopold Smith, the professional assassin. 'What can I do?'

Thelma knew exactly what to do. 'Firstly, get you out of Bogotá.' 'There are any number of TMG facilities I can hide you in where you will be safe. The head of the Popayán office is a good friend of mine and I often stay in his house when I am down that way. Certainly, no one from Triple F will be welcome in any of our properties and our security there is at present on high alert. In fact, I'll fly down with you – I have to return to our operations there – and I'll be with you every step of the way, in an escorted bulletproof limousine both to and from the airports and I'll be sitting next to you in the plane. How is that?'

'Will you really do that for me? For us both?' Karin looked down at Peter, now asleep in his mother's arms. 'I don't know what to say, how to thank you, but … but I am frightened to my core here, at the moment.'

'Morten is a very dangerous, very clever and scheming individual. We have to match that and do better, place you somewhere where he could never dream of. But let us start with Popayán. You know it, don't you? El Mono mentioned you had a finca near there, Claudia.'

Claudia and Karin both smiled at that.

'Oh yes, we know it,' said Claudia. 'I think it is fair to say that we know it very well and it's long past the time when we should return there. Don't you think, K.?'

Karin looked down at her son, not wanting to face her friend. 'I haven't thought about it for months,' she said in a low voice. 'I've put it out of my mind entirely.' She was fright-

369

ened of what she would find if she opened up that little black box inside her.

Thelma didn't quite follow that interchange. 'Does Morten know that you know that place? Is that somewhere he might want to search for you?'

Karin looked up. 'No. I've never mentioned it to him. Never. It is a part of my background that I've put behind me and I've never wanted him to interfere with. I've not been there for ages. I have seen some of his senior personnel from their Popayán office here in Bogotá, however. If I were to go out on the streets there, one of them might recognise me, I suppose ....'

'Hmmm. It is a risk, Well, we can hide you in my colleague's house for the time being and take it from there. Don't worry – we will sort this out.'

Thelma turned to Claudia. 'Karin and Peter can stay here tonight and we will fly out together tomorrow. What will you do? Carry on here at work?'

'That's a joke! Morten has just sacked me. There is no way that Triple F want me now, or I want them. I'll stay with Nelson for the time being, however. Then maybe I'll come down to see you, Karin, in Popayán ... before you disappear again!'

'Please do,' said Karin. 'But please don't get followed when you do come.'

'Have no fear, K. After today, I have learned my lesson in that regard. Really. Once bitten, twice shy!'

7

Reunion

Karin woke late in the morning but she was at last rested and thankfully recovered from the exhausting, emotionally draining escape from Bogota. Baby Peter was agitated, however, and needed a feed. Whatever else might happen, whatever fears, anxieties and hopes she might have, Karin knew that the one constant in her life now was that her son came first. She went to the cot beside her bed, lifted him out and, cradling him in her arms, she returned to the bed and settled back to feed him. She loosened her nightie at the front, the baby's head instinctively turned towards her breast and little eyes opened to focus on his mother. A gurgle of contentment followed. Karin struggled to hold back the tears. She was feeling exceptionally vulnerable and emotionally fragile at the moment. Looking down on such a beautiful but such a small, helpless and totally dependent little baby almost broke her heart. An all-consuming sense of love and a desire to protect him against whatever and whoever might stand in her way threatened to overwhelm her.

Minutes ticked by in silence, save for the tiny sounds of a baby's breathing and rhythmical sucking. At last Karin was at peace. Then the bedroom door slowly opened and a head peered round.

It was Claudia: 'Can I come in?'

Karin gave a muted squeak of delight. She didn't want to

disturb the baby but she had not seen her friend for days and she desperately needed her support.

Claudia hovered at the foot of the bed, looking first at Karin and then looking back, out of the bedroom. 'I've brought someone to see you, I hope you don't mind,' she whispered.

The door opened a little wider and Daniel appeared. Daniel whom she had not seen for two years and yet who looked exactly the same, unchanged. Daniel with those dark-blue eyes that bore into her and that gentle, beautiful, bewitching smile. Daniel.

Karin simply didn't know how to react. She was dumbstruck. There seemed to be a great, vacant void inside her that filled her entire body and baby Peter must surely be feeding on nothing. Her eyes lowered: she could not look at him. She realised she felt ashamed.

'You look lovelier than ever,' he said

Claudia tactfully crept back out of the room and closed the door.

'Can I come closer?' Daniel asked.

Karin nodded; she still couldn't speak.

Daniel quietly approached, lifted the bedclothes carefully across so that he might sit without interfering with mother and son, and gazed at the little baby busily feeding away. 'A lovely boy!' he said.

He was close enough now that Karin could smell the scent of the mountain on him. She could even measure the length of his eyelashes as he looked down upon her baby. Why did he have such divine eyes?

Suddenly she was crying. Silently. Defenceless. Empty.

Daniel looked at her and understood. There was an awkward pause. He reached for her hand for a second and then withdrew. 'I'll wait for you outside,' he said.

Karin wanted to say something, anything, in reply but could only watch dumbly, tears drizzling down her cheeks, as he retreated.

372

Claudia came quickly into the bedroom as Daniel left. The door was shut tight, protecting their privacy. Karin's wet face looked up into the worried eyes of her friend and at last she found a voice. But it was not words that came out, just an inarticulate cry from somewhere deep inside.

The two women put their arms around each other. Baby Peter was detached from his mother's breast and somehow arranged between them. Karin started to sob.

'I'm sorry, I'm sorry, forgive me,' Claudia pleaded. 'I thought you would like to see him.'

Karin shook her head, then just as quickly nodded, emphatically. 'I do, I do, but what do I say? How can I see him? What must he think of me? Look at me!' Floods of tears began to flow.

Baby Peter began to get restless, crying for attention. 'Oh, this is hopeless!' Karin wailed.

But he could not be put off. Despite the emotional tidal wave sweeping over his mother, Peter had to be comforted, returned to the breast again and prompted to resume feeding.

As always, his needs helped focus his mother but the great hollowness that had opened up within her would not go away. The two women looked at each other. What to do?

'I'll ask Daniel to wait a bit longer and then, when Peter is settled, why don't you come out and see him?' Claudia said. 'You've got to see him, you know.'

'Yes, yes. I will,' Karin agreed. 'Go tell him. Please apologise for me and say that I really, really want him to stay.'

The next ten minutes were passed concentrating on her infant. Karin was not able to think of anything else, and could not think beyond him if she tried. But she knew she had to try. She had to face the one person, more than any other, from whom she could not hide.

Peter eventually stopped feeding, was held up gently to rest over his mother's shoulder and had his back rubbed and caressed. He was the centre of Karin's world and she could not now see Daniel without him. So now was the time.

She pulled herself together as best as she could and went outside. Daniel was sitting patiently in the next room, waiting. Claudia and Thelma were nowhere to be seen and Karin guessed that they had known, as she did, that she had to meet Daniel alone in order to relate all that had happened to her and why. They were probably wondering, just the same as she was, how he would react. They were probably not so scared as she was, however.

'Please forgive me, Daniel. I've been behaving foolishly,' Karin said, rather stiffly.

Daniel just looked at her, seeing right through the shell she was trying to put around herself.

'Don't apologise. You don't need to hide your feelings; not from me. The last time I saw you, you were so different I didn't recognise you. This time I see the person you really are. You're beautiful again.'

How does he do it? Insults and compliments that get right under her skin. Her blood surged inside her just as it used to: Karin didn't know whether to laugh or cry.

'What do you mean – I was so different last time? When was that when you didn't recognise me?'

'I went up to Bogotá about a year ago, looking for support for something I was organising. I visited the National Parks Organisation and of course I wanted to look at the Triple F headquarters where I knew you were working. I thought of asking for you but then I saw you rushing, or rather tripping, outside on your high heels. Like I say, I nearly didn't recognise you. You certainly never saw me, even though you walked straight past me with this, this Morten Fields.'

Karin shook her head, mortified. She didn't know when that was. She felt desperately ashamed that she had missed him but she was living a different life then. What she knew for certain was the fact that she was not at all the same person now.

'Daniel – have good look at me,' she demanded indignantly.

'Can't you see that it's now that I'm different? I am a mother! Everything has changed. Everything! Perhaps you haven't seen him properly yet: let me introduce you to Peter. He's my son!'

Karin had been through so many extremes of emotion so recently, so rapidly, that now everything came spilling out of her. Did she feel guilty that she had run away from him and his world, had never contacted him, had married another, had had a baby that was not his? She felt guilty, uncertain of her own buried feelings for this man, uncertain of the value of the life she had been constructing without him, absolutely certain of the love she felt for her son, but uncertain of how all these conflicting feelings could somehow be reconciled. The result was all heat and fire and passion.

Daniel smiled disarmingly. This was the woman he knew. 'Oh come on, Karin. Be honest with yourself. You know what I mean. The last time I saw you, you were the city executive. So cool; so collected; so efficiently superficial. You were busily moving from one place to another, but it seemed to me you were not looking too deeply into where you were going. I hated you for not seeing me. Now you are real again. I guess your son has done that. Thank you, Peter, for bringing back the woman that I recognise.' He finished by echoing her sarcasm, but with a voice touched with tenderness: 'Perhaps you haven't heard me properly yet: you're lovelier than ever ...'

Karin's fire dissolved. He had penetrated right to her very centre, exposing everything she had refused to admit to herself and still did not want to look too carefully into. And then he had reproached her for her sarcasm yet in such a gentle, warm and supportive manner.

She stammered: 'Please ... please don't. You ... you ... always do it. You hurt me in such wonderful ways. If I'm hateful, how can you say I'm lovely?'

'It's when you open up ... when you say what you really feel. That's when you let me see the beauty inside you. It's inside.

Not in the clothes you wear, your city make-up, the image you present. True beauty resides in your soul and shines out of your eyes, through the expression on your face. I look at you now and there is nothing more beautiful than a mother with her baby. It has inspired painters and artists throughout history!' He finished with a flourish.

Karin smiled at that. 'You do talk a lot of cheesy tosh at times!' But it had raised her spirits.

They looked at each other, not quite sure how to take things from there. Karin turned sideways and brought her baby to see his visitor. Peter obliged by opening his eyes and yawning.

At last Karin felt courageous enough to say what she knew she had to.

'Daniel, I'm married to Morten Fields. This is his son …'

'I know.'

'I haven't seen you for ages. Everything has changed between us. How can you still say nice things about me when I have treated you so badly?'

'You haven't treated me badly … What do you mean?'

'Well, I haven't treated you in any way at all. I've left you and denied whatever it was we had. That is the worst of it. After everything we have been through together, after such a friendship that has meant so much to both of us, I go off and leave you with no word, nothing, ignoring everything you mean to me. And I marry someone who is the opposite of you in every way and have his baby. What must you think of me?'

Daniel ignored this last question. 'Do you love him, your husband?'

Karin could not meet his eyes. She turned away and walked her baby slowly up and down, comforting him; comforting herself.

'No. I thought I could love him, but I know now that it was a terrible mistake. I feel such a fool telling you this. How many other silly women throughout the ages have said the same? Been taken in by some attractive, smooth-talking partner only to find out he was the biggest bastard on the face of the earth? I never thought such a thing would ever, ever happen to me. I was too sensible, too intelligent, too worldly-wise to ever fall into that classic trap. How stupid, short-sighted, proud and tiny-minded of me. How can I have been so foolish?' She stopped and looked at Daniel and asked him again: 'What must you think of me?'

Karin saw Daniel look into the distance, deliberately avoiding her gaze. It was his turn now not to be able to meet her eyes. She suddenly dreaded what he was about to say.

There was no answer for a while. Then he started, slowly at first but quicker as his thoughts began to flow: 'I hated you. You had become part of the world that I detested, and worse: you had done all that I'd told you I was opposed to ... How could you do that? You were captured by all the superficial materialism of a world that you knew I hated and so ... I hated you. I couldn't help myself. I took off over the mountains, burying myself in my world that was everything yours was not.

'And that saved me. You see things so much more clearly up there. Why was I so angry with you? Because I wanted you to see things my way? What right did I have to demand that? I was the one who was wrong, not you. You have every right to do whatever you want; not what I want. I was the one to feel stupid, selfish, and to fall into the trap of tiny-minded pride.'

Daniel turned quickly to flash a glance at his companion. 'I know this sounds crazy – corny even – but it's the only way I can describe how I feel. I have travelled miles and miles across all the mountains immersing myself in their life. Following the falcons and condors in the air; the serpents, deer and puma on the ground. Every creature follows its own particular destiny. And then I realised that that is what I had loved so much about you. I used to watch you moving on the mountainside and, more importantly, moving on the streets of town, talking to people, laughing, interacting with your world. You were following your own destiny, as you must do, and you became the lovelier the more you did so. I've told you that before.

'Going off to Triple F, immersing yourself in the world of the big multinational corporations, was something you had to do to be true to yourself. Striding around in those high heels, becoming the efficient executive, marrying Morten Fields, it was all part of your journey. It took me some time – ages – before I realised that ... and of course he was the opposite of everything I represent. That was what hurt me most at first ... until I realised that that was precisely why you married him. You had to give yourself to him and through that to find yourself. The big cats taught me this, and I see it, too, in the condors: they go everywhere, try different worlds, looking for where they truly belong. Most of the time they are still out there, searching for answers. I love to see that. I realised then that, you and I, we are both doing the same too.'

Daniel stopped for a moment, reflecting. 'I loved seeing you first of all; then I hated you; then I hated myself for being so stupid. Now I see you clearer than ever. You and I are both on our separate journeys, looking for our respective destinies. We may cross paths now and again. Only know this ...'

He stopped again, took Karin and her baby and turned them both to face him, and said: 'I love you. I always have. I always will.'

Karin closed Peter to her breast and pushed herself into Daniel's arms. 'Hold me,' she said. 'Hold me tight and never, ever let me go.' She was weeping again.

Daniel kissed the top of her head. 'I have to let you go, Karin. I have to. I can't give you what you need in the world where I belong. You belong to another. You must know that.'

Karin shook her head. Folded in his arms, curled up with her baby against his chest, she shook her head again.

'I've had enough of my world, as you put it,' her muffled voice rose up to him. 'Let me try yours.'

There was something certain that Karin had locked away

inside her. It had been there for years: wrapped up, shrunken down, locked away and buried deep down somewhere where she had not wanted to find it. Yet as soon as Daniel had walked into her sight it had flared up and demanded her attention. Seeing him, listening to him, absorbing all that he was, that certainty now overcame her – filling her entire being. She loved him. She loved him like she could love no other; she wanted him with a passion that made her body tremble and she could not now imagine living without him. Where had she been these last two years? Chasing a career and living a life that she thought she ought to follow instead of listening to her heart and her deepest feelings that were telling her something completely different.

She looked up, her eyes holding his in gaze of fire. 'Come with me; let me put Peter down.'

He let her go but she held on to his hand and, cradling Peter with the other, took him into the bedroom and made him watch as she laid her baby down in the cot. Daniel looked down, of course, with such an expression of tenderness that only made her want him more. He had no right to look like that at another man's baby! Why did he look at the world with such loving eyes?

Now she could hold herself back no longer and so flung herself at him and kissed him with a fervour that she had never felt before. Daniel was, for a moment, taken by surprise. This beautiful woman whom he had said he loved was wearing only a thin nightie and he could feel her naked body pressing into him, sending him a message that was unmistakeable. Flames engulfed him in an instant. He stripped off quickly himself and then the two of them fell on to the bed together, entwined with one another. Her nightie was discarded and Daniel kissed her and kissed her, touching every part of her body with his lips, smothering her with the love he had always felt for her but had never expressed until now.

They made love so intensely, unrestrainedly that Karin

almost fainted. She cried out with such buried and repressed emotion that its release made everything spin around. Then she clung on to Daniel and held him down on her, inside her, with such a surge of fire as if her arms would break. She never wanted to let him go.

It took an age before Karin came down from heaven. Daniel was waiting, looking at her, still kissing her as gently as he could.

'I'm not letting you go!' said Karin when she could find her voice.

'Are you going to break me in half then?' asked Daniel. 'Can I move?'

'No. Never.'

'What if Peter cries?'

'Don't you dare blackmail me! That's a cruel trick to try and pull. Besides, I'll just have to drag you with me to the cot. I've told you – I'm not letting go!'

Then the passion rose within her again and she was kissing him, struggling with him, turning him over so that she could climb on top of him, caress him, press her lips all over his body, push herself on to him and take him into her once more. She cried out again and this time tears of love fell on to his body, hot tears that should have fallen long ago. She shook her head from side to side, trying to shake aside how stupid she had been, never to admit what she truly, deeply felt. Then she collapsed down on top of him, exhausted.

They lay together, enfolded in each other for an age.

'Do you understand now why I can never let you go?' Karin asked.

'Mmm.'

'Do you not feel what I feel and think that you cannot live without feeling this again?'

'Mmm.'

'Communicative, aren't you?' She dug him with her fingers. 'Talk to me!'

He turned his head and looked at her, an inch away, and growled at her.

'Look, woman! Much as I love you, much as I dream of you, you know nothing of the life I lead. I sleep in a wooden hut, most of the time. A number of huts in different places, as it happens. Sometimes I don't see anyone for days. Other days, I maybe see someone or two ...'

'Don't tell me you're seeing another woman ... or two?' She knew only too well the effect he had on females. 'You're not married as well, are you? I don't blame you if you are; there must be many who want you.'

Karin for a moment was horror-struck at her own stupidity. Everything had happened to her in the last two years since she had seen him. Why couldn't the same be true for him as well? Surely he must have loved others, married another? She recoiled from him in shock.

Daniel laughed and grabbed hold of her, pulling her close.

'Do you honestly think I could love you like I just have; could have poured out all my feelings for you; let you lose yourself in me, and me in you ... if I was married and loved another? What sort of person do you think I am? One of those city two-timers that you mix with, that *you* marry? Am I like that? Is that all the faith you have in me?'

That hurt. As always his words went deep inside and cut into her soul. She had no defence against him. She had married a man who had lied to her. This one would never be like that.

'I'm sorry. Don't punish me. I know you are not like that. I've just found you ... I daren't even think of ever losing you again ... Please don't let me go. Don't ever say we cannot be together. I don't care where. I really don't. The only life I want to live now is with you. Please believe me.'

Her body was shaking. Daniel held her close and kissed her again, calming her down. He recognised the inevitability of what had passed between them. Making love like they had just done meant the same for him as it did for her. He was committed to her now. It was to change his life as it was hers.

He sighed. 'You always used to do it. You still do. Dammit, woman, you shake my world from top to bottom and turn it upside down. I had no idea that this was going to happen when I came to see you!'

She rolled on top of him and grinned. She hugged and squeezed him against her, so much so that there were drops of her breast milk that wet his chest. She was momentarily embarrassed but he took no notice. She recovered.

'If you haven't loved another woman recently, then you've missed out. All the ways women like me make men like you see the world differently. You can't live a hermit's life for ever. Join us! Come into the real world with me. Just don't even try to look at another woman now you've got this one, understand?'

Daniel laughed again. Goodness, how he loved her! Much as he loved the mountains and all the creatures he lived with, this tornado had turned his whole world around and made him question everything and all that he was and felt. He wondered, idly, if all the creatures he lived with and which instinctively reacted to his feelings would still be the same, or if his love for this woman meant he would lose all the relationships he had with all the other beings on earth. He looked at her again, her beautiful face so close to his. What if he lost everything else? Was she worth it? He smiled.

'What are you smiling at? What are you thinking?'

Yes. This was his new life. He had been alone for so long and now there was someone here who would never leave him on his own again. Ever. Was he prepared for this? He smiled even broader.

'What is it?' She picked up his smile but still insisted.

'Nothing. I love you like I never thought I could. You are going to drive me crazy, I know it, yet I still can't help it. I'm walking straight into this like a fool with my eyes wide open.'

'Not like a fool. Like a wise man who at last has come down from out of the clouds!'

'Have it your own way!' He kissed her again.

Thelma and Claudia were waiting, wondering what was going on between Karin and Daniel, and hoping particularly that Karin was all right and that Daniel would not upset her, given her current fragility and the fear she still carried within her. The longer they stayed locked away together, however, the more they reckoned things must be going well. After an hour and more, things were obviously going very well. They did not want to interrupt but Claudia, especially, was impatiently walking around in the spacious lounge of this house of Thelma's friend, dying of curiosity and unable to keep still.

At last a door opened and Karin and Daniel emerged together from the guest suite, Karin with her face shining like Claudia had never seen before. Claudia relaxed immediately.

'Well, it seems you two have made friends,' said Thelma.

'Thank you for bringing me here,' said Daniel, coming to sit on the large leather sofa that faced the older woman. Karin immediately sat next to him and held his hand. Claudia came over and sat next to Karin. She couldn't stop grinning at her friend who couldn't stop beaming herself.

'Come on: don't tell me all that you've been doing but tell me something.'

'Claudia – I love him to bits. You know I always have and I've not, we've not, ever admitted it. I've been so stupid for so long, it took a little while for me to empty my head of all my idiocies and come to my senses. Now I'm never going anywhere else but with him. He is still trying to change my mind but I'm not listening. I know what I want.'

Daniel nodded. 'She's crazy and so must I be.' He squeezed Karin's hand.

'Can we please be a little more practical,' said Thelma.

'What do you propose to do now you've found each other and before anyone else finds you?'

Claudia had met Daniel on her finca and had brought him down to meet Thelma to brief him on all that had been happening to Karin before he was shown into the bedroom. He knew the danger Karin and Peter still faced.

'There are many material things that I cannot offer Karin that she, and all of you, must be accustomed to. My standard and style of living is very different to all this.' Daniel waved his hand round at the spacious and extensive property that spread all about them. 'But the one thing I can offer you' – he looked at Karin – 'is how to disappear. I do it all the time, after all.' He smiled sheepishly.

'And don't we know it,' remarked Claudia caustically. 'It's a miracle I found you this morning. It's only taken me two days this time. I remember wasting many more days than that, chasing after your shadow on the mountains in the past.'

'Seriously, where will you go? How will you live? What will you do?' Thelma stayed relentlessly focused on the issue at hand.

Daniel looked at Karin as he spoke to the others. He wanted to ensure that she really knew what she was letting herself in for. 'There are a number of options – places I've visited. But I shan't say where, other than it is where the condors fly and the pumas prowl. Very few people go to these places and those that do I would know they are coming from a mile away and can choose whether we meet or avoid contact. We will be out of phone and e-mail range unless we move down to some pueblo somewhere. That means we will call you on occasions but you won't be able to reach us. That is safest, especially if Claudia, particularly, is being watched. Thelma – you will therefore be the one we would call first of all and you can then pass on our messages to Claudia. At first, for I do not know how many months, we won't contact you at all. Fields is bound to have everyone out watching and waiting for the

slightest clue as to where Karin and Peter are. Beautiful one –
do you really think you can take this sort of life?' Daniel gazed
at Karin anxiously.

'I have to disappear somehow. And I can't think of anyone
or anywhere I'd rather disappear with but with you. It is that
simple.'

'Does your ex-husband know that you know me?'

Karin kissed him for that comment – her ex-husband. 'No.
I've never let him into that secret that was locked away inside
me.'

'Good. He'll look in Bogotá, Cali, airports, England even …
but not in the Andes,' replied Daniel. 'I have to say, the last
time I saw you, city girl, you were so refined and elegant, I'd
only be looking for you on catwalks in London, Paris or
Milan. Not the big-cat walks that only I know of.'

'You brute!' she shoved him.

'Honestly – do you think you'll be comfortable in woolly
jumpers and overalls? Bathing in cold mountain streams?
Carrying Peter like the *indígenas* do, not in fancy baby strollers
and driven around in four-by-fours? No business suits and high
heels if you go with me!'

Karin shoved him again. 'Stop going on about me in high
heels. I'll never wear them ever again!' She loved him teasing
her: it was a new experience.

Thelma interrupted. 'When will you leave?'

'Pack tonight. If it's OK, I'd like to sleep here and then we
can leave tomorrow. Can you find transport for us? An all-
terrain four-by-four to get us as high up as possible in the
valley I'm thinking of. Then it's a walk or a ride from there,
depending on whether I can get horses. I probably can. They
know me in the nearest pueblo. They won't know where I'm
going, though. I'll be heading for a mountain hut that is basic
but I've slept there before. It's weather proof.'

He turned towards Karin with a serious look on his face.

'Do you realise what I'm proposing? That we start our life

together there. That we build our home on that mountainside – you, me and baby Peter. I can't believe I'm saying this myself. An instant family!' He shook his head in wonderment at what he was committing himself to. 'I have walked those mountains for decades on my own. I've built my life around the birds and animals up there since there was no one else but myself to share them with. You can't know this but I've spent whole nights weeping, especially after you had gone, wondering if there would ever be anybody who could live with me in my world. But now … but now … if you'll have me, my lonely life tonight, it ends tonight. I'm yours!'

Karin threw herself into his arms. Even Thelma relented: there was no more to say.

8

Desolation

The next couple of months were like an extended honeymoon for Karin and Daniel. They had so much to find out about each other. And at the same time, there was so much to do – especially for Karin: getting used to a way of life that began as if she was camping but which led to them converting a wooden hut into a home. Daniel was accustomed to mountain life – living much closer to the elements, where weather dictated much of what could or could not be done – but thinking of ways to make life easier and more comfortable for his woman and her child was an entirely new way of looking at the world for him. And, of course, he frequently got it wrong. What he thought would suit her – suggesting alterations and extensions to their living quarters, for example – she invariably criticised as being hopelessly inappropriate. But they fell about with laughter each time they got it wrong, then got it right, then got it wrong again. Such was the process of learning to live together for a couple who had often, separately, fantasised about doing this but where the reality, for two people of such different backgrounds, was very different to their dreams.

Routines began to be established. Karin was surprised to learn that Daniel had been asked to do some research on pumas for the National Parks Organisation. They wanted him to become an eco-tourism guide but he had said he needed to become more familiar with their haunts first of all. That was him being the perfectionist, she knew. He could do it now better than anyone if he wanted. But what he really wanted to do was go wandering off, tracking pumas until he was certain of their whereabouts. There was no way that Karin could be left alone for any length of time just yet, however, so Daniel's tracking had to be limited to no more than a couple of hours at a time. Frustrating for him; reassuring for her.

Karin's wanderings were limited to visiting the local pueblo with Daniel. They had agreed that, if Fields was looking for a solo English woman and baby, her best cover was to appear as Daniel's wife, with Peter as their child. She loved that. Visiting the nearest pharmacy was an essential routine and, although the pharmacist had heard of El Mono often, and seen him sometimes like most of the pueblo, he had not realised Mono was married. He was reassured that they had been together for ages, though with a baby just approaching six months his wife had not been able to visit before. Hearing them talk in English, the pharmacist was happy to practise his own. As the one with the highest level of education in the vicinity, of course, he wanted to show off.

'I learn English in university. Part of my studies. My son Felipe he now study English too. Say 'ello, Felipe!'

A boy in his late teens came out from the back of the shop with his mother and were duly introduced. They all wanted to meet the famous Mono and his wife.

'My wife, Adriána, she no speak English,' said the pharmacist, who introduced himself as Mateo Romero. 'Anything you want, Mono, Mrs Mono, we happy to serve you!'

Daniel and Karin said they were delighted to meet Mateo and his family. They thanked him for his excellent service and came away with some baby medicine. Mateo refused to be paid. It was an honour, he said.

A shop in the pueblo sold minutes on a mobile phone so Daniel took the opportunity at last to call Thelma and give her the news that they were fine, Peter was growing lustily and Karin really didn't miss the luxuries of urban life. Well, not much, not yet. Thelma replied that things were quiet in Bogotá where she was at present. Claudia was now with her in the TMG office and held the fort when Thelma was travelling. Fields may still have people out looking all over for Karin and Peter but contacts inside Triple F knew nothing. Oh, and did Daniel know that National Geographic were scheduled to release a programme on Colombian wildlife in which he was apparently going to appear? It was going to be on their television channel which she would be able to see in Bogotá.

Daniel laughed at that news. He had remembered some woman and a television cameraman chasing after him above the Fernández estate and interviewing him. He had told them if they wanted some footage of some of the creatures he mixed with then they had to very carefully follow his instructions. The woman said she wouldn't be around for very long, she just wanted an interview, but that the wildlife camera work was a much longer commitment. As it happened, he fixed up what they wanted within a week and the camera man was astonished. He said he was used to working for months at a time in the field waiting to get the right shots. Daniel just nodded. He wondered what the programme would be like and if he would be on screen for long. The interview had not lasted for more than a few minutes.

Karin was in the butcher's shop bargaining over how much they would give her for the pigeons they had brought down to sell. The peregrine falcon was a terrific hunter; a real asset to them. And Karin was a great trader, far better than Daniel in dealing with people – especially men – enjoying the cut and thrust in bargaining and leavening the whole process with much teasing and laughter.

Karin came away with almost twice the amount of money that Daniel could have got for the same pigeons. He was duly impressed. He passed over the news from Thelma: that Claudia was now heading up her office in Bogota; that Fields was undoubtedly still looking for her but everything was quiet and, oh yes, he was to be included in some National Geographic television programme.

Karin stopped suddenly and Peter nearly jumped out of the sling she was carrying him in.

'Where can we see it?' she asked.

'I have no idea,' he replied. 'I don't even know if they pick up National Geographic in this part of the world.'

'We have got to see it – you might be famous! I wonder if that electrical repair shop will have a television that shows it, or maybe the Internet café? When is it going to be on?'

'I don't know. I didn't ask.'

'You are absolutely hopeless, do you know that? What do you mean, you don't know? Aren't you interested? You might be famous! They might make you a television star and you will earn pots of money! I love you to bits but you've got as much sense as Paddy O'Reilly's dog!'

Daniel laughed out loud. 'Who the hell is Paddy O'Reilly and what breed of dog does he have? Is it a hyper-intelligent sheepdog? Those Border collies are wonderful.'

'I expect his dog is a flea-bitten mongrel that doesn't know one end of a bone to the other and Paddy O'Reilly is undoubtedly a drunken layabout who sleeps all day while his wife does all the thinking for him. Like me!'

'And I'm the drunken layabout who sleeps all day? Is that what you're saying?'

'If the cap fits ...'

While this little spat was going on, Daniel was looking around the limited number of dwellings nearby that might host a television or Internet connection. If the mobile phone networks were working here, then they had a chance.

Daniel gathered his wife and her baby in his arms and gave her a kiss. 'There's a place opposite that might help us. Why don't you go in, beautiful, and ask whatever you want to ask about this television programme?'

Karin looked into the low, one-storey building across the street that was crammed with all sorts of gadgets. There was a woman in there behind a crowded counter.

Karin grinned up at Daniel and returned the kiss. 'It's a female there. Your speciality. Go and flash your beautiful blue eyes at her and do the asking instead of me!'

Daniel gave in and did as he was told. He went into the shop.

He came back after a while. 'She says we can look at the television guide they have and find out. But you have to do it. I can't read ...'

Karin looked at his face. Flat. Expressionless. He had stopped in the middle of the road, distant, isolated, an island. He was holding the magazine he had been given, with one page folded open, but he was not looking at it – he held it limply at his side as if it was worthless. For Daniel, it was. Karin had forgotten all about that little important detail. After all the highs they had experienced together, after all that morning's banter and game playing that had done so much to raise their spirits and consolidate their love for one another, suddenly Daniel had come down with a crash and hit rock bottom. Karin felt terrible. This was one of those reasons, and a big reason at that, why Daniel hated the city and yet she had completely forgotten about it. On the mountainside he was the one that ruled supreme. In the city he would have trouble reading shop signs and café menus. Confronting it now, she thought he must suffer from some form of dyslexia but diagnosis was small comfort for him if he couldn't do anything about it.

She went up to him. 'I love you like I never thought I'd ever love anyone. Do you know that? You are the most wonderful, talented and magical person I have ever met in all my life, anywhere – from one side of the earth to the other. Never

391

forget that.' She kissed him, trying to soothe away the pain.

'And I still can't read properly,' he said. 'Fat lot of use I am to you on occasions like this!' He was still expressionless, deflated, ashamed.

'Take Peter,' Karin said, removing the offending magazine from his grasp. She passed over her baby and went back to the shop. Reappearing a few minutes later she caught up with Daniel who was still stranded, unmoved.

'It's not on the television so far as I can see. Not for some time yet at any rate. Your fame may reach the rest of the world but not here. We will have to catch up on your programme at some other time and place. Come on, let's go home now.' She put her arm through his and they walked back up hill and out of the pueblo.

They didn't talk about the television, nor Daniel's dyslexia for some time after that. But Karin had not forgotten either. It was a couple of months later when she called in on the pharmacy and mentioned, while she was chatting to Adriána, the chemist's wife, that there was this wildlife programme they were waiting to see. Adriána went to their living quarters at the back of the shop and returned almost immediately, excitedly saying there was this programme on the National Geographic channel on Colombian wildlife, scheduled to be screened in two days' time, and maybe that was the one? Some negotiation between the two women established that they should all come and watch it together – even if this was not the one featuring Daniel, it would anyway be entertaining. Adriána and Mateo would be pleased to have them visit and stay for a meal.

Daniel protested that he wasn't interested in the television programme, but he was nonetheless escorted down the mountainside by his determined partner to the pueblo to visit the chemist, his wife and son at the required hour. Adriána served up a plentiful supply of chicken soup, with rice and salad, for the entire company while they waited for the programme to come on. Karin was impatient to see what was going to be screened; Daniel feigned boredom; Peter was gurgling comfortably in his mother's lap.

At last the programme began. It was mostly in English with Spanish subtitles. It began with a television reporter from National Geographic addressing the audience.

'This is Elizabeth Manning reporting from somewhere in the Andes mountains of Colombia. We have some amazing footage of rare wildlife in this programme, in particular those champions of the air: Andean condors – the world's largest bird – and some truly remarkable, never-seen-before shots of pumas, otherwise known as mountain lions or cougars, and finally we finish with an even more amazing individual – I shall introduce you to him a little later.'

Karin interrupted. 'It had to be a woman reporter, didn't it?' she said to Daniel. 'I can guess you absolutely mesmerised her!'

Daniel told her to shut up; he had done nothing of the sort.

The programme then focused on some beautiful aerophotography of condors flying, wheeling, soaring over clouds and mountains. There were close-ups and long shots, even some taken in the air as if flying close by from one condor to another.

The screen switched to a puma walking, resting, cleaning itself. Next came tremendous shots of a puma accelerating, leaping prodigiously and killing a small deer. It turned and snarled at the camera as if protecting its kill. All the time the commentary was remarking about how this was unique camera footage of a very rare, solitary animal, exceedingly difficult to find and extremely wary of human contact. The commentary finished by emphasising that these were very dangerous animals; every year there were people attacked by pumas and on average one person a year was killed in North America alone.

Elizabeth Manning came back to front the presentation and

to state that some viewers will undoubtedly want to know how this rare camera work was achieved. And this, she said, was the most amazing story of them all.

The camera shifted to a series of interviews of people in Colombia, some native Andean Indians, others local farmers, also National Park wardens and officials, then finishing with a number of English speakers. Karin sat absolutely glued to the spot, unable to tear her eyes away from the screen. There were several people she instantly recognised and they were all talking about the same person.

'He commands the birds out of the skies.'

'Dogs, horses, cattle, they all seem to do whatever he wants.'

Two women came on screen. 'He sent a bull to charge men who were attacking us,' said the older. 'He's just wonderful,' said the younger.

There was Alfonso, from Claudia's finca: 'If one of our horses is ill, just ask El Mono. He knows the problem and how to cure it – I've no idea how he communicates with them.'

The head of Colombian National Parks spoke in English to the camera. 'El Mono is exceptional. Go and see him. He will bring condors down from the skies and pumas out of the *páramo* to talk to you.'

Then, of all people, there was Thelma Marshall, interviewed in her office, the supreme executive, not given to hyperbole: 'He rescued me from a mugging. Don't ask me how he did it but he sent a swarm of bees after my attacker. The brute was right up close, waving a knife in my face, and then he was covered in so many bees I couldn't see his head. Not one of those bees came around me. They focused their attack solely on this mugger and when El Mono told them to come off, so they did.'

Elizabeth Manning came back on to the screen.

'The man you are going to see now only promised one short piece of footage with the animals because he says these are all wild creatures and not pets. He has most definitely not trained

them, he says. The way he puts it, they are just his friends –
but let's let him do the talking now.'

And then here was Daniel, facing the camera telling it how
it was:

'Peregrine falcons are the fastest creatures on earth. When
they stoop, or dive out of the heavens, they can exceed 200
miles per hour, yet their control is startling. Follow my arm.'

The camera looked up along his arm as he pointed into the
blue sky. It focused on nothing in particular, then a small dot
appeared, then something larger and then, quicker than could
be caught on film, bang! There it was. Daniel's arm dipped as
the bird hit the glove and came to rest. Wow!

'Pumas are really beautiful cats. If you ever see one you are
truly blessed. Just look at this one, a large male.'

As he spoke, a big cat appeared from behind him and looked
at the camera. For a moment it was still and then, with barely
any warning, it leapt seemingly effortlessly over the top of the
screen and out of camera shot.

'Condors are at the end of the food chain. They scavenge up
any dead meat – large carcasses mainly. If anything is wrong
with the ecosystem, then it will show up with the condors and
vultures, which is why, here in Colombia, you will only find
these amazing creatures far away from human pollution and
interference. But just gaze at their command of the thermals
and their dominance of the highest peaks. You will hardly ever
see them flap their giant wings.'

The camera followed two birds circling ever closer, ever
larger, coming in for one final sweep right across between the
camera and Daniel, blotting out all light as they did so.

Then Elizabeth was talking to Daniel, holding up the micro-
phone and asking him how he did it. Karin knew his answer. It
was always the same.

'I don't do anything. I don't issue any commands. I don't
have any control over them. They do what they want. I'm just
lucky they want to involve me, that's all.'

'But, Mono, they come to you – from out of the sky and off the mountain. Everyone we talk to says the same. Our cameras have just captured it and thousands, millions of viewers have all seen it.'

'But you can see I don't *do* anything. They just come and make friends with me.'

'How about the claim that you sent a swarm of bees to attack a mugger.'

'Yes. That can happen when I get angry with someone. Like with the bull. Some thugs tried to beat up a person I once knew and I was so angry with them that a bull picked up on my anger and charged at them.'

Elizabeth Manning reacted as if she could not believe her ears. 'Are you saying that animals, birds, bees, can read and act on your feelings – if you are angry or sad? Is that what happens?'

'In a way. Have you seen a cat lick the face of its kittens if they are wailing? That happened to me once, some time ago. But it was a puma licking me when I was distraught, not a domestic cat. Then there was the thief once who tried to rob a blind man. I was so incensed! And so was the bulldog that bit the thief's leg. The dog knew what I felt and felt the same.'

'You must be a dangerous man to try and upset.'

'Not really. I guess I get upset when people try to disturb the perfect harmony in nature. Then nature bites back and I am its witness. But you are perfectly safe right now, for example.'

The camera backed away from these two people talking on the side of the mountain. As it did so, it revealed three big cats, sitting in a circle looking at them. The interviewer, turned to face the camera as it was zooming out, and said with a grin: 'This is Elizabeth Manning signing off from the Andes of Colombia and saying goodbye to El Mono and three, er, *friendly* pumas.'

The television programme ended and the credits went up. In the back room of the pharmacy there was lots of clapping and cheering as all present but one celebrated what they had just seen. Mateo, the chemist, stood up and slapped Daniel on the back.

'El Mono, *el famoso!* We are honoured to have you with us!'

Adriána and Felipe were looking at Daniel with wide smiles on their faces. Karin had tears in her eyes. What a tribute! She had had no idea.

Daniel shook his head. 'I'd forgotten all about it. It was ages ago now and when they came to see me I really did not know what they were going to do ...'

'But Daniel – you were the star of the show. Didn't they tell you?' Karin was still amazed at what she had just seen.

'Not really. They asked if I could show them some wildlife. They had heard of me from someone, somewhere, so I said the two most impressive creatures to film were condors and pumas. That's what I got for them. The girl reporter was with me for only half an hour or so. The cameraman stayed for longer, but it was all over and done with very quickly and that was over a year ago. Before we got back together ...' He looked at Karin.

Adriána and Mateo Romero were absolutely delighted. 'What a programme! Everyone around here will want to see you now, Mono!' he said. 'They know you live close by, so you can expect some visitors!'

Daniel was worried. 'If anyone asks, Mateo, please tell them that I cannot show them what we have just seen. These condors and pumas must be left in peace. The last thing I want is to have everyone searching all around here. None of us who live here want tourists combing the area. This film footage was anyway taken further north, near the Volcán Puracé. Tell anyone who asks to visit the National Park there.'

'I understand, my friend. You want to live your life in peace. But you cannot stop everyone who lives in this pueblo from thinking you are the hero! You *are* our hero! You make this place famous around the world!'

Daniel blushed. Karin kissed him. She thought that this could be the breakthrough that might just bring two worlds together. She wondered if there was some way this sort of programme might tempt him out of his shell, get him to come down off the mountain from time to time and join the rest of the humanity. It was a distinct possibility now, although her own situation complicated things. Nothing was ever easy!

For Daniel, the programme that they had watched reminded him that he wanted, needed, to re-establish contact with pumas, none of which he had seen since his move across the Andes to his new home. Condors soared all over the skies and were no problem for him to find; falcons, too, he had seen and his favourite female had not lost much time in searching him out. But pumas? They were a much more elusive species. He warned Karin that he would take longer and longer on his wanderings until he picked up their trail. She wasn't too pleased about that – she insisted that he never spend the night away from her – but she understood his need to find them.

One evening Daniel returned home with his eyes alight.

'I found the male that was in that television programme. Or rather he found me! We recognised each other at once. He came to say hello and then off he went. I think he is following a female around and so I'm just a distraction at present but this is great news. I'm hoping they will mate.'

'Well, I'm very pleased for you. Now will you come in and follow your own mate, please?' Karin could see she was going to have some fierce competition to get his attention.

The next few days confirmed that impression. Daniel returned home later and later and each day with greater and greater excitement. He had found the female. He called her Venus. Of course, thought Karin. That's all I need now – one of history's all-time beauties transformed into a big cat and keeping my man away from me.

398

Daniel explained that once they mate, male and female pumas do not usually see each other again. The female is left alone to give birth and the male disappears.

'Bloody typical!' snorted Karin. 'Isn't that just the way of the world!'

Daniel reprimanded her for being so cynical. In this case, he had insisted, the male will stay, if not close, then nearby.

'He's not going to reinforce your stereotype of menfolk,' Daniel said. 'I've asked him to stay with us and Venus, as a sort of guardian angel. I call him Mercury. He is very volatile and unpredictable, but we will see what happens.'

Weeks passed and Daniel was out almost every hour of every day now, checking up on Venus. He would come back at night reporting to Karin how the female was pregnant and growing bigger every day. He grew daily more agitated as Venus approached the time for giving birth. Karin was at the same time getting more and more agitated for a not unrelated reason. She was trying to wean Peter off breast-feeding. She wanted to become fertile again. She had gone down to the pharmacy to see Adriána and the two women had been talking about it. Karin had returned home with a tin of baby formula. One way or the other, pregnancy was very much the topic of conversation that surrounded Karin's life.

Then finally the day came that Daniel had been waiting for. It was late, very dark and very cold. There was no cloud and only a sliver of a moon. What light there was on the mountainside came from the millions of stars that stretched across the heavens. A sound drew Daniel's attention. Looking out in the cold, still air, he could hear – high up and at some distance – the screaming of a puma. He turned to Karin.

'That's Mercury, the male. Tonight's the night, I think. I'm going to go up and find them.'

Karin objected. 'Do you have to go? I know you can't resist other females but this one wants you here in her bed. I want you more than ever. When am I going to have you assist *our* baby's birth?' The more she thought about it the more jealous she became. She wanted a child with Daniel.

'Beautiful one, I'll be back in the morning. It won't be long but this is going to be a tremendous honour – to help with a puma's birthing. Venus will let me go near her, I know.'

Karin reached up to him with love in her eyes. 'OK, go if you must, mountain man. Go to your female. But don't forget, Daniel. When you've finished with all these others – I want you with me when it's my turn.' She held his hand down so he could feel her abdomen, still soft and empty; she held him with such a direct and unmistakeable gaze up at him that he had to smile. Then she kissed and released him. Daniel grabbed a warm coat and left, turning at the door to glance back and blow her a kiss. Karin watched him disappear, her heart racing as he went. She loved him so much she ached inside; ached to have his children.

Karin woke late with Peter snuffling for a feed. He was a healthy, growing child, almost a year old and surrounded by love and attention and, despite the discomforts of their small, isolated home, he lacked nothing important in his little life. Karin was indescribably happy. Her life had turned round and around over the last few years but she had finally attained the peace and contentment that comes when her deepest desires were fulfilled. There was only one thing missing now that she wanted: a brother or sister for Peter given to her by the love of her life.

At last she heard footsteps outside making their way to their home. She put Peter down and left the small bedroom, crossing over to the front door to welcome Daniel back. But when she opened the door to greet him, it was someone else.

It was Leopold Smith.

Ice gripped her heart. Karin almost bent over as her insides contracted with fear. She recoiled back into the house. Smith didn't move at first. It was someone else who stepped in front of him and framed the doorway: Miguel Cortés.

'Look what we have here: the English wife of El Mono!' he snarled. 'That's a good story!'

Both men entered the house. Karin shrank away, blood draining from her face, and backed into the bedroom. She stood in front of the cot beside her bed, facing outwards towards the monsters that threatened her entire life, forlornly hoping they would not see what she was desperate to keep from their eyes. But, of course, they would not be denied. Smith brushed her aside like he was dismissing a fly.

Karin screamed: 'Don't touch him!'

Smith, impassive as ever, stopped and looked at his companion.

'You can pick him up,' said Cortés to Karin. 'You're useful to us so long as your son needs you. Of course,' he sneered cynically, 'that will only be until he is returned to his father.'

Karin pushed past Smith to the cot. Water was in her veins; her body was trembling like cobwebs in the wind but her face was as defiant as only a mother's, in defence of her offspring, can be. Fear and hatred battled between them inside her, but she lifted Peter into her arms and wrapped herself around him as if to shelter him from all the evil in the world. Evil was certainly surrounding her: she tried to resist the feeling of hopelessness.

There was a sound outside. Someone else was rapidly approaching. Cortés lunged at Karin and pushed her with her child against the wall of the bedroom, his hand covering her mouth. He looked back at Smith.

'It's Mono! Finish with him while I hold her here.'

Karin did her best to scream a warning but a hard fist buried itself into her stomach while the other hand stayed locked over her mouth. All air was squashed out of her, but the physical pain she felt was nothing, however, compared to the disabling fear she now felt for Daniel, walking into a trap.

Imprisoned at the back of their small bedroom and shaking uncontrollably, Karin heard the front door open. Daniel started to say something and then there was an almighty crash. Then the slump of a body falling. Karin twisted her face free to let out a cry and tears flooded out of her.

'No, no, please no ...' she cried in utter despair. But it was not only her. The heavens seemed to erupt. Birds were screaming outside; there were dogs howling in the distance; horses, cattle, donkeys and other unidentifiable animals were all bellowing somewhere. There were even clouds of insects rising up and covering all the bushes around. The whole mountainside was alive with the sounds of protest. The noise was deafening.

Cortés dragged Karin out of the bedroom, holding on to Peter as if her life would end. Smith stood stock still over the body of Daniel, crumpled beneath him. That sight burned into Karin's soul – she let out a howl that came from her innermost depths, that emptied every emotion within her, that rose up into the sky and communicated her despair to the four corners of the earth. She collapsed in tears, losing the use of her legs. Stumbling over her, Cortés cursed and brutally hauled her out of the building. Smith was unmoved, standing like a statue, so Cortés had to shout at him to get his attention.

'Burn the place down on top of him! Move it!'

Karin and her son were dragged out of the building, down through bushes and on to the horse-track below, until Cortés could drag her no more. Kneeling in the dirt, clutching Peter to her breasts, Karin looked back at her home being pulled down in front of her, on top of Daniel. Smith was outside now, dousing it in petrol and setting it alight. Karin's face was a mask, lined with horror and anguish. She was on the edge of oblivion; her life was emptying out before her. Sounds of indescribable desolation rose up, unbidden, from her throat.

'Don't worry, Mono won't feel anything,' Cortés laughed mercilessly. 'He's already dead – Smith only needs one hit!'

Karin's unearthly wail redoubled. She remained immobile, transfixed in the dirt, rocking slowly back and forth. Smith slowly walked towards her, the flames consuming the house behind him, turning all her dreams to ashes.

'I'll go and fetch the pick-up,' Cortés said to Smith. 'You stay with her.'

Smith did not respond. He was even more expressionless than usual. Cortés shook his head in wonder at his companion's woodenness.

Smith knew that what he had done was wrong. He didn't know how he knew, but he did. As he was swinging his mighty hand to break Mono's neck, in that very action he knew it was wrong. He had never questioned any of the lives that he had ended before but this one felt different. The amazing noise that rose up on all sides as El Mono slumped down only confirmed it. All the creatures on the mountain knew it was wrong and were signalling that to him. Every sound from every direction was rising up in protest. Birds, dogs, horses, even the insects said so: he should not have killed that man.

Cortés was shouting at him and that only served to confuse him even more. Burn it down, he said. That seemed right. What he had done wrong should be swallowed up in fire. But that was not in the plan. Nor were this woman and her son howling at him. Stop that noise! Smith's head was reeling inside; he couldn't have that noise outside as well. Stop it!

The only way Smith knew to stop people was to lay them out, to kill them. His eyes were closed, his ears were ringing, but he had to stop that clamouring that was blocking all his senses. Bang! He lashed out and the woman and her child flew across the ground and fell silent. The baby bounced in the dust out of the woman's lifeless arms.

The noise outside had stopped but inside Smith's head it was still turmoil. An old red Chevrolet pick-up now drove bouncing up the track and here was Cortés again, shouting at him.

'What have you done, you maniac? What have you done?'

'I had to stop the noise!'

'But look at them. You've killed them, too!' Cortés was out

of his mind with rage. 'Fields is going to kill you and me, as well, when he finds out. Look at them!'

Karin and her baby were sprawled out lifeless in the middle of the dirt track.

'I've killed them all,' reported Smith in a dull, monotonous voice.

Suddenly there was a rasping, blood-curdling screech and Cortés was hit on the side by an enormous big cat: a mountain lion, a puma. Neither man saw it coming and Cortés went down with the lion savaging his neck.

Smith jumped back towards the pick-up, his eyes goggling at the scene in front of him. It was a quick, efficient kill. The puma had bitten clean through to the man's neck vertebrae, blood gushed up everywhere and Smith, in shock, then noticed that the cat was now poised on top of its prey, but was lifting its head and glaring, snarling at him. Two yellow eyes burning with venom were boring into his own.

Smith, still numb by the suddenness of the assault, had the sense to move his frozen limbs and get into the cab of the pick-up. The big cat had now leapt up on to the bonnet of the car and its bloodied mouth was open, its vicious canines dripping, and its steady glare was boring into his own eyes through the glass. There was no clearer message. I want you next, this killing machine was saying.

Smith went deeper into shock. Where did this animal come from? He meant it no harm. Was it too telling him that he had done wrong and it had come to seek nature's revenge, to deal Smith his deserved fate? Smith didn't know what to do. He drew out his pistol, the Smith & Wesson that he always took with him on operations, but he thought he couldn't kill this vengeful, marvellous creature that had come to level the score, to deliver what Smith guessed he deserved for his wrongdoing. For a second, the two faced each other through the windscreen, then in a blink of Smith's eyes, the cat had gone. One enormous leap and it had disappeared.

Smith sat there like a corpse. Stunned. He waited a few seconds and slowly got out. There were three bodies in the dust before him: a baby, a woman and a man with his neck bitten through. What to do? None of this was in the plan. Smith raged. He kicked the front wheel of the pick-up. He thumped his hands down on the bonnet, then raised them up and cursed to the skies. What do I do?

He picked up the woman and dumped the body in the back of the pick-up. He threw the baby on top of her. Last, with blood dripping all over him, he picked up the man who had once been Cortés and threw that body on top of the other two. Then he got in the cab, started the engine and backed it out of the place it was parked. Smith spun the wheel and drove out of this hellhole, following the rough horse-track down and off the mountainside, back to the pueblo where he had earlier come from. Behind him the house, once a home – before that a simple wooden mountain hut – was now disappearing in flames and smoke.

The pick-up bumped and crawled its way off the mountain, across the fields and down to the pueblo below. Smith had not the slightest idea what he was going to do with the three bodies he had loaded at the back. The first building he came to, at the beginning of a proper road, was a church which stood overlooking the pueblo. This was as good a place to stop as any. He got out. There was no one around. He wandered across the road, away from the pick-up, and found himself opposite the pharmacy. He fumbled for his mobile phone and dialled Fields's number. His head was still spinning and everything around him seemed to be passing by in slow motion, as if in a dream. As he was trying to make the call, the pharmacist, Mateo Romero, spotted him and called out in his heavily accented English:

"Ello, *gringo*! You find Mono and his wife?"

Smith looked up, vacant: 'They're dead. All dead!'

405

'*Qué?*' The pharmacist did not understand.

'Mono is dead. The wife is dead. Baby is dead. Cortés is dead. All dead! Look!' Smith waved his hand back in the direction of the pick-up.

The call to Fields came through at that moment. Smith could hear Fields saying he couldn't quite catch what was being said – could he say it again? So Smith duly repeated every word again.

There were two violent reactions to Smith's statement – one on the roadside beside him, the other on the mobile phone Both were horrified.

'Mono dead? He cannot be. Not Mono!' Mateo ran over to the pick-up to see what this big *gringo* was indicating.

'My baby boy dead? He can't be. What's happening there? Tell me!' Fields was shouting down the phone.

Smith didn't know where he was going. He walked back towards the pick-up talking to Fields and the pharmacist both at the same time, not knowing what he was saying or who he was saying it to.

'Mono is dead. I killed him up at his house. I pulled the house down on top of him and set it alight. He's gone. No more. I hit the woman and baby. Both now dead – look in the back of the pick-up. Dead, dead, dead. It all went wrong. Cortés is dead. He got killed by a puma. Yes – a puma, it took revenge on us. Because what we did was wrong. All wrong. They're all dead. And it's all WRONG!'

Smith's voice was rising and rising as he was talking and finally he lost it. He could hear Fields shouting at him down the phone but he started shouting back. He stamped on the road, turned round and ran down hill roaring like a little boy who had lost his temper. Smith threw his mobile phone as far as he could into the air – it flew away, describing a perfect arc over the top of the pharmacy and fell to earth the other side; he knew not where and didn't care. He kept running.

Mateo Romero the pharmacist was confronted, horrified,

with three bodies in the back of the pick-up. The *gringo* had run off.

There was one man with his throat ripped out. Clearly dead and cold. There was a baby covered in dust, but as he looked he saw it moving, whimpering, and becoming agitated. There was a woman, the chemist noted – Mono's wife – who was similarly covered in dirt and dust but she was warm to touch, partly covered by the body of this man, completely unconscious, but as far as he could tell she was alive. Just.

Mateo shouted for his wife and son to come and help. The wife, Adriána, emerged from the shop and saw her husband struggling with a body in the pick-up. She called her son Felipe and then the two ran over to help. Pulling Karin out from under the corpse was not easy, even for the three of them. The baby was now crying. Adriána took charge of the baby, leaving her husband, Mateo and son Felipe to drag the unconscious Karin over to their shop. She was too heavy! Mateo asked his wife to put the baby down for an instant and come back and help.

Somehow, between all of them, they managed to get Karin into the shop, through the back and lay her on a bed. Baby Peter was by this time crying freely. Mateo quickly cleaned himself up, made up some baby milk from one of the tins of powdered milk in his shop and asked Felipe to feed the baby while he went to help his wife with Karin.

Karin was in a bad way. She was still unconscious. The side of her head was red and swollen; there was dried blood all the way down her left side and she was absolutely filthy. Adriána very carefully bathed Karin's face and tried to clean her hair and clothes as well as she could without moving and disturbing her too much. The blood, fortunately, was not Karin's but must have come from the corpse that had been lying over her. Adriána was distressed. What had happened to this beautiful mother and her child? she asked her husband.

Mateo was clearly very upset by everything that had

happened. He recounted all that he had seen and heard and how the big *gringo* had said he had killed Mono and burned his house down. The three of them – Mateo, Adriána and Felipe – were all equally horrified.

There was nothing they could do for the time being other than care for the mother and child as well as possible and see if both recovered. Of the two, the baby was by far the better off. He must have taken a fearful tumble like his mother, but he bounced back into health and was basically unhurt. He had taken his feed without hesitation and was now more settled. Mateo judged, however, that the mother was badly concussed and she would need time and complete rest before she regained consciousness. There was no blood on her head and none leaking from her mouth, nose or ears, which was a good sign, but her lovely face was swollen on one side and would undoubtedly become very bruised in due course.

Meanwhile, outside, there was an abandoned red Chevrolet pick-up with a dead man in the back. There was nothing that anyone could do to help him. He was left alone.

9

Broken Dreams

Fields was absolutely furious that his wife had run off with his son. One day she was totally domesticated and settled into her role as the perfect mother and wife, someone he could present to the world as an elegant and cultured partner befitting his status, and the next day she was running all over town carrying his son away from him like a thieving gipsy. His son in the clutches of some common woman of the streets. How dare she force such a lifestyle on his boy! And what had happened to the wife who had been poised, refined and picture-perfect? One day apart and she had turned into some devious, interfering and fire-spitting harridan. Where was the devotion and cultured tolerance he had come to expect? She was going to have to beg if she ever wanted some sort of forgiveness.

Meanwhile, his son's whereabouts was Fields's major preoccupation outside of work. Smith had almost got him back, but every day that passed after the failed snatch outside the supermarket meant it was going to get more and more difficult to trace his wife and son's movements. Professional detective agencies plus his own network of Triple F staff were all instructed to keep eyes and ears open for the movements of an Englishwoman and a sixth-month-old baby. Surely, there couldn't be many in Colombia that fitted their description?

Inside work, the all-consuming concern was how to turn the

fortunes of Triple F around and start to bring in the profits. In the long term everything depended on this. All things would become easier: more people would be willing to serve you, more women would become available and more money and power would fall into his lap. Operations in the Puracé mines of Cauca, however, were still very disappointing. Something had to be done.

Fields called Alejandro González to report back on the findings of the geological survey team.

'The problem is that, even with all the latest sophisticated technology, in prospecting for gold you cannot escape the element of luck,' González said. 'Either you get lucky or you don't. We know the conditions where gold formations are likely to be found; we have two mines now active on either side of Volcán Puracé where conditions are ideal; lots of gold has been recovered from the TMG site, so other finds are quite possible ... but equally possibly, not!'

'I can't deal in possibilities,' said Fields, getting irritated. 'Tell me what our options are with regard to investing more time, effort and capital in Puracé, and give me the probable chances of success in each case.'

'OK. First option, which is cheapest, is to flush out our existing mines with a weak solution of sodium cyanide. That dissolves traces of gold in our existing workings, which we can then recover from the slurry that washes out of the mine. Second option is to work on the vents that come out on the mountainside, where there are the hot springs and plumes of sulphur. Some of these volcanic pipes that come up from below will have gold deposits in. We undertake open-cast mining so that we can get at these pipes. That means a sizeable investment in stripping off the top layers of soil and rock. We might find gold deposits directly in the pipes we unearth or, if not, we can resort to hosing all the debris we create in a cyanide solution to leach out the gold as in the first option.

'Third option is to dig deeper. Blast away underground in

our existing mines and open up more rock face. More expensive than either of the other options but if there is more gold down there then, in the long term, it's the only way to find it.'

'What are the probabilities in each case?' Fields was getting impatient.

'The first way we will certainly get something. Tiny gold traces which cannot be seen will be concentrated in the cyanide solution and we can recover those. It's a bit like filtering through the waste products that TMG didn't bother with when they found the first deposits. Because it's a cheap process relative to the other two options the revenue will likely cover our costs. I should emphasise that the waste water will be polluted with cyanide – that will create a stink with the local livestock farmers. The release of waste waters will also probably attract hordes of artisanal miners, poor people who like to go panning for gold. They'll probably start camping and working below where the waters will emerge from the mine, so that will cause a conflict between them and all the local people who live around here.'

'Well, that is a cost we won't have to bear,' said Fields. 'Our mine brings benefits to some locals and costs to others. They can fight it out among themselves.'

'The open-cast option is bound to create even more trouble,' continued González. 'Stripping off the *páramo* and the rock beneath, then hosing down the workings will repeat the same scenario but on an even bigger scale. The rewards in terms of gold recovered are likely to be bigger, however.

'Of course the greatest probability of success comes with deeper mining. The costs rise exponentially the deeper we go, however. Ironically, because it's underground, the reactions of the local farmers and whoever else lives up top will be minimal, certainly at first, unlike the other two options. But there is one risk.'

'What's that?'

'The area is geologically unstable. It's a dormant volcano

that was last active in the 1970s. There is a chance that blasting away may start some reaction deeper down. It is difficult to quantify that risk, but, if we are careful, it should be low. Blasting deep down is the most expensive option, but it's also the one with the biggest potential payback.'

'Mmm. Thanks. The way you present it, it seems obvious that we should start with the first option and then, depending on results, progress from there either to the second or to the third.'

'I agree,' said González. 'But before we start, can I mention one major headache?'

'Go ahead.'

'El Mono – he has the potential to cause all sorts of trouble and that means all sorts of cost increases. He is still out there somewhere and we haven't been able to neutralise him yet.'

'Agreed. Time to solve that problem. What do you know of his whereabouts?'

'We covered the area around Puracé but have heard nothing. He's not been seen. Cortés can send people out further afield, if you wish.'

'Yes,' said Fields. 'Tell Cortés to sweep wider and wider, further and further, until we pick up something. He can't have disappeared and we can't afford the trouble he causes. Meanwhile, start ordering the men and equipment you need to flush out your mines with cyanide. We are in the gold mining business: let's find gold!'

Cortés was pleased to get the go-ahead for a search mission to capture and dispose of Mono – an operation that in his view was long overdue. He hated having unfinished business, and sorting out this character should have been accomplished months back. His approach now was to buy a couple of anonymous vehicles, put men in each and tell them to run up to the end of every road that led up into the Andes and to ask, in any of the last inhabited stretches of each road, if they had seen Mono recently. It was a long, time-consuming business but Cortés reckoned that so long as no significant pueblos were omitted, he must find out something, sometime.

When Cortés heard of the screening of a National Geographic programme that featured Mono he reckoned that finding his quarry would be easier. Public interest in this man would be greater; searching him out would not be so unusual – probably many others would be looking for him as well, though for entirely different motives.

Weeks and weeks passed with no sightings and then one of his scouts called in with fascinating news: El Mono was reported to be living high up in a valley further south with his English wife and child.

An English wife? And a child? Cortés asked if there was any idea how old the child was. The story came back with no confirmed age but it was a babe in arms. Cortés phoned Fields immediately. This sounded like they could kill two birds with one stone.

Fields nearly jumped out of his chair when he heard.

'Excellent! Tremendous news! Well done, Cortés!' Fields always liked the man. 'But watch out. We know El Mono is dangerous, so be very careful how you approach him. I'll send Leopold Smith down to you. With regard to my son, if it really is him with his mother down there, then make sure my boy is kept safe. What I do with my runaway wife is something I can decide later when I find out what she has been up to – if it is her, posing as another man's wife. What a nerve, eh? Right now I feel like wringing her neck, but my son will probably need to stay with her until I get him back here. So, keep an eye on Mono's movements and don't make a move until Smith gets to you. Then make sure there's a fatal accident. Report back as soon as you've disposed of Mono and got the others. OK? Great. Congratulations again.'

Fields flew down to Popayán with Smith in anticipation of recovering his son. There was a copy of the National

Geographic programme in the regional office which González had recorded and it was shown to Smith so that he would have no trouble identifying his victim. Smith went quiet viewing this film ... but that was hardly a surprise for someone so non-committal. Cortés told Fields he had hired an old pick-up and he and Smith were going to find Mono and his English wife and son the following morning. Fields said he would follow close behind in a Triple F vehicle and wait below for confirmation of the operation's success. He had no doubt that Smith would recover his son and eliminate El Mono. What happened to his wife he was less interested in. Cortés said he would phone in as soon as they had finished their mission.

That was the last Fields ever heard from Cortés.

The next call that came in was garbled and shocking and sent Fields into paroxysms of rage. He had driven down and parked close to the pueblo where El Mono had been last seen, was ready to drive up and collect his son, but now he could not believe his ears. He did not want to believe his ears. It was Smith telling him that he had killed Mono, Fields's wife, his son, and that Cortés was dead as well. It couldn't be! Was that all true, he had asked, were they all dead? Oh yes, Smith had confirmed. All dead, he had said. Smith had wiped out his son and, with him, all the dreams Fields had harboured for years, if not decades.

Fields went berserk. What sort of idiot was he dealing with? he had shouted down the phone. Smith had been instructed to kill Mono and capture his son unharmed and now he had killed them both. Smith was a brainless, mentally disabled weirdo who belonged in an asylum. He deserved to be locked away for ever. He was not welcome back to Bogotá, to Triple F and to be anywhere near Fields. Get lost, permanently, Fields had told him.

Fields had heard Smith ranting and raving at the other end of the phone but he had lost all patience with the half-wit and shut the phone off.

Fields was speechless with fury. It was just as well he was alone in the Triple F Toyota he had driven out from Popayán – he wanted no one near him. And he wanted Smith as stone cold dead as the three corpses the maniac said he had created. Putting the vehicle in gear, he drove quickly up to the pueblo to find his bodyguard, the autistic assassin who had failed him so miserably.

Fields found Smith half running, half stumbling down the road, out of the pueblo, along the deserted track towards him. Fields slewed the Toyota round and brought it to a halt in a cloud of dust halfway across the rough, unmade carriageway. He opened the passenger door as if to welcome inside his trusty deputy. But in the cloud of dust that the vehicle had kicked up Smith did not notice its driver pull out a handgun. As Smith held the passenger door open to climb in – blam! blam! blam! – Fields fired three times at point-blank range into Smith's chest. Smith fell back and collapsed in a heap. Fields reached across to close the car door. He put the engine in gear once more and drove off, leaving his loyal deputy and stepson dead in the road.

Twenty-four hours later, back in the pueblo where Smith had abandoned what he had assumed to be three dead bodies, the woman among them was now waking up. Unconscious for a full day, Karin was at last beginning to stir. She had not wanted to open her eyes, her head hurt too much, but they flickered open in spite of herself.

Karin had no idea where she was or what had happened – it was too painful to think. Yet images burned into her brain, refusing to keep away, images that came and went, swirling like fire. Fire … burning! That meant something!

Karin suddenly blurted out: 'Where's Peter?'

Her voice sounded like an explosion going off in her head but in fact it was more like a strangled croaking. Loud enough, however, to attract Adriána who had been close by, waiting for signs that Karin was struggling back into consciousness.

'He is here, precious one. He's fine.'

Karin opened her eyes to stare wildly around her. She still couldn't take in where she was, but here was Adriána, holding Peter. She tried to haul herself up in the bed to take him but her head complained vigorously – lights started sparking and everything spun around. Karin sank back into the pillows. She closed her eyes again.

'Careful. Take it easy. You have been out cold for all day and all night. You still need to rest.' Adriána's voice sounded a long way away but it filtered through into Karin's hearing.

Images again played in her mind: burning. Leopold Smith. Daniel's crumpled body.

'Daniel!' This time it was a scream. Karin's whole body shook with pain but it could not stop the alarm from tearing out of her lungs: 'Daniel! Daniel!'

Mateo came into the room to be with his wife. They both tried to calm Karin down, but she was now awake and sobbing her heart out. The pounding in her head was harder than ever but the pounding in her heart had opened up a vast empty void within her and panic had taken over and had filled every part of it. She was shaking uncontrollably and even her baby's cries could not stop her.

'Please no … Adriána, Mateo … tell me: Daniel?'

Karin was staring at them. She remembered! She couldn't shut the horrifying pictures out of her head: images of Daniel lying inert on the floor and then Smith pulling everything down and setting light to it. Daniel covered in fire.

The face of Mateo; the expression of sadness and sorrow in his eyes; the memory of all the birds and animals sounding their fury as flames reached up to the heavens: it all meant one thing.

'NO! NO! NO!' Karin's misery poured out of her. She sobbed like she had never sobbed before: every last ounce of her being was wracked in grief and hopelessness. '*Daniel!*'

There was little that Mateo and Adrián could do. They stayed with Karin until the crying slowed a little. They did their best to comfort her. Peter's crying began to meld into that of his mother's and at last Adriána was able to hand him across. Karin held him to her breast and that, as always, kept her attention and helped calm her a little, but there was nothing that could be done now to soothe away the massive void that dominated her being. Her face was bleak; her eyes were dull; her soul was dead within her. She knew: Daniel was no more.

Peter was feeding ravenously and Karin held him to one breast, then the other. It took a good ten minutes before her baby began to slow and become less desperate. Then Karin turned her head to look at Adriána. She spoke without expression, without hope.

'He's gone, hasn't he? Daniel?'

Adriána couldn't speak for the tears in her own eyes. She nodded.

'I know.' Karin felt empty.

For the rest of the day Karin felt nothing, could do nothing. Adriána continued to nurse her, to feed her a little, to help her lay Peter down and to encourage her to sleep herself. Karin's body had taken a terrible battering and now her psyche was irretrievably damaged. A black depression consumed her. Sleep came in fits and starts and Karin feared closing her eyes for the awful sights that would spring up out of the darkness. Her one comfort was Peter and for every passing hour she thanked God that he too had not been taken from her or she would surely have died of utter despair.

As it was, Karin felt as if she were sinking ever deeper and deeper into a bottomless black pit. She had understood now that she was being cared for in the back of the pharmacy: Mateo and Adriána were looking after her with an absolutely selfless devotion that she could never repay. But she was dead inside. Physically and emotionally, everything hurt.

In between sleeping, waking, feeding Peter and being fed herself, Karin lost track of time. Days had passed but she did not know how many. She slowly became stronger and was finally able to get out of bed. She went out of the back room where she had been quartered and found Adriána and Mateo. At last, she was able to thank her hosts properly for all the care and attention they had shown her and her baby. For their part, the chemist and his wife were pleased to see that the wildness and fever in their patient's eyes had receded and, even if the light that had once been there had not returned, at least her expression showed she was back to health and normality.

Karin asked her hosts how she had got there – How was it she had woken up under their roof and had received their protection? The full story of how this big *gringo* had arrived outside and said he had killed everyone was related to her. Karin had to ask then: Had anyone gone up to check what remained of her home; what had happened to Daniel?

Sadness filled the eyes of Mateo once more. He said it as gently as he could for fear of the anguish he was delivering. Yes. He had gone up to look around. There was nothing left of Karin's home. Everything had gone. Only ashes remained: El Mono's among them.

Karin lowered her head and held her son to her. She had nothing left in the world now except him. She could not speak.

The side of Karin's face was covered in bruises. She looked in the mirror at the person that Daniel had once called beautiful. That person had gone now. The black and blue might disappear sometime; the swelling may go down; but the face that looked back at her would never again carry the light from her soul that Daniel had said he loved. Karin wondered what she would do with her life. She did not want to do anything but she knew that she could not stay where she was, in the pharmacy, exploiting the kindness of her neighbours any longer.

What to do? Ironically, she thought, now that Smith believed her to be dead, she was probably safer now than before. If she could remain dead, so far as her ex-husband was concerned, she would not need anyone's protection any longer. That thought bored into her soul. She wanted Daniel's protection! She wanted his protection so badly ... but she would never, ever receive it again. What should she do? Where should she go? Who could she be with?

Claudia! Karin must talk to the one person who might possibly help her and to whom she owed an explanation for such a long silence. Karin asked to borrow a phone.

As soon as Karin heard Claudia's voice, tears began to stream down her face.

'Claudia ... it's me ... Karin.'

Claudia knew instantly there was something awfully wrong. Karin did not sound like Karin.

'K.! What's happened?'

Karin tried to stop it but, yet again, an unearthly wail emerged from deep within her, threatening to make any words she uttered unintelligible.

'Claudia, they found us ... they killed ... they killed Daniel. Help me, please!'

The howl at the other end of the phone line echoed Karin's own cries.

'Karin! No! ... It can't be! But ... but are you OK? And Peter?'

'We're here, both now OK. But he tried to kill us, too. Leopold Smith it was ... but we survived and he's gone away. But Daniel ... Daniel's been killed! Oh Claudia, please get us out of here! Somehow! We have nothing left. Not a penny. Everything has been burnt down and Peter and I have nothing, nothing left in the world.'

'Don't worry, we'll get you out. Where are you, for God's sake?'

'Remember we asked to be brought to the end of the road in this pueblo, before we started walking? We are in that pueblo right now. One of the last buildings – the pharmacy, opposite the church at the top of the village. Can you get the same vehicle and driver that brought us here to come back and pick us up? Can you? Please?'

'I'll sort that out straight away. But where shall we hide you now? Where do you want to be taken?'

'Claudia, Morten will think I'm dead. Smith will have told him so. I should be safe anywhere ... but can I see you? There's no one else I want to be with now. Daniel's gone. Oh Claudia, I can't bear it. Daniel's gone!' Karin dissolved in tears.

'Karin, I'll come for you. I'll get you to my parents: that's best. I'll send the driver as soon as I can and he'll take you to my parents – in Cali. I'll meet you there. Don't cry, Karin. We will beat them. We won't ever let them get you and Peter. We'll beat them! Karin, talk to me!'

Karin was sobbing but she replied, her voice broken with emotion: 'I hear you, Claudia. Thank you. Thank you so much. I do need you now. I really do! There's no one else.'

As things turned out, it was not difficult for Karin and Peter to be rescued. Claudia contacted Patricia Ramírez, she got through to the TMG transport office in Popayán and they organised everything. The driver knew the territory and was outside the pharmacy in four hours.

Karin did not know how to thank Adriána and Mateo Romero. She had nothing to give them but her undying gratitude. She did ask them to say nothing to anyone about her and Peter, that they had survived: she had already explained how evil people had wanted to kill her. The Romeros told her not to worry. The police had been around asking many questions when they had removed the pick up and the corpse it contained. They had also apparently found another unidentified body on the road below the pueblo. But the Romeros had told them only what the big gringo had said ... that everyone had been killed. It was easier for all concerned to conceal

Karin's existence rather than let the authorities intervene. Mateo and Adriana faithfully promised no one would know of her escape. They kissed Karin and her son and waved them goodbye and good luck.

The long drive to Cali and to Claudia's parents took all night. Every mile of the way, however, Karin felt better: she felt as if she was in the process of being delivered from some awful nightmare. At the end of her journey she felt that someone she knew and loved, and that loved her and Peter, would be waiting and that began to give her some hope. In the back of the large, blacked-out, armoured four-by-four, Karin was exhausted but able to sleep curled up with her child. Some peace of mind at last embraced her as the night, and the journey, wore on.

In the morning, Claudia was waiting when Karin arrived. Floods of tears came again. Trying to explain all that had happened was impossible. Since they had last seen each other, Karin had been to heaven, had lived a life of indescribable joy … and now had descended into unending desolation. Karin seemed to relive it all, recounting it bit by bit to her friend, over the next few days.

Thelma Marshall was the next to visit and, again, the story had to be retold. Practical as ever, Thelma wanted to know what Karin proposed to do, and how could she be helped. They talked over this for some time.

So long as Fields thought Karin and his son were dead they were both safe, but Karin could not stay undercover for ever. She had to start rebuilding her life.

Karin knew there was only one option: to return home to England. She would change her name, and that of her son, and fly out back to the UK. It meant saying goodbye to Claudia, to Colombia, to the life and the world she had come to love. The three women looked at one another. They all understood. This was the only safe way out of the impasse Karin was faced with: there could be no future here.

Thelma was a tower of strength and support. She offered to contact the British Consulate in Cali and set everything up under top security so that the safety of Karin and her child would not be compromised. Karin could not imagine how this woman could cope with the reality of her son's, Leopold Smith's, evildoing and yet keep coming up with so much positive energy and assistance. Karin had held nothing back about what had happened to her and who had been the instrument in breaking all her dreams, of destroying her life here, but all that did was to drive Thelma into more and more determined effort to put right, so far as she could, all the wrongs that Leopold Smith had committed.

Karin had said she had lost everything; she was penniless and that she and Peter had come to Cali with nothing but the clothes they were wearing. She had no papers, no passport or ID, and she was frightened of going to the authorities since she did not want Peter's existence to become known; they were thus condemned to live a life underground. Thelma promised to sort all that out. She would insist that the British Consul accompany her in coming to see Karin and that, if the British authorities were too idiotic and bureaucratic to solve this problem, then TMG would not fail her.

The next morning Thelma arrived with a new playsuit for Peter and some clothes she thought Karin might like. She insisted that Karin and Claudia accompany her straight away to the best outfitters in Cali, to order a whole new wardrobe for Karin to replace all that she had lost. If she was going to fly out to build a new life in the UK, Thelma said, Karin had to start on the right foot, after all.

The British Consul arrived. Constructing a new identity for Karin and Peter was most irregular. This meant breaking all the rules – how could such a thing be countenanced? Easy, said Thelma – don't pretend such things don't happen! A Colombian birth certificate for Peter Mayor had to be produced. A UK passport for Mrs Karin Mayor and her son had to be issued. And this all had to be accomplished in a matter of days. Flight tickets had to be purchased in these names, so speed was of the essence.

There was one final detail to attend to: Karin had to contact her mother in England. How on earth was she to explain everything? Not necessary, said Claudia. Just tell her that her marriage was the biggest mistake in her life; that Morten Fields had turned out to be the bastard she had always feared and that she was coming home. Her mother would understand all that, no problem. For the first time since Daniel had died, Karin laughed. Yes, Mother would understand all that. There was no need for any other information just yet.

The next day the British Consulate in Cali phoned through. Would Mrs Karin Mayor like to call in and pick up her passport? All was ready, they said. Claudia drove Karin directly to the appropriate address and there it was: her new identity. She could not believe it. Flight tickets were purchased over the Internet and boarding passes were printed within a matter of hours. Thelma had seen to everything; had paid for everything. Things had happened so fast that Karin was bewildered, overcome; she did not know how to express her thanks. All really was ready. Karin and Peter had only to step on the plane, say goodbye to Colombia and their new life would begin.

Both Thelma and Claudia accompanied Karin to the airport. The flight was Cali to Miami and Miami to London, Heathrow. First class all the way. Karin's mother would be waiting at the other end to welcome Karin back to the UK.

It was tears again at the departure gate. Karin thought Peter was going to grow up a real cry-baby if he never saw his mother in any other light, but she could not help it now. She had so much to thank these two women for and no idea when she would see them again. Promises to keep in touch were made; all fervently hoped that the next occasion, whenever that might be, would be an altogether more joyful one; and then it was goodbye: last embraces and waves were exchanged and Karin and Peter left to start a new life with new identities on the other side of the world.

After six months, Karin had had enough of living with her mother. She was commuting into London working as a financial assistant in a large bank and, although it paid well, it was deadly boring. Peter was now eighteen months old and flourishing in a local playschool: his grandmother took him in and picked him up so that Karin could work a long, bigger-income-earning day. It was good for Peter to know his grand-mother, to have a family beyond his mother, she told herself, but after all the changes she had been through, was this the life she wanted for them both?

There was an advertisement in the paper that caught her eye: the International Office at the University of Durham was looking to appoint a new member of staff to take responsi-bility for developing contacts with Latin American universities. Staff and student exchanges, postgraduate recruitment, devel-oping research possibilities, all fell into the job description. A graduate with good Spanish and/or Portuguese, and some experience of working in Latin America was preferred. Some travel possibilities existed.

The pay was not fantastic but the intellectual stimulus would be far better than her present occupation offered. Karin told her mother she would apply. If she got the job, it meant leaving to live up north. Her mother was a bit upset – having her daughter at home after such a long time away was some-thing she had really enjoyed. Did Karin really have to go away again?

Yes. Of course, Karin got the job. The post might have been written for her: there was no one who could compete with her qualifications and experience. She couldn't wait to tell Claudia: there was a good hour's worth of chat on Skype involved there. Almost like the old days. *Almost*.

Sorting out her domestic arrangements in Durham was all

that remained. Finding the right nursery or playschool for Peter came first. She would live somewhere close by once that was sorted and, as a university town, Durham had plenty of rental accommodation available, so Karin was not too worried on that score.

Then it was a matter of packing up, moving and settling down again elsewhere. Karin had done that so many times under so many different circumstances that she wondered if she could ever stay in one place for years at a time. Maybe not – only the future would tell and she had long ago stopped trying to guess that.

A few days into the new job and the Head of the International Office, Siobhan O'Donnell, introduced someone whom she thought Karin might know.

'Karin, come and meet Matthew Williams from Earth Sciences. He is not so long back from a research project in Colombia ...'

Karin could not believe it. She had spoken to him, knew all about his work and indeed had been instrumental in setting him up before Morten Fields and Alejandro González had got to him, although she had never actually met him. She wondered if he would know who she was. Siobhan had probably told him that Karin had been employed with Triple F for a while but wouldn't know any more. If Mathew didn't recognise her voice, he probably wouldn't know who she was, or had been.

'Hello, Matthew, good to meet you. How was Colombia?'

Matthew clearly did not recognise her voice. He grimaced.

'I didn't see much of Colombia,' he replied. 'Only the insides of a Triple F office in Popayán. Do you know it?'

'Popayán? Yes: a lovely place. Your office I guess not. How was your research?' Karin dreaded to hear the answer.

'It could have been good, but Triple F didn't want to know. They axed my funding after a while. Siobhan said you worked for them, too. What did you think of them?'

'I couldn't sum that up easily,' Karin smiled. 'It's complicated!'

'Would you like to have lunch with me? I've been back a while and when I mention Colombia people switch off. They have no notion of what it's like. You are the first person that has shown any interest, so let's exchange notes, would you mind?'

He was a nice-looking man who she knew had had a rough deal with Triple F. Not quite as rough as herself, she thought, but she accepted the offer.

'Thank you, Matthew. That would be lovely.'

Karin had to chase up a member of staff in one of the colleges in town, so she suggested they meet up in a pub or café just off the marketplace rather than in the cafeteria in the university offices. Matthew agreed.

They came together for a drink and sandwiches. It was all very civilised but Karin couldn't help thinking this was decidedly unreal – meeting up in a Durham pub in October and talking about a world that might be thousands of miles away but was so close to her, so vital to her life, that she felt she could almost reach out and touch it. For Matthew Williams, of course, he had no clue about any of this – his was just a research project that had ended disappointingly quickly. He explained that he had felt badly let down; he had been brought out on false pretences.

Karin let him speak and unload his frustrations. He clearly had not met anyone in Durham who was prepared to listen or understand. After twenty minutes or so of quite animated conversation Matthew eventually asked about Karin's experiences. She didn't really want to go into too much detail. She mentioned her early student exchange in Universidad de los Andes, her internship in Triple F and her subsequent appointment as a personal assistant, though she did not say with whom. Karin did wax lyrical about Popayán, however, about Claudia's finca, and her eyes shone when she spoke about the

426

páramo and meeting someone – she did not say who – who had acted as her guide to the mountain environment.

Matthew picked up on that. 'You were very fortunate. I wish I could have seen more of the Andes but never really got out of my office for long enough. Did you ever see that programme by National Geographic about Colombian wildlife? Really amazing. A guy who lived with pumas and condors. Quite spectacular. I've never seen anything like that.'

Karin smiled shyly. She looked down. 'Yes, I saw that programme. I agree: spectacular … I did see condors up close once. They are magnificent. I never got that close to pumas, however!'

Matthew was increasingly interested in this attractive woman with whom he could share a common experience. He tried to drag out the lunch hour for as long as possible, he was enjoying her company so much, but when she started looking round to pay up and leave Matthew asked if they might meet again. Some evening maybe?

Karin smiled at him again. Maybe. She warned him, however, that her son came first in her life.

Was she married? No. Separated some time ago.

Matthew took the plunge: 'Karin, do say you'll come out with me. Don't give me maybes. Make it yes or no?'

He smiled at her. He was a nice-looking man. Not the sort to treat her badly, she thought, but who was she to judge character these days?

'OK, Matthew. I'd like to. But I have to find someone who might babysit for Peter if it's an evening. Give me your mobile number and I'll call you if and when I get something sorted.'

Matthew went back to Earth Sciences with a spring in his step. She was an absolute beauty and with such a sad, shy smile. He'd given her his number and hoped he hadn't come across too strong. He was so keen he had told her his number wrong twice before he was sure she had got it right! Don't call me, I'll call you, she had said. Here's hoping I won't have to wait too long before she calls, he thought.

Karin worried if she could go through with it: meeting another man so soon. She regretted it the moment they had parted. It was true her social life was non-existent but that was for a reason. She couldn't face going out and being jolly. He was so nice and well-meaning, however, she almost felt as if she could not disappoint him. Having accepted his offer to go out, she couldn't back out now, so she resolved to enjoy his company but she would keep him at arm's length and try not lead him on.

It took Karin a little while before she could find help with looking after Peter for an evening. She was renting a small apartment in a block with married postgraduate couples and so she did a deal. She offered to sit with one couple's children for an evening if they could return the honour.

She phoned Matthew with the news that she could go out the next Friday evening. How would that do? Matthew sounded so enthusiastic Karin could not help smiling. Yes, that would do nicely, was the reply. It was a date.

Karin worried about it all week. What was she thinking of? She felt as if she could give nothing of herself to anyone. It was plain that Matthew was keen on her. She had found out that he was single and that he'd not had a steady girlfriend for a while, and so it was obvious he was looking to develop a relationship with someone ... but she knew it could not be with her. She had to tell him. She didn't know how to explain it, but she had to tell him.

Friday evening came. The wife of the couple upstairs came down to take over duty and, when Peter was sleeping, Karin phoned Matthew to say she was ready. He drove round to pick her up within ten minutes.

Matthew was on top form: effusive, chatty, complimenting her on her outfit, and asking about Peter. That was a nice touch. Karin thanked him for his concern. Matthew smiled, said he had booked a restaurant for them both and confessed he was simply dying to carry on the conversation between them where they had last left off. Karin smiled shyly and looked down. It was the reaction that Matthew had first found attractive and now it made him decidedly hot under the collar, if not all over.

They arrived at the restaurant and parked. It was not exorbitantly pricey. Nothing like she had got used to with Morten, Karin thought, but she didn't want that sort of experience again, thank you. No – this place was nice. Appropriate. Intimate without being claustrophobic.

They chatted, The first course came and went. Karin kept it friendly without giving too much away. Matthew was trying his best to get to know her but Karin wasn't giving anything for him to go on. She began to feel bad about the whole evening. Then, trying another approach, Matthew asked about Peter's father and what had happened to him. This was it. Karin stopped. She had to think carefully what to say.

'Matthew ... I have to tell you that ... that Peter's father treated me very badly. Very badly indeed. It's been a nightmare. I can't describe it. The result is that I can't form a relationship with any man just yet. I can be friends. But I have to tell you ... I'm very sorry ... but it cannot be more than that. It is going to take a very long time for me to get over what has happened. I should have told you this straight away. Don't think badly of me but ... but I can't really go any further with you than this. I hope you understand.'

She looked at him with such sadness in her eyes that he didn't need to be told twice.

'Yeah ... I can see,' he said. 'Thank you for telling me that at least.' He stopped pushing and trying to get her to open up and changed the subject. 'Well, tell me what you think about your return to Durham and your job at the International Office. How's that? Not so painful to talk about?'

That shift in approach brought tears to Karin's eyes. She looked down and felt for a napkin.

'I'm sorry,' she whispered to him. 'You deserve so much better than this. I'm very sorry.'

Matthew said nothing at first, just waited for her to recover. 'Don't worry,' he said. 'Take your time.' He reached across the table to feel for her hand, to console her, but she took it away.

It was half an hour later when Matthew drove her home. She kissed him on the cheek, thanked him and apologised again for the evening. Then she ran in and left him in the car. She spent the rest of the night in tears thinking how hopeless everything was and wondering how she was ever going to rebuild her life again.

10

Pumas

When Daniel went out on to the mountain that cold night he knew that what he was about to do would cement the special relationship he had been working on with the pumas. He was going to assist with the birth of Venus's cubs. This was something that had never been attempted before: wild females were famously dangerous if anyone attempted to approach their young. For Venus to allow him into her lair would be a tremendous honour. Not even Mercury, the cubs' father, would be welcomed there.

As Daniel climbed up to the ridge, to the rocky outcrop that harboured a cave where he knew Venus would retreat to, he called out to let her know he was coming. He wanted no surprises; no added worries to what would anyway be a stressful experience for her. Darkness covered his movements but the sound and smell of him should alert her to his approach.

A low growl emerged from somewhere alongside Daniel. He jumped. That was Mercury letting him know he was here. That alone was confirmation that Daniel was gaining success – male pumas did not stay with females after mating. They were usually creatures of the night – solo operators who travelled far and wide and, in Mercury's case, were volatile and unpredictable. But this male was sticking around. Daniel was delighted. He hoped Venus would not drive him away.

Gaining the ridge and working his way towards the cave, Daniel heard hissing and screaming issuing forth in the air. If she had not produced already, Venus was suffering fierce contractions. Daniel called out to her again in what he hoped she would interpret as a soothing voice. He slowly and deliberately entered the cave, ducking down low to gain access.

Venus was lying on her side, snarling in pain but not reacting to his presence. The floor to the cave was covered in grasses and was clean and clearly as comfortable for the mother as she could make it. She had not produced as yet. Daniel kept talking to her, reassuring her. She was a young female and this was her first pregnancy: it was inevitably a nervous, worrying and unprecedented experience for her. Daniel stroked her beautiful head all the time she was hissing and growling. A yelp of pain; a fierce contraction and Venus started pushing. Nothing yet but a birth was coming soon. Venus struggled and snarled and moved restlessly in pain. Daniel continued to stroke her and keep his voice as calm and reassuring as possible.

More growling and hissing: contractions were coming stronger and stronger and more and more quickly. Venus gave an almighty howl and pushed and pushed and pushed. At last a tiny kitten emerged from her hind quarters. Then more pushing – another! Daniel gathered them in his hands and brought them around to their mother. More screeching and pushing and a third kitten emerged. All were blind – eyes tightly shut – but mewing for their mother. Venus began licking them, cleaning the blood and mucus off their tiny bodies, bonding with her offspring. These tiny cubs immediately started pawing with their front feet, an instinctive reaction designed to get their mother to release milk from her teats. Daniel steered them round so that they could latch on and start feeding. Mother laid her head back. Exhausted. But the three cubs were now all lined along her belly, greedily taking their first feed. Daniel was elated. It was an emotional

432

experience for him, let alone for Venus!

Daniel crawled back a space so as not to crowd the happy family. He lay back, sprawled across the entrance to the cave with a big smile spreading across his face. He could hardly believe what had just happened! This was something he was sure no one else had had the privilege to share. But he was tired and it was time for him to rest as well.

Morning came early. High on the ridge, the sun's rays from the east lit up the outcrop in a beautiful rosy glow. It matched the feeling of Daniel lying there – looking at the mother of three beautiful cubs, peace and contentment in her face. Venus looked straight at Daniel and purred. What a wonderful experience: Daniel felt part of the family.

Daniel lay there a moment thinking over what he had just seen. He slowly got to his feet. Maybe he should not intrude any longer. When all was said and done, he belonged to another family and Venus, Mercury and their cubs should be left to find their own way in the world. Daniel started slowly walking downhill, his footsteps returning to his home, his woman and her son. He belonged there now; not here. It was his job, he realised, not to live on the mountainside any longer but to give children to Karin and – as she had forcibly reminded him – to assist in her birthing, not that of other creatures.

He was excited, honoured, delighted by what he had seen and helped with but it was a thought-provoking experience in what it had taught him about his own role in the world. Mercury came over to growl a greeting as Daniel descended, lost in his own meditation. Yes, he thought, we males have got to figure out our roles with the particular females we have chosen to mate with. He dropped a hand to stroke Mercury, as if connecting with a brother, but Mercury was not having any of that. He was too proud and independent. He simply growled again and slid away. More to think about: Daniel was still coming to terms with the fact that the life he had led so far – independent and solo like a male puma – he had chosen to end. He had chosen to share his life with a woman whom he loved. And all choices involve sacrifices. He could not continue chasing pumas.

Such thoughts as these dominated Daniel's mind as he approached his house, so he wasn't looking out as carefully as he might have done and did not notice the subtle signs the mountain was sending him that others had visited this place. He opened his front door and walked straight into an enormous, swinging fist that threatened to end his life. There was an instinctive attempt to duck but it was too late. Daniel felt an almighty crunch and blackness descended. His body slumped down as if lifeless.

The next sensation Daniel felt was heat. Heat all around him. And hot breath down his neck. What on earth was happening? There was smoke now, entering his nostrils. And he was moving. Being dragged. Daniel's head was aching as if he had been smashed unconscious, so his senses were confused and he had no idea what was happening. He opened his eyes and saw flames, but he still felt hot breath down his neck and the sensation of being dragged backwards. And someone was growling determinedly in his ears.

Stupid with pain and with a head that felt twice its normal size, Daniel suddenly realised what was going on. Mercury had a hold of his collar and was pulling him upslope, out of a burning building. The building, Daniel slowly recognised, was his home that was going up in flames. Dragged now under the bushes, Daniel was safe but his head was still scrambled. He turned on his side to try and thank Mercury, who was panting, tired but looking for all the world as if he was satisfied for a job well done. Concussed as he was, Daniel could not help but wonder at the tremendous qualities of these marvellous animals. He had just been dragged from a burning building! Mercury had saved his life!

But what was going on? Daniel felt as if he had been

smashed on the head precisely because he had been smashed on the head! Scrabbling under the bushes, Daniel circled round to try and see what was happening on the mountainside below him.

His house was now consumed in flames. Where was Karin? and Peter? Aching with worry as well as with pain, Daniel kept low and out of sight among the bushes, moving round to see who had attacked him and his home. He felt Mercury doing the same alongside him.

Lower down, on the horse-track that led to his home, an old red pick-up was bumping its way upwards, towards the burning building. Daniel could see the back of a big man standing there – one he had seen before, long ago. Who was it? That man who had levelled a pistol at him on the *páramo* of Volcán Puracé and who had fallen from his horse and been knocked out. That was the one. But where was Karin?

The pick-up stopped and a man got out. He was shouting at the big man. All at once, the horror of the scene in front of him hit Daniel with full force. They were arguing over the fact that the big man had just killed Karin and Peter. Their bodies were sprawled in the dust on the other side of the two men. Crouching down as he was, Daniel had not seen them at first.

Daniel kneeled there, under the bush, absolutely crushed. Desolate. Numb to his core. Karin was spread-eagled in the road in front of him. Lifeless. Clubbed to death it appears by the big man. And these two idiots were arguing about it – about ending the lives of the ones he loved. Daniel's senses were still foggy but the awful reality that lay before him could not be denied. Shaking his head free from the confusion that still clogged and clouded it would not erase the horror that had happened. Karin had been killed here in front of him just a matter of seconds ago. Anger began rising in Daniel, a blind anger that he had never, ever felt before.

Mercury needed no other communication. With a blood-curdling roar he flew through the air and struck the nearest man down to ground, fangs buried in his throat. The man stood no chance: his neck was ripped open and he died in an instant, his blood staining the ground and dripping from the jaws of the maddened puma. The big man clambered into the cab of the pick-up and Mercury leapt up on to the front, trying to get at him through the windscreen.

Daniel couldn't move. He was still in shock, seeing the woman he loved sprawled dead in front of him. But the big man was waving a pistol in the pick-up and Daniel feared for the life of Mercury now. He urged him to leave. He had killed one. Stop it now and save yourself.

Daniel had no idea how long he knelt there; empty, numb, deaf and blind to everything – as if he too was dead. He had a dull idea that the big man was out in the road, lifting the lifeless bodies of Karin and Peter and throwing them in the back of the pick-up as if they were plastic dummies. The man killed by Mercury was also unceremoniously dumped in the back. Then the big man got in and drove away. He drove away and took Daniel's life and love with him.

Their home was still burning. Everything that Karin and he had built together. In physical terms it was not much, but the dreams it embodied, the love it represented, the seeds of the future that had been planted there – all that was going up in flames. Daniel could still not move.

Mercury came back and sat with Daniel, looking at him, waiting. Still, Daniel was motionless, grief rising within him, guttural sounds of loss somehow emerging from his throat. Minutes passed. Slowly Daniel struggled to his feet. Everything hurt. He walked out on to the horse-track where death and destruction had reigned – blood and dust and oil from the pick-up were all there. At last, Daniel gave vent to his feelings and he roared to the heavens and kicked at the blood and dust around him. Then he started walking uphill. He had seen one family created that morning. He had lost his own, so he started walking uphill to return to the other. That was all he had now.

Daniel could not face seeing anyone for weeks. Weeks that stretched into months. He lived close to Venus and her cubs, watching them grow. He wandered off at times, like Mercury, searching the high ridges and peaks. He went off hunting and feeding when necessary, then returning to see how the cubs were getting on. Peregrine falcons visited him, as did condors and eagles and a variety of different creatures that he met on his wanderings. Living high and wild and spurning human company, Daniel returned to the creatures he had grown up with and who had given him inspiration just as before when he had lost his parents and lost his faith also in the world that humans had built. He was regressing. All that he had learned from Karin about coexisting with and tolerating the city he now began to lose again. The faith that he had built up in her and in the world from which she had come was lost. Anger replaced it. He knew that anger was a negative, destructive emotion but he could not help it. It burned deep within him and glowered from his eyes at times, especially at night, when his thoughts returned to the evil that men did and repeatedly resorted to.

Constantly on the move, Daniel lost weight but gained in stamina. Psychologically, he was changing, too. With the anger that was buried, seething inside him, he felt more aggressive, intolerant of those whose actions he disapproved of. And the fire that he felt and that seemed to surround him wherever he went, any creatures that were close by could feel it, too. There were times when he could feel the rage rising within him and then all the insects, birds, animals around – they all burned and cried and spread that anger around as well, as far as the horizon. You could hear and see and feel the effect across the mountain. The earth itself seemed ablaze.

In a matter of months Venus' cubs had become fiery adolescents. They caught and killed their own food. They were becoming more independent but, just like Mercury, they hovered around Daniel. With his own intense fire, Daniel somehow attracted them. Never too close, but never too far. Every member of this puma family went their own way on occasions – Mercury going further than any – but they would always return.

Daniel started walking north, back in the direction of Volcán Puracé. Something was pulling him there. He had seen condors far in the distance in that direction and they seemed to be signalling that all was not well. The volcano was the highest peak in that part of the Andes, where Daniel of course knew that terrain so well – it was where he had first met Karin – but there was something happening right up there that he had a bad feeling about. Condors were telling him so.

Daniel made a decision to go and visit an old friend. He would go down into Popayán and find El Ciego. He wanted to know what was happening: what bad things were being done; what wrongs needed putting right.

Daniel looked different these days. Older, bearded, more drawn in the face and lighter, quicker on his feet. Months of grief and living on the edge had done that to him. He rather hoped that people would not recognise him as a result. El Ciego would not be fooled, of course. His senses worked differently to more sighted people.

It was Sunday, market day and Daniel took up his old position in the plaza. Apart, standing back from the crowds that circled the stalls, he watched humanity at work and play. Few, if any, paid any notice of him but every animal, bird and insect knew he was there; the heat within him set all of them on fire. The plaza sounded differently as a result. And El Ciego picked it up.

He left his stall and came tap-tapping across. 'By God, you're alive!' he muttered. 'The whole region has been mourning your death and disappearance but I feel you here stronger and more alive than ever before. And there is an element of danger about you I've never felt before.'

Daniel nodded. 'Old friend, I think much the same of you. How you feel these things when no one else so much as glances at me. It shows you've grown also! But do you know why I've come back? Do you know that as well? Can you guess?'

'Triple F have started causing trouble. Back in the place where the old TMG mine operated. Where Carlos Díaz was killed. But there is more. There's some internal conflict, too. I can't be sure, but Triple F is not a healthy place right now. All sorts of contradictory rumours circulate and the only thing that tells me is that it is boiling up inside, like a dormant volcano. But enough of me. What have you been doing? Every creature in the plaza seems to be on a knife edge. There's something boiling up inside you as well.'

'You're right, Juan Sebastián. Triple F again: they killed my woman, the love of my life, and her child, too. Anger has been growing inside me for months and I feel like I will erupt soon – before the volcano. Soon. It only needs a trigger to set me off. I guess I've come looking for that.'

'Take care, Mono,' said El Ciego. 'But go to the Puracé mines and maybe you will find what you are seeking for there. Perhaps you need to erupt to purge you of all the fire that's burning up your insides. If so, be careful of who gets hurt in the process. Good luck, and take care.'

'Thank you, my friend. Keep this visit quiet, won't you? There are few people in this town, or anywhere, that I trust these days but you are one. We will meet again some time.'

Daniel had the information he needed, indeed expected, so he withdrew from the plaza taking his barely suppressed fire with him. It was a long walk to the old TMG mine on the other side of Volcán Puracé and he knew he could find a horse easily enough to ride there, but he wanted time on the mountain, to feel the earth under his feet, hoping that the long journey would help still the raging torment within him. It didn't. Sleeping out en route, with pumas prowling restlessly around him, might have calmed him a little, but in the months since he had lost Karin nothing yet had quelled the flames inside, so one more day, one long walk, had little effect.

There was one more diversion on his way, however, that was bound to impact on him. So much so that he was unsure whether or not to stop by. He was almost frightened to test his feelings and see how he would react when he saw them: Valentina, Natalia and little Lucho – Carlos Díaz's family that he knew he loved. He had barely thought of them from the moment that Karin had re-entered his life; he felt guilty about that, but he also wondered about his own buried feelings for them all.

It was late morning when he surmounted the last rise and descended into the valley where he used to stay over in the old converted cattle shed. It had been a home of his of sorts. Not too near, not too far from Carlos and his family. The falcons with him knew where he was heading – the pueblo close by, over the next ridge – and flew ahead.

Valentina was out hanging clothes to dry when she noticed condors wheeling high above her. Looking up she also noticed some other birds also – circling high as well, though not quite so large. Surely they were eagles? What were they doing here, a long way from their usual haunts?

Blinking in the bright sunlight, Valentina could not keep gazing upward so she looked down to collect her thoughts. Something was happening.

'Mother! Mother!' It was Natalia running back home from the houses in the pueblo below, shouting excitedly: 'Look!'

She was running, spinning and pointing at one, two, three peregrine falcons that were zipping around her and which flew up and then came to rest on the poles and wires of the pueblo.

Mother and daughter looked at one another. They both knew what all these signs meant.

'He's alive, Mother. He's come back to us!' Natalia was crying with joy.

The two women turned to look at the mountainside stretching above the pueblo up to the distant ridges. To the west, from the neighbouring valley, a lone figure was walking over towards them. It was Daniel walking down to them slowly, his emotions in turmoil. He heard a voice: not-so-little Lucho was shouting: '*Hola*, Mono! *Hola*, Mono!'

Before he got to the pueblo Natalia threw herself at him. Lucho was grinning, running up to grab a leg. Valentina hung back a little at first and then she too had to come close and give him a hug.

Daniel kissed the top of the two women's heads, losing his face in their hair. He had his arms around them both, then raised his head to grin down at Lucho. Tears filled his eyes. He should have come to see them before.

Valentina lifted her head to him. 'Everyone said you were dead. That you had gone for ever. We couldn't believe them.'

Natalia shook her head. She kept her face buried in Daniel's chest, unable to look up, weeping profusely. Her voice, muffled by Daniel's rough clothing and her own emotion, rose up to him: 'We never, never believed it.'

Valentina continued: 'But you look different, Daniel. What's happened to you?'

'I've been living rough for months now. Unable to settle. I've been living with the pumas.'

'It's not that.' Valentina smiled up at him and held his face in her hands. 'There have been other times when you've looked rough, like some urchin who's been playing in the streets. But there is something hard and violent about you I've never seen before ...'

Natalia still held him, still wouldn't raise her head, but she shook her head. She didn't agree with her mother. Daniel was still Daniel and she loved him whatever he looked and felt like.

Daniel sighed. Valentina had cut through to his inner feelings straight away. He nodded. He did his best to control his voice in answering her.

'Triple F killed the woman I loved. She was my wife in everything but the law. I was knocked out and couldn't protect her and they killed her like she was nothing, nobody. I have never felt such anger before. I thought that if I went back up to the mountains then in time I would calm down ... but I haven't. I'm still angry. Deep inside.'

Natalia let him go. Valentina gathered Lucho and Natalia together by her side. They all looked at him.

'We heard something of all that. We also know what it is like to lose someone you love. You know we do. So why didn't you come and see us before?' Valentina reproached him so gently but so pointedly.

Daniel couldn't answer. He shook his head and looked desolate. He changed the subject. 'I came to see what was going on at the mine nearby. What problems they're creating. Do you know?'

Natalia answered for him: 'Half the pueblo is up in arms – they're polluting the waters again. The other half has given up protesting without you or my father to lead them.'

'Leave that for later, Daniel. Come inside.' Valentina was immediately practical. 'You look a mess and we need to cut your hair and clean you up!'

The next hour was taken up by the two women attending to Daniel's physical appearance. Lucho was despatched to play outside while Valentina got out the scissors and cut Daniel's beard down to a manageable length. Natalia went off to boil water and bring her father's old razor. She promised she would not cut him if he would trust her to shave him. This was a luxury he had never experienced before. Valentina watched as her daughter wielded the razor. When Natalia had finished she kissed Daniel on the cheek. She lingered over it, her eyes shining.

Valentina stepped in and flashed her eyes at her daughter, as if to say: Watch it! She produced the scissors again and began in earnest at cutting Daniel's hair, turning his head one way and then the other as she busied about.

The process did not only affect Daniel's appearance. These women and particularly Valentina's sure-footed management of him had penetrated the shell he had worn about him for so long. They loved him. It was obvious and he had been too wrapped up in his own hatred until now to search out the one medicine above all others that would cure him. Their love touched him deeply; it warmed his soul. Sitting there, with Valentina now holding his head and looking at him, Daniel reached out and circled his arm around her. He pulled her close and laid his head against her breast. Anger within him seemed to dissipate and something more loving began to rise in its place.

Natalia's big round eyes took all this in and she retreated. She went out into the road outside to look for Lucho.

Left alone together, Valentina bent her head down and kissed him. Daniel responded.

She whispered to him: 'I've always loved you, did you know that? Even married to Carlos, loving him as I did, I loved you also. Can you believe that?'

Daniel nodded. 'Yes. I knew then. Thank you for telling me now.' The raging inside him was fast disappearing and he felt something of the person that he used to be returning. He stood up and drew Valentina to him, kissing her gently, once, twice. 'It's easy to love someone when they are so lovable.'

'Daniel: stay with me.' Valentina said. 'Start tonight: in my bed. And stay here with us all. I've lost my husband; you've lost your wife. We're the same, you and I.'

Daniel looked at her. How could he refuse? Yet somehow he knew he had to. He wasn't ready.

'I do love you, Valentina. It is a sort of love that has always been there because you seem to draw it out of me. And we are the same, like you say. But I'm not yours – I'm not anybody's.

If I belong anywhere, I still belong on the mountainside. I can stay tonight if you want me ... but I cannot stay always. Can you understand?'

She smiled a slow, sad smile. 'I thought you'd say that. I hoped you wouldn't but I do understand: you don't belong here; not yet anyway, if ever. Like me, the period of loss and mourning leaves a long shadow. But let us love each other tonight, at least, and leave the future for another time.'

Valentina cooked a meal for them that evening. She sat Daniel at the head of the table and served them all just as she used to when it was Carlos, and not Daniel, sitting there. They sat round looking at each other, taking in this new domestic arrangement, trying to react normally. Lucho was grinning like crazy and being noisy and excessively friendly. Valentina sat there, love and affection oozing out of every pore of her being. Natalia was holding everything back, watching her mother and Daniel like a hawk and trying not to let it show. Daniel was not sure how to react: he had not been at this table, in this house, since Carlos had died. He had not been in any house since his and Karin's home had burnt down. Somehow he made polite conversation.

The meal finished. Daniel helped to clear everything away while Valentina put Lucho to bed. Natalia stood very close to Daniel while he was in the kitchen, washing up. She was now nineteen, possessing a flowering femininity as well as her father's fiery temperament. Her closeness and deliberate silence in Daniel's presence crackled like an electric current next to him. Daniel noticed she had dyed her long black hair a reddish-brown colour – he guessed that the pressure of city fashions and her peers must have led her to do this. He disapproved. In an effort to break the pregnant silence between them he spoke to her.

'You don't need to colour your hair to make yourself look any more beautiful ...' he started.

Natalia dropped the cloth she was holding and ran out. Oh dear, Daniel thought. Wrong move.

A moment later Valentina came to see him.

'What have you said to Natalia? She has just locked herself in her bedroom in tears.'

'Nothing,' said Daniel. 'I was only trying to be nice to her.' He explained what he had said.

Valentina came close and put her arms up to him. She turned her head to press her lips to his neck and then whispered: 'Be careful with her, Daniel. She's had a crush on you for years and now, having you back here after we were told you were dead, it has been intensely emotional for her ... For us all!' Her eyes sparkled at him.

Daniel nodded thoughtfully. 'I know. You don't have to tell me ...'

The two of them finished the chores in the kitchen then cast around for other things that needed attending to. They were looking for things to do to fill the silence and space between them, but they could not stretch out the quiet and graceful dance between them for much longer. Valentina stopped and looked at him.

'Come to bed?'

Daniel kissed her. 'Mmm.'

They made love slowly, lovingly, selflessly. They owed it to each other. If they never made love again, then tonight represented all time. It was a love that was not possessive, exclusive; it allowed each to give to the other completely for now and now was all that existed.

The dark night covered them.

Daniel woke in the small hours next to this wonderful woman but he knew he could not stay there: he could not signal to her, to her children, to himself that this was his place. He had to leave. Quietly he rose, dressed, embraced her for one last time and prepared to steal away. In the half-light, Valentina lifted one naked arm towards him as if trying to hold him back, the bed sheets fell away from her revealing her breasts that seemed to reach for him also. She looked painfully beautiful. Their eyes met. Not a word was spoken – it was a moment frozen in time but they also knew it meant goodbye. Daniel melted away into the night.

The walk in the dark along the track up over the ridge to the next valley, to his converted cattle shed, took an hour, but throughout that time Daniel's mind was in a different place. His feet seemed to know what they were doing but his head was in another dimension. Emotions were swirling around; the anger, hostility and intolerance that had filled his life for the last months were now all dissipated. He had learned to love again. On reaching and entering his old quarters he noticed how spotless and tidy it had been kept – someone's love for him had even reached here and kept it ready for him in his hoped-for return. How selfish and self-absorbed he had been for so long that he had not realised how much others cared for him. He did not deserve all this. Daniel collapsed on to the straw mattress. He felt humbled, guilty, ashamed. And then at last sleep prevented him from feeling any more.

It was not yet morning when he was woken by the rush of a body into his bed. Natalia! She was tearing at him, kissing him, licking him, sucking him, burying herself in his flesh. Daniel was astonished. He struggled to stop her but she was crying, rubbing her head and tears against him, refusing to release him, moaning aloud.

'I love you! Let me love you. Don't stop me!' Wet with tears, she reached her face up from below to look at him defiantly, eye to eye. 'I won't let you go, do you hear me? Don't try to push me away. I love you and want you and I've waited for ever for you!'

Natalia climbed on top of him, pushing aside bedding, clothes, everything that might interfere with their two naked bodies. Her hands were scrabbling, scratching, searching Daniel's bare flesh as she mounted him and took him into her.

She cried out with passion and fury, her eyes glaring at him, daring him to try and stop her. She rocked to and fro on top of him, lifted her head back and let out a cry to shake the heavens. Then she burst into tears, collapsing down to cling to him, holding on ferociously like an eagle grasping its prey. Her long hair splayed out all over Daniel's face and shoulders, and as she moved and tried to kiss him once more so it became wet with her saliva and tears.

Daniel came out of shock and instinctively reached to kiss and caress her. He was still amazed at what was happening and tried now to examine his own feelings. The speed and passion of the advance that had overwhelmed him at last gave him time and space to respond.

'Natalia, Natalia, look at me!' He tried to turn her face towards his.

She shook her head away from his grasp at first and then, free to move her head as only she wished, she glared at him: all fire and flames and fury. She knew he'd given himself to her mother and not to her. She was insanely jealous.

Good God! thought Daniel. What a woman! He kissed her eyes, first one then the other. Something of the fire subsided, then flared up again.

'Tell me you love me!' she demanded.

Daniel smiled. He did as he was told: 'I love you,' he said.

'Do you mean it?' she asked fiercely.

Daniel smiled even more and kissed her lips, slowly, letting her feel him.

'Natalia, you don't have to demand it, you don't have to cut me open and drag my love out of me … You are a lovely girl; a beautiful woman. You do not have to do anything. Just be yourself, relax and let love come to you.'

He gently rolled her over on to her back and came on top of her. He looked into her big round eyes. The fire was still there, so he kissed her again and again until she began to relax. Then he entered her and loved her and held her as she moved and moaned and cried out her feelings and all her aching emotion.

She shook her head violently again and then clung to him once more, pulling him down, holding him inside her and glaring up fiercely into his eyes. 'Do you know that there have been lots of men that have been looking at me, following me, trying to get me for themselves ... and I haven't let anyone near. Not one of them. I wouldn't let anyone so much as touch me. Do you know that?'

Daniel shook his head.

'Do you know that I've got friends my age already married. Some already with babies. And men, some of them husbands, are chasing after me trying to bed me, do you know that?'

Daniel shook his head again. He could imagine that, at her age, with the figure she had, with her mother's eyes and her father's passion, she must have half the men of Cauca desiring her.

'All this time, even when they told me you were dead, trying to catch me, I wouldn't let them near me. I knew you were alive somewhere. I kept coming here, looking after this place, keeping it clean, preparing this bed, waiting for you to re-appear, to find me. Did you know that?'

Daniel shook his head.

'I love you! Only you. All this time it's been driving me crazy. And now you are mine and I want you always!'

Daniel kissed her again. She was only nineteen.

'Natalia ... you've got me. Here and now. I love you. Here and now. But don't talk about always. You are a beautiful woman with a whole world out there waiting for you that you don't know about. Don't limit yourself to me. Don't deny yourself all the wonderful experiences that are out there beyond me that others can give you, not me. You don't need me and I could never give you what you deserve.'

He rolled off her, trying to put space between them, but she wasn't having any of that. She swung round, flinging her arms around his middle, throwing a naked leg over his.

'Don't try to get away from me, do you hear? Don't try and tell me all sorts of rubbish and slyly refuse me? OK? I'm not stupid. I know what I want and I won't listen to your rubbish, your lies.'

Daniel looked at her and marvelled at her wild temper.

'I don't lie. Understand? I won't lie to you and I would never treat you like you were stupid, not you, never. But I'm not talking rubbish!' He kissed her, trying to disentangle himself from her at the same time.

'Natalia – you can't have me. You shouldn't want to have me. Really!'

Daniel got up on his knees and pulled the bedclothes over her naked body, between them, so that he couldn't look at her beautiful figure and distract his thoughts. Heavens above, he thought. It would be so easy to stay with her: I need all my will-power to resist her!

'Natalia – I have to push you away from me. Not just for your good but for mine also. Glorious and desirable that you are, I can't love you for always. I can't give you what you want. I have to refuse you, do you hear? Listen to me!'

Natalia was shaking her head, putting her hands over her ears, glaring at him. 'No, no, no. Daniel. NO!'

She leapt up like a puma and flung her arms around his neck and dragged him down on top of her. Daniel had to use all his strength to untie her hands, haul them round and force them back above her head, trapping her beneath him. He looked into her face. She suddenly grinned and wickedly moved her body beneath his. Although the bedclothes were now between them, she writhed under him, opening her legs and pushed herself up at him, trying to entice him to return to her.

Daniel went red in the face. 'Behave yourself,' he told her.

There was no talking to her, Daniel realised. He had to go. He jumped up and started pulling his clothes back on. Natalia tried to stop him but he was now determined and annoyed.

With his clothes half-on, half-off, he made for the door. Natalia panicked: she was driving him away.

'Daniel, don't go!' she cried out. 'I love you: don't leave me!'

Daniel paused in the doorway. 'If you really love someone, Natalia, you give them room to grow. Allow them space to be what they want to be, not what you want them to be. That's why I know that your mother loves me!'

Natalia was left howling after him. That hurt her deeply.

Striding off as rapidly as he could, heading up slope to circle round and above the pueblo, Daniel was heading for the access road that would take him to the old TMG, now Triple F, mine. Anger had built up again inside him, though unlike before this was directed at Natalia, and especially at himself for being so stupid as to try to love her as the mature woman she had not yet become. Worst of all, what had just happened made his relationship with that family impossibly complicated. How could he ever resolve all the issues that now existed between them? He felt he could not visit them again. Why did he not stop her? Why did he not stop himself? Well, of course the answer was obvious – Natalia's sexual energy and appeal had been irresistible. Now he had to pay the consequences.

Daniel's mind was reeling. So many images and thoughts competed for his attention – two lovely women, each beautiful in their own way – and all the time he was punishing himself for the way he had behaved and the excessively complex situation he had got himself into with them. He stomped away uphill. A couple of hours or so of steady walking and directing his thoughts towards what might be going on way up in front led him eventually to calm down a little. It was not easy but he had now to concentrate on the business at hand and leave the turmoil in his head to another time.

The access road that he could see leading off towards the mine higher up the mountain looked a lot different to what he remembered: the valley that it followed was now badly eroded and it was very obvious that this was a recent development –

there were swathes of mud, silt, pebbles and boulders that littered the meandering and braided river. Beside the road was a camp of rough dwellings made up of plastic, rags, scrap timber and whatever else could be scavenged and pressed into service. And alongside this collection of shacks were people, and even from a distance as Daniel approached he could see that the atmosphere in this gathering was confrontational. There was trouble brewing.

Two Triple F-marked jeeps were parked on the road a little higher up, manned with security personnel, but the trouble that Daniel could sense did not include them. They were there as mere observers, keeping an eye on what was going on in case the trouble came in their direction. No, the focus of attention was some rivalry between a group that had come together on the road and another group that was strung out along by the rough encampment.

There was an explosion of noise and a number of men from the dwellings darted forward in an aggressive stance towards the group on the road. Sticks were raised and then came down, raining blows: some people were clubbing others. The sound, travelling slower, came up to him with a delay – shouts and screams as fighting broke out.

Daniel started running. There was one particular thug in the middle of the road flailing a club around viciously – he didn't like the look of that. Fast as he could run, however, he noticed something even quicker break cover and streak down towards the fight that was now spilling over the road: it was Mercury the puma.

Daniel was frightened – he had really little control over what Mercury was going to do. 'Don't kill him!' he shouted out to the big cat just as it gained the road and launched into the air.

Pandemonium broke out. Mercury flew at the big thug in the middle and brought him crashing to the ground, fangs locked into the man's shoulder. There were men, youths, women and a few children scattering in every direction. The

451

puma had landed on all four feet, straddled across his victim. He released his fangs and snarled ferociously in the man's face, ready to strike again. Daniel hollered out: 'Don't move!'

The fight had stopped. Fear and amazement had replaced it. A circle of people formed around the puma and his prey as individuals were caught between the desire to get as far away as possible and their fascination to see what was going to happen. Daniel broke through them to try and prevent any tragedy. He spoke first to the big cat.

'Mercury, get off him!'

The puma didn't budge. He turned his head to snarl at Daniel as if to say: This is my catch. You leave me alone!

The poor man, pinned down by the big cat, tried to move but as soon as he did so the puma opened his jaws and snapped forward as if to tear the man's face to shreds.

'Don't move!' said Daniel. 'I'm trying to stop him killing you!'

Daniel summoned up all his will-power and told the big cat to let the man go and come to him. Mercury was clearly reluctant to do so. He shifted his paws one way, then another and snarled his discontent at all and sundry. But he eventually backed off his victim and slunk across to Daniel, growling with bad temper all the way. As he did so there was whoosh of air and a falcon zipped down from the skies to land on Daniel's shoulder. The peregrine had returned to watch proceedings.

The circle of people grew bigger. A buzz of noise went round them – sounds of astonishment and incredulity. The evidence of a puma and a falcon by this man's side needed some explanation. Someone shouted: 'It's Mono! He's back' – which prompted a ripple of applause from a few. Others expressed awe and delight that Mono had apparently reappeared from the dead and communicated this to others. Some doubted who he was, which only prompted more discussion.

Meanwhile, the man who had been floored by Mercury

struggled to his knees. He was clearly in extreme pain – his shoulder had been savaged, and there were claw marks that had ripped down his back and front. The puma, now crouched low on his haunches beside Daniel, was still watching him and occasionally turning his head to snarl at others around.

Daniel looked at the growing numbers that gathered about him. He thought Mercury had better be gone now. Mercury thought the same and bounded off before he was encircled. Searching for faces he recognised, Daniel saw Pepe, one of Carlos's steady companions when he was alive.

'Pepe! What's all the fighting about?' he asked.

Pepe took his time to respond, a little shy at being addressed by this ghost from the mountains, but those by his side pushed him to answer.

'It's all about the water that's been pouring down here,' he said. 'These people – they've come to pan for gold. They don't care that the water is poisoning the earth; poisoning the living of all us farmers. So we want the waters stopped. We want them off this land. Go find some other place else to poison!'

One of the women in the encampment spoke out against this. 'We don't have some place else to go. We need to make a living as best we can and these waters from the mine – they've given us the best chance for ages! People here should not be so selfish, so greedy. They don't own these mountains – they are for us all.'

'You people are fighting each other when you should be uniting against those who are the cause of all these problems,' said Daniel. He asked the name of the spokeswoman of the encampment who had spoken out. She called herself Manuela.

'Manuela,' Daniel asked, 'do you really want to work these waters when they will poison you as well as the land? A friend of mine who spent years panning for gold in polluted streams is now nearly blind – is that what you want for you and your family? And Pepe – it is not these poor people who are your problem, it is the contamination from the mine. We need to work together and get them to clean it up. Can't we agree to that?'

Argument followed. Some agreed and others disagreed as to what the parties really wanted. But at least discussion and disagreement was better than the fighting that threatened to become an outright pitched battle. Daniel let them keep talking and arguing, watching to see if there was some ground for a compromise, a joint action where they would all support each other. The potential for agreement seemed to be fizzling out, so he seized the initiative.

'Look, if I organise a protest over pollution and demand that the mining company do a thorough clean-up, would you all support that? If we bring out cattle, horses and all manner of animals and people in a protest march, would you head it up with me? Both parties here?'

'Yes, Mono! Do it! We will join in this time!' Pepe explained to all the others that the animal protest that the famous Mono had organised the last time against TMG made news all over the country and even overseas. TMG had to clean up their act as a result. Triple F will have to do the same, he said. The waters that remained would not be poisonous.

The argument came at last to an agreement that contaminated waters were in neither party's interest: a combined protest was the face-saving solution that both sides could support. A number from the encampment who had been panning for gold and had not before met Mono were persuaded that he was indeed the best leader they could hope for. Mono's reputation among the local farmers was not questioned. If he guaranteed the safety of any livestock, they accepted it. They agreed therefore to return the following morning and bring what cattle and horses they could spare. Mono was asked about the puma.

'Pumas will come if I need them but they are unpredictable,' said Mono. 'There are less dangerous creatures that might help us instead. We shall see.'

The crowd that had come together on the road eventually dispersed – farmers walking back towards the pueblo and various other homes in the district; the gold panners returning to their encampment. Two Triple F jeeps whose occupants had been observing from a distance backed up and turned on the road, heading off to the mine. They had seen enough and would eventually report back. That left only Daniel alone on the hillside – alone except for the falcon on his shoulder. He set off to go back to his old cattle shed, fervently hoping that there was no one there waiting for him.

11

Finale

Fields was to spend months in a bad temper over the loss of his son. Work, however, could not wait. The flushing out of the Puracé mines with cyanide solution had to proceed and Fields was anxious to hear if there was any payback yet. Things started well at first, he was pleased to hear – after weeks of preparation, the required solution had washed through the first mine for a month or so, and traces of gold had been recovered as the waste water had been filtered and discharged. But then he received a phone call that astonished and infuriated him.

Alejandro González called. The road up to Triple F's deep mine had been blocked in a local protest. Cattle, horses, dogs and crowds of people had filled the access road and nothing could get through. A couple of trucks had tried to barge into the mêlée and knock anyone out of the way but they had to be abandoned. Apparently, a cloud of hornets had risen from the river bed and got into the truck drivers' cabs. The drivers had got out.

González assured Fields that they had tried their best. Local Triple F employees had really given their all to reopen the road – even a bulldozer was brought into service, the driver swathed in netting and protective clothing, but a puma had appeared and dragged him off his machine. After that, González said, no one would go against the protest. El Mono was back, he said.

FINALE

Everyone thought he had been killed but now everyone was saying he had come back from the dead. None of his staff were willing to risk going up against him. And now the newspapers and television people were here, interviewing everyone.

Fields lost his temper. He ranted and raved down the phone. He never thought much of González anyway: the man was too weak.

'What do you mean Mono is back from the dead! He's not immortal! Don't tell me he is resurrected like a Second Coming. He isn't Jesus Christ, for Christ's sake! What's the matter with all you people? If no one down there, including yourself, can sort out this man and the problems he causes then I'm coming down myself. I'll be there tomorrow! In the meantime, I want as much information as you've got on Mono and especially I want to know his whereabouts – where we can hit him. If you have only got myths and rumours, then do some proper research! Gettit? Find out something believable before I get to you or start looking for another job!'

Fields slammed down the phone in a rage. The fact that the media people were down there made it even more infuriating. He phoned Carolina in a foul mood and warned her that she would be called up soon, if it had not already happened, and she should prepare the standard response. He slammed the phone down a second time and paced the carpet, swearing out loud. Then he told his assistant to book a flight to Popayán for himself and his new bodyguards.

Two people meanwhile raised their eyes upward in despair. The top boss was in a tantrum and had thrown all the toys out of the pram again. Both Carolina Santos and Alejandro González wondered what was going to happen next: Alejandro knew that whatever he did would probably not be good enough; Carolina was starting to really worry about the lies she was being required to circulate and how she could possibly defend them.

Alejandro had the biggest problem and the shortest deadline:

one day to try and get some more information about Mono. He asked around the office and received a tip that he had once picked up months ago: if you want to know what is really going on in and around Popayán, he was told, go out and find El Ciego.

During the week, with no Sunday market stall to locate El Ciego, it meant a bit of walking around and asking people where the blind man was likely to be found. It did not take long: after half an hour he found El Ciego in a café, chatting to the waitresses. Alejandro González went straight up and introduced himself.

'Señor González, the Regional Head of Triple F – this is indeed a surprise!' El Ciego said. 'To what do I, a poor blind man, owe this great honour?'

'Poor or not, blind one, I need some information and you, I am told, are the man to give it to me. What do you know of El Mono and his whereabouts?'

'Information, my dear sir, is what I trade in,' replied El Ciego. 'Before I can tell you anything, what information can you give me in return?'

González sighed. He looked about and could see that in this café there was no one in earshot. He wondered himself how much he could safely disclose but decided he would open up a little.

'Firstly, what I am to tell you is that you did not hear this from my own lips. OK? I cannot betray my own business. But I can tell you this: I am personally tired of all the problems, protests and killings that have been going on for years over mining in this part of the world. If there was an easy way out, I would take it. But I cannot see any way out at present. Now: tell me what you know of Mono!'

'Well, Señor González, first of all what I know of El Mono is that you are not the only one who wants to find him! I have been asked for his whereabouts by someone else just recently. Unlike you, however, others love him. In your case, if you tell me that the killing cannot stop and yet you are looking for Mono, then it is clearly obvious whom you want next in the firing line! Triple F did not get him at first; so you want me to help you get him a second time? Am I so foolish to help you? No. But I will tell you this for nothing: you will not find him. He will find you; or whoever it is that seeks to hunt him down. Tell your business superiors that.'

'How do you mean – he will find whoever it is that hunts him down? Does this man have extra-sensitive radar or something?'

'Yes, he does have something like that,' said El Ciego. 'He was nearly caught once. He will not be caught again. If you do not know this already, then let me tell you now: this man has an immense influence in this region. Ironically, he does not even know that himself. When people thought he was dead, the mountains here felt dead, too. But now they are alive and singing. People have seen him for the first time in ages and everyone is talking about it. Word has travelled from pueblo to pueblo, town to town. As a result, now he is around, you can feel it. And, in my case, if he is close by, I can hear it – everything sounds different. He is not close today, I can tell you that. If you want to find him; if your hunters want to find him, go up on to the *páramo* above the Fernández estate. He is there somewhere. But you won't catch him again. You will not even get close. He will know you are coming. Señor González, if you are really tired of the protests and the killing, then you will have to come to an accommodation with El Mono. You will not beat him. Not now: he is stronger than ever.'

González sighed for the second time. He knew that El Ciego was telling the truth, but he also knew that he could not say all this to Morten Fields. He would never accept it. Like all dominant leaders, he could be told only what he wanted to hear. Well, González decided, he would have to tell him only that.

'Thank you, blind one,' said González. He passed over a packet of cash to pay his informant. 'Your information, or as much of it as I can, I will pass on to my superiors. What they will do with it, I cannot say. Or, rather, I fear that they will not believe it. In which case, the hunters will be out – I hope El Mono's radar is working well! Goodbye.'

'Have no fear for El Mono, Señor,' replied El Ciego, pocketing the cash. 'His radar has undoubtedly already told him that you have come to see me. As you leave, look up into the sky. Your eyes will see what mine cannot. Goodbye.'

With that cryptic message, Alejandro González left the café and returned to his office. He did look up on his way, however. There were condors circling far above him.

In Durham, England it was five hours ahead of Colombia and Karin was down on her knees, playing with Peter in the last few minutes before his bedtime. He was nearly two; a lovely boy with his mother's dark hair, blue eyes and an expression at times that Karin could only guess came from her side of the family. Her own father maybe – though she had no idea what he looked like. It was certainly not a look that she had ever seen in Morten Fields.

Karin wondered, not for the first time, what sort of life, family and upbringing she could give her son. All by herself she felt inadequate. There were times when a bottomless sadness filled her days and she desperately wanted to avoid giving any of that feeling to Peter. But what could she do? Deny her own feelings? Transmit a flat, expressionless nothingness? Hardly an appropriate upbringing. They say that time heals all wounds – Karin wondered just how long a time she was going to need to heal hers. Meanwhile, Peter ran across the carpet chasing a ball and she inevitably found herself thinking that her son needed a man to kick the ball or throw it back to him. When was she ever going to stop thinking like this?

It was just as she was toying with these questions and worries, trying to stop going down blind alleys in her mind, when her mobile phone rang. Claudia, the message said.

'Karin, Karin, is that you?' Claudia sounded as if she was jumping up and down with excitement.

'Yes ...?'

'Karin ... I have to tell you this ... I've checked and checked and asked lots of people ... but everyone is saying that Mono is back. Karin: Daniel is alive!'

'Claudia!' Karin cried out in shock. 'Claudia ... it can't be ... he can't ... Please tell me! What do you mean?'

'I came to our finca last night, Friday night, and Alfonso told me. He said everyone is talking about him. Karin, I rushed down to Popayán to see if I could find El Ciego – you know, the blind man who is the source of all news and information – and I've just got back. I begged him to tell me what he knew. Karin, El Ciego has seen him. Daniel looks different he says. Much sadder and angrier. He thinks that they've killed you, he says ... but he's alive. Karin, Daniel's alive!'

Karin exploded in tears. 'Claudia!' She couldn't speak. She went through every emotion in the space of seconds: fear, doubt, joy, happiness, then fear again.

'Tell me again ... Claudia, tell me again ... tell me it's true.'

Claudia shouted: 'It's true. Daniel's ALIVE!'

Karin began to wail. She didn't know how to react. Peter became alarmed to see his mother so emotional and ran across into her arms. Karin picked him up and kissed him and kissed him and hugged him as if she would break him in two. She smiled through her tears and told him that she loved him like never before. All the floods of emotion surging through her body she directed at him – there was no other way she could express herself. She was laughing, crying, on the verge of hysterics. She tried to speak to Claudia.

'Give me an hour or so to put Peter down, then Skype me. Please Skype me. I have to see you Claudia ... Tell me I'm not dreaming. Tell me it's all true. I love you, Claudia ...'

Karin finished in tears again and had to put the phone

down. She had no idea how she was ever going to get Peter to sleep after this.

Peter was puzzled and unable to read his mother's feelings. All sorts of contradictory emotions came at him so he took longer than usual to go to bed – he kept looking for reassurance that everything was all right. Was everything all right? He guessed so. His mother certainly had a strange light in her eyes and she was smiling and grinning and then looking away into the distance. Were there tears in her eyes? He wasn't sure. But then she was smiling again and telling him everything was fine and that he should close his eyes and go to sleep. Eventually, sleep did overcome him and so he never found out that his mother's heart was racing and her stomach was in knots.

Claudia came through on the Internet and for the next hour Karin went over and over again all the details of what had been happening on the other side of the globe. She had to keep on asking: Was she sure? Was it really true? What exactly had she heard and who had she talked to? Eventually, Karin began to believe the impossible. Maybe, just maybe, Daniel was alive. Of course, there was no doubt in Karin's mind now – she had to take Peter and return to Colombia. The next morning she would have to talk to Siobhan in the International Office and say that for urgent personal business she had to fly out, for how long she did not know. It also meant visiting the bank in Durham and asking for a loan. She would have to take the very first flight she could find, change in Bogotá and go straight on to Popayán. Claudia would meet her there and then they would go to her finca. Just talking about it all made Karin's heart leap. She could visualise it all. The most amazing and most nerve-wracking thing of all would be trying to find Daniel. She still couldn't quite believe he was there somewhere, back in the *páramo* where she had first met him all those years ago, despite the fact that Claudia kept on telling her, every couple of minutes or so. It must be true. It must be true. Daniel must be alive.

Emotional exhaustion eventually got the better of her. Karin said goodbye, switched off her computer and retired to her bed. She lay there for a moment. Was it all a dream? Do dreams come true? If it was true, it was something that had changed everything. Something she could now hold on to and begin to live again.

Fields was true to his word and took the flight from Bogotá to Popayán the next morning. He arrived at the Triple F regional office in in the early afternoon with two bodyguards and the three immediately went into a meeting with Alejandro González.

'Right! Tell me what you've got on Mono.' Fields was as impatient as ever.

'Well he is up on the *páramo*, where he lives,' began González. He was wondering just how exactly he was going to explain what he had been told. 'I'm informed that he lives above the Fernández estate, which you can reach by going due east from here – parallel to, but further south from, the access road to our Puracé mine. But apparently he knows you are coming.'

'How the hell can he know that?' Fields demanded. 'Have you been telling everyone?'

'Of course not. But I'm told he has friends everywhere, that nothing escapes him, that you won't get near him, you can't kill him. That's the story. Believe it or not.'

Fields had two ex-US Special Forces bodyguards, Ryan and Tom. The younger of the two, Ryan, spoke up.

'You mean he's in hiding, that we won't find him?'

'I'm told he will find you. Like I've heard, he will see you coming.'

Fields had had enough of this claptrap. 'I get it. The guy is superhuman. He sees all and knows all. People here believe he cannot be killed. Well, we will find out if bullets bounce off him like Superman. We will take a high-powered rifle with scopes: if he sees us, then we can see him.'

Tom the more experienced bodyguard wanted to know about transport: 'How do we get to the area where you say he hangs out?'

'You can travel by four-by-four until the roads run out,' said González. 'One track takes you to the Fernández estate, which is not that far. The access road to our own mine will get you up to four thousand metres – a lot further and a lot higher. Where you go from either place is anybody's guess. There's a lot of mountain and you will have to go on foot or by horse. The *páramo* stretches for ever, and if you want to cover a lot of ground I guess it will have to be by horse.'

Tom was no fool. 'Mr Fields, sir, let me sum it up for you. We are chasing a single individual on the side of a mountain. He knows the terrain and we do not. He has all the support of the local populace. Up there, with no clear idea of where he will be, we could be searching for days. So, first, we need more men. Second, we will need altitude – it will be a lot easier moving downslope than looking uphill. Third, if we have men on foot or on horseback strung out in a line sweeping the area – which is the only way to pick him up – then he is sure to see us coming first. That is easy to predict. He may choose to run or hide – either way it will take time chasing him. Lastly, this son-of-a-bitch is hard to find and hard to kill. We know that. So we need experienced hunters. I suggest you recruit as many such men as you can find and we don't go until we've got 'em. That's it.'

Fields cursed. He wanted action. But he had experienced soldiers with him and he would be stupid to go against their advice. He turned to González.

'What sort of security personnel do we have here?' Without Cortés, Fields had no idea who was any good and whether any of them could communicate in English.

'Juan José Gómez has taken over from Miguel Cortés,' said González. 'Gómez is reliable and he and his men know the area around our mine. His English is pretty limited, however. None of his men knows more than a few basic commands in English, but if you go through Gómez and he understands what you want, then he'll get through to the others. I suggest we ask him how many men he has who are up to the job.'

'How long will it take to get him here?'

'He's over at the old TMG mine, so if we get through now it'll be at least a couple of hours before we can have him here,' replied González. 'If we ask him for his best men and some are there, some are here, then it will be dark before they can all assemble. You won't be able to set off searching before tomorrow morning at the earliest. Maybe later.'

'Get him here as fast as you can and tell him to bring his best men with him,' said Fields. 'You've heard what we are going to do – pass the message on to Gómez and get him to summon whichever men he has that are up to it. I don't want security guards that sit around drinking coffee all day checking visitors to our offices. We need fit and strong characters who can cover the mountainside. And we want them quickly. Go to it!'

The protest at the old TMG mine had gone well: the two different groups of local people had worked together successfully to block the road and Daniel was pleased to see that animosity between them had disappeared in the face of a common objective. Daniel had asked to see the Triple F personnel at the mine to present their concerns and by the end of the day he had secured a certain understanding on all sides.

The security chief there, Juan José Gómez, wanted his men unharmed. They had all heard of Mono the magician and now they had seen what support he could conjure up from hornets and pumas and consequently were somewhat in awe of him. Mono just wanted to talk to the mine chief and stop the pollution. The chief agreed that they would stop pumping immediately but he insisted that he needed authorisation from the regional boss in Popayán if the temporary halt was to be prolonged – and he in turn would need the permission from Morten Fields in Bogotá if the waste solution was to be adequately filtered and decontaminated as a permanent measure.

Daniel reckoned he had bought time, probably a week, before either the order was sent to restart pumping out contaminated water, or investments were begun to detoxify the effluents. That was an achievement at least. It did his reputation no harm. He set off south, into territory that he knew blindfold and which carried rich memories and many heartaches.

There was something in the air that bothered him. Condors were circling far away over in the west, towards Popayán, and then returning. They could see some disturbance of some sort and were signalling this to him. Daniel wondered whether or not he should journey into town himself but decided against it. He would stay high on the ridge above the Fernández estate for the time being and, if he went into town at all, it would be to see El Ciego on the next market day.

Daniel did not want to come down too close to the Fernández estate. The memories stirred by the place were just too painful. It meant not seeing Alfonso and María, who must have heard he was around by now, and he regretted that but after recent experiences he was very wary of going back and visiting old friends. Maybe later, he told himself – not now.

Just over the other side of the ridge, on an east-facing slope with a view of a vast, unpopulated panorama, Daniel had a bivouac spot tucked into caves in a large outcrop. Venus and her three offspring, all big these days, had shown him the place and were there now, busy prowling around, getting restless, thinking of hunting, as the darkness began to descend. There was not a lot of food for four, sometimes five, pumas in the territory below him, so Daniel guessed it would not be long before the family – now his only family – split up and went their different ways. It was highly unusual for these pumas to stay together for so long as it was – a tribute to Mono's influence – but there had been an increasing number of territorial disputes, with Mercury, of course, as the youngsters had got too close to their father. The day of parting would not be far off.

Daniel wondered about Mercury and why he had stuck around with him for so long. He reckoned that the puma was waiting for something; he could sense something, so Daniel could sense something as well. One way or the other, a big day was coming.

The next morning that sensation was confirmed: condors were directly overhead, eagles were wheeling a little way over to the north and three peregrine falcons were perched on the outcrop above the cave where Daniel had slept. Venus was up, growling and uneasy, and her three adolescents – one male and two females – had been dispatched in all directions. Mercury was nowhere to be seen. Something was definitely afoot.

Daniel climbed to the top of the ridge and, lying down at the best vantage spot, he scoured the mountainside to the north – in the direction of the Triple F mines, where the eagles were flying, where all the previous problems had come from. The sun was rising in the east on a beautiful, blue cloudless day. There was still a heavy mist hanging over the *páramo* below him but that would eventually dissipate when the sun got higher. The frailejones were in flower – like a carpet of gold, twinkling in the condensation – and insects were busy about them. It was such a blissful morning that Daniel had to pinch himself to take in the signals of alarm that were coming to him from all around. What was it that was in the air?

He waited. He could see nothing yet. He still waited. Minutes ticked away. Time seemed to stretch out and challenge him: Are you sure that something was destined to happen today? Daniel began to have doubts.

Then far away he saw a horse and rider. Was this it? A horse and rider slowly walked out of the mist that hovered over the *páramo*. One became two then, as Daniel peered across into the distance, he could see another and another. Yes, this was definitely something, that something he had been waiting for. It was a line of horsemen coming towards him, slowly zigzagging across the mountain slope from high on his right, eastwards, to further down on the left, westwards. The mist hugged the vegetation, so the horses were partly obscured and the riders appeared to be floating. They were methodically searching the *páramo* – he could now see five riders moving together – scouring the land across a broad front. What were they searching for? It hit Daniel with a shock that they were probably looking for him. He had just made a nuisance of himself at the Triple F mine, and Morten Fields would have seen that. Up until now, Fields would have thought – like everyone else – that he was dead, but now it was obvious that the first attempt on his life had failed, so this must be the second. Yes, that must be it. They were looking for him.

Daniel concentrated on the highest rider, the one who would eventually follow the line of the ridge that led up to him – he was the nearest and the one least obstructed by any vegetation. What was he carrying? Difficult to see at first but as his horse slowly moved up and crossed one way then another – there was a clear silhouette of a gun, a rifle, which came into view.

Daniel checked across to see the other riders – were they similarly armed? Impossible to tell at this distance, but one was enough – it was an ominous warning. His first concern was for the pumas. They were all out there somewhere. Daniel thought his best strategy was to head downslope himself and lead the hunters down with him and away from the higher ground, away from the outcrop he had just spent the night under.

Daniel set off. This was a familiar walk in very unfamiliar circumstances. He was moving downslope towards the Fernández estate with quite possibly a posse of gunmen a short distance away searching for him. Their paths were soon to cross.

Daniel dropped quickly downslope, on paths that three years before he had taken with Karin. Despite the danger that was approaching he was filled with nostalgia – the boulders where they had first met were just below him.

Daniel looked up: condors and eagles were shadowing the hunters, looking down on them as they were looking down for him. These wonderful birds were signalling that the horsemen were now spread out across the mountain slope in a V formation. Daniel reckoned that, if the one at the top, the one with the rifle he had seen, was gunman number one, then he was now low enough to have passed gunmen two and the head of the V, number three, must only be a short way ahead.

Sure enough, just below him, a horse and rider appeared out of the mist. Daniel wondered who he was and what he would do; he didn't recognise him. In fact, he didn't look like a local man, not even Colombian. Rider number two then appeared, just upslope. Daniel recognised this one at once: it was Juan José Gómez.

'*Hola*, Juan José,' said Daniel. 'Are you looking for me?'

Gómez nodded. His face was serious. He looked across at the other man. 'It is Mono!' he said, speaking heavily accented English.

The other rider produced a handgun.

'I think I ought to warn you that if you do not put that gun down,' said Daniel calmly, 'you will seriously regret it ...'

The bodyguard, Tom, the more experienced of the two that Fields had hired, was surprised at this reaction. People did not talk like this when he was about to shoot them. Such unhurried, perfect English in this place in these circumstances made him hesitate for a second. Nor did he really want to shoot someone dead in cold blood who was just standing there, smiling at him.

Riders four and five now drew up from below. Daniel had time to get a good look at them – all local toughs, he thought –

before returning to address the first rider who had found him.

'I really think you should lower that gun or else ...'

Before he could say any more to the gunman, there was whistle of air and, coming down at frightening speed, a falcon hit him full in the face. The poor man screamed, dropped his gun and put both hands up to his eyes. He had been blinded.

Almost at the same time there was an eruption of frenzied snarling and screaming and pumas seemed to rush out from all sides. Horses bucked and reared, riders toppled, pumas lashed out at a variety of targets. There was pandemonium.

The blinded bodyguard hit the ground with a crash – he had little idea what was now happening other than that his horse had thrown him. He stayed down, still covering his eyes with his hands. Riders four and five, the only local men that Juan José had been able to recruit to go up against El Mono, had both been dragged off their mounts by pumas. Frantic with fear, they had both tried to scramble away, only to be caught and savaged by the big cats. They ended up being hauled back, kicking and writhing with pain, staring wild-eyed at the pumas spitting and snarling in their faces. Blood was staining both men's arms and upper bodies where they had been seized by their ferocious attackers. Juan José had been pitched off his horse before he could be assailed by a puma. He had hit the ground with a bang which had concussed him but at least he had the sense to stay down as the big cats darted around and seized any man trying to escape.

Daniel called the big cats off – it was Venus and her three offspring – and surveyed the scene in front of him. All the horses had bolted. Juan José and his two men were shaken, bloodied but alive and in various states of injury. They had been severely mauled. They struggled to their feet but huddled together, still scared out of their wits, as the four pumas circled about them, glaring at them and spitting with rage. The first rider, the bodyguard who had been hit by the falcon, was grovelling on the floor crying desperately for his lost eyesight. Daniel gestured to Juan José to go and help him stand.

It was at this point that another horse and rider appeared from below.

A voice cried out. Daniel was so focused on the four men grouped in front of him that he did not recognise it at first ... but the voice sounded uncomfortably familiar.

'Daniel! Daniel!' The cry came louder and more insistent. He knew that voice. It came from a memory buried deep within him, from out of dreams that had haunted him, from out of a desolation that had filled his nights for what seemed a lifetime. His blood ran cold and then hot. His hairs at the back of his neck stood up, running up into his scalp.

'Daniel! Daniel!' The voice was now closer, demanding his attention. Nightmares were returning to him and warning him not to give into the horrors of the past. Images of a burning building and a body stretched out in the dust flared up in his head. How could he ever rid himself of such torment?

Despite himself, Daniel had to turn and look downslope, at the path up from the Fernández estate that had brought so many memories, which had led him to someone who had come from another world, who had transformed his entire life. He looked at the person now approaching who was riding out of those dreams. Daniel's whole body was rigid with shock, his face was blank. He could not believe it. A ghost was dismounting and running crazily at him, ignoring everything around her; she was oblivious to everything and everyone but one person. It was Karin.

She flung herself into his arms with tears streaming down her face. Daniel was still in shock, unable to move. Pumas growled and paced nervously around them but seemed to know that this newcomer was no threat. They stayed focused on the four captives they had unhorsed. But time had stopped for Daniel. He was in another place. In dreamland.

Karin had to shake him, to kiss him, to drag his eyes down

to focus on her. 'Daniel! Look at me! It's me! Your Karin!' She was alive with laughter, electricity was surging through her veins, her eyes was alight and shining into Daniel's. And all the time her lover was like a lifeless plank of wood, stiff and insensible.

There was a crack of rifle fire from a distance and a bullet screamed past, just missing Daniel, hitting and ricocheting off the boulders below. An outburst of snarling accompanied this and four pumas crouched low, ready to leap at their adversaries in front of them.

Daniel snapped out of his dream. He turned his back to cover the woman that had thrown herself at him and croaked a warning, albeit in a voice that he scarcely recognised as his own: 'Steady, Venus! No need to attack!'

Daniel looked up to the ridge from where he had descended and from where the rifleman must have taken aim. He saw a tiny black dot plummeting earthward from out of the blue sky.

The hunters were getting restless. There was also a glorious woman beside him whom he was now desperate to acknowledge but Daniel resisted the temptation. He spoke to his would-be assassins:

'I'm afraid your friend with the rifle has now suffered the same fate as your friend here.' He indicated the blinded man, who still held his hands up to his bleeding eyes. 'There will be no victory for you today.'

Daniel put his hand up, high into the air. There was a whoosh and a bang of feathers and a falcon appeared on his arm. There was blood dripping from its tiny talons.

At last Daniel could look down at the woman who was clinging to him.

'You're alive …' His face crumpled in tears. This was an impossible situation. How could he talk to this vision who had just appeared out of his dreams when these men were still corralled before him? He had to get rid of them.

'Juan José, take your friends away from here. Go down this

path and you will find the Fernández finca. You can call an ambulance from there. Someone will have to go and fetch your friend from up on the ridge as well. And Juan José … take a look around you as you go. The pumas will be stalking you. Think about that and forget trying to catch or kill me. Tell your boss the same. You will only lose more men if you try it. Now go.'

Daniel waited for the group of bloodied hunters to move off but as he did so there was yet another interruption. There was one final scene waiting to be played out: the appearance of the last evil hunter, the one who had ordered the search and destruction of Mono, whose hatred had blighted the lives of so many as surely as it had contaminated the lands around the mines he controlled.

Morten Fields came bursting upon the gathering, riding in as fast as he could from a position that he had held back in reserve. He was furious, armed and ruthlessly determined to exterminate this Mono, this individual who seemed to frustrate all his plans, this one who they said could not be killed. Well, if others could not be trusted to eliminate him, then he would do it himself. He urged the horse to ride down upon his foe as fast as he could, firing a pistol blindly in front as he bounced around in the saddle.

Daniel did not move. He held Karin behind him but told the pumas to retreat and leave him alone. The men they were guarding were unable to do anything but cower down. The reckless, onrushing, half-crazed assault carried Fields into their midst but brought only disaster. Daniel knew the horse that was whipped up into a gallop would never finish its charge and, sure enough, well before it reached him, it reared up in anguish, pawing the air, ejecting its rider at speed out of the saddle. Fields hit the mountainside with a sickening crash.

All the anger, hatred and murderous intent that had grown like a cancer in this man over a period of years was brought to a sudden, awful climax. One glance at a gruesomely broken body was enough to confirm that Fields had snapped his neck.

Daniel quickly moved Karin away from this scene of anger, bloodshed and carnage. The two of them held hands and hurried upslope, traversing the *páramo*, following animal trails, just as they had done years before when they had first got to know one another. They did not speak. They could not speak. There was simply too much bottled up inside of them.

They climbed and climbed and at last they reached a ridge some distance further above and beyond where the final confrontation had taken place. Karin stumbled to her knees with relief but Daniel just laughed and hauled her up, dragging her on higher and further along. He wanted still more space between them and the violence they had left behind. Karin didn't know where he was taking her, nor did she care. They were together! Then they both collapsed down for one last time, high on the mountain with the blue sky above and the Andes falling away on either side, the sierra stretching out for ever into the far distance.

Daniel lay on his back with condors and eagles wheeling in splendour above. There were no more threats in the air – only a glorious woman clambering on top of him, covering him with kisses, her tears wetting his face, as this vision of loveliness from his dreams was at last in his arms again. Life surged within him. He would never live without her now again. All sorts of possibilities for the future reappeared that he had earlier discarded, thrown away in anger. He would let go of all the animals, birds and creatures that he had ever loved, all in exchange for the love of this one woman. There was only going to be one family for him from now on and that was to be her and their children. They could be anywhere in the world, so long as they were together.

They looked at one another. His eyes were mirrored in hers. His dreams were now reflected in hers. They clung together for all time. They rolled around in the dust. When they eventually stopped making love, they both fell back and looked around, taking in the vast, beautiful Andean panorama that stretched around them, limitless and rich with possibility.

'Daniel ... I'm alive again!'

'I must be dreaming. It is you, isn't it? Tell me I'm not dreaming ...'

Karin rolled over to hold his head inches from her own. She kissed him one last, passionate kiss.

'If you think that that was a dream, you've been living with your head in the clouds for far too long. Come back to me, mountain man!'

Daniel smiled. 'Yes, I think I will,' he replied.

And a big cat, Mercury, started purring just above them.